A PICNIC TO REMEMBER

He lay back, sprawled on the blanket beside her, face toward the blue sky above them. Amanda looked at the length of him there and felt things she knew she shouldn't. How simple it would be to stretch out beside him, to nestle by his side, to listen to his breathing.

"How could you want to marry me?" she said.

"I don't know myself why I persist. There are hundreds of other wealthy young ladies. Why is it that since I've met you, I have not been able to concentrate on any of them as prospective wives?"

"How can you say that?"

He sat up. His arm went around her, and he pulled her against him. "I don't know. Why is the sky blue? Why is it that when I see you I want to kiss you, I want to make love to you a thousand times? Why do I want to possess you?"

She didn't know how it happened, but suddenly their mouths were together, hungrily kissing each other. The warmth she had wanted a moment ago was now hers as he embraced her, held himself back no longer with deep, probing kisses and urgent caresses.

"Edward, Edward," she whispered, "why do you do this?"

"Becaued in a hoarse whisper.

PATRICIA WERNER
VELVET DREAMS

ZEBRA BOOKS
KENSINGTON PUBLISHING CORP.

ZEBRA BOOKS are published by

Kensington Publishing Corp.
475 Park Avenue South
New York, NY 10016

Zebra and the Z logo Reg. U.S. Pat. & TM Off. The
Lovegram logo is a trademark of Kensington Publishing
Corp.

First Printing: May, 1994

Printed in the United States of America

After the ball is over, after the break of morn—
After the dancers' leaving; after the stars are gone;
Many a heart is aching, if you could read them all;
Many the hopes that have vanished after the ball.

—from "After the Ball," words & music by
Charles K. Harris

Chapter 1

New York, 1893

Amanda Whitney fidgeted in the plush seat of her family's opera box. Though on stage Faust was bargaining for his soul with the devil, Amanda had her opera glasses trained on the boxes opposite. Francis Newton, the young man with whom she had a secret understanding, had not shown up at intermission, and she could not fathom what had happened to him.

Through the round circles of glass that were focused on the parterre, where New York's wealthy owned their cream, red and gold boxes, Amanda hunted for Francis.

A hand distorted her vision, and her mother, seated to her right, hissed, "Do you mind, dear?"

Amanda surrendered the glasses to Louisa Whitney, the woman who arranged everything about her life. The only triumph of Amanda's privacy were a few hurried and secret meetings with Francis that her mother, as yet, did not know about.

Mrs. Whitney took the glasses in her gloved hand and raised them to her eyes. Though the opera had progressed to Act II, the new electric lights in the rebuilt opera house had dimmed only enough so that those who wished to could follow the action on stage. Most of the glittering audience as well as those who had paid a dollar for standing room in the family circle, were more interested in what was going on in the boxes.

There, bejeweled ladies in the latest décolleté Paris gowns sat in the front of the curved boxes, with a number of white-tied gentlemen in tailcoats behind. And though intermission was the proper time for the ladies to receive visits from gentlemen from other boxes, champagne corks popped and glasses clinked throughout the performance.

Amanda's gaze slid across the faces in the boxes nearby. Where had Francis got to? Though Amanda passionately loved the drama of opera, her attention was fractured. She disliked the anxious feeling in the pit of her stomach, and resented the fact that Francis had not lived up to his promise.

Mrs. Whitney dropped the opera glasses to her lap, and Amanda's hand snaked over to reach for them. Her mother absently handed them to her, and she quickly lifted them to focus on the stage. From there, she slowly shifted the view.

A gasp escaped her lips, and she nearly dropped the glasses.

"What is it?" whispered Mrs. Whitney.

"Nothing," answered Amanda in the same pronounced whisper.

Though she didn't use the glasses to look again, she could clearly see that the dark-haired gentleman in the box directly across the opera house was smirking at her. For her survey had revealed that he was engaged in the same activity as she was, and his glasses had been directly focused on her. Now he lowered them to reveal a handsome face, though she couldn't see the features distinctly from this distance in the lowered lights.

To her humiliation, she saw him nod to her, his face laughing and his mouth suppressing an ironic grin. Whoever he was, he was certainly impertinent. Of course, it was her own guilt that made her feel that way.

On stage, Faust trembled with ecstasy over his meeting with the pure and beautiful Margarete. The devil, Mephistopheles, laughed in sly victory, and the village square filled with a whirl of dancers, lost in reckless celebration. The blue velvet curtain fell, gloved hands in the audience united in applause, and the house lights came up, the five electric chandeliers overhead blazing down on the elegant audience.

The door to the anteroom behind the Whitneys' box opened, the chatter of voices raised to a din, and Amanda turned to see if Francis might at last appear. But her first glimpse at the men and women crowding into the anteroom to pay calls revealed her friend, Emily Van Burton, an attractive young lady of the same age as Amanda and of nearly the same proportions, but with very different looks.

Emily's dark hair, gracefully coifed with pearls wound around the chignon, and her swanlike neck above sloping shoulders, always made Amanda feel stiff and graceless, even though her own dress of Spanish lace over satin trimmed with fur was one of the most expensive in the opera house. The puffed sleeves dropped off shoulders she considered too square, and a gathering of lace at the front covered her youthful bosom, where Emily's décolleté gown showed off a great deal more abundance. In short, for all her money and breeding, Amanda did not really consider herself attractive. Her hair color was too nondescript, and it took hours with the curling iron to train it to do anything. And her own brown eyes were so ordinary beside Emily's flashing green orbs.

"Amanda," squeaked Emily, making her way between the gentlemen who had stood up at the back of the box. "I'm sorry I didn't come last intermission." Emily pulled a wry face. "Mother insisted I stay and greet my cousins."

While Amanda was glad to see her pretty friend, she kept an eye trained on the door, through which her brother, Max, was now departing. And then her eyes widened, for there was Francis at last, sweeping in, red satin-lined opera cape still about his shoulders, top hat in one hand, sand-colored hair mussed over his attractive forehead.

Francis handed the top hat and cape to the valet in the anteroom, straightened his white bow tie, tugged at his black waistcoat and nodded and smiled his way through the little crowd. Finally he caught sight of the two girls whose gowns draped over the seats in the box and hurried down the two steps separating anteroom from curved box.

"Good evening, ladies," said Francis. "Sorry I'm late. I was detained."

He touched his forehead in a quick gesture of exasperation, then reached for Amanda's hand and bowed over it. "How lovely you look," he proclaimed, dropping a kiss on the long white glove that covered her hand.

"And you, too, Emily," he said, performing obeisance likewise to the other pretty young lady. "Such beauty," he said, a smile lighting up his rakish face. "My eyes are blinded by the radiance all around me."

He placed a hand over his heart in a gesture of being overcome with emotion and moved one of the little chairs so he could sit between but a little behind the two girls.

"Perhaps you are blinded by the new electric lights," said Emily, referring to the bulbs glimmering from rosette ornaments, not only on the fronts of boxes and balconies, but in the chandeliers that reflected in the myriad tiaras, earrings, chokers and necklaces of the women in the audience.

"No doubt," said Francis. "And how is the opera?"

Amanda could not help the twitch of annoyance that fluttered across her brow. She would refrain, of course, from reprimanding him for not appearing during the first intermission. No man liked a harping woman. But it had been many days since their whispered conversation at Mrs. Schyler's tea.

Amanda had only come out last year, and though at parties all her brother's friends asked her to dance, she hated the affairs. She wasn't a good dancer, and she always felt that her partners were doing their duty for her brother's sake. Francis had been the only young man who sought her out several times and rained compliments enough to quite sweep her away. She believed he liked her for herself, and he had begged for future private conversations. What girl wouldn't be smitten by his gay blue eyes, attentive looks, warm squeezes of the hand and clever, off-hand manner that succeeded in making her feel she needn't worry about what she said.

Emily was busily filling Francis in on a combination of what had happened on stage and who was sitting in what box in the audience. Amanda's attention was caught by a reference to the man sitting in the box of Mrs. Paran Stevens. The man who had been staring at her.

"None other than the Duke of Sunderland," said

Emily, with awe in her voice. "Personally, I find him very good looking."

"My, my, a duke no less. Well, where is the chap?" asked Francis.

Amanda turned quickly toward the Stevens' box, which, like their own, was filled with visitors, but she didn't see the man who had been spying on her. She turned back toward Francis.

"I'm sure he holds no interest for me," she said self-righteously.

Francis flashed her a grin and reached to give her hand a quick squeeze. "That's what I like about you, my dear. You don't go all amush at the mention of some sniveling aristocrat."

"How do you know he snivels?" asked Emily, looking around them for a possible glimpse of the duke in question.

"Well, I haven't met this chap, but some of those other English lords who invade our society strike me as affected, to say the least. Haven't got our spirit, if you ask me. Too much inbreeding, I'd say."

Amanda smiled at Francis. She was no good at this kind of repartee and wondered when they might get another chance to speak privately.

As if perceiving her thoughts, Francis said, "I hope both you ladies will be attending Mrs. Astor's ball this Friday. I must have someone to dance with who doesn't step on my feet." He flattered Amanda with a quick wink.

She blushed slightly. "Mother speaks of nothing else. I'm afraid it will be a very long week."

She gave a wry grin, thinking of all the preparations her mother would put her through to make sure she was as presentable as possible. Amanda was not stupid. She was aware of Mrs. Whitney's plans to marry her off to the most socially well placed young man she could find for her daughter. But if she must marry, which unfortunately seemed inevitable, Amanda thought she might like to marry Francis himself. Their relationship had not progressed that far, but the hints Francis had dropped could not but lead her in that direction.

Now Francis favored her with a long look. "It will be long for me as well." His words were heavy with meaning.

Emily was distracted by Mrs. Orme Knoedler, who entered the box with Amanda's mother. Mrs. Knoedler's breadth required several more yards of brocade and satin to cover it than did Louisa Whitney's thin, straight-backed figure. She cooed over Emily's lacy cream-colored gown with perky puffed sleeves set off by a cameo at the throat. While the two ladies spoke to Emily, Francis leaned briefly toward Amanda's ear, his breath fanning the curls that framed her face.

"Meet me on the Mall in the park at eight tomorrow morning," he whispered urgently. Then he was out of his seat and bending over her hand. In a louder voice, he said, "It was lovely to see you, Miss Whitney."

Then he rose, as if just now noticing the older ladies behind him. "Ah, good evening Mrs. Whitney, Mrs. Knoedler. Enjoying the opera?"

"Of course, my dear young man," said Mrs. Knoedler, examining him carefully. "One is always appreciative of the age-old struggle between good and evil. Do not let the splendor of the drama hide the truth behind the myth. Especially at your age, there is much to learn in these great works."

Francis cleared his throat. "I'm sure there is, madam. You are quite right, of course."

All the while Louisa Whitney was frowning at him out of her hawklike face. Unlike her fair-haired, rosy-complected daughter, Louisa Whitney had sharp features, severe dark hair which she dressed with diamonds, and a tall, straight-shouldered frame. Her harsh mouth formed into easily readable expressions, whereas Amanda's enigmatic mouth often hid thoughts that she knew would be too radical to express. Her domineering mother made no attempt to hide her wishes; wishes that were carefully ordered to enable her to achieve her goal of leading New York society.

"Good evening, Francis," said Mrs. Whitney, giving him her hand. It was a dismissal, not a greeting, as all who heard it knew.

Francis scrambled up the two steps and disappeared between the shoulders of a group of gentlemen and a few ladies in the anteroom. Amanda leaned over to share a few words with Emily.

"We'll probably leave here after the act begins. Mother never stays longer than Mrs. Astor does."

Even on Monday night, the most fashionable night at the opera, Caroline Astor, the acknowledged Queen of Society with a capital *S*, was in the habit of arriving at nine P.M., regardless of curtain time, receiving guests in her box during the next intermission and then leaving for supper at the Waldorf or one of the Fifth Avenue mansions belonging to her friends. Those who imitated her felt they could leave the theater, too. The show in which they were most interested was over.

True to Amanda's prediction, Louisa now intervened.

"I'm afraid I simply must whisk Amanda away," said Mrs. Whitney. "The opera is long, and she must get her rest."

"I'm really not tired yet, Mother," said Amanda, annoyed at the way her schedule was being regimented.

Unlike many of her class, she actually enjoyed the drama and music of the performance, following with interest the careers of the stars. It would be nice to see an opera in its entirety just once. And now that she had made arrangements with Francis for tomorrow, she could relax and enjoy this evening.

"But you will be tired," replied her mother. "Come, our guests are leaving. Now would be a good opportunity to fetch our wraps. We have an engagement at Sherry's. Oh, dear, where is Max? We can hardly be expected to depart without an escort. He knew I wanted to leave after the intermission."

"Maybe he lost track of time," said Amanda, winking at Emily, to whom Louisa's back was turned.

Emily cupped her white-gloved hand over her mouth to hide her laughter. The way Amanda covertly mocked her domineering mother never failed to send Emily into fits of glee.

"Well, let's go anyway. We'll no doubt see someone on the mezzanine who can escort us. Everyone will be leaving. Someone will take pity on us if that renegade brother of yours fails to show up again."

Amanda shrugged her shoulders and stood up, casting one last yearning glance toward the emptying boxes and the curtained stage. She wondered how the singers felt performing for a half-empty house of music lovers who kept their seats in the balconies after the socialites left from below.

She took a step toward the anteroom and then jumped out of the way as her near-sighted cousin Henry stumbled into the box. He missed the top step, set his foot on the bottom step and did a half turn, catching himself with a hand on the back of one of the chairs. One hand went up to keep his gold-rimmed spectacles from flying off.

"Oh, sorry," he said to no one in particular.

Seeing that Henry was now stationary and that her train was no longer in danger of being torn from its seam, Amanda moved closer to him.

"We're going, Henry," she said. "You'll have the box to yourself unless Max comes back. I don't know where he's gone, do you?"

"Well now, I don't believe I've seen him in some time," replied Henry.

A likable fellow, and not unattractive behind the spectacles, Henry Whitney was a rather bookish young man. He and Amanda had grown up good friends, playing quiet games together as children when taunted by the older, louder rascals who ran with Max's crowd. As young adults, they still often clung together for security when faced with the demands of social life.

Henry did his best to take his place in society, but was always hampered by his near-sightedness, which caused him to stumble toward the most fragile object in any room. In Amanda he had a friend who genuinely enjoyed discussing history and to whom he could explain his theories of science and what made things run without the fear of being laughed at.

On second thought, Louisa said, "Or would you like to join us at Sherry's? We seem to be in need of an escort at the moment."

"Oh, my, in that case." He cleared his throat and puffed up his chest a bit. Like Amanda, he enjoyed the opera for its own sake, but if duty called, he was prepared to go.

The valet handed them into their wraps, sable for

Amanda, chinchilla for Louisa. Henry took his cape and top hat, and the party swept into the corridor to mingle with countless others who were likewise taking the opportunity to escape to the more congenial surroundings close by.

Sherry's restaurant, located on the Grand Tier of the opera house, was a favorite gathering place during intermissions and for after-theater suppers. When their party entered the gilded room, it was already full of society people. The maître d' led them between linen-covered tables where feathered and furred ladies were already raising champagne glasses with their formally attired escorts.

When the maître d' reached a circular table suitable for their party, Louisa suddenly veered away, intent on a group of acquaintances standing around a nearby table and focused on a distinguished gentleman with impeccably cut evening wear. His snowy, stiff, stand-up collar and white cravat set off dark hair. He was being introduced around by Mrs. Paran Stevens, to whom Louisa now applied her social graces.

Henry seated Amanda. Then, while he deliberated anxiously on which of the other two seats he should take, Amanda peeked at the gentleman, whom she recognized as the one who had been examining her through his opera glasses. At closer range, he appeared to be a decade her senior, but with handsome features, a high forehead, marked cheekbones, a rakish, sardonic smile and laughing, almost haughty, brown eyes. But even his impeccable manners, and the excellent cut of his clothes, did not hide the fact that there was something of the outdoorsman about him. He was taller than the women surrounding him, but the feathers and tiaras on top of the hair that was piled upon the dazzling feminine heads kept her from seeing him clearly.

Then she heard him laugh out loud at some witticism, and he turned in her direction. To the charming grin on his face was now added a raised eyebrow, and Amanda quickly turned her gaze away, embarrassed to be caught staring.

Henry finally settled on a chair and had no sooner got into it than Louisa came back. Henry sprang up to hold her chair, knocking his own over in the process.

"Good heavens, Henry," admonished Louisa. "Do watch what you're doing."

A waiter rushed over to assist, and between them, the two men got the chair righted and Henry back into his seat. The waiter handed out oversized menus, the gold tassle of which now plunged into Henry's crystal water glass.

Louisa leaned toward Amanda and used her menu to shield her words from the party to whom she had just been speaking.

"That's the Duke of Sunderland," she hissed. "He's going to be at the Astors' ball and wishes to meet you."

Amanda bristled. "Oh, Mother, really. How can you know that?"

"He noticed you, that's how. He saw you at the opera, and when I mentioned that we would be at the ball, he said he would be charmed to make your acquaintance."

Amanda drew a sandy-colored brow down. "He would say that of anyone. He was being polite. Why should I need to meet a duke?" But she knew the answer and wished she hadn't even formed the question.

"Because, my dear, he might like you. You have the money and the breeding to please him. One never knows." Louisa sat back in her chair with a self-satisfied air about her, and Amanda could imagine the scheming that was taking place in her mother's head.

What could she possibly have in common with a duke, Amanda wondered silently, staring at the items on the menu. While they ordered bisque de creme followed by canapé of crab, Amanda spotted a group of gay young people just entering. Partially blocked by a garlanded marble pillar, she had to wait until they were shown to a table to see that Francis Newton was among them. She bit her lip, wishing that her mother weren't here, for then she and Henry might be able to invite the group to join them. Her brother Max straggled in as well, and when Louisa spotted him, she raised a gloved hand, getting his attention. Max turned to speak to his two tailcoated comrades, gesturing to the table where his mother sat and, from the looks of it, excused himself to come over to their table.

"Oh, there you are, Mother. I've just come in with Winthrop Rutherfurd and Julius Vanderbilt."

"I have eyes to see that. You evidently forgot we wished to leave the opera at the second intermission."

"Oh, so I did," said Max, unperturbed. "Well, it looks as if old Henry here has come to the rescue."

Max's easy going manner and lack of shame in the face of his mother's criticism only increased the displeasure on Louisa's face. Amanda's eyes turned in exasperation to the embossed, gold-painted ceiling as Max smoothed away his mother's acid tongue by dropping the names of the friends his group planned to join.

When Louisa Whitney saw that her children were advancing their connections in social circles, she could hardly complain. And the fact that Max was going around with Vanderbilts, Sloans and Morgans did him no harm. For though the Vanderbilts had actually only become accepted in society in the third generation, their money and pretensions had succeeded in penetrating society's Four Hundred, which until recent times had been made up of much older families.

Amanda's great-grandfather was George Abercrombe Whitney, a self-made man who had made a fortune in rug manufacturing. In his day, he'd had no time for New York snobbery. Not so his granddaughter-in-law Louisa. But new money still carried a taint among the inner circle of New York's Four Hundred, that exclusive social set currently circumscribed by *The* Mrs. Astor and that grand arbiter, Ward McAllister. McAllister drew the line at four hundred because, he said whimsically, that was the number that could easily fit into Mrs. Astor's ballroom.

Even a palace on Millionaire's Row, that stately length of mansions lining Fifth Avenue from Thirty-fourth Street to the Sixties and Seventies, did not automatically bring an invitation to the most coveted drawing rooms of the older society families. But Louisa Whitney had succeeded in breaking into the upper crust. As Amanda was all too painfully aware, her mother was happy only when she was dominating those involved in her plans, and now she had it in her head to find a titled husband for her daughter.

Amanda searched the glittering crowd to see where Francis had gone with his group of friends. She spotted them at a large, round table in a corner, and to her dismay saw Francis lean his head very close to the ear of Melanie Goelet, one of Amanda's acquaintances. Even from this distance, Amanda could see that Francis was sharing some enticing tidbit with Melanie, who smiled and placed a hand over her mouth to suppress her mirth.

Jealousy sprang into Amanda's breast. How dare he be flirting with Melanie!

The waiter now held a bottle of Chablis for Henry to examine, seeing as how he was the only gentleman at the table now that Max had left to join his friends. Henry squinted at the year, and then nodded as if he had been able to read the label at that distance.

The waiter poured; Henry lifted the glass, sniffed and swirled, a few drops flying out of the glass to land dangerously close to Louisa's fan. He tasted, swallowed and pronounced it fit to drink.

Amanda's jealousy was now capped by the horror of seeing wine drip onto her mother's lime green satin.

"Henry, do look out," said Amanda crossly. She knew her words were sharper than he deserved, and she stole another glance across the room at Francis, who seemed to be having a gay time without her.

Rage and exasperation vied for first place on her face, coloring her cheeks with a flush, and it was at that moment that she chanced to feel a gaze upon her from the other direction and looked up. The devilish duke appeared to be listening to Mrs. Stevens, in her gown of pink brocade trimmed with pendant jets, but his eyes were on Amanda.

Amanda blinked, swallowed and reached for her glass of wine, to which she was limited a single one. Her eyes concentrated on raising the crystal glass to her lips, but then her glance slid toward the duke once more. Now she burned in embarrassment. He managed to smile at her while nodding attentively to Mrs. Stevens.

The nerve of him, thought Amanda. For his look was at once superior but curious. It was a look that sent waves of natural charisma to envelop a female creature while at the same time making Amanda feel as if he viewed her much as he might view a piece of art or sculpture. The look unnerved her, made her feel somehow immodest, though she had done nothing at all to deserve it. But perhaps it was because every time the man looked at her he caught her guiltily searching for Francis or in a state of emotion in which she did not wish to be observed.

She picked up her fan and unfolded it, using it as a screen to protect her. Emily and her mother entered the restaurant, and luck brought them this way. As there was space at their table, Amanda leaned over to her mother.

"Mother, here come Emily and Mrs. Van Burton. Shall we ask them to join us?"

"Why not, my dear?" said Louisa, turning and gesticulating to Florence Van Burton.

Emily and Amanda grinned at each other, happy at the chance to be together again, while Henry stood helplessly as the waiter placed the newcomers in their chairs.

"Sit down, Henry," Emily finally said when she and her mother had taken their seats.

Henry cleared his throat. "Wine?" he offered.

"Yes, thank you," said Emily, giving her friend a wink.

Emily's seat gave even a clearer view of the duke at the Stevens' table, and as soon as she saw him, she lifted a dark brow, commenting to her friend, "Well, well. There's some nobility for you. Doesn't look to me like he deserved Francis's slurs. Just jealous, I suppose."

"What's Francis got to be jealous of?" said Amanda, loyally.

"Oh, come on. There's the title, for one thing. And probably a stately mansion somewhere in England. Oh, my, how romantic," swooned Emily.

"Hmph," said Amanda.

Across the table Louisa and Emily's mother were discussing the fashions all around them, and when the bisque came, Amanda thankfully plunged her spoon in it. She was becoming annoyed by the bursts of laughter from her friends who were having such a gay time at the table where Francis sat. His back was to her, so of course she couldn't even signal him. How the hours would drag until eight tomorrow when she promised to meet him in Central Park.

"When do you sail for Europe?" asked Emily.

"In two weeks," answered Amanda with a long, wounded sigh.

"I'd be excited if I were you," said Emily, her bright green eyes contrasting with Amanda's downcast face.

But when Amanda thought of the upcoming journey, her heart turned over. For at eighteen, she felt that her world was on the verge of collapse. With her coming out, her previous joy at simply living had become tarnished by her mother's ambitions to see her married.

No more the carefree days of summer when she, her brother and cousins picnicked in the country. No more bicycle races with her friends in Central Park. No more sleigh rides in winter with her own circle of confidantes. For many of her female friends as well were either busily receiving suitors or already engaged.

At last the strained supper came to a close. Amanda had hardly heard what passed across the table as chatter. But she did notice that as they stood to go, Francis's group got up as well. Henry attempted to help the ladies on with their furs, and then they paraded across the restaurant. Now Francis turned and saw her coming. His face lit with a smile, and he stood aside to let the ladies pass.

Since Louisa led the way, it was possible for Amanda to lag behind the others and cast a loving glance in Francis's direction. He seized on it and fell in with her, squeezing her hand as they passed through the door.

"I haven't forgotten tomorrow," he said. "On the Mall." He raised her hand to sneak a quick kiss to her knuckles.

Her heart, which had been so heavy, sang, her lips curved upward, and her eyes glistened. Thus enraptured, she joined the little group awaiting her in the lobby as Francis made himself scarce. As she turned around, her heart lurched in embarrassment.

The Duke of Sunderland was just leading Mrs. Stevens out to the Grand Tier mezzanine, and his amused eyes were upon Amanda. She knew at once that he had seen everything.

Chapter 2

Not being one to miss an opportunity, Louisa reached a gloved hand for Mrs. Stevens, who could not do otherwise than bring the duke to a stop in front of the group of ladies just as Henry backed into a potted fern.

"Why, my dear," cooed Louisa to Mrs. Stevens. "I was just telling my daughter about your distinguished guest."

"In that case," said Mrs. Stevens, unable to do anything else, "allow me to present the Duke of Sunderland. Your Grace, you remember Mrs. Louisa Whitney, and this is her daughter, Miss Amanda Whitney."

The duke smiled and first bowed over Louisa's hand. "A pleasure."

As he turned to Amanda, she imagined she noticed his lips rise in an ironic grin, but his eyes were sober as he took her gloved hand.

"Miss Whitney," he said and bowed with all due ceremony.

Mrs. Stevens also presented Emily and her mother, then, almost as an afterthought, Henry, who could not escape the corner.

"How do you do, Your Honor?" said Henry, shaking the hand that was offered.

"Very well, thank you," answered the duke.

The duke was by now at ease among these Americans, and had gotten used to most of them getting his title and the proper forms of address wrong, as Henry Whitney had just done. At least he had schooled his hostess, Mrs. Stevens, as to proper introductions.

"His Grace has been seeing something of the United States," Mrs. Stevens went on. "But soon he will be returning to settle down at his ancestral home in England."

"Oh?" said Louisa, her interest clearly piqued. "And where is your home, Your Grace? You will forgive me if I am unfamiliar with the many great manor houses of England's nobility, limited as we are with their acquaintance."

"My home, Elsenheim Palace, is located in the fairest countryside of all England," he said with a smile. "We are a few hours from the sea, but near enough to reap the benefits of seaside air when the wind is right."

"How lovely," said Louisa, smiling at the poetic description.

Amanda distinctly felt her mother's hand in her back nudging her forward. But Amanda tried not to look at the duke, who for some reason she was certain could read her mind.

"Will you be bringing the duke to Mrs. Astor's ball?" inquired Emily of Mrs. Stevens, evidently too hesitant as to how one spoke to a duke to ask him directly.

"Most assuredly," answered Mrs. Stevens. "Oh, there is Caroline now. I must just say hello to her. If you will excuse us."

The duke bowed again to the little assembly, admiring the many jewels that lay on the mature bosoms presented in low-cut satin before him. But his fancy lay more in the direction of the pretty young ladies, whose jewelry was more discreetly wound in the coils of their hair.

His eyes were drawn to the lovely Amanda, whose expression hid tantalizing secrets, for hadn't he caught her distinctly looking for someone several times this evening with such a displeased expression that he felt he could almost decipher her thoughts? Now his dark eyes flicked over the smooth skin above her expensive gown, revealing shoulders of pearly white. Her bosom, which he suddenly longed to view, was covered with enough lace to prevent any man from gazing directly, but somehow the modesty of her dress only inspired him to see more.

Edward Pemberton, Duke of Sunderland, was a virile man who admired women greatly. In his twenty-eight years he had always kept his dealings with women discreet, limiting himself to an affair here or there that would in no way bring scandal to the weighty title to which he had been born. And women admired him. If he had been more indulgent, it would have been nothing to sow his seed in the many pastures that presented themselves to him.

But not only would that have produced the possibility of many bastards, which would be expensive to support, it might have wrecked his distinguished reputation. And he was not about to incur the wrath of the house of Sunderland. He owed it to his ancestors to uphold the name and produce legitimate heirs.

It was the production of such heirs that had brought him to the United States. For alas, the house of Sunderland was financially impoverished. Maintaining a palace took a lot of money, and maintaining it in state even more. On his deathbed, the late Duke of Sunderland had admonished his son to do everything in his power to carry on the traditions and to marry well. His mother had died many years ago, and now his grandmother, the Dowager Duchess of Sunderland, had run out of patience and shooed him off to the United States with orders to bring home a wife, and a rich one at that.

Now Sunderland examined the two young ladies before him, much as he might examine horseflesh, for it was his duty and the purpose of his trip. The darkhaired one had a lovely neck and a generous bosom. But her tinkling laughter was hollow, and he instinctively felt that in years to come her shallowness would become impossible to live with.

The other one, introduced as Amanda, made him laugh inwardly. This one had a temper, he could see, and her mind dwelt stubbornly on some desire, though he could not tell what it was. The fact that she did not simper or fawn brought her up a notch in his estimation. In some ways she reminded him of his sister, Norah, with whom he was extremely close. Norah, too, was stubborn when it came to what she wanted, but she had an intelligence to match his own.

The party moved away, and his attention was turned toward this Mrs. Astor, whom everyone here treated as aristocracy. For though the duke was given to understand that in America all men were created equal, he could see for himself that some were more equal than others.

The Whitney party succeeded in rounding up Max, and then the four Whitneys stepped from the porte cochere on Thirty-ninth Street into their shiny black brougham, turned out with a perfectly matched pair of bays.

Their liveried groom, Charles, in greatcoat, white breeches, polished boots and silk top hat, held the door, a neutral expression on his face, eyes discreetly avoiding those of his employers, though not unaware of the pretty hat-check girl who had been leaning out of her first-floor window across the street to flirt and visit with him for the last two hours.

When the carriage door was firmly shut, Charles hopped up to the box to join the similarly attired coachman, Stanislaw, years older than Charles, who now applied his experienced hands to the reins.

Amanda longed to wave to Francis, who had just come out of the entrance with his group, but she knew it would only endanger her chances of conniving behind her mother's back to see him when she had the chance.

"Say, Mother," interjected Max. "A few of the old boys are thinking of running out to the Sound for a day's sail tomorrow. I thought of going along."

Louisa arched a brow in the light and shadow cast in the coach windows from the street lamps they passed. "I should think that with going up to Marble Gate next week and then with a three-month sojourn in Europe after that, there would be little time for sailing."

"On the contrary, Mother. My man Louis has all my things ready. I can easily afford the day."

Amanda ceased listening to her mother and brother argue. They dropped Henry at his home on Madison Avenue and then continued up Fifth Avenue past the reservoir, the stately mansions and churches that lined Millionaire's Row and at last arrived at Sixtieth Street. The carriage stopped at the side entrance, and Charles jumped down to hold the door once again.

The brick and marble mansion that George Whitney had built with his fortune had been large enough to serve his offspring into the third generation. The family trooped up the wide front steps past the Greek revival pillars and stepped into the grand three-story entrance hall.

The floor of white marble squares with smaller black diamonds for accent led the eye to the white stone walls. The vertical lines of the paneling led to the second-story level where large paintings of mythical scenes were hung as if in the heavens. Mrs. Whitney believed in simple decoration, and only two Grecian statues greeted the eye in the hall niches at floor level, as well as a Chinese vase in the corner where the stairs took a turn upward.

Amanda hurried up the rose-colored carpet covering the marble staircase, passed the Chinese vase, her hand skimming along the black iron stair rail, its geometric design the chief ornament of the grand hall. When she had been a child, the long, sweeping staircase had seemed an endless climb upward, where she sometimes feared she would be accosted by dark shadows before she reached the safety of her room.

Now over the childhood nightmares, she skimmed along the corridor, reached her room, and pushed inward the carved door with its gilded molding. From the center of the satin coverlet on her four-poster bed a large orange cat named Morgan watched her with big green-yellow eyes.

"Hello, Morgan," she said to him, smiling at her best companion.

She had brought him home from the Brearley School, from which she had graduated last spring. The mother cat in residence at the school had had a litter of kittens, and much to Louisa's chagrin, Amanda insisted on keeping the kitten. Her father had sided with her, and the animal stayed.

Thinking of her father, Jay Whitney, brought another pain to her heart. Louisa and Jay had not gotten along for some time, and rather than put up with his wife's acid tongue, the two were living apart.

When Amanda had been a girl, her father had always been her fun-filled, dashing knight in shining armor. And it was a loss to see him become less and less involved in their lives. Now he appeared only for holidays or family celebrations, but most of those ended in such severe arguments that Amanda no longer looked forward to them. She longed to meet her father alone, and when he was not occupied with business they managed a few lunches or teas; but those times were becoming scarce.

Amanda's maid, Delcia, came to help her out of her gown.

"And how was the opera, miss?" asked the pretty, dark-haired girl, her own thick curls pulled up severely and stuck under a white starched cap with long streamers.

"It was all right, what I saw of it."

She could only partially blame her mother for the fact that she had missed most of the action, since during the first and second acts her own opera glasses had been trained a great deal of the time on the other boxes.

She turned her back so that Delcia could unhook the dress. She knew she daren't let Morgan near her until the lace was safely put away. Off came the dress; then Amanda stepped out of shot silk petticoats. As Delcia loosened the treacherous corset, Amanda breathed easier. Then she stepped behind her dressing screen to remove her camisole and lace frilled drawers, and slipped a cream-and-pink flannel nightgown over her head. When she came out from behind the dressing screen, Delcia held a quilted dressing gown for her.

"And were there many handsome gentlemen there?" asked Delcia, always interested in the romantic world of furs and diamonds that would never be hers.

Amanda shrugged, then picked up Morgan to carry him to the dressing table, where he could sit on her lap.

"A few."

She thought of her exasperation over Francis. She often came dangerously close to confiding some of her secrets to Delcia, for in the years Delcia had served her, she had proven completely trustworthy. But prudence won, and she didn't mention her morning rendezvous.

"I met a duke," she said, thinking to entertain Delcia as the maid unwound the pearls and removed the pins that let down Amanda's long, generally unruly hair.

"You don't say? A real duke?"

"From England, looking for a wife."

"Well now, is he rich and handsome?" Delcia's perky mouth curved upward with interest as her quick hands took the brush to Amanda's hair.

Amanda lifted a shoulder and let it drop as she stroked Morgan, who purred in her lap. "Handsome, I suppose. You might think so. Rich, I doubt. Why else would he be here looking for a wife?"

"Well, miss. You could do worse."

Amanda made a face. "You sound like my mother. She has this notion that I should marry nobility. She's obsessed with gaining a title for the family."

"Lady Amanda," quipped Delcia, spreading out Amanda's hair in a romantic gesture.

Amanda was used to the good-natured teasing of her maid. "Don't be silly. In any case, I wouldn't be Lady Amanda. Lady is only followed by the woman's first name if she's the daughter of an earl or above. I've read about that in books on the peerage."

"You don't say. So what would you be?"

"I'm not going to be anything because I'm not going to marry an English lord at all."

Delcia met her gaze in the mirror over the dressing table. "You will if your mother has her way."

Amanda's lower lip protruded. "I realize my mother has her ideas. But she can hardly make me say 'I do' to someone not of my own choosing."

Delcia blinked but said nothing. It didn't do to become too involved in family squabbles. She changed the subject.

"I'm stepping out myself on my day off tomorrow," she said. "Mrs. Whitney thought I should have a day to myself before the voyage. Kind of her, that was."

"That's nice. I didn't know," said Amanda. "Where are you going?"

"Charles and I are taking a little excursion. Going to Coney Island, we are. There's a steamboat takes you out on the water. We'll even be having tea at the hotel."

"That sounds very nice, Delcia."

As far as Amanda knew, Delcia and Charles were only friends. She hoped so, for the way Charles liked to flirt with serving girls when he thought no one was looking made Amanda feel uneasy about trusting her Delcia with him.

She stroked Morgan's thick, orange fur, lifting him up for a hug. "Good boy, Morgan." The cat licked her face, wrapping a paw about her neck.

Delcia replaced the brush on the table and started to braid Amanda's hair so that it wouldn't become tangled during the night.

"Just think, Miss, we leave on Saturday. I've never been on such a big boat myself. Won't it be glamorous?"

Delcia was to go along as maid to Amanda and Louisa, while Max was taking his valet, Louis.

"Now, don't get too excited, Delcia. The cabins are very crowded. And you might be seasick. There's no telling what kind of crossing we'll have." She stifled a yawn. It was getting late, and she had to be up early.

Delcia turned down the bed. "Is there anything else, miss?"

"No, go on, Delcia. I'll see you in the morning."

Amanda carried Morgan to the bed and placed him on a pillow next to hers where he liked to sleep. Then she made sure her curtains were pulled open so the sun would wake her up. She picked up a copy of Goethe's *The Sorrows of Young Werther*, turned up the gas lamp affixed to the wall by her bedside and located her place. Soon she was lost in the tale. But as the pages turned, her eyes grew heavy, and she finally turned down the lamp.

Up with the sun, Amanda dressed in a blue serge outing dress and braided jacket. Her bonnet with projecting front brim was heaped with flowers and feathers on top. Amanda was a morning person, and since she was the only member of the family who liked to rise early, she always found the house peaceful at this hour. She left the house with a song in her heart.

On other days, she would steal down to the library and spend some hours reading and practicing her languages before having to appear for breakfast. But this morning she slipped out the front door, where she would escape notice by the delivery men who drew their carts around back to hand their goods to Cook and the kitchen help.

The only vehicles out this early were carts and delivery wagons, with the exception of the occasional young man with his fast trotter harnessed to a sulky, going for a run up to Harlem Lane. Amanda darted across the street and down the block to where she entered Central Park.

The dew had not left the grass, and early spring crocus were just beginning to bud in the flower beds. Birds twittered in the trees. It was but a few steps to the entrance to the Mall, a quarter-mile promenade lined with a double row of elms, at the end of which the elaborate stone carved Terrace was a favorite meeting place for ladies and children out for a stroll to admire the landscaped flower beds and lawn of the park. But this early, Amanda was alone. For a moment she wondered if Francis had forgotten, but turning around she spied him coming along the Mall behind her.

The evening clothes of the night before were gone, and in their place were knickerbockers tucked into high boots, a belted Norfolk jacket and cap. When he saw her he hurried forward. How handsome he looked! It was so thrilling to think that he cared for her. Francis Newton had always been one of the dashing young men of their set, and he loved a good time. She could hardly believe he'd noticed her. For she thought he would be more likely to choose someone like Emily, who was adept at flirting and social chatter.

Francis's fair-haired good looks always turned heads, and there was something daring about him that thrilled Amanda, whose life had been so completely sheltered.

"My dearest, how good to see you. My heart has ached since last night. I knew there wasn't a chance of having a word with you from the moment I set foot in your opera box."

She turned to walk with him toward the Terrace.

"Your mother doesn't approve of me, you know," he said with a frown.

"I know." Her voice conveyed her unhappy state of mind. "And now to make it worse, there's this voyage."

"Yes, that is the devil of a thing. Whatever are we to do?"

For a moment, a mad thought seized Amanda, but she daren't voice it. Still, her heart hammered against her ribs as Francis took one of her hands and started them walking again.

"It is possible that I can follow you to France," he said.

Hope sprang in her breast. "Do you think so, really?"

"Well, Father has promised me a trip before I settle down to business."

"Oh, Francis, that would be wonderful."

He smiled, then raised her hand to his to plant a kiss on the chilled knuckles. He looked gravely into her eyes.

"You will marry me one day, now, won't you?"

"Oh, yes," she said on a breath, overcome. For a moment she allowed herself to swoon as he placed an arm about her shoulders. If only Emily could see her now! The bookish, quiet Amanda Whitney with her dashing cavalier.

"But of course our engagement must remain a secret," he said. "Until we can think of some way around your parents' disapproval."

Practicality forced itself on Amanda. "It's just Mother. I don't think Father would care that much. He would want my happiness."

"Well then, the battle is half won."

"We shall be at Marble Gate next week. Perhaps I can explain to Mother then," said Amanda, gazing hopefully into Francis's hazel-green eyes.

"You can send for me if you want me to come there."

"All right, I'll do that."

Satisfied that there was hope for convincing her mother that the absurd plan of hers to find her a husband in Europe was a waste of time, Amanda smiled. Francis took her arm, and they walked along the Terrace. How lovely to have it all planned, she thought, pushing away her resentment that he'd appeared to be having such a gay time without her last night. Now he was all hers, and it made her throat tighten.

"I haven't very much money," Francis said with a sigh. "But don't worry about my ability to support a wife. I've been promised a very good job at New York Central under the tutelage of George Vanderbilt."

"Money oughtn't to be a problem," said Amanda. It never had been, for her father had settled her own money on her, which she could have beginning in two more years. It was something she'd never had to worry about.

"Ah, but it sometimes is. I'll have to speak to your father to see if he can see his way clear to give us a little start. Your family has been blessed with money where mine has not. Such is the way of fortune," he said loftily.

"I'm sure he'll do whatever I ask him to do," said Amanda. "But I won't see him if we leave for Europe."

Her heart twisted. She simply must persuade her mother that she didn't want to go to Europe. She wanted to spend the summer here or in Newport where at least there was a chance of being with Francis.

He patted her hands, and they turned to walk back down the promenade. A few people were entering the park now. Clerks and shop girls cut across it to get to their jobs.

"Then we shan't worry about a thing. And I hope I can at least steal you away for a while during Mrs. Astor's ball."

Amanda pulled a face. "I'm not very good at those affairs. I feel stiff when I dance, even after all those horrible lessons. And you have to keep up such trivial conversation."

Francis grinned. "That's what I like about you. You don't force a man to be clever and witty all the time. And if you don't want to dance, why, we can stroll about the gallery and look at the pictures. I'm sure we'll find something to do to amuse ourselves."

"Do you really think so?" His words almost gave her a reason to look forward to the dreaded formal affair.

"I think so."

They were nearing the end of the Mall, and Francis knew he mustn't be seen by any of her household or there would be the devil to pay.

They were about to cross the road and looked up at the sound of a pair of high-stepping horses that came along at a brisk pace. The curricle that approached was dark burgundy in color with tufted seats of a light mauve. The horses' harness was embellished with silver ornaments. The elegantly attired lady in the carriage wore a satin gown and a large feathered hat with gray veil. Francis whistled under his breath.

The even steps of the matched pair clopped toward them, and Francis stared in wonder, his eyes piercing the lady's veil. She must have felt his gaze, for the ruby lips below the veil curved in a seductive smile as she passed. She held the reins herself with kid gloves, and where a liveried footman should have been standing on the rumble behind, there was none.

Amanda's eyes went to the rubies and gold on the exposed throat, and she was surprised at the low-cut attire visible where the lady's cloak was open at the neck. It was hardly suitable fashion for this hour of the morning.

"I wonder who that is," she said as the elegant carriage passed and the woman turned her head to face front again. "And what's she doing out this early dressed like that?"

"This late, you mean. Most likely an actress," Francis muttered under his breath, for he recognized a woman of the demimonde when he saw one. Actress was the acceptable euphemism in polite company.

He urged Amanda along. It wasn't proper for genteel eyes to dwell on a lady of the night. He bid Amanda goodbye and then made his way back into the park, with promises for the future.

Friday evening arrived with due pomp and ceremony. Amanda, Max and Louisa traveled down Fifth Avenue to Mrs. Astor's mansion in their carriage. The third-floor ballroom glowed with the soft light of wax candles in crystal chandeliers, which reflected in the mirrored paneling. The perspective produced by mirrors placed opposite each other made the room seem endless.

To Amanda's relief, her card was filled, with many young men vying for a dance, so that none of her time was spent on the tapestry-covered, backless seats ranged along the walls. Her ball gown of light blue satin with bead embroidery in an iris design did much to flatter her appearance. Long white gloves reached to short puffed sleeves of the same material under a ruffle of

beaded satin. In her left hand she carried a fan of white
tulle with figures appliquéd in blue lace. A blue ribbon
was fastened around her neck with a small cameo resting at the throat.

Her cheeks were naturally tinged pink, her eyes wide
and glistening.

Francis flashed her a wink from across the room but
had not come to claim his dance yet when Louisa bore
down on her.

"Your grandmother is here, Amanda," said Louisa.
"She wishes to speak with you."

Louisa led the way along gala corridors, finally turning to open a door that led to a small sitting room.
Amanda spied the white head of her grandmother sitting in a wide satin-upholstered Louis XVI chair, which
was roomy enough for her jet taffeta skirts. Amanda
smiled and moved forward to greet her grandmother.

"Hello, Grandmother," she said, leaning down to kiss
the soft cheeks. Amanda adored Josephine Whitney, and
was always pleased to go see her.

"Good evening, my dear, now let me look at you."

Amanda turned for her grandmother's inspection and
only then noticed that Louisa had not followed her into
the room.

"Very nice," said Josephine. "I approve."

"That is good, Grandmother. But I really feel quite
stiff in these clothes."

"Always the little hoyden, eh?" said Josephine. She
gestured to the French sofa in front of the marble fireplace. "Sit down, my girl, there is a matter I wish to
broach with you."

Amanda did as she was told, and fixed her gaze upon
the still-attractive face with soft white hair arranged in
dowager fashion, pulled softly upward and done in a

bun behind. A black feather was fixed in a net with jet combs at the back, giving her grandmother a stately appearance.

"I have been told that a rather important young man is interested in furthering his acquaintance with you," said Josephine.

Amanda stiffened. Now that she was alone with Grandmother Whitney, she wanted to confide in her what she was afraid to broach to her mother.

"I see," she said. But before she could go on, her grandmother continued.

"You know that your mother is greatly concerned that you find the right husband."

Amanda frowned. "I had hoped to choose a husband for myself."

Josephine smiled sympathetically. "I understand your feelings, dear girl. But marriage is a weighty matter. Almost no one your age has sufficient wisdom and foresight to make such a choice unaided by those of more maturity."

"But I want . . ." Her words died with the sharp look her grandmother gave her. Blue eyes alert, gray brows arched.

After a moment, Josephine spoke. "Aha, then there has been a romance budding under our very noses. Come, girl, tell me who it is."

Now Amanda's words rushed forth. "Francis Newton. He has spoken to me and hopes to gain my mother's approval."

At the mention of the name, Josephine's eyes grew brighter. She clucked her tongue. "No, no, my dear. That young man will simply not do."

"Why ever not?" asked Amanda, temper putting color to her cheeks.

"It's not his family one would object to. He is a Whitehouse on his mother's side, and a cousin to the Goelets. But the young man is a profligate, given to extravagances."

Amanda's eyes were wide. "How could you possibly know such a thing?"

Josephine gazed on her granddaughter with patience. "Where you young people are concerned, your mother's generation and mine keep a sharp eye on eligible young suitors. It is widely known that Francis Newton is a bit on the wild side. Attracted to your money, I'd say. He's been about with the wrong sort of crowd, one hears, indulging in drink and gaming too much. Not that most young men won't try that sort of thing. But there comes a time when they should break the habit. Francis has finished his schooling and ought to be settling down to work since his personal fortune does not afford him the pursuit of leisure. But I have it on the best authority that he prefers to spend his days getting into who knows what sort of trouble. Not the sort of husband for you."

Tears crowded Amanda's eyes, but a stiff determination showed itself as she came to Francis's defense.

"I don't believe you. Francis adores me. He has told me so."

"He may have, my dear. And you know I would not want to hurt you. I am simply trying to help your mother save you from a mistake you would spend many years regretting. Your infatuation with Francis is a thing of youth. Why, most people don't know the meaning of love when they marry. That comes only after years of mutual respect and of raising a family together. Common purpose, that is what one ought to marry for.

"I barely knew your grandfather when I accepted his

hand in marriage. But I wouldn't trade my years with
him for all the tea in China, may he rest in peace."

The common sense of her grandmother's arguments
battled with the haze of Francis's attention, which was
still too new to be dismissed so easily.

"But I've promised him."

"I understand, dear. A promise made in a moment of
girlish passion. It need not stand."

"But—"

Josephine raised a finger and waggled it. "You may
be angry with me at the moment, Amanda. But in years
to come, you'll thank me."

Amanda saw black, and Josephine's words fell on deaf
ears. Now both mother and grandmother were allied
against her.

But rather than allow Amanda's anger to simmer, Josephine folded her slender, if somewhat veined, hands
on her lap and continued. "Your mother will be bringing the Duke of Sunderland into this room in a few moments so that the two of you can exchange a few
pleasantries."

Amanda scowled, failing to hear the door handle turn
behind her. "The Duke of Sunderland? Oh, heavens,
not him again," she said in loud agitation.

Then her face turned scarlet as the sounds of a gown
sweeping into the room and a gentleman clearing his
throat made her turn around.

Chapter 3

The Duke of Sunderland walked forward and bowed to Josephine and then to Amanda, whose tongue stuck in her throat. It was Louisa who managed to carry it off as if no one had heard Amanda's insolent comment.

"The duke has asked to join us for some refreshment," said Louisa, swishing around the sofa from which Amanda wished she could flee. Louisa took up a pose beside the mantelpiece as if she, and not Mrs. Astor, were the lady of this house. "Your Grace will remember my daughter."

He gave a crooked smile. "Indeed, how can I forget?"

Indeed, her spontaneous protest at the prospect of his appearance amused him. And she was doing little to cover it up. Many society girls would have twittered and fawned over him as if they had not just uttered an insult. Or at the very least fanned brightly blushing faces, trying to hide their mistake. But Amanda stood there like a stump, glaring at him, obviously annoyed at the interruption. But her attitude only challenged him. He was often at his best when facing an adversary.

"And my mother-in-law, Mrs. Josephine Whitney,

Amanda's grandmother. May I present the Duke of Sunderland, who wishes to join us."

Sunderland strode to where Josephine sat, took the old lady's hand and bowed over it. "An honor, Mrs. Whitney."

The duke's charm was not lost on the older woman, whose other hand picked up her fan to quickly fan herself.

"Glad to meet you, Your Grace. I've heard you've been inspecting these United States for some time."

The duke took a seat on a tapestry-covered chair, stretching one leg before him, the other one bent as he leaned against the chair back, managing to look at the same time relaxed and regal.

Amanda frowned at him. He must have practiced that superior air of his. Charm simply oozed from him. Well, he's not going to charm me, she swore silently. The very reason she'd been attracted to Francis was that he had been her own secret choice.

An array of livery-clad footmen came in with trays of finger sandwiches and pastries. After the ladies were served, the duke took a glass of champagne, but refused any food.

Probably because he'd look awkward with a plate on his lap, thought Amanda. For he happened to sit out of reach of the marble-topped side tables. His long, lithe body was graceful but masculine, and she instinctively disliked him for the ease he appeared to feel in such a circumstance.

For herself, she balanced a plate on her knees and sipped champagne, a linen napkin under the plate protecting her from any spills. Her fear of formality arose from the strict discipline imposed on her by Louisa as she'd been growing up. Don't drop this, don't spill that, the litany of reprimands echoed painfully even now.

Because she felt so awkward herself in formal surroundings, she hated the duke's easy sophistication as he carried on a conversation with Josephine.

"I must admit I was quite impressed with your scenery in the western states, though many of the towns and cities are still quite primitive. I rather favored the graciousness of Charleston, however."

"My other son went west," said Josephine, referring to Jay's brother. "Didn't want anything to do with his father's rug business. Runs a newspaper in Denver."

Louisa winced at the mention of trade, but said nothing.

"Ah yes," replied Sunderland. "The city that sprawls at the foot of the Rocky Mountains."

"I haven't been there myself," answered Josephine. "But he seems to like it."

Louisa intervened, in an effort to call attention away from the business that had made the Whitney fortune, well aware that people in trade were not considered good enough for the more fastidious in high society. But if the duke was shocked, he showed no sign.

"Since His Grace has expressed interest in a visit to Newport, I have invited him to be our guest next week at Marble Gate."

Amanda nearly spilled her entire plate of sandwiches. Not only could she scarcely think of something to say in a room of this size with two others present to carry the burden of conversation, but now she was being asked to entertain this English duke for several days at their home? She knew good and well that Louisa would throw her with him in an effort for some imagined courtship to take place. She'd better speak to her mother about Francis right away, before things got out of hand.

Sunderland settled his gaze pleasantly on Amanda as he said, "I shall look forward to it. And now, I am in hopes that Amanda has a place on her card for me to have a dance."

"My card—"

"Why, of course she does," said Louisa sweetly. "I'm sure whoever she had promised will not mind deferring to our honored guest."

Amanda's jaw clenched. She could hardly refuse to dance with him in front of her mother and grandmother. But she remained seated, making them all wait. Finally, unable to tolerate them all looking at her, she put aside her plate and stood.

"Very well," she said with resignation.

The duke glided upward and toward her, a smile of pleasure lighting his rugged face. "I'm glad to see you are so pleased to accept."

Her eyes blazed at his mockery; but she accepted his arm, and they excused themselves, leaving the room.

She followed his long strides, uncomfortably aware of his commanding presence and the charisma that emanated from him. He was masculine to the extreme, and even in her state of agitation, she sensed it uncannily. By the time they finished the distance from the withdrawing room to the ballroom, she was drawn into the special place he had created for her by his side, and she felt she was being shown to the world as his honored dance partner. She was aware of the eyes that were upon her.

As they entered the ballroom, the master of ceremonies announced a mazurka, a dance at which Amanda was especially clumsy. Her lips pinched together, she followed Sunderland onto the floor, where they joined three other couples for the round dance.

The speed of the dance was not great, and she tried to concentrate on the rhythm, with its stress on the second beat. Some of the dancers marked the second beat with a tap of the heel to the wood floor of the ballroom, creating a certain excitement to the dance, and to her chagrin, Sunderland was expert at it, taking great advantage of the latitude for improvisation the dance provided. But Amanda remained stiff, depending on his support for balance whenever they touched hands.

Puffing for breath, she started for the chairs after the dance was over, but Sunderland held on to her hand. "Do me the pleasure of the waltz, which I believe is next."

"I'm not very good at waltzing," she said.

But he only laughed, slid his hand about her waist and extended her right hand.

"I promise not to step on your feet," he said into her ear as if this communication were meant especially for her alone.

But still Amanda could not loosen up. She counted silently—one, two, three, one, two, three—to make sure she didn't fall down. The nearness of the duke, who she had to concede was handsome in addition to being graceful, didn't help.

For the fresh smell of his stiff collar was pleasing, and his hold on her so firm that she couldn't help being guided along easily. Soon she ceased counting and floated along with him, her feet moving to his rhythm.

Her lips parted slightly, and her eyes came alive. For the first time she was in the arms of an expert dancer, and once she relaxed, the dance ceased to be a struggle. In spite of her resentment, she began to enjoy herself.

Feeling Amanda relax in his arms, Sunderland became more bold and sweeping in his steps, cutting a wide circle among the glittering dancers, who parted to allow them room. He was enjoying himself immensely. Amanda might be an unwilling partner, but he sensed the effect he was having on her. And there was something about her that interested him, perhaps because the spark of stubbornness in her reminded him of himself.

Francis's face flashed by, and Amanda tried to turn her head and send him a look; but Sunderland swept her away, so that Francis was lost from view. When the dance came to an end, Amanda was breathless, an attractive flush to her cheeks.

Sunderland smiled at her sparkling eyes and felt a sense of satisfaction that he had made her enjoy the dance, for he had been quite aware of her awkward hesitations. Yes, there was something about this girl that aroused the instincts of the game. For Edward Pemberton was nothing if not a sportsman. Any hunter knew that most of the fun was in the chase, and Amanda Whitney so obviously had her sights set elsewhere that he felt the challenge of gaining her attentions.

And he was pleased with her clear complexion, the soft curve of bosom above delicate lace. Her lips were full and pink, and he began to feel like tasting them with his own. In other words, she had aroused his desire to explore. She tested his caution, for she was no poor working girl he could invite to his bed casually.

Love was out of the question. That had never been part of the promise he had made to his father. But he had reached an age when he simply must marry. And so he had considered the myriad young heiresses placed before his nose on his travels throughout the United

States, and he had at least tried to find one or two candidates for the position of Duchess of Sunderland who might prove entertaining.

So far he had not even cared one whit whether or not the woman he married aroused any feelings in him. His attentions until recently had been sewn up elsewhere for that matter, though it had become painfully clear to him that he would have to give up his mistress when he married, for the family could not risk scandal. That was but one more burden of the title he bore.

Now he turned his thoughts away from such unpleasant reminders and tried to focus on the conversation coming his way as new acquaintances passed and stopped to speak. He returned Amanda to the chairs along the wall so that she could find the partners who had filled up her card.

"Thank you for the dances," he said to her gravely. "I hope you enjoyed yourself."

She swallowed, looking up at the dark, intense eyes. For the first time she read something human in them. The feeling was so fleeting, she barely put a name to it; but she sensed a trace of melancholy in this otherwise debonair, teasing duke, and it surprised her.

"Ah, Amanda, there you are." Francis's voice reached her left ear.

"Um, oh, Francis."

Sunderland hadn't moved, so she supposed she must introduce them. Frantically she searched her mind for the correct form of address used by Mrs. Stevens and her mother.

"Your Grace," she managed to get out, "may I present Francis Newton. Francis, this is the Duke of Sunderland."

Sunderland gave a little bow and extended his hand, which Francis took. "A pleasure, Mr. Newton."

"Er, um, yes. Well, the pleasure is mine, Your Grace," said Francis, although his half scowl indicated that it really was no pleasure at all.

"I apologize if you are one of the men I so selfishly cut out just now," said Sunderland, giving no explanation of why he had done so. It did not occur to him that an explanation might be expected, he was so used to other men deferring to him.

He bowed and drifted away, to be assailed by other matrons anxious to present their daughters. Francis guided Amanda to the dance floor.

"You looked like you were enjoying yourself," said Francis, a note of challenge in his voice as they took their positions for the stately polonaise.

Left without the duke's strong sense of rhythm, Amanda once again felt adrift as she bent her knee and bowed to mark the beat. It was easy to converse, for the dance was done as a promenade around the ballroom.

"The duke is not a bad dancer," she said.

"Well, well," replied Francis. "Rumor has it he's looking for a wife."

"Is he? I wouldn't know," she fibbed.

Francis sent her a look. "I know you wouldn't be tempted by such show of state."

"Of course not, Francis. Don't be ridiculous."

Satisfied, he moved on to what was on his mind. "Have you had a chance to speak to your mother yet?"

"No," she said, panic rising. "Though I did mention your name to my grandmother."

"What did she say?"

"She didn't approve," Amanda said in such a hesitant voice that Francis had to ask her to repeat herself.

"She said she didn't think you were the type to settle down," she said in a stronger voice, considering this a good enough definition of profligate.

"What does that mean?"

There was no time to answer, for they had to turn and go the other way. Now she saw that the duke was dancing with Emily, and she and Francis nodded to them as they passed.

By the time they reached the other end of the room and the dance came to a close, Amanda hoped that Francis would suggest they go off somewhere where they could talk, but at the announcement of the next dance, Francis shook his head.

"My, my, I've got to go, old girl. Promised this one to Melanie Goelet. You will excuse me?"

She blinked. "Of course."

Just as she thought she would be left alone, her brother Max came along. By his relaxed gait and the agreeable expression on his face, she could see he was having a good time.

"Hello there, sis. Having a nice time?"

"I suppose so," she said, pulling her mouth in a sideways grimace.

He laughed. "Oh, come now. You've danced with nearly everyone here. Why don't you flatter your poor old brother with the next one? Let me see your card."

She fished the card out of her reticule, and Max examined it. "Aha, Winthrop Rutherfurd is supposed to claim you next. But I witnessed myself the very fact that Winthrop is off with Consuelo Vanderbilt having a tête-à-tête in the gallery. It didn't look to me like they wished to be disturbed." He presented his arm. "So what do you say?"

Since Amanda was used to dancing with her brother

from the many dancing lessons foisted on them as children, she followed him out. She could even dance and listen to him talk without too much difficulty in this, another waltz. Max was not as good a dancer as the duke, but he was fair, and he had all the confidence in his dancing that Amanda lacked. So at least he kept a firm hand on her and prevented her faltering.

"So you've been hounded by all these young pups this evening, hmmm?"

She shrugged. "What do you mean hounded, Max? Most of them are just being polite by dancing with me. Some of them are your own friends."

"Hmmm. It's not my friends I'm worried about, but all the young fortune hunters who are bound to come sniffing around now that you've come out."

Amanda pressed her lips together, afraid she was going to hear yet another lecture. But Max's tone was different. They were fairly close, and as he continued, she understood that he was actually concerned for her well-being.

"Don't tell Mother I said so, but it's my opinion that the men she'll introduce you to will only want to marry you for your money."

"Grandmother says that Francis is only interested in my money. But I don't believe her."

"Francis Newton, eh? I'm not so sure about him, sis. He's a likable enough fellow, but a bit of a wild card. I would be careful if I were you."

Max's disparaging remarks came closer to bringing her to tears than all the high-handed lectures from her elders. She tried to swallow her grief, and as they passed Francis, whirling Melanie Goelet across the floor, he sent Amanda a dazzling smile.

Amanda finally found her voice. "Mother's invited

the Duke of Sunderland to Marble Gate next week," she said.

"Yes, so I've heard. Sorry I won't be there much to help you entertain the old fellow. At least he's honest about what he's after. Wants a wealthy wife. Most suitors fail to admit that as their motive."

"But I don't even like him," protested Amanda, shocked at her brother's matter-of-factness. Max shrugged.

The dance ended, and Amanda was handed off to her cousin Henry, whom she hadn't had a chance to talk to all evening. Henry being a worse dancer than even she, Amanda suggested they take some refreshments instead.

"I'm famished, Henry," she said. "I didn't get to finish my sandwiches in the other room. Let's get a plate of food and sit down somewhere. You haven't told me what you've been up to lately."

"Ummm, right," said Henry, adjusting his spectacles and offering his arm to escort Amanda to the refreshment room.

Had she followed his lead, she would have walked right into the pillared architrave surrounding the doors, so she steered Henry slightly to the left.

"You really must take a look at Fergusson's *History of Architecture,*" Henry said, launching into a discussion of the stimulating book he'd been reading. The fact that a discussion of historical precision and technical expertise was rather heavy conversation for a ball escaped him.

He and Amanda passed through several gala rooms to the one where refreshments were displayed on a long table. They chose from sandwiches, flavored ices, fruit, and pastries, finding a quiet corner to sit in. Though normally enthralled by topics like Fergusson's *Architecture,* and Hamilton's *History of Philosophy*, she was distracted more than usual this evening. She saw Francis from a distance several more times, but he did not dance with her again.

The evening finally came to an end, and Amanda could not wait to leave. Riding home in the carriage, she had to listen to her mother's incessant observations on society and what everybody wore.

"And what did you think of the Duke of Sunderland, my dear?" Louisa finally asked.

Amanda lifted a resentful shoulder. "Pompous, if you ask me."

"But a good dancer. I noticed how well you did with him."

Amanda prickled. She had thought the same thing, but wasn't about to admit it. She judged it the wrong time to bring up Francis. So confused were her feelings that all she wanted was to be left alone. Upstairs, she got out of her gown with Delcia's aid and then climbed into bed, seeking comfort from Morgan, who curled up on her pillow, his head against hers, purring her to sleep.

Normally, Amanda looked forward to time spent at her family's house in Newport. Marble Gate sat back from high cliffs, and she loved the changing moods of the ocean with its misty surges against the rocky cliffs. The view from her bedroom looked over the high stone walls surrounding the house so that she felt at times she could see clear across the Atlantic.

But it was too early for the gardens to be blooming with anything but daffodils, hyacinth, and crocus, and a chilly wind blew in from the sea. Now the grand rooms that Louisa had decorated so carefully were cleaned by the household staff as if for a state visit as Amanda tried to forestall the duke's coming. But such was not to be. The duke arrived as planned, and her first encounter with him was at lunch.

She entered the formal dining room, which seemed to swallow the few people gathered there. The white marble walls were divided by pilasters with capitals of gilt bronze. Four marble niches contained Grecian statues, and the crystal chandeliers were suspended from the carved plaster ceiling.

Besides the duke there were only Josephine, Max, Louisa and herself to dine. They gathered at the side of the room where Louisa was just pointing out the garden, visible from the tall, narrow windows that looked out onto it. Max was entertaining his grandmother with some anecdote. True to his word, he wasn't spending much time at the house, but he had been commandeered for the luncheon.

Sunderland turned as she joined them. The sunlight coming in the windows glinted off his handsome face. He looked no less in command of himself in his frock coat and pearl gray trousers than he had in evening dress. His hands locked together behind him, he bowed to her.

"Ah, Miss Whitney. A pleasure to see you again."

"Thank you," she said.

"Well, shall we sit down?" said Louisa.

She placed the duke on her right with Josephine next to him. Amanda and Max sat opposite them, leaving the long expanse of the rest of the dining room table to stretch empty down the length of the gold and white room. Red roses in a Flemish vase decorated the table, well out of the way of the gold-plated dinnerware, fine china and crystal.

The footmen brought in the lunch, and Amanda searched her mind for something to say. Not that she was ill-at-ease for conversation among her own intimates. But being introduced to this duke made her feel like she was an objet d'art placed on view for possible purchase. Luckily Max filled the void with talk about yachting, a subject in which Sunderland seemed most interested.

"Perhaps after lunch, Amanda can show you the grounds," Louisa suggested, observing that if she weren't careful, Max would have the duke off on some adventure before they knew it.

"Yes, of course," he answered, bringing his attention back to the ladies. "I would like that. I noticed the stables. Do you keep horses?"

"Yes," said Amanda, finally finding a subject she liked. "Do you ride?"

The corners of his lips turned up. "Of course."

"Then I can show you our stables."

Too late, she realized she had now placed herself in the position of going riding with him. But Amanda was more comfortable on the back of a horse than anywhere else when she didn't have her nose in a book in the library. Perhaps it was just as well to escape this stuffy atmosphere.

Sunderland let the conversation drift pleasantly along until they were through dessert. He walked with the elder of the Mrs. Whitneys as far as a white drawing room hung with a fine set of tapestries. Also displayed around the room were chiseled bronzes set on marble-topped consoles. He duly admired it all.

"The andirons were chiseled by Gouthière and were made for Marie Antoinette," said Louisa, pointing to the elaborate figures of what appeared to be draped seminudes holding harps on pedestals supported on the shoulders of two more seated seminudes.

The duke did not ask how they got from Marie Antoinette's family to this one. But if the Whitneys were trying to impress him with their wealth, he was convinced. Though one didn't necessarily know what kind of a dowry Amanda would come with, it was probably a substantial one. The nouveau riche in New York were where the money was, which was why he didn't bother searching for a wife among the well-established families, the Knickerbockers, Livingstons and Van Rensselaers. Many of those older families were as impoverished as he was.

"Well, now," Louisa finally said, "we'll leave you two young people alone to chat. I'm sure you'll enjoy a tour of the grounds, Your Grace."

He bowed. "I shall, at that."

The rest of the family trooped out, leaving the duke and Amanda alone.

"Shall we go to the stables?" she said.

"I would like that."

Anxious to escape the house himself, he followed her through another gilded salon, then to a corridor that led to an exit. Outside, the fresh sea air was invigorating, and he breathed deeply. This reminded him much more of home than New York City with its bray of vendors and hustling crowds.

"A lovely setting," he said as he followed her along a brick walk.

"I like it," she said. She skirted the gardens, too impatient to point out the various flowering plants, and headed through the grilled gate in the high stone wall that separated the garden from the stableyard.

Sunderland's eyes lit up at the sight of the brick stable

with two stories of diamond-latticed Gothic windows and castellated roof. Two grooms were busy with chores, one sweeping the doorway to one of the stalls, the other hosing down the side of the building. It was plain that the Whitneys spared no expense here.

Amanda led him through the central arched doorway, and they stood in the cool stable.

"This stable would do Elsenheim Palace proud," he said sincerely, admiring both the architecture and what horseflesh he could see and now smell. The horses were facing inward, their heads in feed bags, tails swishing.

"I've always spent most of my time around the horses when we're out of the city," said Amanda. "My favorite mount is over here."

She led the way to a stall containing a chestnut mare of good lines. Amanda slipped into the stall, clucked to the mare and rubbed her nose.

"This is Windy," she said. "Because she loves to race the wind."

Sunderland joined her in the stall, running his hands over the fine lines of the mare. The smell of horses was a pleasure to him, and there was nothing more exciting than to see such good specimens, unless it was riding them himself. He smiled as he observed Amanda talking to and petting her horse. He had a sudden impulse to continue the motion of his caress from the horse's withers to the cheek of the girl beside him who suddenly seemed to take on a glow of life that she lacked inside.

Amanda threw him a shy smile. "I'm sure you'd like to see the rest. We have some very fine geldings."

"Indeed."

They made an inspection of the rest of the horses, and the duke continued to be impressed.

"Would you join me for a ride tomorrow morning?"

he asked. "Surely there are some challenging paths along those cliffs there."

She nodded. "Yes, there are. I'm an early riser myself."

"All the better. I can be up with the dawn if the horses will be ready."

She raised her eyes to meet the challenge. "Then we'll meet here at six o'clock."

"Smashing," he said. "I'll be ready."

They had worked their way to the end of the stable and exited a side door, which took them out to where the ground sloped down to a sharp cliff. Edward moved toward the sea to get a better view, the wind ruffling his hair.

"Sometimes it feels as if you could see England from here," commented Amanda, following his gaze.

"Indeed," he said as they walked close to the cliffs and peered down at the foamy water, but not so close as to be in any danger of sliding over the edge.

"Do you miss your home?" she asked, beginning to see the duke more as a person than the figurehead she had at first taken him to be. Out of doors his cheeks appeared more ruddy, and when he gazed across the sea, it was as if he were indeed looking toward something dear he had left there.

He turned and smiled as if caught in his own transparent thoughts. "Yes, I suppose I do. Shall we walk a bit?" he said, and they turned along a path beside the cliffs that led well around the grounds of the other great houses.

The wind lifted her spirits, and Amanda stopped hating him enough to be willing to hear thoughts he might originate. But as soon as she decided that here in the open she could afford to put aside her prejudice against him for a little while, his words barbed her generous feelings.

"They expect me to marry an heiress like you," he said, likewise inspired by the setting to hold nothing back. "In my position, I'm not expected to marry for love. I loved a girl once with all my heart, you see. A shopkeeper's daughter. But it was impossible, because I am a link in the chain."

Chapter 4

Amanda stopped, and turned toward him, her lips parted and her eyes questioning. The wind pulled strands of her hair out of her chignon, and they swirled about her face.

"Whatever do you mean?"

He smiled gently. How could an American girl understand? He turned to walk, and she came along, her head still turned in his direction, though she had to glance at the ground from time to time to make sure she did not fall. He took her arm to make sure the small outcroppings of rock did not trip her. They approached a bench that had been erected so that passersby could enjoy the magnificent view, and he guided her there.

Her wide, curious eyes moved him in a surprising way, all the more reason to be honest with her. He might be expected to marry for money, but he was not about to lead a prospective wife along with false pretenses. And Amanda Whitney was fast becoming a likely candidate. Better to tell her the truth now, so that she would not suffer any delusions.

"When one is born into a noble family," he explained, "one is born to obligations and traditions. I've been raised to respect my duty, for it's not just one's personal life that matters, but all those who depend on it."

She cocked her head, listening in spite of her own distractions. He continued.

"There is the estate, you see. All the tenants and villagers who work it. They earn little, but we care for them in sickness and times of trouble. They depend on us. And the English have a great love for order. The nobility provide a framework for their lines. It is expected that we live up to a certain standard."

"I see," she said, though she still did not entirely.

"I'll not hide the fact that Elsenheim needs money. Our family has none. Thus, I've been sent to find an heiress."

"Just like that? Like a business contract?" She gave a laugh.

He nodded, gazing at the view that so appealed to him. For the white sails of yachts were visible, moving across the horizon, and nearer in, fishing trawlers chugged by.

"A business contract if you wish. It is a small sacrifice for upholding the standard expected of my title. To insure the survival of the family, individual happiness is as nothing compared to the perpetuation of succeeding generations and the care for the ancestral home."

She blinked in surprise at his little speech. "But you would be marrying against your own will," she said, shocked at his matter-of-factness.

He turned his head, his eyes softer as he gazed at her, the melancholy she had seen before now more transparent in his determined face.

"I can subdue my will. It is something I promised to do," he said. "The privileged class is inseparably bound to its duty."

There was an emotion in his voice that stopped her from prying, though she was curious as to whom he had promised. Still, she was aghast that he would compromise his own happiness to such a degree. She thought of Francis and the battles it seemed she must fight in order to obtain her own happiness.

"I don't see how you can do it," she said, more to herself in reflective thought.

Sunderland reached for her chilly hand and wrapped his own around it. "It can be done, I assure you. It need not be unpleasant. I may not be privileged to marry for love, but there are other things to consider."

She did not draw her hand away, feeling the strength of his. And the way his eyes settled on her face made her tremble. Surely, it was fear she told herself, fear that he might draw her into his net, the net she'd sensed when she'd danced with him.

He observed the upturned face, the half-parted lips, the graceful throat above ruffled gown. Her freshness appealed to him, and he began to feel desire stirring again. Her bosom curved softly under the bodice of her dress, and her waist was one that he could most naturally slip his hand around. Relief swept through him as he began to feel that here was a young lady he might take as his bride. Naturally vigorous, he had never deigned to hope that he would find a bride who met his requirements and would tantalize him as well.

With the realization that he might not have to, came the irrational urge to press his mouth onto hers, to explore the curve of bosom with his hand. But he was fully aware that they were exposed to the eyes of any onlookers who happened to glance this way from their windows. And one didn't behave like a beast toward a woman with whom one was considering marriage. Instead he had to satisfy himself with a gentle kiss on the back of her hand.

The intensity of his gaze on Amanda's cheeks made them warm, his lips on her hand made it tingle, and within her a curious new sensation blossomed that left her startled and vulnerable. It disturbed her that he could arouse such feelings in her on the heels of his announcement that he would not marry for love.

It was then that she realized her danger. Edward Pemberton was attractive, and the headiness he made her feel was a betrayal of her promises to Francis. Moreover, to marry for the sake of her fortune was a betrayal of herself. What could her mother be thinking of?

"Tell me," he said. "Have you thought of marriage? To anyone in particular?"

The quick shift of her head to avoid his gaze told him her answer.

"Ah, I see," he said, lowering her hand slowly.

"There is someone," she said, after a moment. Sunderland had been honest with her; she ought to allow him the same courtesy.

She stood up suddenly.

"I . . . I think we'd better go back," she said.

"Just so," he said, standing up, his eyes still dwelling on her face. It was better to start walking and calm the blood that had begun racing through him. The fact that she had a young man did not daunt him. If there were a formal engagement, he would have been informed, but that was not so. Clearly the family considered her eligible, and that was enough for him. Other suitors didn't matter. They could hardly compete with his title and lineage. And he was simply used to getting what he wanted.

"Perhaps you will visit Elsenheim while you are in

Europe," he said as they returned along the curving path.

"No doubt," she said without enthusiasm, for she was well aware that her mother was set on wrangling such an invitation.

Once back in the house, Amanda left the duke to browse among the paintings in the picture room and fled upstairs. Her ears throbbed, and she was overcome with a sense of desperation. She shut the door and crossed the floral carpet to the tapestry-covered lounge placed before gauze-curtained windows and flung herself down. Where was Morgan? She needed to squash him in her grasp and feel his soft fur, pressing kisses on his little head as an outlet for her emotions.

"Morgan." She kissed the air, leaning over to search beneath furniture. "Where are you?"

But the cat must have been taken downstairs to the kitchens. Seeing he was not there, she fell on the sloping back of the lounge and frowned out the window.

After a while her tumbling thoughts turned back to what Sunderland had said. Though she could not understand the ways of English lords, his words were spoken with sincerity, and she had no doubt that he believed what he said. How sad that he had been raised knowing his fate was sealed. And what of this girl he had once loved? What had happened to her?

But the duke's dilemma was not as important as her own. Perhaps Francis had written. She got up and bounced out into the hallway and down the main stairs. Going into the library, she tugged on the bellpull for Morris, their butler.

In a moment the man appeared in his dapper coat, white waistcoat, prim starched collar and white cravat.

He bowed, his partially balding head glistening as if it had been polished.

"You rang, miss?"

"Have there been any messages or letters for me, Morris?"

"No, miss. There have not."

Her shoulders fell in disappointment. "Very well. Thank you. But if anyone should inquire, I am at home."

"Yes, miss."

Thus instructed, he turned to go. Amanda tried to curb her impatience and looked around the library, where she tried to remember what she had left off reading. Drat! She had been here for two whole days. Why hadn't Francis called? He said he would be able to come up to Newport. Well, he wasn't here, but that made no difference. She would speak to her mother at once, before matters got out of hand and before Edward Pemberton got it into his head to broach the business arrangement of marriage.

She sought out Louisa to force an interview, only to discover that her mother was not at home. She and Josephine had gone calling and would be back before dinner. Restless, Amanda went out to the stables.

No one was about when she entered the cool darkness, and she moved quietly along the row of stalls. She was about to step up to Windy's stall, when a rustling from one of the far stalls caught her attention. At the same time, Windy stamped a hoof, and Amanda moved to pat the mare's rump.

Then her hand froze. She distinctly heard a soft human moan. She started to call out; but in the next moment, the sound came again, in a deeper voice, and it made her hold her breath. She sensed rather than heard that whoever it was did not wish to be disturbed.

Curiosity drew her out of Windy's stall and cautiously along. Her ears pricked, and she justified her actions by telling herself that someone might have been kicked by a horse and be lying hurt. Yet she was furtive, sensing she was wrong, for the moan she'd heard had not been one of pain.

She came to the rungs of a ladder nailed to the walls that led to a hayloft above, and she set her foot quietly on the first rung. Then oblivious to splinters, she pulled herself up step by step.

The hayloft was dark as she climbed up to it and let herself down into the hay, drawing her knees up to clasp them in her arms. She had often sought refuge in the hayloft as a girl when she had wanted to be alone. Sometimes throwing open the hay doors, she would let in the brilliant sun and the view of the sea.

But now she sat still, listening to the groans and rustles that seemed louder. She crawled a little way in the direction from which the sounds came, glancing down at the stalls below her. Then she clapped her hand over her mouth and crouched back out of sight. But she was too shocked to draw her eyes away from what she saw.

Her brother sat next to their scullery maid, Annie, and the two were half-undressed and engaged in very intimate activity. The young girl sat with her blouse down around her waist, bulbous breasts dangling in Max's hands.

The girl twisted and moaned under Max's ministrations. He had been dressed in knickerbockers, which were now unfastened, and a tweed jacket, which had been cast aside on the bales of hay between which they were wedged.

Neither of them saw Amanda gaping at them from above, for their mouths were pressed together, Max's leg pinning down the girl's. His shirt was unbuttoned and her hands inside it, massaging his chest.

Amanda shut her eyes, knowing she should withdraw, for what she was witnessing was sinful, or at least private. But she was too stunned to move, and she was afraid they would hear her. After a moment, she opened her eyes again, careful not to make any noise. But what she witnessed next nearly made her stop breathing altogether.

Max's trousers had lowered enough that the girl had her hand at his groin. His grunts were louder now, and it seemed almost as if he didn't care who might walk into the stables at this inopportune moment. His hand snaked under the girl's skirt and pulled it up, exposing white ruffled drawers, which she helped him peel off.

Annie moved her head from side to side, her eyes shut in ecstasy. From their smooth, liquid movements, which began to build to a frenzy, Amanda guessed that they had done this together before. Still, curiosity and her own quickening blood made her stare down at the entangled pair.

When Annie cried out and their gasps rose to Amanda's ears, she crept backward, scrambled to the hay doors to open them, and inhaled a breath of fresh air, lying against the hay and breathing deeply, her eyes closed. She waited in the loft until she could hear from the sounds below that Max and Annie were finished. She heard them talking in subdued voices, Annie giggled, and they rustled about, evidently dressing themselves.

For a long time after they left, Amanda lay there until her breath became more even and the perspiration dried on her forehead. The only sound except for the sea breeze was a stall door banging against the stall where the wind opened and shut it hard against the latch someone had forgotten to close.

Somehow the afternoon passed, and when Amanda returned to the house, no one had missed her. When it was time to dress for dinner, Amanda tried to select the plainest dress she had. Even so, the crêpe de chine with small puffed sleeves and bodice trimmed with ruffles accented her figure in a flattering way, and the velvet ribbon Delcia tied around her throat only seemed to show off her shoulders and hinted at her bosom to good advantage.

She gazed at the armoire, trying to think of a more modest gown, as if she could hide herself from the dinner party, blending in with the high-backed chairs so she wouldn't feel like she was on display, and so Max wouldn't read her guilty face. But there was no time.

A knock sounded on the door, and when Delcia admitted Morris, in evening tailcoat, he bowed politely.

"The party is gathering downstairs, miss. Your company is desired."

She rose from the vanity bench. "Thank you, Morris. I'll be along."

Delcia cocked her head for one final inspection, looking proudly at the chignon with curls at the front and sides.

"You look lovely, miss, if I do say so myself."

"Oh, thank you," said Amanda. Then, so that Delcia didn't misunderstand her mood, "You did a lovely job."

Delcia bobbed a curtsy and held the door for her.

There was no need to pinch her cheeks for color; they

were already blazing by the time she reached the white drawing room where the party was having champagne. Sunderland looked up from his conversation with Max by the fireplace when she entered, and she didn't miss the pleased expression that came into his eyes. She lowered her gaze in embarrassment.

"There you are," said Josephine, bedecked this evening in frilly lavender satin. "Come here, dear, and sit by me."

She escaped to her grandmother's side on the brocade sofa and accepted a glass of sherry from the footman who approached with a tray.

"You look lovely, my dear," said Josephine.

She examined her blushing granddaughter closely. The fluttering of eyelashes and the tinge on her cheek were new. She was aware that the duke had taken her for a stroll this afternoon. Could it be that an attraction had formed? Josephine smiled to herself. Perhaps things were going to go easier than they had all expected.

Somehow Amanda got through the meal. Max was in a gay mood, looking her full in the face without guessing her secret. She drank more wine than she usually did and was thankful when the ladies retired to the parlor again to take coffee. With a little of the stimulating liquid in her, and the doors closed against the private man talk that would take place in the dining room for the next half hour, Amanda found courage to speak her mind when her mother's inevitable interrogation began.

"Did you enjoy your afternoon, dear?" asked Louisa, after Morris had served them their coffee and shut the doors after him.

Amanda set her china cup and saucer on the side table beside a muted, fringed globe lamp.

"I had an honest discussion with the duke, if that is

what you mean," she said, keeping her eyes slightly averted from her mother's.

"And?" asked Louisa.

"He made his purpose clear about finding a wife who could support him."

A sound between a gasp and a choke issued from her mother. "Amanda, that is no way to speak."

"Well, it's true, Mother," said Amanda, her voice and her eyes rising with more defiance now. "His family is impoverished, and he has a house that's too big to run."

Louisa's face darkened, her eyes turning to steel. "It's not a house but a palace. He has described it to me."

"I don't care what it is, I'll never set eyes on it."

"The duke has invited us to visit Elsenheim while we are on our tour."

"So I've heard. We will have to decline. I wouldn't want to lead him on. For I could never marry him."

"Why not?" Louisa's voice built in volume just as Amanda's words picked up speed.

"For heaven's sake, Mother, he doesn't love me or any other heiress for that matter. He is after a business arrangement."

"Many arranged marriages turn out successfully," stormed Louisa, standing up now, unable to contain her anger. "You are simply too young to know."

Amanda, too, jumped up, her fists clenched, and Josephine waved ineffectually from the sofa as if to stop the two of them from knocking over any of the china in their anger.

"I shall never know because I intend to marry someone of my own choice, someone I love."

"And who might that be?"

"Francis Newton." She nearly shouted it.

There followed a dead silence, during which Louisa's

face turned from red to mauve then went white and then red again. Her jaw seemed locked while Amanda's own flashing eyes stared her down. Finally Louisa drew a wheezing breath and spat out, "Not that hopeless gigolo."

Now it was Amanda's turn to gasp. But Louisa seized her chance. "Francis Newton would only want you for your money."

"So does Edward Pemberton."

"That is different."

"How is it different?"

Louisa blustered, but then spewed forth, "Everyone knows that Francis has affairs. He's been seen about town with women of questionable reputations."

Amanda drew herself up. She had no idea whether or not this was true, nor was she even sure any longer if she really loved him. And any indiscretions in the past were explainable because Francis was not yet married. Though people did not talk about it, it was understood that men had a way of gaining certain sexual experience denied to ladies. And of course any such adventures would cease once he was married. Witness Max and the maid. She would sooner go to her death than tell anyone what she'd seen. That was Max's business. Instead of defending Francis, she attacked the duke.

"Sunderland has most likely had affairs as well. He told me himself he was in love with a shopkeeper's daughter."

"Surely he will give her up once he marries," said Louisa.

"As would Francis. So you see, Mother, you have not gained a point."

"There is a further difference."

Amanda did not miss the threat in her mother's voice. "Oh?"

"Edward Pemberton has a title."

Tears sprang to Amanda's eyes, and her lips trembled. "So you would sell me for a title."

"Amanda," said Louisa, truly shocked. "I am only thinking of your welfare and security. You are too young to make this decision by yourself."

"Then I shall not make it at all. I don't have to marry. I want to see the world. Perhaps I'll join a convent."

She meant nothing of the sort, but shouted the first thing that came into her head, emotion running rampant.

If Louisa had any sensitivity toward her daughter's dilemma, she did not show it. Rather, she clenched her jaw and moved toward her.

"I tell you this, my girl. I will shoot any suitor of yours of whom I have not approved."

Amanda's eyes opened wide in horror, and she stared open-mouthed at her mother. Was the woman mad? For the first time she wondered about the sanity of Louisa's obsession. Her mother had always been at her strongest when dominating others. No wonder her father lived apart. Who could tolerate such domineering? The threat silenced Amanda completely, not in surrender, but in dumb shock.

A knock sounded at the door, and a second later it opened. Max and the duke entered the stony room. Their laughter at some humorous incident died on their lips as they faced the glares of the two women posed with fists clenched and the white-faced Josephine on the sofa, who quickly grasped her beaded fan and began fanning herself.

The duke was the first to salvage the situation. "Max was just telling me about some friends of his who got stranded in a rowboat without an oar. It could have been rather dangerous except that a fishing boat rescued the party, returning them all smelling like fish."

No one laughed. Max came around to where his mother was standing by the mantel.

"Shall we have a little sherry in here? It goes down well after the coffee." For answer he pulled the bell rope and, when Morris appeared, issued the order.

By now Louisa had stifled her anger and found her tongue. "Please have a seat, Your Grace. I have just been telling Amanda about Elsenheim."

Sunderland glanced at Amanda's face and thought that if her expression belied her feelings about what she'd heard of Elsenheim, she certainly would not want to hear any more about it just now. So he merely said, "You must visit us and see it for yourself."

"Ah yes, the voyage," said Louisa, as if reminded of a topic about which they could make conversation. "We set sail in a little over a week."

"And where will you stop first once you cross the Atlantic?" asked Sunderland politely.

The sherry came in small glasses on a silver tray, and Morris served, then left the tray with a carafe on a side table.

"We shall go to Paris first," said Louisa. "I have a sister there who insists on entertaining us."

In her agitation, Amanda gulped down her sherry. Now she listened to her mother babbling on about the latest fashions in Paris. A few times Sunderland slid his glance her way, and though he was able to carry off the social situation, she felt instinctively that he was not enjoying himself much more than she was. He was simply used to making inane small talk when necessary. For the second time today, she wrenched her attention away from her own problems to take his view.

Rising and helping herself to another glass of sherry, she thought about him, probably stuck in a hundred drawing rooms like this one since he came to America on his relentless search for a wife. She couldn't help but feel sorry for him. If it was true that he bore such responsibility for his title, then he couldn't lead a very happy life either. Well, it wasn't her problem.

"Excuse me," she said suddenly when her mother had reached a period in a sentence and the duke had drawn breath to reply. "I think I should go up."

All eyes turned to her. Sunderland rose. Max lumbered to his feet likewise.

"Don't forget our ride," said the duke. "Six A.M. in the stables."

"Very well," she said. Then she turned and fled up to her room.

This house was a prison, she thought to herself as she struggled to get undressed. Finally giving up on being able to reach the fastenings at the back, she sent for Delcia, but after the girl got her out of her dress, she dismissed the maid, saying she would brush out her own hair. In truth she wasn't in the mood for a late night gossip with her maid. Instead, she sent her to fetch Morgan.

She extinguished the lamp and lay on the bed. Not even the sounds of the sea rushing in against the rocks soothed her. No book would take her mind off her ridiculous situation, and she hopelessly tried to plot ways to foil her mother's plans. She'd finished her schooling. There was no hope of hiding out for another year of education. There was nothing a young lady of her social class was expected to do except marry and produce children.

There was a light tap on the door, and then Delcia came in only far enough to drop the cat on the rug. Morgan meowed and trotted to the bed.

"Come here, boy," she said, patting the pillow where he jumped up and then settled himself down. He purred as she stroked him and continued her own thoughts.

There was her intense interest in scholarship, but what could she possibly do with that? Oh, there were a few women who broke the rules and published some little pieces, but she had no talent for writing. Charity work was expected, of course, but not as a full-time vocation. She felt trapped in a marble prison. Was there no way out? She could of course run away with Francis; but she didn't think she could face the scandal, and then she punished herself for her spinelessness. She needed to talk to Henry. She must have him come up to console her.

Well, she had stood up to her mother tonight, and that wasn't the end of the matter. Tomorrow morning she would have a talk with Sunderland and tell him of her feelings. Then perhaps he would go home and stop pursuing the matter. If she could insult enough titled lords on their voyage to Europe, perhaps she could make herself so unattractive that no one would ask for her hand, and she would have a chance to decide for herself what she wanted to do with her life. She did not want to be rushed about that decision. Francis or no Francis, she wasn't going to allow anyone to tell her what to do any longer.

Satisfied at last that she might indeed have the ammunition with which to fight back, she allowed herself to relax enough to go to sleep.

* * *

Her eyes flew open as the gray light of dawn tinged the curtained windows, and she sat up. Morgan crept nearer and licked her face.

"Yes, kitty. We'll go downstairs for your breakfast."

She arose, turned up the gas lamp, for it was still too dark to see in the shadowy room, and then, putting on dressing gown, picked up Morgan, shifted him so that his paws clung to her shoulder, and carried him into the corridor. Her slippers trod noiselessly on the runner, and the house was dim and cool, nothing stirring as she made her way downstairs and then through the corridors that led to the kitchens on the side of the house.

Here there was activity aplenty, and she handed Morgan over to a kitchen maid named Jillian, who cuddled Morgan herself and then took him outside. She was glad it was Jillian and not Annie who took the cat, since she was afraid she wouldn't be able to hide her secret knowledge.

"Good morning, miss," said Sarabeth, their big, jolly cook. "Up early to bring Kitty down, I see."

"I'm going riding this morning," said Amanda.

"Ah, well now, that's a healthy thing to do."

Amanda grinned in wry humor. "I have to entertain our guest."

"Well now, he looks to be a fine man to me. Have a nice ride."

On her way out, Amanda stopped by the big cast-iron range and sniffed the hot cereal that Sarabeth had begun to simmer. "I'll be hungry when we come back," Amanda said with a grin.

"Well, then, we'll have to make sure that brother of yours leaves you something to eat for breakfast."

Amanda left the kitchen and started for the stairs. Normally she didn't think anything of going about the house in her dressing gown at this hour, for the simple reason that no one was ever up except the staff who had to begin their chores in the darkness of early morning. So she was startled by the footstep behind her as she passed the door to an anteroom where a few displays of armor were kept.

She paused in the corridor. To her surprise she heard another step, and then Sunderland appeared in the shadows, dressed for riding. She was so surprised at seeing him that she could not find words.

"Good morning," he said easily. His smile conveyed that he liked what he saw. He cleared his throat and came a step closer. "You're not dressed yet."

Her hand flew to the ruffles at her throat. "I was just going to dress," she said. "I didn't know you'd be ready this early."

"Oh, it isn't quite six yet, but I was eager for the exercise. I've already been to the stables to watch the groom saddle the horses."

He had steered her into the anteroom, out of the corridor. The shadows made the room very dim, and the armor mounted on stone walls made it feel like they had stepped back in time. His arm was on her elbow as he moved her closer to him.

"We should go, then," she said, trying to step back. But he did not relax his grasp on her arm.

"There's no hurry. This is rather pleasant. Perhaps you can tell me about this collection."

The ease of his conversation and the state of her dress were unnerving, but she opened her mouth to comply. "My father liked to collect things, and Max rather fancies them as well. We've brought home some of these pieces from our travels in Europe. All medieval."

Her words faltered as he slid an arm about her waist and pulled her nearer, his lips brushing her hair and cheek.

"Really?" The word sounded so sensual that Amanda trembled.

"I ought to dress for our ride," she said, trying to turn and go, but she only succeeded in facing him, for his arm was still about her waist.

"I like you this way," he said, a smile of pleasure in his voice. "It's very nice to see how a prospective bride appears in the morning after her beauty rest."

"It's not really proper," she said, but too late, for his lips had found her chin and left a kiss there.

Her eyes opened wider, and her lips parted in surprise. How dare he behave this way!

The parted lips and shining eyes were a temptation he made no effort to resist. He lowered his mouth to touch hers and snaked his other arm about her trim waist. The taste of her was delicate and stimulated his senses so that he pressed her against him gently.

Amanda's heart pounded against her chest as he gathered her up in his arms. She had never been kissed this way, not by Francis, not by anyone. Blood pounded in her ears as he let his hand drift up her back to loosen her hair.

"Amanda, my dear, you are lovely," he said when he raised his mouth, but still he held her in the embrace.

She found to her surprise that her arms were twisted about his neck. Her collar had come open, and the frilly nightgown underneath displayed its pink bows. Sunderland took her face in his hands, his thumbs caressing her cheeks as his eyes bored into hers.

"Very lovely. More lovely than I had hoped."

She was speechless with embarrassment and feelings she had no name for, but when she took a step backward, she swallowed. He let her go. How dare he do such a thing! She blinked and then fled from the room. She thought she heard his laughter as she ran up the carpeted stairs, gown flying behind her, hair splayed over her shoulders.

She shut her door and threw herself on the lounge to catch her breath. But she knew that her breathlessness was not only from running up the long flight of stairs. As she caught her reflection in the mirror she saw a new awakening on her youthful face that had not been there before.

Chapter 5

Amanda pulled herself off the couch and went to the armoire to get down her green riding habit. In moments she was into the white blouse with high white collar and neck stock, long skirt that covered trouser legs, fitted jacket, sturdy riding boots and hat with green veil.

The veil doing a great deal to mask her face, she went downstairs again and out to the stables. There was no question of not keeping the appointment. She could not allow Sunderland to think that he had flustered her that much. As to fleeing from his embrace, that was explainable, due to the impropriety of the incident.

As she made her way downstairs she became more certain that the man was a cad. He himself had admitted he would not marry for love. Indeed his whole upbringing and his idea of marriage proved to her that he was a hypocrite. For love he cared nothing, but for his own pleasure, he evidently cared a great deal. And experienced in matters of the flesh, he must be.

She straightened her spine and marched to where Charles had her own Windy and another Morgan horse saddled and bridled with proper English gear. Sunderland was commenting on the tack to Charles, whose responses indicated that he must have thought the duke knew what he was talking about. For Charles was reticent with strangers unless they loved horseflesh.

Sunderland checked the snaffle bridle and the cinch on the black gelding he was to ride.

"Stargazer has a fine disposition," said Charles. "Give him his head. A light touch to the reins is enough to let him know what you want to do."

Sunderland nodded and turned to wait for Amanda to join them. Windy snorted and turned her head as her mistress approached, and Amanda gave her some sugar.

"All ready?" asked the duke.

"Yes, quite."

He bent to give her a leg up to her sidesaddle where she took up the reins. He saw immediately that she had a good seat, and Windy stood, alert, attuned to the mistress on her back. Sunderland smiled then mounted his own horse.

"You lead the way," he said.

They walked the horses out of the stableyard to the street in front of the house and then proceeded down the avenue, for they must pass through town to get to the countryside. Smoke from other chimneys indicated that households were beginning to stir, and a baby's cry from an upstairs window indicated that someone must be hungry.

At the edge of town, Amanda turned onto a path that led through the elms. A grassy meadow stretched away from the cliffs, and she urged Windy forward. The horses eagerly broke into easy canters, and Amanda thrilled as she always did at the movement, the sound of hoof on ground, the cool breeze assailing her face. Her hat was firmly pinned to her chignon, so she was not afraid of losing it.

After a short ride, they pulled up along a wide stream that rushed along. From here an old waterwheel was visible where some of the first settlers to the area had ground their meal in the mill built at the edge of the water.

Edward pulled up beside her to admire the lovely New England scene. "Very nice," he said.

"That's the old mill. We used to love to explore it as children," she told him.

"Still working?" he asked.

She shook her head. "The millstone's broken, but the owners of the property keep it up for visitors."

They found a place where the horses could drink. Sunderland dismounted and helped her down. She tried not to look him in the face as she rested her hands on his shoulders and slid down, his hands at her waist, easing her to the soft ground. They were in a dense thicket, fresh with the smell of spring. The water rushing by provided a lively background, but not so loud that they couldn't talk.

After the horses drank, they hobbled them to graze and walked along the path. Here Amanda pointed to bloodroot beginning to show their buds.

She hadn't gotten over her disconcerting feelings about this man, and really didn't care to make trivial conversation. Perhaps the truth was best, but she waited for him to broach the subject that must be so much in the front of his mind as well as hers.

"You might like England, you know," he said after they had examined some jonquils. "There, nature flourishes in the lush soil and the moisture. You would find many flowers and birds to amuse you."

She straightened. "There is quite enough American flora and fauna to suit me."

He laughed at her haughty reply. "Then I take it you are not looking forward to your upcoming voyage."

"No," she said ingenuously. "I'm not."

"I see."

He took her hand and led her to a fallen log, which he brushed off so that she could sit on it. He leaned against a white birch and crossed his arms.

"Now, tell me about this young man of yours."

She blinked. Her look of surprise gave her away, and she knew it. For in the light that had now brightened the spring sky, his eyes could easily penetrate the green veil. She quickly looked away, but it was too late.

He saw the blush on her cheek that the veil did not hide. His heart missed a beat. Couldn't he, himself, sympathize with her? Hadn't he been in love with a shopkeeper's daughter? A girl so sweet her kisses melted his lips. And skin so soft it was like silk beneath his fingers. Thoughts of his old love brought a twinge to his heart. And he turned his head, his own pain akin to Amanda's.

She saw him glance away, saw the fleeting emotion cross his face. Of course, she realized, attuned to his thoughts. Her secret was exposed. And he had made no secret of the girl he had perhaps wished to marry but could not. The silence that followed was heavy. Sunderland shifted his weight, then finally spoke.

"Tell me about him," he said. "Why is it your family does not wish the marriage? Assuming, of course, that the young man has mentioned marriage to you."

"Of course he has," she said, chin going up. "He is a respectable young man. But alas, not rich. And not titled," she said with bitter meaning.

"Ahhh," Edward sighed. He looked directly at her. "Then I am sorry."

For a moment she believed he actually was. But his next comment brought with it his old air of indifferent acceptance of his fate.

"But we can't always have what we want, now can we? We who are bred with a silver spoon in our mouths. The masses envy us. What they do not know is that we have been brought up in stricter discipline than the poor child who spends its days in the kitchen with all the love of a doting mother who makes goodies to satisfy its every whim. With our money and positions comes responsibility. Yours is to marry and raise children."

She rebelled at his lecture and sprang up from the log. "I am not ready to marry. And when I do, it will be to someone of my own choosing."

He chuckled, following her through the grass. "When you are ready, do you think it will be any different for you? You will have to marry a husband acceptable to your social position and to your family. Surely you realize that by marrying an English title you will have a greater chance of leaving your mark on the world, of doing worthwhile things with your money. Have you stopped to think about that?"

She stopped, turned on him, angry now. "I thought you wanted my money to redecorate your house."

He grinned humorously. "I would hope to put my future wife's money to other good uses as well."

She glared at him, smarting at his comments. "You haven't even proposed to me yet."

"Would you like me to?"

For answer she uttered a strangled sound, turned and stormed back to the horses. She released Windy from her hobble, walked her to a stump so that she could mount by herself and, once seated, trotted off.

When she reached the open space, she nudged Windy

into a canter. Thundering across the grass helped release some of her own pent-up energy; then she slowed the horse to a trot and then a walk, making for the path along the cliffs.

Below, the waters swirled and eddied, and Amanda lifted her face to the ocean, breathing in the salty air. But looking at a steamer far out on the horizon only reminded her that soon she would be ocean-bound herself unless she could think of a plan. She urged Windy along, and when they turned into the stables, only then did it occur to her that she'd left the duke behind.

Charles took her horse, and she slid off on the mounting block. "His Grace will be coming along," she said.

"Very good, miss," said Charles.

She didn't miss the cocky look in the groom's eyes, but she knew he would hold his tongue for fear of his job. She wasn't in the least worried that Sunderland would find his way.

Amanda hurried through the house. In the entry hall she stopped Morris. "Have there been any messages for me?" she asked.

"No, miss. There have not."

She sighed in disappointment and went to change for breakfast. She would prefer not to face the duke again, but she wasn't going to starve herself on his account. Stories of physical martyrdom on account of love were ridiculous, to her way of thinking. There were better ways. She said little as Delcia helped her into a morning gown of crisp dotted swiss.

When she entered the breakfast room, Sunderland was already there, carrying on his usual conversation with Max and Louisa. They all turned to greet her.

"Have a nice ride, dear?" asked her mother.

Amanda kept her eyes focused on the coffee cup as she sat down. "Yes," she answered.

"That's good."

Her mother sounded noncommittal, and Amanda exhaled slowly. Of course the duke's manners would be too impeccable to make any indication of their quarrel. Indeed, when she got up enough courage to glance at him, he seemed indifferent to anything that had passed between them.

Sensing her glance, he turned and nodded as if nothing had happened. She suddenly recalled his lips on her face and throat and looked away. How she hated him for playing with her like a toy, making her experience sensations that ought to be reserved for a lover.

But such thoughts only made her blood simmer even more. A man so sensuous would be the worst type of husband, for he would probably prefer a collection of mistresses to tantalize him with their variety. Oh, how she hated men just at that moment, especially worldly ones.

Well, she would just turn her thoughts from that. She must get a message to Francis today and arrange to see him. She hated to risk using the telephone they had at Marble Gate. The telephone was so public. Servants always answered them, and then one never knew who might be listening in.

A note would be better. She could get one out in the morning post. Excusing herself as soon as she had finished, she went to the sitting room upstairs and took paper from the writing desk, uncapped the ink bottle and dipped in her pen. What to say?

Francis knew where she was, but perhaps he had been put off by the knowledge that the Duke of Sunderland was staying here. And if Francis was still in the city, he would not get this until tomorrow. Since the family was returning to New York the following day to prepare for their trip, she would try to meet Francis at St. Thomas Church at noon on Friday.

Satisfied with her communication, she sealed the note. She started to take it downstairs and deposit it on the silver tray where the family placed outgoing mail. But then she thought better of it. What if Francis had written, but she hadn't gotten the letter? It was not above her mother to screen her mail. So Amanda had a better idea and called for Delcia.

When the young maid entered the room, Amanda shut the door behind her, then handed her the letter.

"Please take this down to the post office yourself, Delcia. I want to make sure it gets out."

Delcia cocked her head. "But the post has not yet been picked up this morning."

"I know that. But this is a confidential letter. I don't want you to mention it to anyone."

The maid's eyes became lively, and she looked at the letter in her hand. "Oh, my. A secret. Of course. Well, I'll see that it gets mailed."

Thinking she'd better explain, Amanda lowered her voice in the event that someone might be listening at the door.

"My mother doesn't approve of this young man," she told Delcia, who listened eagerly to her mistress's plight. "But we have pledged ourselves to each other. He's probably afraid to show himself here, so I have arranged for a meeting in the city."

"How romantic," said Delcia with a secretive smile. "Although I do think your English lord to be a handsome devil."

"He's not my English lord."

"No, no, that's not what I mean. Still, to marry royalty and live in a castle, oh, my," the maid swooned.

"He's not royalty, Delcia. A duke is considered nobility. His ancestor was granted the title. He has no royal blood."

"Oh, well, all the same."

"But I promised myself to Francis Newton," insisted Amanda. "And he to me."

Delcia gave a sigh and said somberly, "Then we mustn't stand in the way of love."

She tucked the letter into her pocket, assuring her mistress it would reach the post.

The duke left Marble Gate the following day, and the Whitneys returned to New York on Thursday. As they rode along in the plush seats of the railroad carriage that clacked over the rails, Amanda failed to feel the relief and anticipation she had expected to. Sunderland had more or less ignored her after their one morning ride and had taken himself off without even saying goodbye. But why should she care about his rudeness when she, herself, had told him what she thought of him? Now perhaps he would do his fortune hunting elsewhere.

Neither had she heard from Francis, but she suspected that was due to Louisa, who could easily have ordered Morris to report all calls and messages to her first. The immutable butler would have obeyed his mistress without question or show of expression.

Once at home, Amanda was immediately caught up in packing, and only narrowly escaped the house and made her way down Fifth Avenue to St. Thomas Church, slipping in with other noontime visitors who came to meditate in the cool, quiet, lofty church. At first she didn't see him; then she spied Francis studying a stained glass window and went around the pillar and down the aisle. He turned at her footfall and smiled. They took seats in the last pew, and he squeezed her hand.

"You got my message," she whispered. There was no one very near, but they had to speak softly so as not to disturb those who sat farther forward, contemplating the artistry of the dark interior and their own thoughts.

"I did. I hope you will forgive me for not coming to Newport after all," he said in hurried, low whisper. "Social engagements I couldn't get out of. My cousin is down from Boston, and I had to show him around, alas."

"Oh." She felt a moment of disappointment.

"But don't worry. I have it all worked out to sail to France in a month. I shall surely be able to join you in Paris."

Hope renewed. "Oh, Francis, that's wonderful."

He gave her hand another squeeze. His voice turned more serious. "Perhaps I should have a word with your father."

Her hands began to turn clammy as she recalled her interview with her mother. "I did try to bring up the subject with Mother."

"And?"

"Oh, Francis, she was dreadful. Said you only wanted to marry me for my money."

Francis swallowed and blinked. "Did she now? Well, perhaps your father will see differently."

"I don't know. I'm going to see him after I leave here. I managed to telephone without anyone knowing it. He's meeting me at Delmonico's."

"Ahhh. Good."

She faced front. A group of boys, young and old, were filing into the chancel and being directed to take seats. A rehearsal of the boys' choir was about to commence. She turned to Francis again.

"I tried to think of a way to get out of this voyage, but it seems the plans are all made. Aunt Zoe in Paris is expecting us."

"Then you must do your duty and go see her."

Strangely, his words reminded her of Sunderland's. "Francis, do you believe the privileged class is inseparably bound to duties?"

"What? Duties? Why, I suppose so."

She waited for him to expound, but he did not. Of course, why should she expect him to analyze and dissect his views on life when he had never done so in her presence before? But she suddenly wanted to hear Francis give reassurances that would carry her across the ocean, spout noble philosophies that would guarantee her he would follow her to the ends of the earth and wait a thousand years if necessary.

Instead, he said, "It is getting near time for lunch. You don't want to keep your father waiting."

She looked at him, and he smiled brightly, then lifted her hand and bowed his head for a quick kiss to her knuckles. Then he slid out of the pew and helped her to her feet. Before the altar the choir boys were beginning to sing, and their angelic voices followed her as she stepped out the door into the sunlight.

When the ship left the docks of New York harbor, Amanda felt that all that was familiar was being torn from her. Her luncheon with her father had only increased her nostalgia. He'd listened to her plight and agreed to see Francis when he came to call at the apartment he kept in a town house on Grammercy Square. But he also suggested she keep her mind open as to other suitors.

"Your mother and I don't see eye to eye on very many things," the dapper forty-five-year-old man had said, as he'd sat back in the comfortable chair at Delmonico's, "but I'm sure she wants the best marriage for you."

"But, Father, why can't people marry for love?"

Her father smiled indulgently. "What do you know of love, my sweetheart? The flutter of heartstrings does not always last. Too often we find our mates to be entirely different persons than we knew them to be at the time of our marriage.

"Look at your mother and me for instance. She was beautiful and energetic when she was young. Little did I know she would turn that energy into running not only her life and our household but my affairs as well. I'm sorry. I promised her I would not poison you against her. But I'm just trying to explain that you should not always be ruled by your heart."

"If I cannot see the future, Father," she had said, her brown eyes snapping, "how do I know that any marriage I make will turn out well?"

Her father had reached across the linen tablecloth to pat her hand. "You don't, my dear. One does one's best, but one cannot know for sure."

Now she stood on the crowded deck watching the skyline recede. There was nothing before her but the gray ocean. She had crossed the Atlantic several times before, and she always looked forward to seeing Europe, the beautiful monuments, the great masterpieces and the ancient villages. But then she had not been forced to look for a husband. And to make matters worse, Francis had not come to see her off.

A niggling doubt began to assert itself as she contemplated this failure on his part. While she could not bring herself to admit that the others could be right about his character, she had to grudgingly admit there was something wrong.

The words of love he had spoken before now resounded hollowly in her heart. Tears brimmed on her lashes as she was forced to consider that he had not exactly shown the devotion she had expected in a suitor who loved her for herself and not her fortune.

The voyage was uneventful, and at Southampton they changed to a steam ferry that took them across the Channel and deposited them at Le Havre. Here, Max left them to visit friends in Monte Carlo. Louisa, Amanda and Delcia entered Paris by train.

Aunt Zoe's town house was located on a picturesque square of similar houses that stood behind iron-grilled fences facing a flowering park. And the sweet scent of hyacinth filled the air.

They were ushered in from their carriage by the French housekeeper named Marie, a tall, thin woman of about Louisa's age, but with her light hair pulled into a bun under frilly mob cap. Her sharp tones ordered the rest of the staff about in clipped, excited French. Footmen in livery appeared to carry luggage, open doors and take wraps.

Aunt Zoe herself appeared through a door at the other end of a tastefully furnished drawing room that admitted sunlight and a view of the square. She was a rotund lady of indeterminable age, but she carried herself as if she were royalty. She was shorter than either

Amanda or Louisa, but her penetrating blue eyes bore down on everyone within her sphere, leaving no doubt that she was grander than anyone present in the room.

But she was full of affection. She turned a cheek for Louisa to peck.

"Zoe," said Louisa. "You look marvelous. How good it is to see you."

"Thank you, my dear. And look at you, Amanda. Come here, my girl. I haven't seen you in two years. Turn around so I can see you."

Amanda did as she was told, the ribbon on her hat twirling behind her.

"Hmmm. Well, we'll have to see about some clothes for you. If I am to present you to society, we must dress you properly. Can't have you looking like the ugly duckling."

Amanda stifled her laughter. Only Aunt Zoe could call her an ugly duckling and not insult her. "Yes, Aunt, if you say so."

"I say so."

Zoe rang for refreshments and made Louisa and Amanda sit and tell her about their voyage before she would release them to their rooms. As Amanda munched fruit and pastry, she realized from the demure expression her mother kept that here was one person who was not intimidated by Louisa's martial habits. It might be rather refreshing to stay with Zoe, Amanda mused.

A shopping spree followed, and for once even Amanda enjoyed the visit to the rue de la Paix establishment of Charles Worth, the only couturier that mattered for rich American ladies. But soon that joy was dimmed as Louisa began to once again assert control. When the models paraded several lovely evening gowns before them, Amanda pointed to the yellow tulle with white lace.

"That's a lovely one, Mother," she said.

Louisa frowned, and motioned for the model to come nearer. "The color would make your complexion look horrible. We'll take the blue," she said to the saleswoman who waited on them.

"Very good, madam."

And so, dressed in the blue, Amanda was displayed at her first Parisian ball, accompanied by Aunt Zoe, who introduced her to counts, barons, ambassadors and an array of military gentlemen, some of whom were old enough to be her father. All of them danced with her. Some spoke no English. But Paris differed from New York in one important respect for Amanda. There was a sprinkling of intelligentsia here that mixed easily with men of great fortunes. Such intellectuals were shunned at home, and Amanda began to find stimulation in talking to young writers, artists and musicians. For literature was her passion, and she had read all the great French works.

During one of many soirees, in conversation with a delightful young Frenchman who had published several essays and taught young scholars, Amanda lost herself in a discussion of literature such as she had not done since her meetings at home with Henry. Emile Reveillere had himself tried his hand at short stories and was most taken with Amanda's interest.

They stood at the edge of the guests in a gala salon of Madame Isabelle Fichet. Having discovered their mutual love of books and plays, Amanda's eyes came alive. Her cheeks took on color, and her naturally pink lips chattered on gaily about great books and characters she had loved.

The poor scholar, Emile, was enjoying himself immensely. His boyish good lucks and his impeccable manners and perhaps, too, his sad brown eyes and his ability to compliment his hostesses continued to gain him entrance to these gay soirées where he had a chance to eat his fill and drink better quality wine than he could afford in his garret.

His parents were of modest means, but they had eked out enough to send him to university, where his intelligence had gotten him honors. He had lived the gay life of a Left Bank student, and now was part of the Bohemian world that so attracted artists and amused the great society hostesses, who always included a smattering of them at every party to entertain their guests.

Speaking of his interests seemed to animate the lovely young American with the pretty face, soft curls that drifted along temples and high cheekbones, and tendrils that accentuated a lovely neck. And when she spoke of things she loved, Emile began to enjoy himself even more than he had before at one of Madame Fichet's soirées. He always came to eat and drink his fill. But as he gazed at the face turned to him in rapture, he began to entertain other naughty thoughts.

"It is unusual to find such an interest in writing in a woman, *ma chérie*," he said. "Especially such a pretty one."

She gave him a guilty look. "I know. It is a great problem at home. I am thought some kind of freak. My family simply ignores my inclinations, all except my cousin Henry. And he is eccentric himself."

Emile handed his champagne glass to a passing footman and took her hand to lead her into an adjoining gallery where fewer people mingled. Here they were surrounded by tasteful oil paintings of peasants bundling hay and of ladies picnicking by waterfalls.

Suddenly he was seized with a cough and stopped talking, waiting for the spasm to pass.

"Are you all right, monsieur?" she asked, looking at him in concern. "Do you need a glass of water?"

In a moment the coughing stopped, and he smiled. "It is nothing. Let us continue." The color returned to his face, and he accepted a glass of wine from a waiter.

"I would like to see your work," said Emile, knowing that the way to a woman's heart was through flattery. Not that he wasn't truly interested in her intelligent conversation, but since she was both literary and female, naturally his inclinations turned to the possibility of a lovely interlude. "How long will you be in Paris?"

She sighed deeply, and Emile at once felt his heart turn in the direction of romance. He knew he was infatuated.

"Not long enough, I fear," she said. "We are to go to England next week. We've been invited to the palace of Elsenheim."

"A palace," he said, his eyes sweeping from her face to the curve of her neck and then to her delightfully low-cut bodice. He brought his eyes to her face again.

"Such a cold-sounding place. I think," he said in serious tones, gazing deeply into her eyes, "that you are a woman who prefers a cozy nest."

Amanda swallowed. His sensuous lips were so near. Gooseflesh began to form on her naked arms, and she was at once reminded of the kiss the duke had given her.

Suddenly she was able to forget her disappointment in Francis. Here was a young Frenchman who seemed to love the very things she loved. His hand warmed hers, and his attentive manners touched her heart. Emile admired her literary interests, and he treated her like a lady. And he liked her in spite of the fact that he had no knowledge of her wealth. She looked away from him, determined to test this last.

"How well do you know my Aunt Zoe?" she asked, for perhaps Emile had heard that a young American heiress was to be invited tonight and was cozying up to her for that reason.

"Madame Zoe? Which one is she?"

Amanda smiled. "The short little warship with purple and jet feathers adorning her coif."

He smiled. "Ah, Madame Zoe, but of course. A lovely lady. But alas, I have only met her briefly. But if she is your aunt, I would very much like to make her acquaintance."

Amanda smiled inwardly. "Then you have heard nothing of the American Whitney family?"

He shook his dark head. "Not until tonight, *ma chérie.*" His eyes glanced off her charming bosom and narrow waist. How he had to restrain his hands from wandering up to touch her delicate cheek.

Emile's ingenuousness impressed her, and the smile she returned to him was equally shy and sincere. Emile inclined his head closer. "We must meet, *chérie.* Fate has thrown us together. We must not waste our chances."

Her heart raced. If for no other reason than to escape the strictures of her mother and Aunt Zoe, she was determined to meet Emile. His daring attracted her, and talking to him was one way of getting back at those who would confine her acquaintances to men of their choosing and not hers. It made Amanda feel pleasantly wicked to contemplate a friendship that her mother would not approve of. She glanced over her shoulder, certain that at any moment now their absence from the gala salon would be noticed.

"I rise early," she said, giving way to the temptation of adventure. "In the quiet of the morning I am in the habit of a walk since Aunt Zoe's library is so scant."

He smiled, his victory showing in glistening brown eyes like her own. "Where shall I meet you?"

"I don't know Paris very well," she said. "But there is a park across from my aunt's house. We can meet there at dawn."

Love in the morning, thought Emile with a surge of desire. He could hardly contain his excitement at the proposed rendezvous.

"Give me the address, *ma chérie*. I shall be there before dawn to await you."

She whispered the name of the square, excited at her proposed adventure. Emile would show her the Left Bank; he would stimulate her thoughts. She felt instant rapport with him, as she had with no other young man her own age. Suddenly glad she had come to Europe, her eyes glistened. For here was a friend of her own choosing who would help her escape her own constricted life. It was a chance to rebel against the duties and responsibilities those who were born with a silver spoon were burdened with, as the duke had put it. Well, she was not ready to settle down to the life proscribed for her without this one small adventure first. Surely it could not hurt anything.

Just as she expected, Aunt Zoe penetrated the room, a middle-aged gentleman with ribbons on his chest in her wake.

"Amanda, my dear, you've been hiding. I wanted you to meet Count Valtin from Belgium."

She made the introductions as Emile slid away.

"Charmed, my dear." The balding count bent stiffly from the waist.

Buoyed up by her new friend, Emile, Amanda was able to face the rest of the evening. As for Emile, he was especially entertaining and charming to all he met, his heart aflutter with newfound love and his blood racing with desire that he was certain would be satisfied upon the morrow.

Chapter 6

Returning home later that evening, Aunt Zoe handed Amanda a letter that had come with the evening post. Delighted when she saw it was from Emily, she hastened up the stairs to the guest room that was hers. On the landing she turned to kiss Aunt Zoe good night.

"Thank you for a lovely evening, Aunt," she said.

Zoe smiled, seemingly pleased. "I'm glad you enjoyed yourself, my dear. Though you must learn to divide your time more equally among suitors."

"Yes, Aunt. It is just that the company was more stimulating than I expected. In New York, one does not get to meet such talent."

Zoe smiled condescendingly. "European culture is more broad-minded, my dear." She stifled a yawn. "Sleep well, my dear. I regret that I will not see you at breakfast. Tomorrow morning your mother and I will be visiting the Sisters of the Holy Cross Hospital. It is my charity day."

Amanda nodded. More time for her walk with Emile, she thought happily. "Very well. I will amuse myself with your books."

Zoe was not too sleepy to raise her nose an inch.

"Such a studious young girl. All very well for you to entertain yourself reading. But do not forget that most men do not like a woman who is too bookish. You must cultivate your feminine abilities, my dear.

"When you marry, you will be expected to run a household, and that includes proper seating of distinguished guests at your dinner table. You will find several volumes on titles and nobility in my library. You should make a study of them before losing yourself in those German plays you seem to love. You'll be in England soon, and you'll need to be aware of the peerage."

"Yes, Aunt."

Louisa was coming down the hall, and Amanda turned to let her mother peck her cheek. "Good night, Mother," she said.

"Good night, dear. Be sure and get your beauty rest."

Amanda took her letter with her to her room and sat at the little round table with muted globe lamp to read it. Hungry for news from home, she devoured the first page of Emily's chattery gossip written in her spidery hand. But when she came to the second page, her face began to warm in consternation.

"I'm afraid your Francis has not been behaving well," Emily's letter said. "He went off to visit friends in Massachusetts and has been seen escorting Abigail Van Ryck about town. You may remember her. She was widowed about a year ago and is very wealthy. I do not tell you this to hurt you, dear Amanda, rather to protect you. I know that you fancied Francis, and you intimated that you had an understanding with him even though your mother did not approve.

"Perhaps he gave up on persuading either of your parents and has gone off to seek romance elsewhere. I do not think you should spend any time grieving for him, but rather free yourself from thoughts of him and have a gay time in Europe."

The rest of the letter went on to tell of Emily's visit to North Carolina, and Amanda skimmed it to see if there were further references to Francis. But there were none. When she reached the end of the letter her hands fell heavily in her lap, and she crumpled the paper. Emily was right, she thought as she wiped a tear from her cheek. Francis wasn't worth it if he could so easily forget her. She had been mistaken about him from the start. Oh, how foolish she had been.

She held out a small hope that there might be a note of explanation from him, but since she had had no word from him since she'd been here, she doubted it. She hated to think that all who had advised her against him were right, that he was merely a fortune hunter. How she had liked his laughing blue eyes and his breezy manner. But she should have seen the signs herself. He always seemed to manage a gay time even without her.

She crushed the letter into a little ball and threw it into the fireplace. Then she extinguished the lamp and took herself to bed. Cursing herself for having been a fool, she vowed to hold her head up. She must write to Emily and thank her for telling her. She would rather have heard it from her friend than let some idle gossip catch her unprepared.

After a night full of bad dreams, she blinked her eyes open, remembering that she had an appointment this morning. There was nothing like having something to do to help her get over the loss and humiliation of having pledged herself to a man who could betray her so easily. She rose and dressed in a fine linen gown the color of Persian lilacs, threw a light woolen cloak about her shoulders against the early morning freshness and put a horse-hair bonnet on her head with lilac streamers down the back.

Slipping downstairs, she tiptoed across the marble-tiled entry hall. She wasn't as familiar with the servants of this household, and was not sure how early they started laying the fires. She twisted the doorknob silently and was thankful that Aunt Zoe's household kept her hinges oiled. Soundlessly she emerged from the house and pulled the door shut behind her.

The early tinge of dawn still muted the sky; but there was light to see by, and Amanda smiled at the freshness of the spring day, the strong scent of hyacinth in the air, and the smoke coming from chimneys in the other houses that lined the street. A few carts were being pulled along the brick street by delivery men, and a chimney sweep hopped down from a wagon driven by an older man, then ran through the gate and down the steps to the cellar entrance to be admitted by a servant.

She had just set her foot on the other side of the street when she saw Emile sitting on a bench and smelling a lavender hyacinth he had most likely plucked from one of the gardens. His collar was turned up to help warm him, his face rapturous with the scent of the flower. And then he saw her, roused himself and came along the walk to greet her with a guilty smile.

"Ah, mademoiselle, I was enjoying the flowers, but they pale in beauty beside your charming face."

Amanda laughed and allowed him to kiss her hands. "I am glad to see that someone else likes to rise as early as I do."

"Ah, *ma chéri*. Life is so short, and there is so much to enjoy. I get up early in the morning so that I may savor it all the more. And today of all days I was awake while it was still dark, for if I had wings, I would have gone down to the other side of the world to pull the sun along faster so that I might be with you sooner."

She warmed to his poetry. Francis be damned. He had never spoken to her like that. Perhaps her American compatriots could learn a few things from these debonair French.

"Show me Paris, Emile," she said, in a rush of enthusiasm. "Show me the real Paris. I am sick to death of dressmakers and salons, though the soirées I have attended are far more interesting that the dull parties we have back home."

She sighed, her excitement building. "I didn't want to come on this voyage," she said. "But now, perhaps I'm glad I did."

"And I also, mademoiselle. Now, let me see, where shall we go first?"

"You must show me where the artists live," she said, her face livening to the idea. "Show me everything about the student's life, all the things that aren't deemed suitable!"

"As you wish. Come along, then. You do not mind walking? You will see more if we go on foot."

She laughed. "I love to walk."

He paused, and glanced across the square at the house from which she had emerged. "You will not be missed?"

"No one is up this early, and my mother and aunt have charity duties this morning. So you see, I am free." She gave a conspiratorial laugh. "When I return I will say I have been out for a walk. They may not approve of my going out into a strange city alone, but I don't care, Emile," she said in a rush of determination and rebellion at all the strictures surrounding her. "I just don't care."

"Ah, *ma chérie*, how your eyes sparkle when you speak so."

He took her hands in a rush of emotion of his own and kissed them warmly. He must find a way to hold on to his turtle dove, now that he had found her. Emile gave little thought to the difference in their stations, or the fact that his newfound love came from America. A hopeless romantic, in his mind love could conquer all.

He placed his hand about her waist and gave it a squeeze, and they started off down the streets. Emile talked as they went, amusing her with anecdotes of the many salons he managed to visit.

"I have gained a reputation as a tutor and so gained entrance to some of these great houses," he said, swinging an arm toward the town houses they passed. "It keeps food on my table and allows me to drink their fine champagne. In exchange I beat letters and numbers into the thick heads of their children."

Amanda laughed. "Are all the children so dense, then? Do you not enjoy teaching at all?"

"Some are not so dense. Some are promising, and this inspires me to lead them on, to place before their eyes texts that will show them how letters on a page can open vistas of their imaginations."

"It's what I love, too," she said. "I've read all the great authors."

They babbled on about great literature, roaming from Zola, to Goethe, to Henry James, whom Amanda was surprised to find Emile had read in translation. So engrossed were they in their conversation that before they knew it, they had covered the distance between Aunt Zoe's quiet, genteel square and the Pont Neuf, the stone bridge that crossed the Seine to the Ile de la Cité.

Here they slowed their pace so that Amanda could

enjoy the islands that seemed to be gliding down the river with the massive towers of Notre Dame, the golden spire of the Sainte Chapelle and, at the tip of the Ile de la Cité, silver willow, with branches so low they trailed in the water.

"It is beautiful," said Amanda, gazing at the old world facades of the Palais de Justice, the stone lacework of the Sainte Chapelle, and the bronze statue of Henri IV.

"Come, come," Emile said, after a moment. "There is much to see."

Emile proved an excellent tour guide, narrating how Marie Antoinette lived for two and a half months in a cell here in the Conciergerie, and how in the women's courtyard the highborn captives did their washing, and how in the shadow of the guillotine, liaisons were managed even though iron railings separated the men prisoners from the women prisoners.

"It is very sad," said Emile, pausing to gaze at the Palais. "They executed the great poet André-Marie de Chénier."

Amanda found it hard to imagine such blood and terror, for now the flower markets nearby perfumed the air, and the chirping of birds announced spring in Paris.

They hurried on to the other side of the Seine and continued along the Left Bank. Cafes and bookshops lined the street they took, and Amanda was at once charmed. Her blood tingled with the excitement of a new place, and one that reflected her own love of books and art was thrilling.

"How wonderful to live here, Emile. You must show me everything."

Laughing at her tirelessness, they proceeded from one street to the other as the shops began to open and students emerged to attend lectures or merely to argue with each other at the cafes. Several hailed Emile, and he introduced Amanda, though he hurried her along, whispering in her ear that he would not let any of his painter friends gaze at her for long, lest they fall in love and abscond with her to their studios where they would want to paint her picture.

As he himself visualized her posing seminude for an artist, his own blood pulsed. She would make the perfect model. At last they sat at a round wooden table to take coffee and pastry at a small cafe below Emile's own rooms. After their exhilarating walk, Amanda was famished. And when the steaming coffee and the delicate pastries filled with fruit were placed before her, she lit into them with enthusiasm.

Emile ate little, feasting his eyes on the vivacious American girl. And as they ate they carried on about whatever came to mind.

"Tell me about your own writing, *ma chérie*," he said. "Do you write tales of romance? I would like to see them."

She shrugged in embarrassment. "I'm sure my own writing is not ready to show. I would never let anyone see it until I feel it has more merit. But with each effort I get better. Someday perhaps I will have the courage to send off a story for print. Though I could not let any of my family know of it."

He frowned. "Why not?"

"As I told you, my friends and family do not acknowledge that a woman can do such things."

"A great pity, then."

She grew melancholy and declined another pastry, suddenly thinking of the bleak life she lived. She gazed at the lovely catalpa trees with their large leaves and showy white flowers. The trees lined the modest brick street next to tall gas lamps, where young scholars bargained with book vendors at their stalls. She fervently wished for a moment that she could trade places with one of them. How romantic to live the Bohemian life and pursue one's dreams.

Seeing the faraway look of his beloved, Emile took her hand. "What is it, my little one?"

"I hate my life, Emile. I truly do. From the very beginning it's been so ordered, with governesses and tutors, school and social obligations. I feel so . . . so unproductive, like nothing more than an ornament with no purpose of my own."

The bitterness exploded from her lips with passion. Tears moistened her eyes. Thoughts of Francis's betrayal mingled with her mother's expectations, and suddenly the quaintness of the street and the lovely Parisian spring morning combined to fill her heart with a great nostalgia for something she could not name, some unknown happiness she had not yet seen.

Emile quickly moved his chair closer and lifted her hand to his cheek.

"The tears glisten in your eyes, *ma chérie*. I cannot stand to see you cry."

He placed an arm about her waist and lifted her to her feet. Then he guided her to the narrow stairs beside the pastry shop. With one hand he signaled to the shopkeeper that he would settle his account later. The shopkeeper trusted Emile to pay his accounts. Far be it for something so trivial to stand in the way of romance.

Amanda let him lead her up the stairs. If she were to make a show of her emotions, it would be better to do it in some private spot than in public.

"I'm sorry," she sniffled as he handed her a snowy white handkerchief.

"Do not worry, my little one. I will comfort you."

At the top of three flights of stairs, he pushed open a door and led her inside. She blotted her eyes and then opened them to see that she was standing inside a garret with slanted roof, wood floors covered with faded rugs, simple furniture and stacks of books everywhere.

"Is this where you live?"

"Alas, it is not so fine as your aunt's elegant house on the square. But this is my little refuge from the world. Here, sit down, and I will make you a cup of chocolate."

He escorted her to a lumpy lounge chair covered in faded tapestry, its back reclined for restful interludes. But it was situated before an open window that looked out over the roofs to the Seine. The view of the flower market helped to calm her while Emile lit the spirit lamp and heated the chocolate in a tall, slender chocolate pot. He also opened a wooden cupboard and took down a bottle of cognac given him by the parent of one of his charges. He had saved it for a special occasion.

When the hot chocolate was ready, he poured it into an enamel cup and set it on the small wooden table by Amanda's side. Then he took his own cup and sat on a hassock at her feet, sipping his chocolate and gazing sadly at her.

She began to feel soothed. "You are so kind, Emile. It feels delicious to break all the bonds that have been holding me back. Perhaps there is some hope that life can be enjoyed, though I do not see how, in my present circumstances."

He gave her a melancholy smile. "You must share your burdens with me. What is it that troubles you besides being dressed up in silks and satins and forced to idle conversation with balding dinner partners during ten-course meals?"

The way he put it amused her, and she managed a laugh. "I was betrayed by someone I thought I loved," she said.

Suddenly Emile's sincere interest opened a floodgate of words, and she told him all about her brief courtship with Francis, her meetings with Edward Pemberton and everything she felt. Her words were unorganized, rolling off her tongue in great volume. Never had she been able to confide in anyone so thoroughly, and Emile was an attentive listener. Even Henry, whose calm friendship always helped bolster her, had never been a confidant in matters of the heart. Henry had had no experience in that arena, and so was more comfortable in the matters of the mind that Amanda shared with him.

Emile rose to refill her mug of chocolate and then opened the cognac bottle and filled two round brandy snifters, yet another gift from wealthy patrons. Interjecting sympathy when she paused for breath, he learned much of her life and of the way these American society girls were pushed toward marriage. It was all very sad, for they seemed to live in gilded cages with none of the freedom and love of life that should be theirs at such a blooming age.

Amanda drank the chocolate, cried once more, laughed as she described her umbrage at the duke, and sipped the cognac, which mellowed her and made her feel even more expansive. She even told Emile about Edward kissing her in the armor room. All this Emile followed with great interest. He moved his hassock closer, slowly sipping his own cognac. He smiled when she told of the naughty duke stealing a kiss in the shadows of the medieval knights' armor. What a place to take a kiss!

He leaned over her, smiling at her rosy lips. "Did he kiss you like this?" he asked, and he bent to taste the brandy on her lips.

The kiss was warm but gentle, and Amanda felt the surprise of his lips on hers, his hand on her shoulder. A tremor rippled down her, and she replaced the brandy snifter on the little table, gazing wide-eyed at him. Her lips parted as she drew in a breath.

"I . . . I, don't remember . . .," she said with breathless vagueness, unaware of how tempting her answer sounded.

"Ah," said Emile, concentrating on the best way to find the answer to his question. "Perhaps it was more like this?"

He set his own brandy snifter aside and took her in his arms, one hand cradling her shoulders, the other at her waist. His mouth was more demanding this time, tasting the delicious lips, parting her lips to let his tongue dance against hers. He moaned in pleasure, letting the kiss go on, explore, delight, send warmth coursing through his veins.

Heady rapture filled Amanda. Sinful newness coursed through her. Through the haze of the lull the cognac had induced, she thrilled to the kiss, moving her lips against him, accepting his embrace, though she knew she shouldn't. When at last he moved his lips to tease her ear, and then her throat, her hands were on his shoulders.

"Emile," she murmured.

"My beauty," he whispered in a caress. His hands drifted to her face, her hair, while he continued to kiss her lovely skin, his lips straying lower and lower on her throat to taste the softness against her collar. "You are so lovely," he whispered.

"Emile," she said again, lost to the sensations he was causing in her. She knew she oughtn't to let him do this to her. It was sinful, wasn't it? But the disappointments she had just shared with him brought them closer, and the loveliness of his seeming devotion and his tenderness moved her. So unlike the duke's material motivations.

She had come with Emile this morning to explore a world that could never be hers. Now she was carried away on a cloud of excitement. Being in Emile's arms was a way of getting back at everyone around her who proscribed such things as free choice and the pleasure to be oneself as beyond the pale. This would be her secret, these kisses, this desire. These would be hers and hers alone. She cared nothing for the consequences. Giving way to the delight that filled her, the naughty revenge she was taking for Francis's leading her on, for all the suitors who wanted her for her money, she returned Emile's affections, for he wanted her only for herself.

Emile was breathing hard. His hands molded her waist, her bosom, but with such tenderness that the warm glow within Amanda was nothing but a new awakening to secret pleasures she knew would be forever denied her in her other life. Her own heart was beating quickly, and she sought his mouth again, wanting again the eager kisses. Wanting to kiss a man because she wanted to, not because it was expected.

Delirious pleasure accompanied his caresses and the moist kisses on her face and throat. His quick fingers undid her collar, and now he was able to bury his head in her bosom, tasting the skin above her lacy camisole, never ceasing to murmur loving compliments as their breath began to come in shallow gasps.

Her hands entangled in his thick hair as his head nuzzled her breasts, and she thrilled at the sensations that came with the touch of his hand on her leg as he found his way gently under her skirts.

"*Ma chérie,*" he finally said as he sat up again to gaze at her face solemnly. "I love you, *ma chérie.* I want to make you mine."

"Oh, Emile," she said breathlessly, unaware of the beauty that radiated from her flushed face. "This is all happening so fast. I've never ... I've never ..." She suddenly choked on her words, confusion filling her.

"Do you want me to stop, my turtle dove? For I want only to give you pleasure. To gaze upon your rapturous face is pleasure enough for me. I could not stand to see you so sad. You are too beautiful to let the tears mar your face."

That he was giving her pleasure was undeniable, and yet she was frightened of what might happen if they continued. But then defiance made her throw caution to the wind. She might never have a chance to do as she pleased after this day. By indulging in Emile's love, she was slapping her mother's plans for her in the face. She was making Francis wrong to miss his chance. She was showing the haughty fortune-hunting duke that he would never have her love.

Emile saw her waver, saw the thoughts flit across her face. But he saw, too, her resolve to taste what he offered her.

On a deep sigh of devotion, he whispered her name. Then, still gazing with earnestness at her eyes, he pulled the unfastened dress off her shoulders, exposing their proud whiteness. He pushed the dress down and smiled at the gay little ribbons that tied her camisole in front.

Now the round bosom that peeked above corset and camisole invited him.

Amanda was filled with daring, and had she not had the cognac to mellow her, she might have stopped him yet. But when his delicate fingers explored her soft skin, she moaned in delight, leaning her head back on the tapestried chair as he pulled at the ribbons to loosen the camisole. Then he pushed it aside to be confronted with the laced corset that pushed her breasts upward.

He gave a shudder and quickly undid the corset so that her breasts sprang forward. The fire that raced through her nearly sent her springing from her chair. Instead, when he lowered his head, taking first one breast and then the other in his mouth, she fell forward in ecstasy over his dark head, for she had never experienced anything like the feelings that now overpowered her in wave after wave.

She clawed at his shoulders, moaning in newfound pleasure, pulling him closer and closer, and then lost herself in sensations as arms, hands, legs entangled, and she found herself drawn lower on the lounge with Emile kneeling over her, sucking the wondrous nipples as his hands plunged under petticoats to caress soft thighs.

From time to time he would lift his head to gaze on the beautiful exposed breasts, then would tweak them between thumb and forefinger in a manner that sent her writhing in ecstasy. Just how he came out of his own coat, and how his shirt became unbuttoned, she was not aware, but soon her lacy drawers were on the floor, her stockings undone and her feet out of her shoes. He held one of her long legs across his lap and transferred his moist kisses to her calf and then to her thigh, his own trousers becoming loosened, his fingers dancing up her leg.

Then he turned his attentions again to her lips, his tongue plunging deeper, entangling with hers, delighting in the hunger he sensed in her, while his hands worked their magic on her thighs. She was drunk with a passion she did not know she possessed, falling faster and faster a slave to the new pleasures he showed her. When at last he fanned the flames between her white thighs, she quivered with new sinful pleasure. And when he showed her himself, she gulped in stunned emotion.

"Touch me, my love. It will make me ecstatic. I cannot wait."

Then he guided her hand downward until she closed it over him, and he shut his eyes and sighed in pleasure. He moved her hand, teaching her what to do, his shallow gasps evidence that her touch delighted him, sending him into another region of consciousness.

And when he covered her with his body, parting her legs so that his maleness could seek her, she dug her fingers into his naked shoulders, frightened at this new prospect.

"Do not fear, my love," he said. "I do not want to hurt you. But you will feel a little pain. Surely a small price to pay for all the rest?"

Indeed the continued waves of pleasure he sent through her body were enough to make her open herself to him. Her eyes were wide, her head thrown back and her mouth open with an intake of breath when he penetrated her.

"My love, my love," he uttered as he found the tight, moist center.

Such pleasure he had never known. How wonderful that love could be so new each time. For each time Emile fell in love he was completely enslaved.

Three times had this happened, and each time he

had grieved greatly when some unforeseen circumstance or pettiness had separated him from the woman he loved. That he threw himself headlong into his affairs and did not foresee any difficulties never occurred to him. For Emile, love was everything, and when the real world took his love away, he moped like a puppy until the natural French aptitude for all that life offered one so young finally dragged him out of his lovelorn grief. And then he would find love again. Ah, happy chance, and the cycle would begin again.

And so while he loved Amanda, he would be with no other. Just how he planned to retain her, he had no idea. For the moment he floated on the ecstasy that carried him.

Amanda winced at the first shock of pain. But his mouth pressed hers, and soon she became used to the rhythmic movement, still numbed by the thought that she was with a man, against all the creeds with which she had been brought up. She gave herself to Emile, fulfilled that his pleasure was as great if not greater than her own. His movements increased. He clasped her shoulders, his cries filling her heart, and at last he gave a great groan, pressed and pressed against her, shuddering and heaving ecstatically on her breast, while moisture spread between their legs.

"Oh, my love," he said, drawing a deep breath. "At last, at last, I have found heaven."

She cradled him against her, and they remained thus, entangled on the wide, deep lounge. She smiled, sated with pleasure, the sun, which had risen higher, warming her face.

Emile lifted his head and kissed her gently, murmuring sweet nothings as he dropped tender kisses on her face and lips.

"Then I am the first to show you the pleasures of love," he said in a voice full of emotion.

"Yes, Emile. You are."

She felt sinfully righteous, secretly thrilled that no one of her circle would know what she had done. But the fact that she was now made a woman elevated her in her own mind, proved to her that there was more to life than the decorum of society's so-called pleasure pursuits. For her, pleasure was attainable in a ratty garret with a student prince.

They spent a long time in the aftermath of love. He touched her hair. She caressed his chest, and soft kisses passed between them. This was beautiful, she thought. All of Francis's chaste kisses and protestations of love had been nothing, she now realized. If she had married Francis, she would never have known this rapture. Ah, lucky her, to have come to Paris to find love in springtime.

At last they rose and rearranged their clothing. She used a small cracked mirror to try to twist up her hair, which had become disheveled in their lovemaking.

When they were again presentable, they prepared to face the daylight and went to the door, she a changed woman.

"Are you hungry, *ma chérie?* It is almost lunchtime."

She smiled at him lovingly. "I am starving. But I must return home. I will have a hard enough time explaining where I have been. If I delay any longer, they will send out the gendarmes to look for me."

They laughed; he held the door for her and led the way downstairs.

With the sun on her face, Amanda felt that surely everyone who saw her must know what she had done. But fortunately for her, the Latin Quarter was much more liberal in its views of love. Such matters were private. If anyone noticed their impassioned eyes or their sated countenances, they saw only two hearts in harmony and did not question what went on behind closed doors.

Her aunt had told her to cultivate her feminine abilities, but Zoe would be surprised at just how seriously Amanda had taken that advice.

Chapter 7

Emile saw her back to the square, but they kept well away from the house. He bid her goodbye, extracting a promise that she would meet him again tomorrow morning.

"I'll be here waiting," he said.

She knew it would be dangerous to continue seeing him; but the danger was fraught with pleasure, and it was Amanda's way of defying her mother and all she stood for.

"I will be here, Emile, but I'll have to be back in time for breakfast. I cannot stay away for so long."

He looked suggestively into her eyes. "Then we will have time for either a leisurely walk or time to make love. The choice will be yours."

She blushed at such frank talk. He raised her hand to his lips and then let her go. She hurried across the square and then slowed to a walk before she entered the house. She tried to assume a neutral expression, her heart still pounding in her chest, hoping she wouldn't meet anyone but the servants until she got to her room to change. Marie opened the door to her.

"Hello, Marie," she said, only giving her a glance.

"I've been for a walk. I'm sorry I missed breakfast. I wasn't hungry."

She didn't stop for a reply and hurried up the steps, not looking back. If Marie had a judgmental look on her otherwise professional face, Amanda wasn't going to risk it.

Upstairs in her room she took off the dress that had gotten so rumpled. She gazed at her figure in the oval mirror hanging over the white and gold dressing table and hugged her arms to herself. A body that had been made love to. The idea gave her gooseflesh all over again. Whether she loved Emile in the way that would last, she had no idea. It had all happened so fast.

She sat down on the vanity bench and removed the pins from her hair, brushing it with long strokes. Delcia was out, which was just as well. Her own maid knew her so well; she was bound to see through her. Amanda needed some time to adjust, to find ways to keep her secret.

She thought at once of the haughty duke they would be seeing in England and smiled sardonically to herself. He admitted to having a mistress. Well, now she had a lover. The thought made her flush all over again, and she worked hastily on her chignon, wrapping her hair in a roll that she pinned to the back of her head, leaving only a few curls to frame her face. Then she chose a prim muslin day dress with lace about a high neck. In such conservative clothing she might look less like she was no longer chaste. And the soft dress protected her tender breasts, petticoats hiding the ache between her legs as if it could be seen outwardly.

She went downstairs, finding that her mother and Zoe were still not back. Triumphant that she was carrying things off so well, she took herself off to the library and found the books on peerage that her aunt had recommended. She took down an elegantly bound volume in crimson morocco.

When Louisa and Zoe returned an hour later they observed her sitting at the gold and white table in the center of the room, a large volume of maps open on one side of the table and Amanda studiously poring over English genealogies.

She heard their voices in the hallway, and then when the door opened and Louisa entered, Amanda looked up.

"Hello, Mother. How was your outing?"

"Very tiring, but quite necessary. We distributed gifts and visited the patients, helping the good sisters arrange flowers for all to enjoy."

"How nice." She stretched her shoulders as if she had been sitting for a very long time in one place. "My goodness. I didn't realize it was so late."

Zoe bustled in. "Ah, there you are, child. Reading, I see?"

"Yes, Aunt Zoe. I did as you suggested, and after I indulged myself in a little of the German poets, I began to look at *Burke's Peerage.*" She shook her head in dismay. "Most confusing. How shall I ever get all the ranks straight?"

"You will have to practice. I've faced the very same problem when I've invited my friends to lunch. Sometimes shades of rank are so slight that an unintended insult as to placement around the table will burn in the breast of the offended forever."

Normally the mention of such social necessities would turn Amanda into a petulant beast, but she felt so satiated, so sinfully victorious, that she could afford to be generous. She smiled agreeably, shut the book and got up.

"Then you shall have to instruct me on the finer points, Aunt Zoe."

Zoe smiled. "Well, I'm glad to see you taking some interest. It is difficult to turn an American princess into a lady fit to attract European nobility the way your mother seems set on doing. Of course your wealth helps. But you must also make yourself acceptable to the society in which your prospective husband moves."

"Providing I find an acceptable husband," said Amanda, unable to resist at least one jibe.

Louisa watched the exchange with suspicion. It was not like her daughter to acquiesce so readily to these lessons. But if Zoe had been able to make headway where she had not, she was only thankful. She could not beat her child into submission. She could punish her for not doing as she was told. But action, Louisa was only too desperately aware, must spring from within the girl's own breast.

Amanda was so agreeable at lunch that both Louisa and Zoe began to look at her curiously. She began to feel that she mustn't meet their eyes, lest they guess her secret.

"Well now," Zoe pronounced as soon as the last plate was taken away. "I believe we are expected at Monsieur Worth's for a fitting."

"I can take her, Zoe," said Louisa. "Surely you need to rest after this morning's expedition."

"Nonsense," said Zoe. "I may be older than you, my dear, but I shan't stop getting about when and where I please. When you cease being active, you might as well lie down and die. Besides, although Amanda's French is passable, it is not good enough for the finer points that might be needed in any such transaction. I shall be ready in an hour."

They all rose as if understanding orders from their general.

"I believe I'll walk in the square, Aunt. It is such a gorgeous day, I cannot bear to be inside a moment longer."

"Very well, as long as you don't stray from the square. If you get lost, I would not trust your Americanized French to get you home again."

She laughed inwardly. If only she could tell her aunt how much farther than the square she had been this morning, but then, of course, she'd had Emile's French to rely upon.

When everyone was ready, they took Zoe's handsome cabriolet, the top pushed down so they could enjoy the fine spring day. As the horse clopped along the brick streets, Amanda breathed in the Parisian air. Where was Emile now? she wondered. Most likely leading his little students through their lessons. At the thought of him, she felt the stirrings that reminded her of her newfound experience, and she reveled in it.

It was as if someone had pulled aside a curtain within her, revealing a deep sensuality she had never known she possessed. She dared not think past the newness of the revelation. But if she felt she could ride along on her cloud of ecstasy for long, she was wrong. All too soon reality thrust itself at her, and she was reminded of what she was about.

"We leave for England Tuesday morning," Louisa said as they turned into the street where the famous couturier had his establishment. "That only leaves us five days to complete your wardrobe, together with all necessary accessories. And one of those days is a Sunday. We shall be very busy indeed."

"Five days," said Amanda on a wail. "So soon?"

Louisa glared at her daughter. "I did not know that you were growing so fond of Paris."

Amanda's chin set. "Well, I rather like it here. And I've had no chance to see anything. What about . . . the Louvre?"

"The Louvre can be seen if there is time," said Louisa.

"Oh, come now," said Zoe. "Don't argue. There ought to be time between making purchases for the girl to see something of paintings and monuments. You Americans are so sadly lacking in culture that it will do her good to spend some time among the masterpieces. Do not forget, dear Louisa, that it is her mind as well as her face and figure that I am trying to enhance in such a short time as you have given me to make her presentable."

There was no time for further discussions, for they had arrived at their destination, and once inside, Amanda was made to stand in a dressing room in her undergarments being measured and fitted. She tried on gown after gown, the seamstress, Madame Sophie, mumbling to herself in French. But when the woman pulled fastenings around Amanda's slim waist, she yelped.

"That's too tight. I cannot breathe. And if you expect me to eat anything in this, I must have some room."

"Give her a little room, Madame Sophie," instructed Zoe in French. "But only a little." To Amanda in English she said, "At your age a slim waist is important, even if it means you do not indulge too heavily at meals."

Amanda frowned at her reflection in the mirror. Why

must all pleasures be denied her? Good food when she had a healthy appetite was something she enjoyed. She purposely expanded her diaphragm when Madame Sophie pulled the material together at the waist. She wasn't about to let the dressmaker choke her to death. And she had no plans to remain standing at a party in a dress that would split at the seams if she sat down.

When the dressmaker fastened the back of the material, Amanda had to admire the fit and the silky material that would become a gown. But the bodice seemed cut much lower than her usual gowns. A tinge of color formed on her cheeks as she noticed how revealing the low-cut neckline was. If Emile saw her in this dress, he would be driven to distraction, and she wondered with a coy smile if he would be the jealous type, furious that other men at the soirées where they were likely to be would get such a generous look at her bosom.

Or would he be proud of her, knowing that he alone had kissed and caressed her creamy skin? He alone as long as they could contrive to be together. Then her mother's words echoed in her heart. Five days. What could she do to make it longer? How could she intrigue to return to Paris and to Emile after the dreaded visit to England? She must think of something.

She caught her mother's stare in the mirror and turned guiltily, busying herself in getting out of the costume and into the next one. But she had caught the speculative look on Louisa's face, and Zoe's words confirmed that they had noticed a change in her.

"I do believe these clothes flatter you, my dear," said Zoe as Amanda next tried on an evening gown of white China silk. The deep scoop neck was ruffled as were puffed sleeves that ended at the elbows, and the same deep ruffles ringed the skirt. "A white ribbon of the same material tied around your neck would be just the thing, and chrysanthemums in your hair."

Louisa's face took on a look of satisfaction. "Yes, you're right. I do believe we've succeeded in doing something after all." But she continued to peer at Amanda as if not quite sure what had made the difference.

Amanda would not meet her mother's gaze, knowing very well what had made the difference. They left the dressmaker's and returned home so they would have time to rest before dinner. Tonight they were off again to the house of the Comtesse St. Germond for dinner and then an evening of musical entertainment. Zoe rattled off the names of the guests, saying vaguely that usually a number of the comtesse's circle stopped in after dinner for the entertainment, which often proved quite amusing as a sprinkling of literary figures and artists usually added to the party.

"I cannot get used to the fact that in Paris you rub shoulders with the literati," said Louisa in the carriage. "In New York, such people are considered too far below the salt to be invited."

"Hmmph," said Zoe. "Such snobbery is not necessary here. In France no one can live without the arts. Where politics and different classes and coteries so sharply divide us, art and literature unite us. Intimacy and the continuity of our permanent friendships provide the basis for our social life, but the occasional new blood provides such interesting stimulation."

Louisa blinked in noncomprehension, but Amanda smiled inwardly, liking her aunt more and more. Whether or not Emile succeeded in getting himself through the door of tonight's party, she dressed with gaiety. Delcia noticed her mood and commented.

"You are finding Paris to be most enjoyable, miss?"
she said as she arranged pearls and feathers in
Amanda's hair.

"Yes, indeed. More than I had hoped."

Again it was on the tip of her tongue to confide in her
maid, but she daren't risk it. She would save that confidence for the day she needed to send Emile a message
and could trust it to no one but Delcia.

Once again gowned and wrapped in a satin cape,
Amanda set her feet in the cabriolet, together with Zoe
in jet gown with emerald jewelry, and Louisa in her finest brocade. They rode through the streets, the muted
globe lamps sending a hue of radiance into the night.
The sweet scents of gardens and flowering trees from every square seemed to say that romance filled the night.

At last they came to the eighteenth-century mansion,
standing between mossy turf and garden in the rue de
Grenelle. They were relieved of their wraps in the grand
entry hall, which glistened with candles in the chandelier.

Upstairs, they were ushered into the first of a series of
three drawing rooms, a small room hung with red damask against white paneled walls. Here the comtesse
greeted them. She was a small woman with prematurely
graying hair, and she had to use a cane. But her nobility
showed in her stance and in the manners with which
she greeted her guests . . . and in her diamond tiara and
necklace. She smiled in welcome.

"I'm so glad you've brought your niece, my dear Zoe.
She will do much to enliven our little group."

After a few more words, they passed into the second,
larger drawing room, where the dinner guests were
gathering. Amanda was presented to the Compte
Alexandre de Laborde, who she soon discovered was an

expert on illuminated manuscripts. She had no sooner plunged into a discussion with the eminent gentleman than she was whisked away by her aunt to meet the other guests, comprised of the French ambassador to St. Petersburg and his wife, a gentleman attached to the British embassy in Paris, and several other august diplomats as well as a German prince.

As soon as she could, she drifted back to de Laborde, and the two of them escaped into the third drawing room, this one lined with gilded glass-fronted bookcases full of rare books in precious bindings.

"I didn't know the comtesse was so fond of books," said Amanda in delight.

"She is a collector, not a reader," said de Laborde in an authoritative tone. "She admits it herself. Whenever one of her guests is raised to honors in Academia, she buys his last work and tries to read it, but with no results. She must always ask friends she trusts if the book is any good."

Amanda laughed. The guests were called in to dinner, and she saw that several other young men had joined them. For a moment she held her breath, for one of the young men looked like Emile. But when he turned, she saw it was not him.

In France the rules for seating at table were the reverse of what she was used to. Here, host and hostess sat opposite each other in the middle of the long table. The guests were seated right and left according to their rank, dwindling to the table ends where the untitled, unofficial, witty young guests were seated. Two of them this evening were playwrights, one a poet, and one a novelist. Amanda found the mixture of guests quite entertaining and began to enjoy herself as the brilliant witticisms sallied forth from the ends of the table.

Contrary to dinners at home where one was constrained to talk to the dinner partner on one's left or on one's right, in France it seemed that the whole table indulged in general conversation, each guest vying to outquip the other. Mostly the men carried the conversation, but the women present appeared absorbed and attentive. All but Louisa.

Amanda was laughing at a joke told by de Laborde, when she caught her mother's eye. The look of slight displeasure was all too familiar, and Amanda's laugh slowly died. Then her mother's eyes flicked to Prince Schlipf, and Amanda understood the implication. Louisa was in hopes that Amanda would pay more attention to the German prince.

So she turned her head in the direction of the prince, who was having trouble getting the peas to stay on his knife. For some reason this struck Amanda funny, and she began laughing all over again. By the time the ladies left the table, Amanda was flushed with enjoyment, and Louisa was taut with ill humor.

"My dear," she said in a low voice as they made their way to the drawing room where they had first assembled, "you really must not make such a spectacle of yourself."

"Oh, Mother," said Amanda. "The French are so lively. I must say I am enjoying Paris more than I thought I would. It's too bad we must cross the Channel to England. I should really rather stay here."

"Hmmph. You don't know what you're talking about."

After a short time during which the ladies chatted, the gentlemen joined them, and the groups began to rearrange themselves. It was then that a boisterous group could be heard in the entry hall, and the comtesse's butler announced them. Several were friends of the comtesse, and she began to introduce them to those they did not know. Amanda's pulse had quickened, for if Emile were to make an entrance, it would be now. He said he was often invited to the comtesse's salons and knew these eligible young bachelors who added to the party after dinner. But as her eyes took in the group, she saw that he was not among them. Thinking that perhaps he would appear later, she followed the others to the music room where they were to be entertained by a string quartet. She took a seat by de Laborde, who explained that this quartet was very good and that they played here very often.

The musicians took their places and began. Amanda listened for a while, but her thoughts began to wander. De Laborde seemed absorbed, so she did not speak to him. It was then that she felt the tap on her shoulder.

A strange voice whispered in her ear, "Do not turn around, mademoiselle. When this piece is finished, excuse yourself and go to the back of the room. Your friend is waiting for you there."

Her heart quickened, and she sat up straighter, waiting for the piece to end. As soon as the musicians lifted their bows, she popped up.

"Excuse me," she said to the people who let her rustle by. Then she walked calmly to the back of the room, ignoring the stare from her mother.

"Powder room," she hissed in her mother's ear when she passed Louisa's chair. Her mother would hardly follow her if she thought that her daughter was only making a visit to the necessary room.

She made it to the door just as the musicians began their next piece. A doorman opened the door and let her through, and she found herself standing in a small anteroom, lit by a gas chandelier. The French doors were opened, and the long damask drapes blew inward. Amanda moved forward.

"Emile?" she called tentatively. Then she stepped out to the tiled balcony.

For answer, he reached for her hand. She gave a start, but he held his finger to his lips and then pulled her away from the door and into his arms.

She gave a delighted giggle as he held her, leaning his body against the stone wall. Then he quickly slipped his arms around her waist and parted his lips to kiss her. She returned the kiss gladly, and for a moment their passion heated. Then he lifted his mouth and simply held her, his cheek against her temple.

"Come," he whispered, "you must see Paris at night."

He released her and then led her to the edge of the balcony from where they could view the city. It sparkled like diamonds, and through the center snaked the dark Seine like spun satin, the lights reflecting on its broken surface.

"It's beautiful."

"I shall always remember it this way, standing here with you."

She nestled closer. "Don't say that, Emile." His words were a reminder that their time was short, unless a miracle intervened.

"Emile," she said, turning to look desperately into his eyes. How could she have found so much joy and then be torn away from it so soon? There must be a way. A frightening sense of panic began to fill her.

He smiled sadly. "You are right. We must make the most of the time we have together. And then, who knows? Life is always full of surprises. Come, we must not waste another moment."

He started to guide her away from the balcony and back into the house.

"We can't go in there," she said. "My mother is in the music room. She'll see us."

He gave a conspiratorial laugh. "I do not intend to take you to listen to that dull music. I have arranged a private bedroom for our use."

She gasped. "Just like that?"

"Of course," he said. "As I told you, I am known at this household. All it took was a whisper in one servant's ear that I had a rendezvous tonight with one of the guests. Do not worry. We will not be disturbed."

"My goodness," she giggled. "The French are very accommodating. It would not be so easy in an American household. The entire family knows what each member is doing."

They turned up a staircase, and Emile dropped kisses on her temple while she continued to chatter in a con-spiratorial tone. "My poor brother Max had to take his paramour to the stables at our home in Newport."

"The stables. Oh, dear, among the horses?"

"In the hay," she said, feeling drunk, though she had only consumed a little wine at dinner.

"How uncomfortable."

They turned at the landing, and made their way along the shadowy corridor. Emile counted the doors.

"Here," he said. "The serving man said third bed-room on the left-hand side." He pushed the door inward.

A globe lamp glowed on a round table by the win-dow. Amanda eyed the bed, feeling her heart beat in naughty excitement. The time before it was almost acci-dental. This time she was a willing participant. But she didn't care. Amanda was still filled with a heady need to spread her wings, to flaunt society and, in her own way, to get back at her mother.

She turned to Emile, standing at the foot of the bed, and grasped his lapels. "Make love to me, Emile," she said.

He was filled with excitement. "Of course, my dear."

His arm slid down her side, and he sought her eager mouth. She returned his kiss, and then his lips left hers to explore her face, the back of her ear, her throat. As he murmured softly against her hair, his hands massaged the softness of the material covering her breasts until an almost painful urgency filled her.

"Come," he said gently, guiding her toward the bed.

They could not risk damaging her clothing, so they paused while he helped her out of the hooks. Then the dress was over her head and draped on a chair. Emile removed his coat and trousers and then turned his attentions to her lacy underthings.

She had cast aside her petticoats and started to untie the laces of her bodice.

"No wait," he said, smiling. "Let me do it."

While he released her from her camisole and corset, her hands worked their own magic under his shirt, shyly seeking the object between his legs. When she touched him his mouth sought hers, and they lay on the bed, fervently touching and responding to the sensual buildup. Their mouths joined hungrily while his fingers probed, tantalizing her breasts.

The tingling between her legs ached, and Emile moved against her thigh. Skin against skin, he pressed, caressed, breathed faster, his fingers and tongue moving and tasting all of her.

"Amanda, I love you," he whispered, never forgetting

in his passion to speak compliments and communicate his adoration.

It was this brand of lovemaking that moved her so, that encouraged her to give herself to him. She was lost in a fantasy world that perhaps had nothing to do with the rest of her life, but she was hungry for it, dazed, in love.

"Emile," she whispered. "This is all so new."

"I know, my pet."

He guided her hand again to his throbbing maleness, her touch driving him mad until he moved to mount her, kissing her, gazing at her soft, round breasts, finding a place for himself between her white thighs. She drank in every inch of him, thrilling with the daring that she had felt when they had first made love.

Then he began his rhythm, her head moving from side to side as he made long, sweet, sensuous love to her. Time stopped, and Amanda was barely aware of where they were or how long they'd been there. When at last Emile's thrusts quickened, she followed him to dizzying heights, and he crushed her in his embrace. Stars seemed to appear overhead, and her heart was full to breaking when she let out her own cries of joy and ecstasy. This time her pain was less, and she was swept away with a release that drove her out of her head.

The pleasure lasted some moments before they began to return to earth. And she held him against her, thoughts dazed and fuzzy, wanting only to kiss and caress his brow. At last he lifted his damp forehead and kissed her again, long and lovingly.

Amanda felt a well of grief build inside her. Love with Emile was so beautiful. There must be a way to hang on to it.

But he kissed away her melancholy and finally rolled

onto his side. "All too brief," he said, "but the concert will be ending. You must return before it is over and your mother starts looking for you."

"Good heavens," said Amanda, crashing back to earth. "My mother."

She sat up and began to replace her clothing. Emile helped her, still enjoying the feel of his fingers on her creamy skin. When they were again clothed, and Amanda had checked her appearance in the gold-framed mirror over the dressing table, they quietly returned to the passageway.

Emile escorted her downstairs and then folded her into his arms for one last kiss. "I will join the party, but of course we will appear as acquaintances only. But I will meet you in the park in the morning, *ma chérie*. I regret every moment not spent at your side."

His romantic words pleased her, and she gave him a coy smile. Then she turned to rejoin the group listening to the final piece in the music room. Rather than make a stir by marching down the aisle and reclaiming her seat by de Laborde, she slipped onto a cushioned chair beside the door. No one seemed to notice her entrance.

When the concert was over, she smiled and clapped gloved hands just like the rest of the guests. The matron beside her gave her a nod. "Charming music, don't you think?"

"Oh, yes, very pleasing," said Amanda.

She saw her mother get out of her chair and scan the room. In another moment she would be bearing down on her. But she saw her route of escape. The row of chairs where she sat was beginning to empty, and the German prince was standing at the other end.

Amanda slid along the row until she was standing by

his side. The gentleman with whom the prince was speaking broke off, and the two men bowed.

"And how did you find the music?" asked the prince politely.

"Very nice," she said. "Your German composers so outdistance the French," she said cleverly.

The prince responded with a pleased smile. "Of course. That goes without saying. Still, there are a few French pieces I myself enjoy for the sake of relaxation."

Amanda launched into a conversation about German music and literature, which surprised the prince. But her ploy worked. For as Louisa approached, she found the prince so engrossed with her daughter's conversation that she dared not interrupt them. So she turned away.

The rest of the evening went off well. Emile mixed with the gay, chattering group and came to speak to Amanda. Both acted as if just remembering each other from Madame Fichet's. Their conversation gave nothing away, until he raised her hand to kiss it. Then he whispered into her ear.

"Tomorrow morning, my dear." And he left her.

It was past midnight when Louisa declared that they should go. She had to round up Zoe, who was still moving from group to group. But Louisa had reached her limits.

"Come, Zoe, Amanda needs her rest."

"Of course, my dear. Let us send for our wraps."

And so the three women thanked their hostess and emerged into the sweet-smelling Parisian night. Amanda was sated with love and adventure, and was thankful for the darkness of the streets as they rode along. Not enough light illuminated the carriage for her face to be scrutinized by either Louisa or Zoe.

She began to wonder about Zoe. The woman had

lived in Paris for several decades. Had she, too, been caught up in the romance of the place? What kind of a past did she have? Amanda would have loved to have a talk with her aunt, and get her to confide her youthful adventures. And Amanda herself was beginning to want to pour out her feelings about her newfound love to a confidante. But there was no one she could trust.

The next morning she was up before dawn, and true to his promise Emile met her in the park. After a few brief kisses, they hurried along to the riverbank, where Emile bought flowers from the flower peddler for her. Then they sat on a park bench, nuzzling each other and talking in low, intimate tones as petals from the flowering redbud drifted down to her hair.

Emile quoted love poetry to her, and her heart beat with affection.

"Oh, Emile, I wish it could be like this always."

"Hmmm." He sighed in melancholy.

Suddenly he was seized with a cough and leaned forward.

"Oh, Emile, are you all right?"

The seizure lasted some moments, but he finally got ahold of himself. "A slight cough. It is nothing."

"I hope you are not becoming ill."

He shrugged. "Sometimes I have a dry cough. But it is gone now. Come, let us walk along the river before you must return to the house."

They strolled hand in hand until it was time that they return. Amanda couldn't risk being out too late in the morning. It was always possible that some of her aunt's acquaintances might drive by and recognize them.

She bid Emile adieu at the end of the street, and he promised that if he could, he would attend the evening's soirée. Amanda smiled in appreciation of the fact that he had ingratiated himself so well with so many hostesses. He seemed to be able to go anywhere. But then who wouldn't welcome his company? He was witty, handsome, artistic and with just that trace of melancholy that made a young scholar attractive.

"Then I shall hope to see you tonight," she said as he kissed her fingers, reminded that the time when she must leave Paris was ominously near.

The day passed quickly, and when it came time for the evening's outing she dressed carefully, paying more attention to her appearance than Louisa was used to seeing in her.

"Are you well, my dear?" her mother asked when she came in to examine Amanda's dress.

"Quite well, Mother."

"Hmmm. It seems you are enjoying yourself in Paris more than you had planned to."

Amanda looked contrite. "Yes. The society here is more stimulating than I had expected." She gave an ironic smile. "The gay Parisians are so attracted to the arts, you know. It is refreshing to be able to discuss music and literature with Zoe's friends."

"Hmmph." Louisa could think of nothing to say to that. "Just be careful who you speak to. You don't want to encourage the wrong sort of young man. I'll be keeping an eye on you, Amanda. You must remember our purpose here."

"Of course, Mother."

The dinner party they attended was not unlike the others, and Amanda amused herself with conversation while Louisa scrutinized all the eligible gentlemen present. When the party moved to the salon for dancing, Amanda began to look for Emile, hoping he had managed to slip in. But she did not see him.

After dancing with several gentlemen, she took a seat at the side of the room. A young man of medium height with dark brown hair sat beside her. As the musicians were tuning for the next dance, he leaned toward her, but did not look at her.

"Mademoiselle," he said in a low voice. "I am a friend of Emile's. My name is Maurice Letiens."

She turned toward him. "Where is he? He said he might be here tonight."

The young man's eyes held sympathy. "I am sorry. He has taken ill."

"Ill?"

"It is a cold. Until the last moment, he thought he would be well enough, but he decided it would be bad mannered to appear with such a cold. So he stayed at home in hopes that he will be better tomorrow."

Amanda looked around to make sure no one heard them. "Perhaps I can see him tomorrow."

"He said that if he is able, he will meet you in the morning as usual. But if he is not there, you are to stay away."

Maurice smiled as if he knew perfectly the lovers' situation. "He would not want to expose you to his cold, of course."

"Oh, I see. Thank you."

She turned around to face front. Poor Emile. But of course it would not be pleasant for him to come to a party if his nose was running and he had a cough. She remembered he had coughed slightly the other night when they had met and again this morning. She must think of a remedy and take it to him tomorrow. For if he was ill enough to stay home tonight, she did not believe the cold would be much better in the morning.

Better for him to stay at home in bed, and she would visit him.

When the dance began, she stole a few words with Emile's friend again.

"Tell Emile to stay in bed tomorrow morning," she instructed. "I will bring him something for his cold."

Maurice gazed at her with a romantic, melancholy look. "Such devotion. No wonder he is in love with you."

She glanced away in embarrassment. "You must excuse me," she said, not wanting her aunt or her mother to become suspicious about her preference for young French nobodies.

For the rest of the evening, she was exceedingly pleasant to all the diplomats, the princes and the academicians, especially enjoying de Laborde's drollery. And when it came time for her mother to sweep her home, Louisa could find no real fault with her daughter's behavior. Still, it was apparent that Louisa was looking forward to getting Amanda to England and the promised visit to the duke. Though Louisa would not admit it, the French were a bit too colorful for her taste. Better the staid traditions of the English. At least they spoke the same language, more or less.

Amanda was up early and stole downstairs. She made her way to the kitchen where Zoe's kitchen maid was lighting a fire in the iron cook stove. Amanda was relieved that it was the maid instead of the cook, for she thought she'd be able to get what she wanted more easily out of the girl. Amanda's French was good enough to make herself understood, and she told the girl she thought she had a cold coming on.

"Do you have some herbs for a cold remedy?"

The girl cocked her head and thought. *"Mais, oui,"* she answered and led the way to the pantry where she brought down jars of mullein, mint, horehound, anise, thyme and cloves of garlic.

Amanda recognized the herbs, which she had used before to fight off nasty colds and sore throats. She measured some out into a small jar, took the garlic cloves and also some honey and thanked the maid.

"I'm sure I will feel much better. It's really not bad yet, and this will prevent it growing worse. *Merci."*

She took the jar upstairs with her and tucked it into a net bag that she could carry with her. Then she went out for her walk. Fortunately she had been observant the other morning, and she remembered how to get to Emile's. She followed the streets they had followed, and when she came to the Seine, she knew she had come the right way. She hurried across the Pont Neuf, smiling at the flower vendors who were setting up their stalls.

She took a wrong turn in the Latin Quarter, but as soon as she discovered her mistake, she went the other way and soon came to the cafe above which Emile lived. The proprietor was sweeping his sidewalk, and looked up as she came along. When he recognized her, he smiled in greeting.

"Bonjour, mademoiselle."

"Bonjour, monsieur," she replied. "I've come with a remedy for Emile. I've heard he is ill."

"Oui," said the proprietor, shaking his head. "He took to his bed last night. His friends say he is not well at all. Poor Emile."

"I'll see if my remedy can help him," she said.

"Bon." The proprietor rattled off his sympathies, saying how lucky Emile was that he had one so beautiful to care for him in his infirmity.

Finally Amanda excused herself and mounted the stairs. At the top, she hesitated before she knocked. Emile might be sleeping, and she wouldn't want to wake him. Trying the door, she found it unlocked and slowly pushed it inward. The little garret was in shadows, except for the sunlight that poured through the half-open window. She heard his raspy breathing and then saw him tangled in the sheets of his bed under the sloping ceiling at the side of the room. She tiptoed across the room and stood looking at the sprawled figure, one arm thrown across his brow. Poor Emile. His nose was red, and his mouth half-open.

Then a cough racked his chest, and his eyes flew open. They widened in recognition, and as he coughed he tried to sit up. She knelt on the floorboards beside him.

"Don't sit up, *chéri,*" she said. "I've brought you something to help."

When he lay back on his pillow, she helped him untangle himself from the sheets and smoothed them over. Already he looked happier and more comfortable.

"Heaven has sent an angel to care for me," he said, taking her hand, when the coughing was over.

"I was so worried. You rest now while I heat water on the spirit lamp and make my remedy."

"You should not have come," he said.

"Don't worry. I used to nurse my cousins and my brother. I have a very strong constitution." She smiled down at him. "Besides, how could I stay at home knowing you were ill?"

His eyes filled with gratitude, and he did as he was told. "There are matches in the cupboard," he said as she crossed the room.

Finding the matches, she lit the fuel in the spirit lamp and filled a teapot with water from the tap over the dry

sink. She made her concoction, then returned to Emile
to wait for the water to heat.

She fluffed up his pillows, tucked in the blanket and
straightened the night table.

"Clean handkerchiefs in the top drawer," he
wheezed, and she crossed to the old chest of drawers on
the opposite wall. Rummaging about the things in the
top drawer, she found a stack of worn, but clean handkerchiefs, which she brought him.

As he dabbed at his nose, she looked at his bloodshot
eyes and shook her head. "You should have a doctor,"
she said.

But he shook his head. "It is only a cold," he said in
a raspy voice. "And besides"—he smiled sadly—"I cannot afford a doctor."

"I can," she said in a no-nonsense voice. "Is there one
in the Latin Quarter?"

"Mademoiselle," he objected, "I could never per-
mit—"

But she cut him off. "Don't be silly, Emile. This is a
very bad cold, and unless attended to properly, it could
get worse. Give me the address of the doctor, and I will
fetch him. You can pay me back later, if you wish. Right
now, it is your welfare I am concerned about."

He blew his nose and then struggled for breath. "All
right, a loan, then. You will keep a record. Dr. Machard's rooms are in the next street. Ask directions
downstairs."

She nodded. The water was hot, so she poured some
into a cup with the herbs and added the honey. After
bringing the hot mug to Emile, she lifted him by the
shoulders so that he could drink it down. He breathed
in the aroma of the tea, and Amanda hoped the drink
would help his congestion while she went for the doctor.

Chapter 8

Dr. Machard was found in his surgery, and as soon as he finished wrapping a sprained ankle, he came to Emile's room. A rotund man with a white head, he huffed up the creaky stairs behind Amanda. She let him in, then went back downstairs to allow the doctor to examine the patient in private. As she was taking some coffee provided by the cafe proprietor, along came Maurice, and seeing her, he waved a greeting and came to join her.

"Ah, mademoiselle, I see you have ignored Emile's orders and come anyway."

She sighed. "I could not let him languish in a sick bed when there might be something I could do. However, I cannot stay long. My family does not know I am here."

"I understand."

"I am only waiting to hear what the doctor says, and then I fear I shall have to go, though I hate to leave him alone."

"Do not worry, mademoiselle. His friends can see to him. But you must care for him very much to risk the criticism of your family. Emile is very fortunate indeed."

She smiled sadly. "I do care for him. And I am worried. His cough is deep. It is hard to believe it came upon him so suddenly. Only yesterday he seemed fit."

"He was fit in the morning. But then he received bad news. When he went to the home of his student to give the boy lessons yesterday afternoon, he was remonstrated for the choice of literature he was having the boy read. The father has a very strict view of what an eleven-year-old should read, and he and Emile had a violent argument. It ended in Emile's being relieved of his position."

"Oh, dear. And then he became ill."

"Yes, it is sad. But perhaps now that you are here, he will be revived."

"I hope so. And surely he can find another position."

Maurice shrugged. "He still has several students, but we all struggle along who live here. I paint pictures, and so far, few have sold. But one must keep one's spirits up."

"Of course. Someday your fortunes will change. I am sure of it."

"You are very hopeful, mademoiselle."

She lifted her chin stubbornly. "I have to be. You may think that because I was born wealthy the way is smoothed for me. But that is not so. I have as many fetters as you do. You just do not see them."

"It may be so."

"For example, I must leave for England in a few days. What if Emile is not well by then? I cannot refuse to go. My mother has threatened to shoot any suitor of whom she does not approve. Alas, she would punish me severely if she knew about Emile, for she is determined to marry me to some titled nobleman."

Maurice sympathized. "Oh, no, no, no. You cannot do that."

"I will not, if I can help it."

They looked up as the doctor lumbered down the stairs. "Ah, *mes amis,*" he said when he saw them. "I have seen the patient." The kindly doctor frowned slightly. "I do not like this congestion of his. But we shall keep an eye on it. I shall send an unguent, which should be rubbed on his chest. That plus the herbal remedy Mademoiselle Whitney was so kind to prepare ought to bring some improvement."

In the distance the bells of Notre Dame chimed their vibrant medieval ring, and Amanda became aware of the time.

"Oh, dear," she said. "I must go."

Maurice saw her anxiety and put a hand on her shoulder. "I shall look after the patient, mademoiselle, do not worry."

She stood up, and Maurice did likewise. "All right. Please tell him I will be back when I can."

"I will give him the message."

She turned to the doctor. "Please tell me what your fee is. I should like to pay it, as well as for the medicine. I want Emile to have the best of care."

"Mademoiselle is too generous," said the doctor.

But with the right amount of humility and concern for the patient as well as gratitude that he would be paid, he named a modest figure, which Amanda extracted from her reticule. Fortunately her father had given her spending money before she had left for the trip, thinking she would want to spend it on baubles and at flower stands, no doubt. But she could think of no better use than to give it to the doctor for Emile.

Maurice pressed her hand, the doctor bowed to her, and she hurried away, crossing the bridge over the fast-flowing Seine once again, too worried to take in the morning beauty of the city coming to life.

She was out of breath when she got back to the square, but she needn't have worried. Zoe had taken breakfast in her room, and Louisa had not yet showed herself. Amanda went to the breakfast room where she accepted a plate of creamed biscuits. By the time she had finished, her mother joined her, dressed in a frilly dressing gown, and looking severe.

"What is this about a cold?"

Her eyes flew upward until she remembered that she had claimed to have a cold herself in order to procure the remedy. She sniffed and cleared her throat.

"A tightness in my throat," she said. "I thought the remedy might help it."

Louisa took a cup of coffee from the silver coffeepot on the sideboard. "This is a most inconvenient time to become ill. Shall we call a doctor?"

"No, no," she said hastily. "It's not that serious. The cold remedy has always worked before."

"Then see to it you've plenty of rest. I don't advise you go out of the house today."

Amanda panicked. She had to think of a way to get to Emile. "But a little fresh air and sun is the best thing for a cold."

"Hmmph. Not if you take a chill."

"It's very warm. I shall stay in this morning, but get a little sun in the afternoon. That is, if we don't have any plans. I really don't feel up to receiving visitors." She contrived to look wan.

"I'll tell Zoe you must rest today. Do try to get better by tomorrow night. We are attending the opera."

"Dear me."

"You sound disappointed. At home you always seem

to enjoy the opera so much you never want to leave before it is over."

"Well, yes, of course I want to go. If I am up to it."

She placed her napkin on the table and slowly moved to get up. She gave a slight cough as she left the breakfast table and went out of the room. In the corridor she moved more swiftly as she went along to the library. Frustrated that she was stuck here until afternoon, she paced the room. But when she heard a rap on the door, she threw herself into the chair at the table where fortunately one of the books on British titles of the nobility was open.

Zoe came in. "How are you feeling, my dear? Your mother tells me you are indisposed."

Amanda swallowed. She was not sure she could fool her aunt. "It is nothing, Aunt. A little scratchy throat, that is all." She cleared her throat.

"I see." Zoe came closer and lifted Amanda's chin. "Hmmm. You do not want a doctor?"

"I made a cold remedy this morning. Already I feel better. I don't think a doctor is necessary."

"Hmmm. You have good color. One would hardly know you were ill." Zoe lifted her brows. "Sometimes illness comes upon us at convenient times. Could it be true in this case?"

"I don't know what you mean, Aunt Zoe."

The aunt let go the chin. "Perhaps you did not want to go out today. Or you wanted more time by yourself. Perhaps this round of social visits and shopping is too much for you."

Amanda swallowed, choosing her words carefully. "It is true that my mother's plans for me are a bit baffling. I had hoped to enjoy Paris on my own terms. Sadly, I have not had that chance. And besides, you know my enjoyment of reading. We will leave for England soon, and I fear I will not have had the chance to examine your collection."

"Hmmm," said Zoe. "Very well. Perhaps a day at home will do you good. I will cancel your plans to attend Lady St. Helier's for dinner, saying that you are ill. Unfortunately Louisa and I must go. It is too short notice to inform madame that she will be short three dinner guests."

"I'm very sorry, Aunt Zoe."

"Never mind. Just use the day to rest. Perhaps you will find yourself in better spirits tomorrow." She turned to go.

At the door, she paused, turned around again and leveled Amanda a look. "Oh, and your book is upside down."

She shut the door after her as Amanda glanced at the volume before which she had only just managed to sit down when her aunt entered the room. To her horror, her aunt was correct. The print read the wrong way. She slowly turned the book around and shook her head. She did not read the pages. Instead, she got up and perused the rest of the volumes lining the bookshelves, barely paying any attention. But she selected the plays of Racine to take upstairs with her.

There, she lay down on the lounge, which faced a sash window, and with the book in her lap, gazed out at the trees and houses of the square, thinking about Emile.

The day dragged by slowly, and Amanda saw no opportunity for escape all day. But when her mother and aunt dressed to go to Lady St. Helier's, she saw her chance. It was Marie's night off, and now was the time Amanda would take Delcia into her confidence. The maid would help her escape.

As soon as Zoe's carriage left, she called Delcia to her room. The girl came, an anxious look on her youthful face.

"Are you feeling better, miss?" she asked. For she had brought tea and hot lemon juice to Amanda's room all day.

"Quite, Delcia." She motioned the girl farther into the room, making sure the door was firmly shut. "I need your help. I must go out."

The maid cocked her head. "Oh, I thought you were to be at home tonight."

Amanda bid Delcia sit beside her on the lounge. "I must trust you with a confidence, Delcia. You have served me well in the past, and I believe you can keep a secret."

The risk was lessened here in Paris because the rest of the Whitney household servants had been left behind in New York, and Amanda knew that Delcia was not close to Louisa.

"I have met a young man who is very ill. I must go see him."

Delcia blinked. For a moment her look was confused, and Amanda knew she must clarify, for Delcia had posted the letter to Francis in Newport. She attempted to explain.

"The letter I sent to the young man from Newport was the last communication I shall have with him. He is . . . socializing elsewhere. We have broken off."

"Oh, I see, miss."

"I met a young man here, a scholar, the other night at a soirée. I have learned that he's come down with a bad cold. I am very concerned about it and must go see him."

"But your own cold, miss. Would it not be worse for two invalids to see each other when you are both under the weather?"

"I'm not under the weather, Delcia. I said that so I could get out of this frivolous round of calling and take him a remedy. I must go to Emile tonight, and you must help me."

Realization crept over Delcia's face, and her love of intrigue shone in her dark eyes. "Ah, now I see. But of course. What do you wish me to do?"

"First, you must ascertain where the other servants in the house are. I know it is Marie's night off. Find out where the rest of the staff are. I can't risk anyone seeing me go out."

"Very well."

"Then when you have done that, you must go out to the street and find me a cab. Have it wait at the end of the block facing toward Ile de la Cité. When all is clear, I will go. When I come back, before midnight, you must see that the front gate is unlocked, so that I can gain entrance. Again, you must make sure the servants have gone to bed, and if there is anyone still up, you must contrive to wait for me by the gate outside to give me warning. Wear your dark cloak so that you are not seen."

"I understand, miss."

Delcia left on her mission, and when the coast was clear, Amanda went down to the pantry to fetch more of the herbs to use for nursing Emile. Then she waited in her room until Delcia returned to say the cab was waiting for her.

"Thank you, Delcia. Now don't forget to look out for

me just before midnight. If for some reason my mother and aunt return before then, you must tell them I have gone to bed. But I don't foresee it. They usually arrive home from these parties well after midnight."

"Don't worry, miss. I will place pillows in your bed to make it look as if you are sleeping there in case someone should look in. I can be very convincing."

Amanda appreciated her maid's part in the plot, and she knew that eventually it would be something Delcia would tell her own children about. But for the moment, she thought her secret was safe.

Amanda scurried out into the night. Giving the hansom cab driver the address, she settled back in the carriage. A gentle mist had arisen, and the gas lamps looked even more muted as the carriage rolled along the streets. The Seine reflected the misty lights in her waters, making Amanda's heart ache at the romance of the scene.

Soon they arrived at Emile's address, and she got down and paid the driver. Then she crossed the little street, where gaiety now emanated from the cafe. As she approached the stairs, a familiar figure emerged from the din of the cafe crowd.

"Mademoiselle," the voice called.

She recognized Maurice. "Hello, Maurice. I managed to get out of the house. How is Emile?"

Maurice glanced anxiously up the steps. "Not well, I'm afraid. His cough is worse. I just left him. He sent us all away, saying he did not want to ruin our evening. That is like him."

She bit her lip and looked upward. "I hope he will want to see me," she said. "Is he resting?"

"He could not be asleep so early, I don't believe. I am sure the sight of you will raise his spirits."

"Thank you, Maurice. Could you do me a favor?"

"Anything, mademoiselle."

"I will need a cab when I leave. I will have to get away shortly after eleven o'clock. Can you see to that?"

"Of course, mademoiselle. One only has to walk to the Boulevard St. Michel to get a cab. I will be happy to do that for you." He cast another melancholy glance toward the stairs, and Amanda left him.

She found Emile in the shadowed room, with but a single lamp burning by his bedside. A book lay on his chest, his head sideways on the pillow, and his eyes closed. His eyelids opened at the creak of the floorboards, and he attempted to move his dry lips into a smile.

"Emile," she said as she came to him and drew up a wooden chair beside the bed. She lay her hand on his forehead and to her alarm found it very hot.

His eyes showed his gratitude that she had come, but she saw at once that his symptoms had worsened. "Don't try to speak, just nod yes or no. Did the doctor send the unguent?"

He moved his head up and down and disobeyed her orders not to speak; but his words came out in a hoarse whisper, and she could hear the wheezing of his breath.

"He came again this evening," he croaked.

"Well," she said, trying to hide her alarm. "I have brought some more cold remedy. I will prepare it." She patted his hand and rose to make the mixture.

When she brought it to him, she held his head so that he could drink. He had to break off for a hacking cough, the sound of which she did not like at all. Clearly this was more severe than a mere cold. Possibly pneumonia. She must go to see Dr. Machard at once.

After she had gotten the mixture down Emile, she

straightened the bedding. Then she took the cup back to the dry sink and applied herself to the task of tidying up. With that done, she returned to Emile's bedside.

"I'm going round to Dr. Machard's," she said. "I need to find out what he has to say. Perhaps you need different medicine."

Emile grasped her hands in his perspiring ones and moved his head back and forth. "Don't go," he half whispered.

She got up to fetch a bowl of water and a clean handkerchief and then bathed his face. Then, putting the bowl aside, she said, "I won't be long. I must see what else the doctor advises. I can't stand to see you this way, Emile."

She pressed her lips together, hoping her look of compassion gave him strength rather than frightened him. But his look seemed more full of sympathy for her than pity for himself.

"There's nothing else to be done," he said.

She wrinkled a brow. "I believe you," she said, trying to comfort him. "Nevertheless, I must satisfy myself."

She extracted her hands and rose. "I will be back shortly. Close your eyes and rest 'til I get back."

Contrary to her wishes, his eyes followed her as far as they could; then he exhaled a ragged breath and tried to rest.

Amanda hurried down the stairs and sought out Maurice, who was in the cafe slumped over a table in the corner, drinking wine. Two friends with whom he had been conversing rose when Amanda approached the table. None of them looked gay, and she suspected they had been talking about Emile. Maurice looked up as if afraid to meet her gaze.

"Maurice, I must go at once to see Dr. Machard. Emile is much worse. This is more than a mere cold."

"I'm afraid you are right, mademoiselle. Come, I will go with you."

He drew himself up and escorted her out of the noisy cafe. The street was damp, and the gaslights reflected off the bricks. Maurice said little, turning up his collar against the mist. In the next street they came to a half-timbered house with a shingle in front. Maurice pressed the bell, and shortly they were admitted to a small entry hall by a tall, thin maid in mob cap and bombazine.

"We must see the doctor," Maurice said. "Tell him Mademoiselle Whitney is here."

The maid nodded and indicated a door to a white paneled sitting room with rosewood furniture where they could wait. The woman then ascended the stairs to deliver the message and soon returned to fetch them.

"Follow me."

They followed her up the stairs and across a landing to a study where the doctor got up from behind a large mahogany desk. He came around to offer them chairs. The room glowed from the light of gas lamps affixed to the flocked walls.

"Ah, mademoiselle and monsieur, I trust you've come about Monsieur Reveillere."

Amanda nodded. "I am quite concerned, Doctor. You must tell me what is wrong with him."

The doctor rounded his desk again and took a seat. He looked compassionately at Amanda and drew a breath. "I assume you are a new acquaintance of Emile's, eh?"

She nodded. "Yes. What's that got to do with it?"

His chair creaked as he moved in it. "Then you do not know his medical history."

Her heart hammered as she moved forward in her chair. "No. If there is something I should know, please tell me."

The doctor glanced at Maurice, who gave a small nod of the head. The doctor removed his spectacles and rubbed the bridge of his nose.

"Emile has been consumptive for much of his life."

Amanda's mouth dropped, and she began to tremble.

The doctor continued. "For some years he has been able to overcome the symptoms. But every cold, every tickle of the throat, in his case, is a greater danger than in most. He does not have the immunity of a healthy person."

The clock on the mantel ticked loudly while Amanda struggled to find her voice. When it came out it was hoarse with emotion and surprise. "But we must do something."

The doctor straightened and leaned back in his chair. "The only thing that can be done cannot be done here. In other circumstances I would recommend that the patient be moved to a sanatorium in the south of France. The drier climate and the treatment he would receive there might be able to save him."

She could hardly believe her ears. "Save him? But we must."

The doctor expelled a breath. "He doesn't have the money, to put it bluntly. He refuses to ask his employers to advance so much money when it is uncertain when he might be able to pay it back."

Amanda knit her brows. "Has he no family?"

"Only a sister, whose circumstances are much like his own."

"I see." Again the clock on the mantel ticked. "I might be able to get the money," Amanda said slowly.

Her mind leapt forward to how she could get such a sum out of the trust arranged for her by her father. Her mother would refuse her, she knew, and the money she carried with her was only a little more than would be needed for the doctor's fees.

"Can you make the arrangements, Doctor, saying that I will pay? I must cable my father in America, for I am sure he will send the money to me. Surely you can convince the sanatorium to accept him."

She opened her reticule, taking all the money out except what she would need for cab fare home. After she ran out of what she had left in her dresser drawer at her aunt's house, she would walk.

"This might be enough to cover his transportation. Then you can give me the address as to where to send the rest."

Dr. Machard frowned. "Are you sure you want to do this, mademoiselle?"

"Of course. Of course. If his life is at stake, there is no question."

After a moment's hesitation the doctor reached for a sheet of stationery and dipped a pen into his ink well. Then he scrawled the name and address of the sanatorium on the sheet and slid it across to Amanda.

Her heart ached. "I only regret that I cannot go with him." She folded the paper and put it into her reticule, standing up to go. "My mother swore she would shoot any suitor that she had not approved, and I believe she would keep her promise. Therefore I cannot further risk Emile's life by going with him."

She turned to Maurice. "You must take him, Maurice, and see him settled."

Maurice inclined his head forward. "I will go."

"Good. Then it is settled. Thank you, Doctor."

"I will make the arrangements tomorrow. You can take him on the train, Maurice. It will be a strain for him to travel, but it will be best in the long run."

"Very well," replied Maurice.

They left the doctor and returned to Emile's dwelling, where Maurice left her. "Tell him that I will fetch him in the morning. I have my own affairs to see to tonight," he told Amanda at the foot of the stairs. "Meet me in the cafe a little after eleven. I will get you a cab."

"Bless you, Maurice. I will get him ready to leave. Thank you for going." A sob choked off her words, but Maurice put an arm about her shoulders.

"Do not worry, mademoiselle. You are truly an angel."

He patted her shoulder and then saw her up the stairs. She pushed in Emile's door slowly, then shut it gently behind her. His eyes opened at her approach.

"You are going away," she said, grief breaking her heart. "I have made the arrangements with the doctor. Maurice is taking you to the sanatorium."

His cheeks blazed with color, his eyes widened, and he opened his mouth to speak, but she placed her fingers over his dry, cracked lips.

"Do not argue, Emile," she said. "I am arranging for the money to come from my father. You can pay me back later."

Still, he protested, grasping the hand on his lips. "You cannot do such a thing." But the words sent him into a fit of coughing.

"I can, and I will."

She handed him a handkerchief, and when his coughing fit was over, she bent her head to lay it next to his cheek.

"A loan," he whispered into her ear, his fingers tangling in her tresses.

"Yes, a loan," she replied, squeezing his hand. "Now rest."

She went about the little room packing an old cloth carpetbag with the things he would need. She held each item up, and he nodded yes or no. Then she laid out clothes for him to put on tomorrow. She heard the cathedral bells chime eleven o'clock and knew her time was short. She arranged the things for tomorrow and then came to sit by the bed one last time.

"I do not know when I will be able to see you, Emile. But I promise I will come."

He conserved his energy by merely gazing at her, his gratitude and devotion written on his face. Then she lowered her lips to his for a gentle kiss. He lifted his hand to her hair and returned the kiss with as much fervor as his fever allowed.

"Do not cry, my love," he croaked when he felt her tears drop onto his cheeks.

She lifted her face and tried to smile at him. "Very well. I will not." She stifled the sobs and gazed at him for as long as she dared. Then she pulled herself away.

"I must go."

He nodded. "How can I thank you?"

She tried to smile, but her lips trembled. "By getting well, of course."

This brought a light into his eyes. "Yes, then I will do it for you."

Her heart breaking, she bent to squeeze his hands and drop a final kiss on his forehead; then she closed his eyes with her fingers and stole across the room.

Outside his door, the sob that she had been trying to hold back escaped. Then she fled down the stairs, tears streaming down her face as she found Maurice, who led her to the Boulevard St. Michel and put her into the carriage. Then she leaned out the window for a final word.

"I will be at Elsenheim Palace in Oxfordshire. You must send word there. I'll write to you if there are any difficulties."

"Try not to worry, mademoiselle. Heaven will bless you for your kindness."

"Never mind that. But tell Emile to get well."

She could say no more, and Maurice stepped back so the cabby could flick his whip and the horse pull away. Amanda sat back in the carriage, fear filling her heart. She did not even know if her father would send her the money; she had simply said so in order to get Emile moved as quickly as possible. And as the cab rattled over the Pont Neuf, she wondered if she would ever see him again.

Chapter 9

Fortunately everything went as planned, and Amanda slipped back into her aunt's house with Delcia's help, unnoticed by anyone else. Wanting to be alone, she sent her maid to bed. Then she sat down at the writing desk in her room and composed the cable she would send to her father tomorrow.

The words were hard to come by, for she needed to express urgency, and yet she could think of no way to do it that would not lead her father to believe she had become involved with a penniless young man. And coming on the heels of her infatuation with Francis, she knew it would not sound convincing.

She finally settled on the most simple message, saying a friend was deathly ill and she wished to loan him the money for treatment at a sanatorium. Let her father guess why she wished to do so. She regretted that she could not see her father in person, for in that case, she was sure she would be able to persuade him. As it was, she would have to trust that he would comply.

That done, she was able to go to bed. She tossed and turned until she heard her mother and aunt come in. Then she lay still, expecting that one of them might look

in on her. Just as she suspected, the doorknob turned
and the door opened a crack. She lay perfectly still with
her eyes closed, breathing evenly. Whoever peeked must
have been satisfied and closed the door again.

But she lay awake, thoughts and images turning and
turning, until sometime in the early hours of the morning, she surrendered to sleep.

Amanda awoke, and for an instant did not remember
all that had transpired, and then thoughts of Emile
came flooding back. She threw back the covers and
hopped out of bed, going to the armoire for a dress.
Forgetting that she was supposed to have a cold, she allowed Delcia to dress her hair, and then she went down
for breakfast.

After a healthy breakfast she went out, ostensibly for
her walk. She didn't dare let any of the household staff
know she was going to the telegraph office. The driver
of the hansom cab knew where to take her, and her mission was accomplished in no time. She asked that her
father send the money directly to the sanatorium. As to
where he could reply to her cable, there was only one
choice, Elsenheim Palace.

She would have to inform her host that she was expecting a cable from America. At least at Elsenheim
Palace, the staff would not be under her mother's control, so the cable would be delivered to her. Satisfied
that she had done everything she could, she returned to
the waiting hansom. She had the cabby let her out at
the end of the block so that she could return to the
house from her "walk."

Her face composed, she entered the breakfast room,
where her mother and Zoe were finishing their breakfast.

"Good morning, Amanda," said Zoe, looking up. "How are you feeling this morning?"

"Much better, thank you."

Louisa pivoted around to cast her steely eyes on her daughter. "Out early for one who was so ill-disposed last evening," she said.

Amanda ignored the sarcasm in her mother's voice. "I was feeling so much better that I got up early. Feeling housebound after being sick, I decided to go for a walk. The air is so fresh and invigorating. I don't think it's healthy to spend the entire time cooped up in a room, when it's so lovely outside, with the budding chestnut and flowering lilac to look at."

"Then if you are able to look at the trees, I presume you are feeling able to face the world?" inquired Louisa.

"I believe so," answered Amanda. "The remedy worked marvelously. Only a little tickle in my throat left."

"Good," said Louisa. "Then you'll be ready for the Channel crossing day after tomorrow."

Amanda gave a shrug. "Yes, quite." All reasons for wanting to remain in Paris were gone.

Elsenheim Palace was grandly situated in a park with an ornamental lake spanned by a stone bridge. After a long, curving avenue of elms, a stone arch led into a courtyard around which were situated smaller buildings containing workrooms, the laundry, greenhouse, the porter's lodge and various offices. Several spotted mongrel dogs trotted and yipped after the carriage.

A second stone arch led to the central court, which was surrounded by the main house. There, the north lay open, where a bridge crossed a stream to the high park.

The green glades sloped gently down to the lake. There great oaks stood, some said over a thousand years old, for the park had originally been part of the royal forest of Woodstock. Near the woods were the high lodge, a small house with a lovely view of the surrounding countryside, and a well.

The carriage stopped at the foot of a flight of shallow steps leading to the main entrance of the great house. The Duke of Sunderland himself stood on the top step to greet them. Ranged along the steps were footmen at the ready to carry luggage.

Sunderland came down the steps, and Amanda and her mother alit from the carriage. He bowed to the ladies.

"Welcome to my house," he said. "I hope your journey was pleasant."

"Very pleasant, Your Grace," said Louisa, ready to take charge. "And we are glad to be here. You were most gracious to invite us."

Amanda set her eyes on the handsome, rugged face and remembered the disagreements that had arisen between them when he had been at Marble Gate. She had planned to be gracious, for there was really nothing else to be done. But now that she was here facing him, her stubborn ire seemed to take over, and she swallowed the words she had prepared.

Sunderland saw something of the struggle that went on in her face and inclined his head, an ironic smile touching his lips and questions in his eyes.

"And Miss Whitney, I trust you had a favorable stay in Paris."

Blood washed her cheeks. At his words, she felt as if he had invaded her privacy. How dare he talk to her of Paris!

"Yes, thank you," she snapped, for she knew she had to say something.

The footmen made a caravan of the trunks and baggage that now streamed into the house. Sunderland offered his arm to Louisa, and Amanda trailed behind up the steps with Delcia, who was taken under the wing of the housekeeper when they reached the door.

The doors of the main entrance led into an immense entry hall, and Amanda craned her neck backward to look up at the domed, painted ceiling. She made out a nobly clad aristocrat in a Roman toga driving a chariot and surrounded by clouds. By turning around she could see that he was racing to join Julius Caesar and Alexander the Great.

"My ancestor, the first duke," said Sunderland, giving Amanda a start. He stood beside her, following her gaze upward.

"Oh, I see," she answered. She pressed her lips together and reprimanded herself, for she hadn't meant to gawk.

Below the heavens were large paintings in gilded frames, and Sunderland pointed out the family group. "If you enjoy paintings, there are more portraits in the gallery, which I would be happy to show you."

"Of course," said Amanda, still getting her bearings in the cavernous place.

"If you will follow me, my sisters and my grandmother would like to meet you. They have been looking forward to your visit."

He led the way across the marble floor to a set of doors, which a footman opened. They passed into a grand salon, whose pale green paneled walls stretched from the ornate bookcases and marble fireplace at this end down a length of Turkish carpet past formal furniture groupings to another mantelpiece crowned with an immense dark oil painting at the other end. Only after taking in all these details did Amanda become aware that there were skirts trailing from the brocade chairs at the other end of the room, and that human beings awaited them.

The duke, looking comfortably elegant in his perfectly cut frock coat, strode down the length of the room, escorting Amanda and her mother. Amanda had been in grand houses before, but none so grand as this, and at once stiffened at the formality. How could one ever relax in a place like this?

The elderly woman who sat upright in a thronelike upholstered chair near the oversized mantel was gowned in velvet and satin with a lace bodice that came to a high neckline enclosing her throat. Amanda stared at the dowager, feeling the mighty gaze on her, much as she might feel if she were presented to the queen. That she was being presented for approval, there was no doubt, and her cheeks and jaw became rigid with annoyance.

Louisa stopped beside her, facing the triumvirate composed of the dowager and two younger women, also regally but conservatively gowned.

"I have brought Mrs. Jay Whitney and her daughter, Miss Amanda Whitney. May I present my grandmother, the Dowager Duchess of Sunderland."

"A great pleasure," said Louisa. "We are honored to be here."

The dowager nodded and picked up a large ear trumpet which she held to her ear. Amanda realized she was supposed to say something.

"It's nice to meet you, madam," she said in a voice louder than normal.

"And this is my eldest sister, Lady Isabel Isington, whose husband, Lord Isington, is absent at present."

A tall, thin woman with Sunderland's dark eyes but a squarish chin rose to greet them. She seemed to float toward them, and her smile seemed down-to-earth with honesty. Her woolen dress accented with gold braid was by far the more practical of the group. With her deepset eyes and long nose, she had the constrained English looks. But she was warm with her welcome.

"Welcome to Elsenheim," she said, taking first Louisa's hand and then Amanda's. "I hope your stay here is as pleasant as possible. We shall do everything we can to make you comfortable. Even though the place is two hundred years old, we do have running water."

Amanda appreciated Lady Isabel's frankness and relaxed her fixed features a trace.

"And my other sister," said Sunderland. "Lady Norah Pemberton."

Ah, thought Amanda as the younger sister likewise rose out of her chair and came forward. An unmarried sister. Was she, like Amanda, being presented to noble personages in order to gain a fitting marriage? Or were they planning to marry her off for money? Lady Norah rustled toward them in a frilly gown of dotted Swiss muslin with ruffles across the bodice, trimming the skirt and adorning the wrist under large puffed sleeves.

"It is a pleasure to receive your visit," she said. "I hope we can please you while you are here. You are most welcome."

Her light blue eyes met Amanda's in a friendly smile. Her lighter features and fairer hair made her seem the more delicate of the sisters. But her long nose and pointed chin also gave her an aristocratic quality that spoke of quiet confidence and assurance.

"Thank you," said Amanda. "You are most gracious."

A tea table had been set, and as Sunderland handed Amanda and her mother into chairs, a uniformed maid appeared from nowhere and began to pour tea. A footman offered round platters of finger sandwiches and scones, and soon the party was busy with refreshments. When everyone had been served, Lady Isabel took the lead in directing the conversation since the dowager duchess, whose privilege it should have been, was somewhat hampered by her hearing loss.

"Sunderland tells us you are greatly interested in literature," said Lady Isabel.

Amanda blinked. "Yes, that is true. I'm afraid I always have been. My habit is to rise early and read before breakfast."

"Well then, we shall have to make our library available to you. It is not large; but it is a very old collection, and there might be something of interest for you."

Amanda was not used to having this interest catered to and allowed a crack in her defensive armor. "Thank you. I would enjoy looking at your collection of books."

"Our brother will show you the estate, of course," said Lady Norah. "You will enjoy seeing the village and the countryside. And if you ride, the woods are quite pleasant."

Amanda nodded, forgetting that she was determined not to enjoy herself. Solitary rides in the woods would be the pastime she would choose if she must occupy her time, for she would be free to engage in her own thoughts. Already she was anxious to get out of this confining room. Even though she knew she could do nothing but wait for her father's cable, she felt she could not sit in one place very long. And if she put her mind to it, she knew that she might find a way to go to Emile after this dreadful visit was over. As it was, at least she could write long, impassioned letters to him, begging him to get well.

"I would enjoy riding in the woods," she said, and took a sip of tea. "I ride along the cliffs at our cottage in Newport, at home."

She felt Sunderland's eyes on her, though he had said little beyond making the introductions. When she glanced at him she was surprised at the curious expression on his face and the sense that he was assessing her. She felt at once a spring of recognition, as if they already knew each other well, and he could read her thoughts. But mixed with this was a sense of annoyance.

Louisa began to describe their stay in Paris, but Amanda's mind drifted off. What attention she had for polite conversation was distracted by thoughts of Emile and by trying to shield her thoughts from the commanding presence of the duke. At long last the tea was finished, and they were allowed to go to their rooms to rest from the journey.

"It was a tiresome crossing," Louisa was complaining as Amanda and the duke led the party out of the elegant wilderness.

"Please ask for anything you need," said Lady Norah at Amanda's elbow when they came to the marble-floored entry hall once again. "Dinner is at eight o'clock."

"Thank you," said Amanda.

Rather than leave the party to the care of the household staff, Sunderland chose to escort the ladies to the second floor, pointing out features of the house as they went. As they ascended the wide carpeted marble staircase, he narrated the paintings they passed.

"The Gainsborough landscape is a gift from the Prince of Wales in appreciation of a visit here."

"How nice," said Amanda mechanically.

On the second floor they strolled along a gallery where paintings by Renoir, Corot and Manet hung. In other circumstances, Amanda might have shown some interest. Taking another set of stairs, and turning a corner, they came to a wing that housed the guest apartments.

A footman appeared to open the gilded door of a boudoir into which Lady Isabel showed Louisa, leaving Sunderland alone with Amanda, if one discounted the silent servants that seemed to appear and disappear like apparitions at appointed junctures in the party's perambulations.

"If there is anything I can do for you," said Sunderland, as they walked along the old, but fine, wine-colored carpet with geometric patterns.

Amanda seized her chance. "There is something," she said, as they paused before another white-painted door with gilded molding.

He lifted his dark brows and waited.

"I am expecting a cablegram from my father in America. I am most anxious to receive it, and when it arrives I would like it brought directly to me."

He inclined his dark head. "Of course. I will inform the staff."

Good manners prevented his inquiring about the cable, but Amanda wanted to say something more to indicate that she didn't want her mother getting her hands on it.

"It is a private matter between my father and myself. I wouldn't want my mother upset by noticing it. You see," she went on, feeling she owed the duke some explanation, "my mother and father don't get along well. You may have noticed they live apart."

Again, nothing but intelligent, concerned interest on the part of the duke. "I have noticed, but of course that is a family matter and no outsider's business."

She appreciated his restraint. "Yes. I'm sorry it has turned out that way, but I can't say I blame him."

She looked down, surprised to be confiding so much to the duke. She had meant to keep up her defenses before this frank nobleman, so assured of his importance.

"I see your point." It was said with such quiet empathy and just a trace of amused irony that Amanda was startled into a semismile.

Sunderland curved his lips upward, pleased that he had succeeded in breaking through the formidable ridges that surrounded Amanda, for he was all too aware of her present misery. Something troubled her, and he had a suspicion that it was more than just the discomfort of being presented to a noble family and inspected like a work of art might be before purchase. He could sympathize with her dilemma. For though he had been raised to take much responsibility and do what was expected of him, he was not unfeeling.

That Amanda appeared not to like him much did not bother him. For he sensed the same rapport that seemed to convey itself to her in spite of her resistance. Her own family life seemed to leave much to be desired, and he truly regretted that fact. Such a fiery, intelligent girl deserved a joyous life filled with the stimulation and comfort a loving family could give.

But the more he saw of the Whitney family, the more he saw that clearly was not the case. Her brother Max was likable, but too busy with his own pursuits at this stage to offer his sister much companionship. Max had to become a man of the world, leaving his sister to flounder in a sea of riches unsupported by those who truly cared. He suspected it was this kind of background that led her to make irrational choices, struggling against the gilded cage in which she lived. And so he understood totally the rebelliousness she demonstrated and blamed her for none of it.

At the same time Amanda seemed more attractive to him than when he first met her. Something had happened to her, some blossoming of womanhood. Her radiance was greater; her eyes flashed with determination in spite of her sense of desperation.

This cable coming from her father must have something to do with it. Perhaps she had sent some sort of plea for help and expected her father to come to the rescue. The mystery intrigued Sunderland, who was challenged by every intrigue thrown his way. Instead of being off-putting in her manner, Amanda had succeeded in challenging Sunderland to the chase.

Thus they stood for a moment smiling foolishly at each other in some sort of understanding. Amanda had the ridiculous notion that Edward Pemberton, the Duke of Sunderland, might somehow become her ally in her battle, though how this might be, she could not imagine.

She left him and entered the large apartment comprised of a narrow sitting room that led to a large boudoir, where Delcia was busy unpacking and putting clothes into a tall, ornate armoire. The dominant feature of the room was a huge alabaster fireplace with brass andirons, but it was the bed that most fascinated Amanda.

It stood on a square rug of faded oriental colors, and the blue silk coverlet with gold tassels on its hem was exactly the same color and material as the immense draperies that hung from a canopy with deep scallops of the same deep blue with gold tassels. The draperies could be pulled so that the entire bed was curtained off, and Amanda couldn't help but cover her mouth in consternation. A more smothered mode of sleeping she could not imagine. She stood surveying the rest of the room as Delcia went about her work.

"This is quite the place, miss. How long do we stay here?"

"Too long, I'm afraid," said Amanda.

She stopped gawking and looked at the opened trunks and bags. "Are you finding a place for everything?" she asked.

"It'll do, even if it is out of date."

Amanda smiled inwardly at the understatement. "Two hundred years out of date." She could not resist the quip.

She removed her bonnet and laid it on an antique dressing table. She saw that there was no separate dressing room, only a dressing screen, behind which one could change if one's female friends or relatives were in the room. It suddenly dawned on her that there was no bathroom attached to this apartment. But of course in a house so old, modern plumbing must be scarce.

"Delcia, have you inquired as to where I might bathe. I assume the palace is equipped with a bathroom somewhere in its vastness."

"Hmmph," grunted the maid. "It is. There is one on each floor. But when the house is full of guests, I am given to understand that the staff is used to bringing a hip tub to place right here before the hearth and filling it with heated water."

Amanda's eyes flew open at the description of this primitive undertaking.

It took her a moment to assimilate this news. "Good heavens." Presumably the few bathrooms were reserved for the duke and the dowager duchess.

"Good heavens," she said again.

She walked across the room to look out the tall, narrow windows at the countryside and the forest beyond. She should have believed Sunderland when he told her his family was impoverished, and that it took too much money to run a great house such as this. Whoever he married had better be able to afford to put in bathrooms.

Dinner was a formal affair with the dowager duchess asking questions the answers to which had to be shouted into her ear trumpet. The volume of conversation between the duchess and the person to whom she chose to speak was so loud that it tended to distract the other diners, who might be exchanging a few words with the person seated next to them. Amanda was particularly frustrated by having to talk to the dowager in such a loud voice that everyone else at the table could hear her answers.

"Have you been to England before, Miss Whitney?" the dowager duchess inquired.

"Yes," shouted Amanda. "We've come over several times to visit both England and the Continent. We usually stay in Paris with my aunt."

"Ah, and do you like Parisian society?"

She could hardly answer no. "Yes, very much."

"English society, of course, is much more to the point."

Amanda smiled, as she could think of no reply to this. The duchess continued. "It might interest you to know that our village of Woodhaven had a mayor and a corporation before America was discovered."

"Then it is very old," said Amanda.

She heard her mother cough and at the same time caught Sunderland's amused eye. She hadn't meant to say anything insulting, but she wasn't about to be put in her place by this regal lady. She smiled sweetly and continued her conversation with the dowager.

"When was this house built?" she inquired, loud enough for the dowager to hear.

"The original structure was built in 1700, in honor of the first Duke of Sunderland's military achievements. There have been a few additions since."

"I would be interested in seeing the newer wings," said Amanda.

Lady Norah coughed behind her napkin, and the dowager duchess set down her ear trumpet, pretending not to hear.

"You are in it," said Sunderland, leaning toward her and speaking distinctly, though not so loud as to be heard by everyone along the table.

"Oh," said Amanda.

She concentrated on the currant sauce that smothered the pheasant on her platter.

"You mustn't let my grandmother put you off," said Sunderland in a low voice a few minutes later, as the footmen removed the plates. "She is rather proud of her heritage."

"Of course," said Amanda. Then, not wanting to appear too rude, she continued, "I can understand it. And the house is quite ... interesting." She thought about the shortage of conveniences, but this was neither the time nor the place to mention them.

"And just how did you find Parisian society?" Sunderland continued, signaling the footman to pour more wine for Amanda and then himself. "Was it very gay?"

She did not meet his eyes as she answered. "It was quite mixed. One does not meet so many artists and scholars in New York society," she answered.

"And you are attracted to artists and scholars, I take it?"

Her eyes flew to his at the word "attracted." Too late she surmised he meant it in the broader sense, and yet there was a certain nuance in his voice that made her suspect a double meaning. She lifted her chin a trace.

"As I told you, I enjoy reading and the arts. It was enjoyable to find those in society to be able to discuss literature and such ideas. Since, as your grandmother points out, society is so much older both here and on the Continent, perhaps there have been more generations to have developed time for the arts. Whereas in my country, the focus is admittedly somewhat commercial. That is, among our menfolk."

She sighed. "Sadly, my father was always so busy managing the fortune that was left to him that he had little time for arts and leisure."

"A pity. I do see your point. But you yourself have devoted time to such pursuits. Tell me. Do you have musical talent as well?"

She shook her head. "Sadly deficient in all the arts except languages and letters, I'm afraid."

"Oh, I see." Then he gave her a teasing smile. "For myself, I don't mind. I usually fall asleep in the drawing room when music is performed. Now give me a good game of cards, and I'll be up 'til dawn."

She gave a small nod of the head. "Do you play for money?"

The duke winked at her. "Yes, but only when I am the best player present."

The ladies retired to a cavernous sitting room and took seats near a fireplace with a toasty fire. Amanda wandered down a row of portraits with Lady Norah, who pointed out more family relations. In spite of herself, Amanda became interested in the early portraits, all with features she could recognize in the family. The clothing of the earlier periods was fascinating. One of the ancestors, a young man, looked very much like the present holder of the title.

"Oh, that was Charles Pemberton," said Lady Norah. "He was the younger son of the first Duke of Sunderland."

"I see," said Amanda, studying the handsome, dashing face and the proud stance. "And what happened to him?"

Lady Norah glanced behind them as if to make sure no one else heard her. "Fathered a bastard and died in a duel defending the honor of the child's mother."

Amanda blinked, her eyes wider. Then she curved her lips in a laugh. It appeared that this family was not without its scandals. She wondered just how many more might be tucked away, hidden from the eyes of propriety.

Amanda moved closer to the dark oil painting. "He looks remarkably like the present duke," she said.

Lady Norah cocked her head. "Yes," she said thoughtfully, examining the face. "I see what you mean. My brother does take after him."

Chapter 10

The gentlemen joined them for what Amanda suspected would be a singularly dull evening. Already her thoughts were turning to Emile, and she felt impatient that she had to wait to hear from her father until at least tomorrow. She fervently hoped that Emile was not worse and only half listened to Lady Norah's conversation, while with the other half of her mind, she began to scheme at how she might find a way to the south of France. She was distracted from these plans when Sunderland broke off from a conversation with Lord Isington, and came to stand in front of Amanda.

"I have declined a game of cards with Lord Isington because of my responsibilities toward my guests," he said, smiling down at her. "I thought you might enjoy seeing some of the house tonight. It would be rather tiring to show it all to you tomorrow. It would be rather wise, I imagine, to use the daylight hours to see the surrounding countryside instead."

She did not have much interest in the house, other than her curiosity as to whether or not she might use one of the bathrooms instead of troubling the housemaids to drag a tub and water to her room every time she wished to take a bath. But anything was better than more interviews with the dowager duchess and small talk with the present company. She accepted the hand he offered her and got out of the chair where she sat.

"Very well. I would be most interested."

Sunderland excused them from the party, saying they were going to stroll about the house. "I've given orders for the halls to remain lit in two wings," he told the party.

"The east loggia is particularly lovely at night," said Lady Isabel.

They took leave of the party, and the duke led the way down a long corridor tiled with black and white marble. He turned up a staircase that led upward past drab green paneled walls with stucco carvings of various floral and mythological figures. She soon lost her way as he opened doors that led to tapestried and paneled rooms with painted ceilings and heavy chandeliers. She spent most of the tour looking up until her neck began to feel stiff.

"Such a lot of pictures," Amanda said, shrugging her shoulders to relieve the strain of looking.

They had passed from one drawing room to the next, and Amanda was now quite lost, for they had not returned to any corridor. He opened the door to a short curved room that contained a model ship in a case by a fireplace. The room had not been lighted, but moonlight glowed from a large window.

He walked toward a window seat that gave out onto a small courtyard lit by the full moon.

"I sensed you've been preoccupied since you arrived here," he said. "Is it something you wish to speak of?" He leaned against the window frame, the moonlight half bathing his face.

She shook her head, following the natural inclination to sit on the window seat and gaze out at the moonlit courtyard. Though she had gestured no, she went on. "A friend is ill. I am worried about him."

"Ah, I see." Sunderland lowered himself to sit at the opposite end of the window seat. "That is too bad. Is it serious?"

Amanda pressed her lips together. It was none of the duke's business, but she so longed to unburden herself. If only she could talk about it.

"I'm afraid it might be serious. He was sent to a sanatorium."

She heard Sunderland's expelled breath. "I see."

"It's very expensive, you see, and he can't afford it. I wanted to help him. I have some money of my own, but I had to cable my father to get it. That's why I'm waiting for word from him."

"Ahhh. I begin to understand."

Sunderland observed her keenly. So this was what she had been wrestling with. Her emotional torment touched him, and he was intrigued by her gesture toward the poor young friend. "You are very generous, then," he said. "I am glad you told me."

Amanda looked up then, querying him with her eyes. "Are you?"

"Yes," he said, nodding slowly. "I am."

For a moment neither spoke, then Amanda straightened, half turned and leaned against the inset wall where they sat. As she looked at his dark, interested face, she began to feel embarrassed. Her bare shoulders began to feel chilled so near the window, and she hugged herself with her still gloved arms.

"I'm sorry, I shouldn't be telling you my problems."

"Why not? I am interested in them."

She swallowed. "I don't see why. We hardly know each other."

He smiled, shifted forward. "Isn't that what this is all about? We are to get to know each other."

She frowned. "Then you are still trying to do your duty to your heritage and this house by looking for a wife?"

"I am."

"Then I should tell you I cannot marry you."

"I have not asked you."

She felt the blush tinge her cheeks. How dare he confound her. "Then it would be better if you do not."

He gave a laugh. "I see you are still determined to marry for love, then."

"Of course." She frowned at him, angered further that he could find it so humorous. "Why shouldn't I?"

"Because marrying for love is not always the wisest choice. One can come to love one's mate as one matures."

"That is preposterous. How do you know you would come to love this person? If you marry for money, how do you know you would not come to hate your spouse eventually?"

He leaned closer, enjoying the argument, his mouth curved in a half smile, his eyes sparkling at the irresistible beauty before him. How her eyes flashed, how the emotion lit her face. There was something quite womanly about her that he would swear was not there when they had first met, and he began to suspect what it was.

"And do you still love the young man you spoke of in the states?" he asked, watching her carefully for her response.

She shook her head. "No, no. That was a mistake. He

proved to be an opportunist after all. I have not seen him again."

The duke leaned back, satisfied. "There, you see. You thought you loved him, did you not?"

She shrugged. "I didn't know what love was then."

At once she knew she had said the wrong thing. The silence from the duke was deafening, and her heart hammered as she felt his gaze cloak her, seeing her innermost secrets.

"Hmmm," he finally said, a sensuality coming into his voice that had not been there before. "And you know what it is now?"

His gaze forced her to look at him. She gave a little shake of the head that was neither yes nor no.

"I know what it is." She had said it as a sort of defense, but again, she knew he saw through her.

"Ahhh." The word was pure sensuality. She had taken a lover. He smiled. That was it. She had been introduced to the ways of love.

For a woman of her class it was scandalous, but the thought aroused Sunderland. He had expected he would be forced to marry a virgin who had no experience at all in matters of love, for girls of society were raised to abhor sex, thinking its only use was for breeding children. A sensual man himself, he had hated the thought of marrying someone like that to produce his heirs. But though Amanda persisted in giving him the cold shoulder, he sensed her warmth and passion. Her strong feelings would naturally translate to passion in bed.

"Then, if you are no longer attached to the unfortunate American, who is your lover?"

She gasped, her hand covering her mouth. But as he brought his face closer, she knew she had given herself away. She tried to find the words to deny that she had a lover, but they would not come. Surely he did not realize how far she had let it go. Her throat was dry.

Sunderland reached for her hand and slowly lowered it, his eyes grazing her face and lips. But his words were soft, gently spoken. "Is it the young man who is so ill?"

She swallowed, unable to look away. Finally she nodded quickly. He let go her hand and slowly leaned back again.

"I see."

He looked at her proud, distressed expressions. What was it about this young lady that intrigued him so?

"You're so un-English." He couldn't help saying it out loud, answering his own questions.

She cocked her head.

He smiled, surprised himself to be talking so frankly to her. "English girls, you see, are very sheltered. They are raised by their governesses to please and charm."

Amanda raised an eyebrow. "How dull."

"Exactly," he said. "The difference is what makes American girls so appealing. Some would say forward."

She looked away, but her determined chin and set of her shoulders indicated embarrassed defensiveness.

Sunderland went on. "I find it refreshing."

"How nice. Surely you will not find it difficult to meet other American girls. I believe they visit your shores quite frequently."

"Indeed they do. The London season has become nothing but a marriage market. English girls are brought up from the country; American girls invade our shores for three months of chaperoned exposure to the men who are marshalled for endless dinner parties, balls, and house-party weekends. Here is where the American girl prevails. In the clamor and swish of skirts and flicker of candles, the serene, noble English girl effaces herself into oblivion, while her animated American sister crosses the dance floor to shake a man's hand, her eyes on his, rather than demurely glued to the floor."

"I gather you find that pleasing."

"I must admit I do."

"Then you will have no difficulty finding a wife in the so-called marriage market of the London season, which will soon begin."

"If I wish to look further, I am sure you are right." He was half-teasing, half-serious.

She could not believe his audacity. She had admitted she had a lover. It annoyed her that he seemed to take this in stride, as if any other attachment she might form could be easily swept aside. His extreme self-confidence and businesslike manner was further proof of the lack of feeling with which he approached the matter. Did he think his title so grand that he could dangle it before her like a carrot? Perhaps some of her American friends would be tempted by it, but Amanda had a streak of imagination in her that she had always considered her peers lacked. Surely she deserved something better.

She got off the window seat. "Pray do show me the rest of the palace. I find the exercise of walking stimulating."

He roused himself from his slouched position. "By all means."

They passed from the little gallery into a hall where their steps echoed across the Italian marble floor, and Amanda's eyes were drawn upward by the fluted columns to the open skylights above. Statues of gods and heroes in arched niches watched them cross to the center of the grand space. A frieze with winged lions united the top of the room with covered ceiling.

"Perhaps you find my approach to marriage too businesslike," he said offhandedly.

"Quite," she said, drawing slightly closer to him in the cavernous room simply to avoid feeling so at sea. "It is not logical."

"But it is logical," he argued.

She sighed. "I mean not to follow your heart. It isn't right."

"A hopeless romantic," he said in a teasing tone.

"What if I am? One needs to find some joy in life."

Evidently she had already found it, he surmised, and he wasn't going to press. She was right of course. There were other heiresses whose fortunes would prop up this estate. He had put off marriage for as long as possible. But the necessity to secure an heir and, more practically, the six thousand pound shortfall per year was at the point where something must be done.

Why not take Amanda's advice, button up his dance gloves and take to the floor this coming season? He'd no doubt that some American beauty would capture him beneath the lantern-lit garden of a great London house, and in her atrocious American accent bemuse him with her repartee.

As they continued through the grand house, their way lit by candles in sconces and kerosene in globed lamps on newel posts, it occurred to Amanda that Sunderland, being so up-front with his plans, might be able to help her with her present dilemma. But no, the idea was preposterous, and she banished it. Surely she would hear from her father tomorrow.

"I thought perhaps you might like to drive out to see the village tomorrow," Sunderland said, sounding like the perfect host.

"What? Oh, yes," she answered distractedly.

They had come down a floor and proceeded into another wing with carved doors on both sides of a long corridor. The surroundings began to look familiar, and she thought perhaps she was near her bedroom.

"Very well, then. I'll order the carriage for just after breakfast."

"All right."

He stopped in front of the door that was hers. She felt despondent, anxious, and she wondered if she would be able to sleep. She nearly suggested they sit down somewhere to talk, for she had a sudden fear of being left alone in such a strange place. At least in Sunderland's presence she had the strangely comforting feeling of being with someone in command of his own home.

Though they tended to argue every point, she found him annoyingly open and easy to talk to. But she was wary. He knew her secret, and must think she was a loose woman. He mustn't get the wrong idea. If he made another advance, the way he had in Newport, she would have to show him where her loyalties lay. For she would never think of betraying Emile. No, she must keep things on a formal footing with the duke until she could get away from here.

He bowed before her, his hands folded behind his back. "Pleasant dreams," he said. "I will see you at breakfast."

"Yes. Thank you."

He raised his eyes to pin hers. "For what?"

She swallowed, unsure of why she had used those words. "For showing me your home, of course," she managed to say.

He gave her his cockeyed smile, his face burnished by the flickering candlelight that struggled to light the gloomy hall.

"I only hope it pleases you, even though it lacks certain conveniences that you are no doubt used to."

She blushed, thinking of the awkwardness of bathing in the copper hip tub. But even so, the repartee that seemed so natural between them forced the words to her lips. "I hope whoever you marry puts in bathrooms."

She went in and shut the door. Delcia had laid out her dressing gown, and rather than ring for Delcia to come to her through the labyrinth between here and the servants' quarters, she began to wriggle out of her dress herself. But there was a soft knock followed by Delcia's voice.

"Come in."

The maid entered. "I was informed you were ready to retire, miss," she said, still looking wide awake.

"I wasn't going to bother you this evening," said Amanda.

"Oh, it's nothing, miss. There's ever so much excitement in such a big house. Though I daresay the staff have their work cut out for them here. I've heard all about it in the servants' dining hall."

"No doubt you have."

"And your evening, miss. Was it elegant?"

"I suppose you could call it that."

She shed her gown and wrapped herself in her dressing gown while Delcia undid her hair.

"And the duke," continued Delcia, used to chattering with her mistress when Amanda was in the mood. "Is he a nice gentleman?"

Amanda smirked into the mirror. "I suppose he's nice, though I'm not sure he's a gentleman."

* * *

As soon as she got down to breakfast the next morning, she inquired of the butler if there had been any messages for her. There were none. Entering the dining room, she glanced sidelong at her mother. But she didn't think her mother wielded more influence here than she, herself, did, and so didn't think her messages would be screened. Besides, her mother had no reason to expect that Amanda would be hearing from anyone here.

She greeted everyone all around and took a seat next to Lady Norah.

"Did you sleep well?" asked the duke's sister.

"Yes, quite. The bed was very comfortable." That it was actually a little lumpy, she saw no reason to mention. And she felt no urge to complain. Of the family, Lady Norah seemed the friendliest, and Amanda had no reason to burden her with petty complaints.

Lady Norah lowered her voice a trace. "I am aware of the deficiencies of the estate. It is not possible to entertain in as grand a manner as we used to."

Amanda responded to the woman's sincerity. "Please don't apologize." She wasn't sure how much to discuss with the duke's sister. Certainly they could not be confidential at the breakfast table where all might hear them.

"I understand my brother is showing you the estate this morning," said Lady Norah.

"Yes, I believe so."

"Then after lunch, if you are not too tired, my sister and I would enjoy having you join us at the parish church. We plan to help the vicar's wife make candles."

"Yes, I'd like that," said Amanda.

Evidently these noble ladies were not too proud to get involved with the local parish. Besides, she had to admit she liked what she'd seen of Lady Norah and Lady Isabel, so far. She remembered Sunderland's comment that English noblewomen were raised to please and wondered if that was what gave them their self-effacing dowdiness. For they were not showy, and their wardrobes not splendid. But whether it was that or their assurance that they were born into a titled family, Amanda didn't care. They were easy to be with, and perhaps she would find that they were easy to talk to as well.

After breakfast Lady Norah accompanied her to a courtyard where two matched bays were harnessed to an open carriage.

"I hope you enjoy your tour, my dear," said Lady Norah. "Not so many lands are under cultivation now because of the agricultural depression. During my grandfather's time much more wheat and barley were raised. But now sadly, many of the tenants have moved off the lands. Some of the fields are left uncultivated to provide cover for pheasants, partridges and grouse. Of course, we do our best for the tenants we do have, and they are very hard-working."

Lady Norah seemed to actually care for the tenants of the estate, which Amanda found admirable. But she wondered if Sunderland's sisters had been pressed to make their pitch for Amanda's money as well. After all, she would be more likely to marry into a family where she felt comfortable with the womenfolk.

Sunderland joined them. Dressed in tweed knickerbockers, vest, lounge coat, knee boots and a deerstalker cap, he looked very much in his own element, the outdoors.

"Good morning, Giles," he said to the groom and exchanged a few words about the horses. The groom checked the harness fastenings once more and then handed the reins to Sunderland, who wrapped them about the whipstock. He turned to Amanda and Lady Norah.

"All ready for your ride?" he asked Amanda.

She nodded. "Yes, thank you."

He assisted her into the seat and then climbed up beside her, taking the reins and guiding the pair out of the courtyard. Lady Norah raised a hand to wave, and Amanda returned the gesture. They passed under the stone archway into a larger courtyard and then through another arch and were on the drive.

They returned along the road Amanda had traversed from the train terminus at Woodhaven. Tenants walking along the road stood to the side to make way for the carriage. The men lifted their caps, the women dropped in curtsies, and the duke lifted a hand to them. The smiles on the faces struck Amanda, for the tenants' expressions of pleasure at seeing their landlord seemed sincere.

He turned off before they reached the village, and the road led by ploughed fields and stone fences.

"Many of these people's families are as old as my own," he said. "In England there is great continuity to the land. Sadly, that has changed in the last twenty years. With industrialization, many of them have had to move to urban centers."

His sigh expressed nostalgia for the day when great landowning families had been able to live on their working estates, collect rent and devote time to local or national government. Sunderland sat in the House of Lords, but the pressure put on the aristocracy by the changing economics of England's agriculture and a burgeoning middle class forced him, like his father, to find ways to refresh the family coffers.

His father had sold some of the land, a house in London, his wife's gems, paintings by Rubens, Titian, Van Dyck and Poussin. It had all made a dent, but it wasn't enough. Now it was his son's turn to do what he could to hold the estate together.

Nevertheless the fresh country air filled Sunderland's nostrils with a scent he always remembered, no matter what part of the world he found himself in. The sky was cloudless and blue, and the day promised to be warmer than the damp spring days they'd been having.

When they passed the cottage belonging to a certain shopkeeper and his daughter, Sunderland avoided looking in that direction. He ignored the twinge in his heart, for he could not allow sentimentality to interfere with his thoughts. Rather, he drove on to where there was considerable activity surrounding a huddle of half-timbered structures. He drove into a yard where several men were working at various tasks, all of whom stopped their work, straightened up and took off their caps.

"Good morning, gentlemen," said the duke as he pulled the horses to a stop, set down the reins and got down.

"Morning, Your Grace," came the reply from all the men present. One of them stepped forward.

"Ah, John," said the duke. "I've brought a guest from the United States of America to show her your handiwork."

The man addressed as John swung his cap below his waist and bowed in the direction of the carriage. Sunderland spoke to Amanda. "John is an accomplished chair maker. His work is the most beautiful I have seen."

John bowed again. "I'd be pleased to show the lady if she likes."

Sunderland introduced them formally, and Amanda stepped down, struck by the rugged but interested and respectful faces that looked their way. As they walked toward a wooden building with an oversized opening in front, the men returned to their various tasks. Some were planing wood on sawhorses. Others were fitting hoops to barrels. Another man was carving a wooden spoon, and Amanda stopped to admire it.

The workman held it up for her approval. "Made out of pear wood," he said as he displayed the smooth, light-colored spoon with even, graceful curves.

"It's beautiful," she said, taking it in her hands. Seeing the fine craftsmanship and the man who had made it touched her somehow, and she turned the spoon over in her hands before giving it back. "We don't have such well-made ones where I come from, I'm sure," she said.

The man gave her a gap-toothed grin and bobbed his head. "When it's finished, I'll see that you get it to take home with you, if that's all right with His Grace."

Sunderland smiled. "Of course. We want Miss Whitney to be able to appreciate the fine work we do in Oxfordshire. I believe the present of a handmade spoon would be highly appropriate."

"I'll bring it to the great house then myself," said the craftsman, who bent to the task of smoothing the spoon with renewed vigor.

As they passed on into the chair maker's workshop Amanda felt grudging admiration for Sunderland. These men clearly liked him, and his admiration and appreciation for their workmanship kept them devoted to tasks that surely did not pay as well financially as jobs in some smoky factory. Of course Sunderland would want to keep as many of his tenants as possible, but she saw the sincerity on his face and the ease with which he talked to them. And the reality of English country life began to dawn on her.

Here was their lord and master, whom they were anxious to please. And he repaid their loyalty with a kind interest that never compromised his position.

John the chair maker ushered them into his shop, and she looked around at the cluttered carpenter's room. Half-finished were several chairs in the Windsor style. An older man looked up, saw who the company was and put down his tools to get up and touch his cap.

"Hello, George," said Sunderland. "I've brought a lady from America to see your operation."

The older man wrinkled his face into a smile and nodded. "Pleased to show Yer Grace."

"The smell of wood is wonderful," said Amanda, smiling at the two, who were obviously pleased to be showing guests about their place.

John picked up a chair leg. "We makes the legs of the chairs from oak and shapes 'em with a drawknife."

"They don't use a lathe, you see," Sunderland intervened, "but prefer the appearance of hand-shaped wood."

Amanda touched the smooth wood. "It's quite beautiful."

"Don't believe in stretchers either," said George, from his place where he had begun planing again. "Legs ought to be made strong enough without them."

John showed her where a chair seat was being drilled. "The holes be drilled just right so the front legs end up at an angle, while the back legs splay out at a wider slant."

"Remarkable," said Amanda in all sincerity. "You deserve to have much pride in your work."

George spoke up again. "John's the eighth generation been makin' chairs for Elsenheim," he said proudly. "Some of the chairs gone up to Windsor castle."

"My goodness." She let her fingers drift over the smooth-planed wood that would eventually become part of a chair and stained with color. The continuity was impressive, and she was moved.

Her eyes drifted to Sunderland, who she realized had been watching her, but as soon as she looked at him, he turned away. Something shifted in her heart, and she began to see how tied to these people he must be. She distracted herself with the tools that John demonstrated and the other styles of chairs in progress. When they left, she was made to accept the offer of a chair made especially for her that she could use while she was a guest at Elsenheim and take back with her to the United States.

As they progressed through the other workshops, it was much the same. The proud workmen were only too glad to show the young lady their handiwork. The tinker displayed milk jugs, watering cans and oil cans made of copper and tin. The wheelwright wrought magic in his uncanny feel for wood.

"The wheel's strength depends on the wood itself," he told Amanda. "Wych elm won't split even with twelve spoke mortises cut from it. Oak for spokes because of its strength, and ash from a hedgerow for the rims because it's flexible and tough. You got to season it, too; oak for spokes needs at least four years."

"Then it takes a very long time to make a wheel if you count getting the wood," said Amanda.

"That it does."

From the wheelwright they went on to the wainwright where wagons were being built in the yard. One was nearly finished, and the workmen were applying a coat of blue paint. And on the wagon were the perfect wheels of the wheelwright.

Amanda was fascinated and could have stayed there all day. She itched to try her own hand at some of the crafts at which the women were engaged, such as rope making and dressing the flax, and she said as much to Sunderland.

He was pleased at her interest. "I'm sure my sisters would come back with you so you could try your hand."

"I'm going with them after lunch to the parish," she said to him. "To make candles."

"I see you like to keep your hands busy," he said as they finished their tour and walked back between the two rows of workshops toward their carriage.

"I do," she said. "It helps to keep my mind off greater worries."

The workmen all saw them off, and they were once again on the road. It was only a short distance to the village proper, but it would not do to go on foot.

"Oh, yes, the friend who is ill. You must tell me more about this concern of yours," said Sunderland as he flicked the reins. "There might be something I can do to help you alleviate it."

His words brought the problem to the forefront of her mind. She blinked, then stared straight ahead. Of course, why hadn't she thought of it before? If she got word that her father had not sent the money for Emile's stay at the sanatorium, perhaps the duke would lend it to her.

Chapter 11

They bypassed Woodhaven and circled more of the estate, where their reception was the same. Women curtsied and men doffed their hats. Sometimes Sunderland pulled up to exchange a few words. Other times he returned the salute and they drove on. Amanda wondered in which cottage lived Sunderland's mistress, but it would be too gauche to bring it up.

As they drove beside the stone fences and passed thick groves of forest, she glanced at him out of the corner of her eye. Who was the mistress that received the caresses of those confident, strong hands, the kisses from that sensual mouth, looks of adoration perhaps from the dark, serious eyes that could be so intense.

Burning in embarrassment, she trained her eyes on the scenery as they came to a stone bridge over a stream. Because of her own newfound sensual experience, she was comparing the potential of one man to another. Unfair to poor Emile. She must control her rampant thoughts.

They came to the park where the house was visible with only a few trees and bushes left between here and there. She was reminded of the fortune Sunderland must find to enable him to keep it up. From here, the house sprawled in several directions, and it did not even seem possible to get a complete view of it unless one were a bird.

Thinking aloud, Amanda said, "Can you not sell some of your land to raise the necessary funds to keep up the house?"

He awoke from his own reverie. "There is no one to buy it. The income from investment in land has dropped too radically since the importations of food-stuffs from the far-flung reaches of the empire. Dutch margarine and American wheat have driven down prices of our native products. There are no new tenants moving onto the land."

"It's sad to see so much land go to waste," said Amanda.

"The pressures of changing times," he said.

She thought again of the people they had just seen, so admiring of their lord. She glanced sidelong again at him. Of course, he was showing her these things for one reason, so that she would thaw at the idea of a marriage that would inject her money into his estate. While she was rallying her defenses, she couldn't help but appreci-ate his forthrightness. He might have wooed her in New York and London amidst the high society she was used to, attempted to sweep her off her feet in the glitter of candlelight.

Instead he had brought her to his ancestral home to show her where his new duchess would live, the people she would live among. He certainly could not expect any society girl to take to the oversized, drafty palace, his commanding grandmother and earthy neighbors. What was there here that he hoped to impress her with?

And yet, bring her here he had done. Perhaps because he, too, was resisting marriage. Perhaps in some way, he sought to show her the realities of Elsenheim in the hopes that she would turn away. But she gave up puzzling it out, for she had greater concerns at the moment.

By the time they reached the house again, Amanda had her mind made up. If she hadn't heard from her father in today's post, she would ask Sunderland for a loan.

They pulled into the stableyard, and grooms appeared to take care of the horses. Sunderland escorted her past the stables to a covered passage that led to the house.

"I hope you enjoyed the outing," he said as he opened a door that led to a drafty hall.

"Yes, thank you. It was quite interesting."

"And I'm sure my sisters will keep you entertained on your ride this afternoon."

"I shall look forward to it."

As they traversed what seemed like half a mile of corridor with bare oak flooring, she waited for an opportune moment. When at last they turned into a hall with stairways on either side, she said, "I should like to inquire if my cable has come."

"Very well. Would you like to wait in here?" He opened a door to a drawing room that had sunlight coming into three arched windows that gave onto the park.

"Thank you."

She went into the room and looked around at the furnishings, trying to discern whether this was one of the rooms they had passed through last night. She gazed from the plaster ceiling, slightly water damaged, to the battle standards, armor and portraits, to the Aubusson carpet, evidently stained by one of the dogs. In the day-light she noticed things she had either been too dis-tracted to notice last night or had not seen in the dim candlelight, since no bright electric lights or even gas jets had penetrated the interior of the great old house.

The upholstery had been chewed at the corners, pos-sibly by the same dog that had done the damage to the carpet. The huge Ming vase by the oversized mantel was chipped. The rest of the room was furnished in Louis XVI armchairs grouped around inlaid tables that looked as if they had been brought back from the east. A foot stool in the design of an elephant foot sat not far from a massively decorated fire screen.

To an heiress who had grown up amidst the finest of everything, the room looked shoddy, and it struck some terror into her heart. The next Duchess of Sunderland would be expected to right so many wrongs.

The door squeaked behind her, and she gave a start. Sunderland entered, crossed the room and handed her an envelope. She saw immediately that it was the awaited cable and ripped it open. Sunderland turned his back and crossed the room so she could read it privately.

But as she quickly took in the words, she slumped against the mantel. "Please write me the circumstances in detail. Must make sure generosity not misplaced," the cable read.

Her anguished sigh was audible, and Sunderland turned around. "Bad news?"

The way she crushed the cablegram in her hands was answer enough.

The clock ticked on the mantel, and Amanda stared out the window as Sunderland recalled to himself her words about her unfortunate friend. Something inside him twisted at the sight of her unhappiness, though he tried to keep it in perspective. She was nothing to him but a prospective wife. Why should he care about her little whims? He had been brought up in a tradition where wives were there to beget heirs, run a household for the husband's rest and pleasure, entertain as he decreed and, when he wasn't in the mood for her, keep out of his way.

Therefore he checked his response, the raised hand to touch her shoulder, the kind words of sympathy beyond a brief, "I'm sorry."

He cleared his throat and turned his back again, facing a painted landscape reminding him of exactly where the fourth duke had been governor-general. It was absurd that his responses to this forward American girl were more like those he'd once had for Charlotte. Why did her active mind engage him so, her soft, lively body seem so inviting? A body she had given to someone else? It was outrageous.

In exasperation, he turned around. "Your father refuses to send the money for your friend's treatment at the sanatorium?"

She turned a tear-stained face toward him. "What am I to do? Emile is already at the sanatorium. I only gave Maurice enough for the train fare. I don't even know how they'll get back to Paris."

Who Maurice was, Sunderland didn't know, but he could not stand the sight of tears. His sympathy was sincere as he crossed to her and reached for her hand.

"Perhaps there is something I can do," he said in a low voice before he could stop himself.

She remembered her idea about asking him for a loan, and now his words helped her gather her wits. She swallowed, dared look at him.

"It would be too much to ask, I know. But I would repay you."

A momentary flicker of something in his deep brown eyes made her glance away. "I mean, after I am home, I can discuss it with my father and arrange for the funds."

"I understand," he said.

He took a deep breath. He hadn't meant to do this, but he hated the sight of distress. Her tears reminded him of his Charlotte, when he had told her he must marry well. He had hated himself at that moment. But she had known from the start that he could never marry her.

"Please," he said, drawing a fresh handkerchief from his pocket and giving it to her. Feelings he had thought buried came to the surface. Why did women have to be such soft creatures? So . . . so volatile?

Some sort of guilt over the way he had treated Charlotte moved him to come to the aid of this woman, to whom he owed nothing. Unused to having to deal with this jumble of emotions, Sunderland felt like he was stabbing ineptly with one of the rusted weapons that hung above them on the wall. It made no sense. Amanda Whitney was supposed to bring him money, not the other way around.

"There must be something we can do," he said, his voice louder now, to overcome her sobbing.

"I'm sorry," she said between sniffles.

Desperately she tried to control herself, but suddenly her remembrance of being with Emile and the hopelessness of her situation came pouring out in tears that she had long suppressed.

"Life isn't fair," she sobbed.

In one step, Sunderland was with her, his arm cradling her against him. "No, it isn't."

He felt a lump in his throat as he gazed above her head at the park that spread out from the house. He squeezed her against him, his mouth on her silky hair, quickly mastering himself. Used to being in control, he took responsibility now.

"I will advance you the money. Send it to the sanatorium where your friend is. At least he will be seen to and be taken out of danger. We can discuss the repayment when you return home."

It was what she wanted, wasn't it? But she hated the fact that she had been reduced to begging. Of course he had offered, but it amounted to the same thing.

"I'm sorry," she said, blotting her eyes. "It's not like me to . . . to do this." She swallowed and took a deep breath, sliding out of his grasp. "But my circumstances have changed so radically of late."

"Indeed they have. Coming out is not all balls and teas and white gowns, is it?"

She shook her head, hiccoughing another sob. "No."

He turned away again. Why did she have to be so attractive in her distress? Her straight back and confident, haughty manner hid the sensitivity of a frightened girl. She was not on her own turf. He had the suspicion that if he married her, she would be more than a match for him. Perhaps his offer to help her in her distress appealed to his desire to show her he could take care of such things. It made no sense; but his own feelings were somewhat confused at the moment, and he was at a loss as to what to do about them except plunge on with the practical side of the matter.

"Come now, Amanda," he said. "Dry your tears.

We'll go to my study, and I'll send off a bank draft before lunch."

"I . . . I don't know how to repay your kindness. I mean, I'll repay the money, but your offer of help is . . ." She stumbled and searched for the words to express gratitude, even though it humbled her to do so.

"Please don't mention it. Now, come."

He walked toward the door and waited, and she followed him through a series of rooms until they reached a door that he opened. His study was crammed full of dark antique furniture and low bookcases lining the walls with large enamel vases placed on the bookcases. The walls were dark paneling, the ceiling paneled oak with Gothic carvings. He went to a large desk and pulled open a drawer, extracting a ledger. He wrote out the sum she told him and then on a piece of stationery wrote out the address of the sanatorium as she dictated it. Folding it all together, he addressed the envelope and rang for his butler to have it sent.

"I will also send a wire to say the bank draft is on the way."

"Thank you," she said, not knowing what else to say. "You are very kind." How competent he seemed, and how helpless it made her feel.

When the butler came, Sunderland handed him the envelope and explained where it must be sent. Amanda still felt awkward, standing in the massive study. She had already expressed her thanks, she didn't want to grovel. Luckily lunch saved them. As the butler reached the door, he paused and turned.

"Lunch will be served in the dining room in half an hour, sir." Then he bowed and exited.

"Oh, my," said Amanda, dry-eyed now. "I must change for lunch."

Sunderland escorted her to the door. "Very well."

She scurried off, making a few wrong turns but finally finding her room. She sent for Delcia, who helped her change clothes.

"What a waste this dress is," said Amanda after Delcia had fastened up the lavender satin day dress with a woven motif of golden flowers. For with the black wool shawl she had borrowed from Lady Norah, the dress was all but obliterated.

"No wonder they wear such ugly clothes here. If you don't wear wool and layers of plain muslin up to your chin, you freeze in the drafts, even in the spring."

"A pity," said Delcia. "But perhaps if you sit in the sun, you can take the shawl off."

Amanda sighed. "I suppose. Oh, well, it is only for a few days more; then we will be back in Paris."

"Oh, yes, miss. I will look forward to that."

At least Amanda's maid, if not her mother, agreed that the sooner they got away from here, the better.

While Amanda changed, Sunderland went to meet Louisa, who was waiting for him in a sitting room not far from the dining room. She was sitting near a window, and since the room was small, it was warm enough. Sunderland did not like Louisa Whitney particularly; but the interview was expected, and he faced it much as he would any business transaction.

"Ah, Mrs. Whitney, I hope you have been enjoying yourself," he said when he came in.

She shifted herself into a more formal position in the armchair as Sunderland came around to take up a stance near the mantel.

"Yes, quite. Your sisters are quite cordial, and the dowager duchess very . . . er, forthright." She cleared her throat. "And your outing, was it a success?"

"I believe Amanda enjoyed what she saw. She will go riding with my sisters this afternoon."

"I appreciate the hospitality you are showing us, Your Grace. I am quite sure Amanda is enjoying herself no end." Louisa smiled, but her face looked more like a mask than that of a matron concerned for her daughter's happiness.

The duke was too adept at hiding his reactions under polished, aristocratic manners to show that he knew very much more about Amanda's feelings than Louisa did. He proceeded. It would be too crass to talk of the marriage arrangement directly at this stage. Rather they must talk around it.

"Your daughter comports herself well, madam. She seems at home in these surroundings."

Louisa returned an expression of dignity. "She was raised to take her place in society. As you have seen, she is used to being around a staff of servants, is accustomed to six forks at dinner, for example, and a footman behind her chair."

"Yes. And she seemed to take a sincere interest in the village industries. This afternoon my sisters are taking her to the parish church where they are doing a bit of charity work, something expected of the ladies of a household such as this."

"Amanda is very fond of her charity work. When she was a debutante, she took all her bouquets to the hospitals in New York so the patients could enjoy them."

"Quite admirable."

Of course he knew very well that her mother had no knowledge of the patient on whom Amanda's attention was at present or the lengths to which she was going to succor him.

"I believe she has a great deal of sympathy for the less

fortunate." If any irony accompanied his words, he knew that Louisa would not notice it.

The preliminaries over, the duke continued with what he knew was expected of him. "I should like your permission to pay court to her," he said, adding, "if she will have it."

Louisa suppressed a self-satisfied smile. "You have my permission, Your Grace. I am sure Amanda would be honored."

Or indebted, thought Sunderland, but hid his thoughts.

"Then I will follow you to Paris," he said. "And do what I can to escort her, with you or your sister as chaperone, to some entertainments there."

"That would be lovely. Amanda's aunt has a box at the Paris Opera. You would be most welcome."

He gave a formal bow. "I accept. I will make the arrangements to stay at the Ritz Hotel, where my family always takes a suite whenever we are visiting Paris."

She nodded her head in agreement. "Then all is arranged. I am sure my sister will be most pleased to arrange events that will be amusing to you and allow you time to become better acquainted with my daughter."

"I should look forward to it."

Only a trace of guilt accompanied him as he left the formal interview. They had been bargaining over Amanda's fortune, and they both knew it. But what of the feelings of the girl herself? As Sunderland walked along the long, oak-floored corridor, he felt torn between duty and something else he could not name.

Surprisingly, he realized that if he married Amanda, he wanted her to accept him. The feeling was startling. Always before, it had been the other way around. It had been he who had expected to find an acceptable heiress.

It had never occurred to him that the heiress might not find a duke acceptable to her.

Following lunch, Amanda went to rest for three-quarters of an hour and then to change again, this time into her riding habit, one of the outfits she had acquired at Worth's establishment.

But when she appeared downstairs at the stables, as agreed, she saw at once she was overdressed. Both Lady Norah and Lady Isabel appeared in tweed jackets with riding skirts of plain wool, making Amanda fear that her velvet-collared, perfectly tailored jacket and ostrich-plumed hat with black veil were more appropriate for a ride along the boulevards of Paris than a lope across the country.

She felt a flash of discomfort. She was too showy, her voice too unmodulated compared to these English. How could she ever be expected to fit in with such women, who lived their lives in the country for the most part? The full force of her mother's plan to marry her to English nobility struck her once again, and as she went over to the dappled gray mare the groom brought her, she pressed trembling lips together. She was suddenly filled with a wave of homesickness for all that was familiar and a great longing to be with Emile.

How could her mother expect her to marry a man she hardly knew and come to live on these distant shores, with no friends, no family? And no way ever to see her dear Emile again? It was unthinkable, and she had to fight the wave of grief that welled up, lest the others see her tears.

As she stepped up to the mounting block and then put her foot in the stirrup, she stifled her anxiety. She wasn't getting married; she was only going for a ride across the English countryside. She sighed and tried to relax as the groom handed her the reins. She knew her horse would sense her discomfort and would become nervous, so she banished her angry thoughts and bent to pat the horse on her neck.

"That's Milady Gray," said Lady Norah. "She's a good hunter and responds to a light touch."

"Good girl," said Amanda and turned the horse to follow the two other women on their mounts out of the stableyard.

They traversed the park on bridle paths, and the ladies told Amanda some of the family history, and how this little piece of the kingdom into British history. It was clear that they were content here and very curious about her own life in the United States.

"You must have many American suitors," said Lady Norah. "I have met a few American boys at some balls in London. They seem quite consumed with their team sports and their businesses. Are they all so terribly dull?"

"I suppose so," said Amanda, thinking they were no more dull than an English lord whose only thought was to pay for the upkeep of his estate.

They came to the village proper and this time rode down the center street. As they had done with the lord of the estate, the villagers and tenants looked up from their work. The men doffed their caps and the ladies smiled. Those who were already standing curtsied, but those who were seated in their work did not get up.

"There go the young lord's sisters," she heard a matron behind her call through a doorway. Clearly the sisters didn't have quite the same status as the duke, but they were admired and respected, just the same.

They passed neat cottages and modest shops with half-doors where goods were dispensed to the village customers. At the end of the street loomed the village church, a fieldstone affair with a very tall, pointed steeple. They stopped in front of a stone house with timber roof, which Amanda took to be the vicarage.

They reined in their horses by a stump where they could slide down, then tied the reins to the white picket fence before the house. The door opened, and a matronly lady with twinkling blue eyes emerged, a cheery smile for them.

"Good afternoon, my ladies. Come into the house and have a cup of tea after your ride."

Inside the snug little house, Lady Norah presented Amanda to the vicar's wife, whose name was Agnes Dumbarton. She made them all sit in her crowded but cheerful sitting room while she fetched tea. While it steeped in the pot, they chatted.

"Over from America? My, you've come a long way. I'm sure you'll find our part of the world very quiet compared with what you're used to."

Amanda took to the vicar's wife and felt no sense of being judged for her merits, though the reason for her visit must be obvious to everyone in the village. It struck her that Sunderland might have paraded other wealthy young women through the estates in his search for the perfect wife, and Amanda felt half-inclined to ask about this, so friendly and open was her hostess. But she would not bring up the subject in front of Sunderland's sisters, though they, too, would know the answer.

After their tea, Agnes insisted on guiding them through the village proper to show them the shops, since it was so fine a day. So they all left the house and took to the bricked walk that led along the street.

Woodhaven was a prospering village, and the road

through it connected with a main artery through the countryside, so the townspeople did business with other estates besides Elsenheim. The ladies visited the bakery, where Amanda admired fancy pastries, and Sunderland's sisters ordered some to be sent up to the house.

They visited the haberdasher's, and Amanda tried on bonnets, though she knew she daren't buy any for fear her mother would criticize their country looks. Lady Norah and Lady Isabel stood outside on the sidewalk exchanging news with other women of the parish.

At the little dry goods shop, she looked up from examining a piece of material to see a woman outside with her face pressed to the glass, her hands blocking out the light, staring at Amanda. She gasped in surprise, but Agnes just laughed.

"Oh, don't mind Nellie Beddoes," she said. "She's looking you over. A little eccentric, mind you, very forthright."

It amused Amanda to be thus examined through the glass, and rather than act as if she didn't notice, she put down the bolt of material she'd been looking at and walked toward the glass so the old biddy could get a closer look. When they were nearly nose to nose at the glass, the woman moved off.

Behind Amanda, the vicar's wife chuckled. "That'll show her. News'll be all over town that you are a brash young woman."

Amanda laughed with her, feeling better than she had since she'd left Paris. They left the store, gathered up Lady Norah and Lady Isabel and made their way back to the vicarage.

"Have you ever made candles?" asked Agnes.

"A long time ago. My governess showed me once, but I don't remember anything at all."

"Well, my girl, we'll have you making candles to be proud of in no time."

And true to her word, Agnes took them back to the vicarage where she had a room devoted to such work projects. Here she had a hot vat of melted beeswax. She showed Amanda how to dip the weighted wicks in the molten mixture, then allow the wax to solidify, repeating the process until the candle was as thick as required.

"The beeswax will smell wonderful in the church during our evening services," said Agnes. "You would enjoy it."

"I'm sure I would," said Amanda. "I'm sorry I won't be here this Sunday."

"Oh?" queried the vicar's wife.

"We return to Paris day after tomorrow."

"A pity," said Agnes. "Another time, then."

By the time the young women returned to Elsenheim, it was dusk. A sudden peacefulness seemed to drop over the land as they rode their horses slowly back through the park. Doves cooed and blackbirds fluttered in the branches, settling down for the night. A pink-tinged sky bordered the land from the direction in which the ladies had come, and the lights that showed from some of the windows in the great house gave it a feeling of welcome as it sat on its lush sward, backed by gentle hills that beckoned.

Amanda was suddenly filled with the romance of the setting and murmured, "How beautiful it is."

She was mollified by the pleasantries of the day and relieved that the immediate problem of Emile's situation was resolved, though she knew that as soon as possible she would repay the duke. But as she surrendered her mount to the groom and followed the other women into the house, she felt more at ease than she had when she'd come here.

The corridors to her room had been lit by kerosene lamps, and she knew that her copper tub of hot water would be waiting for her upstairs. But rather than rail against the inconveniences of the monstrous place, she began to absorb its ambiance, letting the centuries of tradition wash over her.

She changed for dinner and went down, ready to shout answers to the dowager and respond to her mother's critical inquiries. She found the duke polite, but not overly solicitous or intrusive. She was surprised then when Louisa announced that Sunderland would be escorting them to Paris to join them for a round of parties and the opera.

Amanda's heart began to hammer in fear. That could mean only one thing. He was determined to pay court to her. She looked suspiciously at both her mother and the duke. They must have arranged something behind her back, and the old deep resentment began to simmer.

So Sunderland still considered her wife material. And now, of all things, she was indebted to him. But if he supposed she would consent to marry him just to pay back the favor he had done her by sending money for a sick lover, he had another thing coming.

Chapter 12

Back at her aunt's house in Paris, Amanda was again thrown into the social whirl, with one difference. This time she had an escort. Edward Pemberton, the Duke of Sunderland, escorted her to the opera, to dinner parties, to balls. They were always chaperoned, of course, either with the ever-watchful Louisa or by the formidable Zoe.

Of course Amanda was not blind to the admiring glances cast his way by the other young women at the balls and parties, and he danced with them all, smiling, flattering, gracious. And he never danced more than twice with Amanda.

As soon as she had arrived in Paris, she had sent a note around to Maurice's studio informing him that she was back and most anxious to hear about Emile's condition. She knew that he had stayed at the sanatorium for a few days to get Emile settled. But she warned Maurice that he must be careful about contacting her, for she did not know if her mail would be watched. She would walk in the square every morning before breakfast, and he could find her there. But in the three days they had been at Zoe's town house, she'd had no word.

She returned to the house after her morning walk,

feeling anxious and out of sorts. When she went in to breakfast, only her mother was there. A footman served Amanda her breakfast and refilled Louisa's coffee, and then left them alone.

"Lovely morning, don't you think, dear," said Louisa from where she had been scanning the society column. Louisa's French was not nearly as fluent as Amanda's, but she could read it well enough to recognize names of hostesses and guests, and she was pleased to see that they had been mentioned as guests of Zoe and that they had appeared last night at the opera escorted by the Duke of Sunderland.

But when Louisa began to prate on and on about it, Amanda cut her off sharply. "Please, Mother, I am tired of hearing about it."

Somehow the temper she'd had to suppress these past few days now came to the surface because of her disappointment at having no word from Maurice about Emile.

"I'm not only tired of hearing about it, I'm tired of doing it. I absolutely cannot stand one more social affair." She sat straight, staring her mother down. "I refuse to go out tonight."

Louisa dropped both paper and fork. Her look of disbelief turned slowly to one of anger matching the challenge she saw on her daughter's face.

"I beg your pardon," she said with all the haughtiness she could muster.

"I said I refuse to go out tonight."

"Don't be silly, Amanda. You must go out. The duke is paying court to you. He must have a chance to see how you behave in public. You do realize he is considering asking you to become his duchess."

"I don't want to be a duchess."

Chairs scraped back, and both women were on their feet. Amanda's fists clenched as she confronted her mother.

"You will be a duchess if he asks you to," said Louisa, a warning in her voice.

"Why?" shouted Amanda. "It isn't your life, it's mine."

Louisa lowered her voice, but it lost none of its threat. "Because you must make the best marriage possible. Married to a titled English lord you would be able to make an impact on the world. Your money would go to good use, you would have a place in society and you could contribute to worthy causes. Your name alone would raise money for charities or garner votes for members of parliament."

"Not my name, Mother, his. I would lose my name altogether if I marry him."

"It's the same thing," said Louisa, losing patience entirely. "I don't understand you, Amanda. You were raised with all the advantages a girl could have. You come from a loving family and have been trained to be an aristocrat. And you want to throw it all away on some gigolo. Are you still in love with that no-good Francis Newton?"

Amanda blinked, having forgotten all about Francis. "No, of course not."

"What, then? Or are you saving yourself for the convent?"

Tears of frustration sprang to her eyelids. "Maybe I should turn to a convent. At least there I could be useful."

"You could be useful to the Duke of Sunderland."

"Oh, could I? How? By providing the money for seven acres of roof on that ruin of a castle he lives in?"

Louisa's eyes bulged, and the blood throbbed in her temples. Had she made all her sacrifices just to be faced with this ingratitude? Her fingers reached clawlike toward her daughter, and she took a step forward. But suddenly pain assailed her, and she gave a purple-faced gasp.

Amanda stared at her, stunned as Louisa's hand flew to her chest and her face wrenched in pain. Then fright overcame Amanda as Louisa began to crumple.

"Mother," she cried, rushing toward her. Then she shrieked as Louisa collapsed onto the floor.

Amanda stumbled to the bell rope and yanked before falling onto her knees beside her mother on the floor. She clasped the clawing hands, tried to prop Louisa up as she struggled for breath.

Servants came from everywhere, and in the background Louisa heard her aunt's voice sending someone for a doctor. Nearly paralyzed with fear, Amanda loosened her mother's collar and fanned her face. The eyelids fluttered open and shut, and her color took on an awful hue. Somehow she was gotten upstairs and into a bed, and then into the flurry appeared the black-coated doctor with his bag. He sent everyone out, asking the housekeeper for hot water and clean linens.

Still stunned, Amanda allowed Zoe to lead her away. Sitting downstairs, Amanda and Zoe waited anxiously for news from the doctor.

"It's my fault," said Amanda. "We had an argument. I probably said some things I should not have. Oh, Aunt Zoe," she sighed in frustration, "is there no such thing as happiness for anyone?"

Zoe patted her hands. "Come, come, my dear. Try not to take it so hard. The worst will be over by now, and the doctor will prescribe something. Perhaps you and your mother have been overdoing it. One's strength can wear out with so many obligations."

Suddenly Amanda's overwrought emotions found an outlet in a flood of tears. "Oh, Aunt Zoe. What am I to do? I don't want to marry the duke. I can't marry him."

"There, there, dear. Is that what this is all about?" She produced a handkerchief for Amanda to use.

"He doesn't love me," she babbled on. "He told me so himself. And I don't love him."

Zoe smiled consolingly. "I see. Well now. Love is a very strange thing. I didn't love my husband when I went to the altar with him, either. That came later. That and mutual respect. We were most fortunate. Now, it seems to me that the duke is a very presentable and kind man. Has he said nothing to you in private?"

"Only that he wants my money."

Zoe raised an eyebrow. "He did, did he?"

"Well, not in so many words. But he spoke to me of his duty. He intends to sacrifice his own happiness when he marries. He is a link in the chain."

Zoe could not help a bit of amusement. Yes, she could imagine such a nobleman saying something like that. Most titled gentlemen did have a rather inflated opinion of themselves and their responsibilities. Still, it was better than being a wastrel. And Sunderland had a good reputation, from what she had been able to find out. No scandalous indiscretions. If he had them, he'd kept them to himself. But Amanda surprised her by mentioning just such indiscretions.

"He's in love with a shopkeeper's daughter. He told me so."

Zoe squeezed her hand. "But of course he cannot marry her."

Amanda shook her head. "It doesn't seem fair. Why should he marry me when he wants her?"

She was thinking more of herself than Sunderland's weighty responsibilities. She looked her aunt in the eye. "Zoe, what if I marry someone I want to? Someone who's not an aristocrat or wealthy or any of those things. Just someone nice, but poor. I have money, and we could live on that."

Zoe had heard about her niece's infatuation with the American and assumed she was speaking of him. She looked into the tearful young eyes.

"Things are not always as they seem, my dear. You mustn't be rash."

Amanda bit her lip and looked away.

Zoe continued. "Nor do things always turn out as we wish them to. If this young man has no money, think how it would be. He would always be beholden to you for your money, and he would have nothing to exchange for it. You would not be able to live as you are used to.

"While romance is in bloom you might think you are willing to live more simply. But your hands are not calloused from housework. If you marry disreputably, you might not be accepted in the society to which you are used to going. You might come to miss things you are accustomed to now.

"You wouldn't have a box at the opera. And what if your young husband went through all your money? Then what would you do? What if, heaven forbid, you were cast out of your home? What if your young man became ill? What if you were widowed? It would not be so easy to make a fresh start."

Amanda winced. Some of Zoe's wisdom penetrated, but she remained stubborn.

"Take the duke, for instance," Zoe continued. "He is a man who would take care of you, provide a home for you and your children. Give you a title which would enable you to have much influence in whatever sphere you wanted to."

Zoe observed the niece she had come to know much better since she had stayed here.

"A titled woman can sponsor literary and artistic endeavors. You could travel, see many things. Whatever your hand touched would be helped by you. Many aristocratic ladies have done much to raise the level of intellectual pursuits and have raised much needed money for many worthy causes."

Amanda blinked, seeing for the first time the useful life Zoe put before her. How different from Louisa's railing. Zoe subtly appealed to Amanda's own interests, instead of badgering her.

"The duke is not unattractive, is he?" said Zoe. "He seems very attentive to you."

An image of Sunderland came to mind, and she had to admit there had been times when his expressions had unnerved her in a way she fought. The memory of his kindness and warmth when she had been so upset about Emile washed over her. She tried to banish the feel of his strong arms around her, of his gentle words and the uncanny rapport she had felt with him. Still, she resisted.

She would not say it to Zoe, but there was another reason she could hardly consent to a marriage to Sunderland. He would be expecting a virginal wife. And though she was not experienced in such matters, she believed there were ways he would be able to tell.

She slumped back on the sofa. "Oh, Zoe, I don't know what to do."

The doctor came down some time later to find Zoe and Amanda in the sitting room.

"Well, what is it?" asked Zoe.

"I'm afraid Mrs. Whitney has suffered a minor heart attack."

"My heavens," exclaimed Zoe as Amanda gasped.

The doctor continued. "I have administered some medicine, and will send some more around with the instructions. She must rest without disturbance. She must be kept calm." He cleared his throat.

"A heart attack," said Amanda, suffering qualms of guilt. "May I see her?"

The doctor looked doubtful. "Right now I think it's best if she not see anyone. Especially if the conversation might be, shall we say, upsetting?"

Amanda's hands flew to her cheeks, and she stood up and walked to the window while Zoe talked to the doctor, escorting him out. They stood in the hall for some moments, and then the door closed. Zoe reappeared, and Amanda turned to face her.

"I suppose it's my fault," she said.

"Now, Amanda. Don't take the blame entirely on yourself. Your mother has a temper; both of you do. Your argument contributed to the attack, but it might have been something else. If she had a weak heart, then whatever she chose to lock horns with would have sent her into collapse."

Amanda sank into the nearest chair. "She'll never relent, will she?"

"About your marriage?" said Zoe.

Amanda nodded. "She once told me she would shoot any suitor of whom she did not approve."

Zoe chuckled. "I believe she would. Let's just drop the matter for the moment. Better for everyone concerned. When she is better we will see how things stand. But for now, I would be kind to her, and whatever you do, don't bring up the subject. If she does, just tell her you are thinking about her advice."

"Yes," said Amanda miserably. "I suppose that's best."

Since Louisa was ill, they sent their excuses to the duke, saying they would not go to Madame St. Helier's tonight. That afternoon Maurice got a note to Delcia, which the maid brought discreetly to Amanda. It was brief, no more than a few words informing her that he had just got back and that everything was settled. As the afternoon wore on, Amanda determined that she must see Maurice. She wanted firsthand information about Emile. She would wait for an opportunity to slip out.

That opportunity came in the evening. Zoe and Amanda dined in somber atmosphere, after which Zoe said she would retire early. They had acquired a nurse to look after Louisa during the first crucial hours after the attack, thus freeing the family of doing anything that would inadvertently worsen Louisa's condition.

Again using Delcia as her coconspirator, Amanda succeeded in sneaking past the footmen and the house-keeper and dashing to the end of the street and into a carriage that Delcia had summoned.

But she did not see the figure hunched in the shadows as she passed by a wrought-iron grilled fence covered with thick hedge. Nor did she hear the noiseless steps of the footpad who slipped onto the sidewalk behind her. His grating voice was too soft as he whispered a few words to his partner, who leapt up to the box at the same instant Amanda reached to pull the door shut behind her.

"Not so fast, my girl," hissed the wraith who yanked the door from her hand and jumped in beside her.

She sprang to the other side to exit through the other door; but just as she opened her mouth to scream, a dirty hand clasped her mouth shut, and an arm pulled her back to the seat. Her screams were muted as she struggled, terror coursing through her.

Then the carriage jerked forward, and she fell against her assailant, who now showed her the blade of a knife, which he held to her throat. She sat rigid, about to bite the hand around her mouth, except for the blade that she felt against her skin. If she moved, she feared that her blood would fill the carriage, and she would not live to go home. The man who'd captured her hissed in her ear.

"Listen careful, my girl. You've got a purse with you. That's all we want. Just a little coin to tide us over."

She strained to see her captor, but he kept his face behind her. She was aware only of his garlic breath. His French was hurried and oily, not the refined French she was used to, but at the mention of her money, she opened the fingers that were wrapped around her reticule and let it drop to the floor. There wasn't much there, but he was welcome to it, if only he'd let her go.

The man released her mouth but pointed the knife under her chin, pinning her to the seat and leaving no doubt that if she screamed, she'd be dead before the sound reached any passersby. He reached for the purse and fumbled one-handed with the strings. But when at last the saw the few coins she had poured out into his palm, he grunted.

"We can do better than that, can't we now?"

She choked back a scream as he pulled at the strings that held her satin duster around her. Then he pushed back the material and peered at her dress. She thought at first he meant to molest her, but then he grunted again and dropped the material with a sneer.

"No jewelry, eh? Pity."

She tried to stammer out some words of protest, but the sounds that came from her mouth were incoherent mumbles. He looked at her face for a moment and then elicited a toothy smile.

"Well, we'll see what kind of ransom you bring."

Her heart pounded in her chest, and she glanced desperately at the door; but his position and that of the knife kept her pinned where she was. Still, if she didn't lunge now, she would lose her chance, for surely they were taking her somewhere from which it would be harder to escape.

They came to a bridge, and out of the corner of her eye she saw the glistening waters of the Seine. She tried to gather her wits and talk to the grimy footpad.

"I have no money," she managed to say before the tip of the knife pressed into her neck, discouraging her from speaking again.

"I see that," he hissed. "But you come from a fine house. Someone there will be willing to pay for your safe return."

"It's not my house," she tried again.

But her words were met with a snarl and the flick of the knife, which this time, she thought, broke the skin.

"Shut up."

Once across the Seine the carriage rumbled into some narrow streets, turning so many times that Amanda lost all sense of direction. Eventually the houses got shabbier, the gaslights fewer and farther between.

Where were they taking her? She must think of a way to get out of the carriage before they reached their destination.

While Amanda was being driven through the streets of Paris, chaos was about to erupt at Zoe's town house. When Sunderland had received a note saying that Louisa was ill, and that the ladies would not be going out this evening, he decided not to go on to the soirée himself, but thought to call at Madame Zoe's. In the back of his mind was the hope for an unchaperoned talk with Amanda.

When he called at the town house, the housekeeper informed him that the ladies had all retired early. He left his card and said he would call round in the morning, then turned to go down the steps. As he approached the iron grilled gate, a slouched figure leapt toward him.

"You there," Sunderland snapped, raising his umbrella with which to defend himself.

But the ruffian only dropped a piece of paper at his feet before gliding away in the night.

Astonished, Sunderland bent to pick up the paper. As he read the scrawl, he became even more astonished.

"Great Scott," he said to himself.

He rushed into the street, but the ruffian was gone. In vain, he looked for a policeman, but there were none to be seen. Following a few more colorful curses, he leapt back up the steps, leaning on the bell.

The same implacable housekeeper answered, and Sunderland brushed past her.

"I thought you said Miss Whitney was in her bedroom."

"She is, sir," said Marie, miffed at his question.

"Not according to this," said Sunderland pressing the note into the hands of the stunned woman.

Sunderland didn't wait for her to read the note but bounded up the staircase, two steps at a time.

"Sir, sir," cried Marie, coming after him. "Please, sir."

But the duke was in no mood to stand on ceremony. "Which way to Amanda's room?"

"Why, there, sir."

Sunderland threw open the door to find a surprised Delcia folding clothing and putting it into the dresser. He saw at once that the bed was empty.

"Where's Amanda?" he demanded.

Delcia started to shake. Not for a moment did she consider lying to the imposing gentleman standing in the middle of the room.

"Gone to see a friend," she said, trembling. "She didn't want anyone to know."

"Some friend. If this is real, I'm afraid she's met with worse luck."

He snatched the note from Marie and handed it to the startled maid. Then he snapped out orders.

"Wake up Madame Zoe. Don't disturb Amanda's mother if she is actually ill. Send someone for the police and bring Madame Zoe to me at once downstairs."

He jerked with his head toward Delcia. "You'd better come, too. Your story may help us untangle what's happened here."

Delcia followed him down to the sitting room. In moments Zoe appeared in a wrapper.

"What's happened?" she demanded.

"Either someone is playing a very macabre joke or Amanda's been abducted."

"Abducted?" said Zoe as she took the note Sunderland had picked up from the walk.

"If you want to see your lady," the note said in printed French block letters, "bring one hundred thousand francs in small notes tomorrow night at ten o'clock to the park in rue de la Capitale. Leave the money at the bottom of the statue, then walk one hundred paces to the south. Wait there. The girl will be brought to you. Come alone. If any police are there, the girl gets a knife in her throat."

Zoe gave a little cry and sank to the brocade sofa. A loud knock banged on the door, and in a few moments a member of the Paris police force was shown to the sitting room. Sunderland took charge.

"We have a girl missing," he said, handing the gendarme the note.

"Hmmmm," said the tall officer in uniform, whose name was Captain Vallet. His drooping moustache seemed to emphasize the gravity of his response.

"Well, this is a clue anyway. We came upon a cabby been hit on the head and thrown off his carriage. Was wandering around, dazed from the wound, looking for his cab. Said he left it at the end of this block."

"You mean . . . ," said Sunderland, jumping to conclusions.

"*Oui*, monsieur." The officer nodded. "The perpetrators must have used the cab to abduct your girl."

"I must see this man," said Sunderland.

"But of course. And may I ask who you are," said the gendarme in a polite, but professional manner.

"Edward Pemberton, Duke of Sunderland, visiting from England."

"I see. And you're the one found this note?"

"I am. Where've you taken this cab driver?" demanded Sunderland.

"He's at headquarters now; his wound's being attended to. I assure Your Grace he will be questioned."

Sunderland paced across the room. "There's no time to waste. The culprits might still be in the area. What time does the cabby remember it being when he was thrown off the carriage."

"Said he heard the church bells chiming eight o'clock."

That was enough for the duke. "I hope you've got men scouring the area. That's not long ago. I want to see this man myself."

Captain Vallet left two more gendarmes with Zoe in case any further instructions from the kidnappers came. They also questioned all the servants in an effort to discover if the man who'd left the note had been seen by anyone who could give a clear description. Sunderland never saw a face, just a hunched over figure that might have been tall or short and wiry. His size was hidden by a cloak.

At headquarters, they found the cabby who'd been beaten, revived by the attentions of a doctor. He was willing to answer the questions put to him by both the police captain and the duke, but unfortunately he hadn't seen much.

"Man climbed up to the box, knocked me in the jaw and cuffed my ears, then dragged me off. I was taken by surprise, and by the time my arms and fists fought back, the man kicked me in the groin and dragged me under a bush. He must have taken to the box and driven away. I lost consciousness. When I came to, the carriage was gone, and I couldn't remember anything 'til I got picked up by the gendarme who brought me here."

"Would you recognize your assailant if you saw him again?" asked Sunderland.

The driver scratched his head gingerly. "He had a low sort of cap on and a collar pulled up around his face. Didn't get much of his face."

"Did you see the girl who got into the carriage?" the duke continued. It made no difference to him that the police had already asked these questions. He had to know for himself.

The driver nodded. "Her maid had arranged for me to wait. I saw her coming along in a long cloak. She gave me the address and then got in. That was when the varmint clambered up and knocked me senseless."

Now the duke was excited. At least they had a lead. "The address," he said to Captain Vallet. "Have you sent your men there?"

"We have," said Vallet. "It's the studio of one painter Maurice Letiens. He says he knows the lady in question but did not know she was coming to see him this evening."

Sunderland felt the blood begin to throb in his temples. "Where does this Letiens live?"

"In the Latin Quarter," said Vallet.

"Give me the address. I must see this man."

Sunderland hired a cab to Maurice Letiens's address. As they entered the Latin Quarter, he looked at the quaint, old streets, the lively cafes where people dined and drank. Music drifted down the street, and lovers paused in the shadows of doorways for hushed words. A dull anger began to pervade him as he pictured Amanda on her way here to see this Letiens, whoever he was.

If her behavior was this loose, then she was no longer a fit candidate to be his duchess. Bound up with his anxiety about her welfare and the fear that she might already be dead, her body drifting down the Seine with her throat cut, was his fury that she had lied to him. He had sent money to a sanatorium for a supposed sick friend. Now he wondered if that were some conniving scheme, of which he could not fathom. For evidently her lover was not some poor, sick, poverty-stricken invalid, but this painter he was going to see. What other explanation could there be?

The cab stopped in a narrow bricked street in front of a line of shops with rooms above. He got down and paid the driver.

"Do you wish me to wait, sir?"

"No, thank you. You're sure this is the address."

The driver pointed to the number over a darkened doorway. "That's it, sir."

Sunderland waved the driver away and tried the door, which was open. He found himself in a narrow stairway; but there was light at the top, so he went up. At the landing, he gazed at a hall stretching back toward the front of the house. Unsure which was the one belonging to the man he wanted, he knocked on the one nearest.

"A moment," came a feeble voice from inside. With luck, he had found the concierge, who would tell him what he wanted to know.

A short, puffy matron answered the door and peered up at the duke in his evening clothes. "Monsieur, what can I do for you?" came the squeaky little voice, seemingly impressed with her visitor.

"I am looking for Maurice Letiens. Does he live at this address?"

"*Oui,* monsieur. But you will not find him at home. Try the Cafe Petite Cour in the next street. That is where he spends his evenings."

"*Merci*, madame."

Back in the street, Sunderland asked his way to the Cafe Petite Cour, and found it without difficulty. Like the other brightly lit cafes, it was full of round wooden tables, its patrons imbibing in wine, lively chatter and laughter. In one corner a poet was on his feet reciting to his rapt friends. As Sunderland closed the door behind him, all heads turned, and an abrupt silence fell.

"I am looking for the painter Maurice Letiens," he said. "I was told he might be found here."

A dark-haired young man in a coat with patches at the elbows rose from one of the tables. "I am the painter Maurice Letiens."

He stared at the obviously wealthy gentleman in evening clothes and thought at first he might be a prospective patron. But then he saw the intense look in the eyes of the man before him. A number of puzzle pieces fell into place in his mind, and he knew at once why the man had come here. He was glad that it was he, Maurice, who stood at the cafe facing the stranger, instead of Emile. For if ever Maurice had seen jealousy in a gentleman's haughty eye, he saw it now.

Chapter 13

"A word with you, monsieur," said the duke, while the cafe patrons listened with curiosity to this exchange.

"I am at your service," said Maurice. And he tossed some coins down and left the table where he had been sitting.

"Where can we talk privately?" said Sunderland as soon as they had quitted the cafe.

"My studio is not far, if you do not mind a short walk. May I inquire your name, monsieur?"

The duke nodded. "A guest in your country. In my own country I hold the title of Duke of Sunderland."

Maurice raised his brows. A duke? But he knew better than to ask any questions. "I am honored, sir. If you will follow me to my rooms." He gestured toward the street.

"Very well. I have been to your house already."

Wordlessly, Maurice led the English duke back to his house. They climbed the stairs, passing the concierge's door, and on the floor above, Maurice took out a key that unlocked the door.

"Please come in." He entered and struck a match to a kerosene lamp.

Sunderland stepped into the painter's studio and gazed at the canvases leaning on the walls. As Maurice lit more lamps, Sunderland's eyes flew across portraits and landscapes. He saw at once that the man had talent. And the thought annoyed him.

"I believe you have been informed that Miss Whitney has been kidnapped," he said, without preamble.

"Oui, monsieur. I was just explaining to my friends in the cafe, when you came in. A most grave affair, though the police assured me they are doing everything possible."

Though Maurice did indeed look worried, there was something about his calm words that struck a note in Sunderland, though he was too coldly furious for it to register.

"She was on her way here, was she not?"

Maurice looked upset as he nodded. *"Oui,* monsieur, though I did not expect her. There was nothing more she could do."

His answer threw Sunderland off. "What do you mean?"

Maurice blinked, then gathered his wits. He had no idea who this gentleman was to Amanda. Perhaps he knew nothing of Emile. He was suddenly placed in the position of protecting his friend and defending a woman's honor who was not even his mistress. But of all the fabrications that he could have told, his instincts told him that there was too much danger to lie. Whoever this man was, it was evident that he had power of some kind. And Amanda's life was in danger.

"I mean," said Maurice, "there was nothing more she could do about our mutual friend's illness. She kindly sent the money to the sanatorium, and our friend is installed there receiving medical attention. She had done her part, and there was little more I could tell her. Still, I suppose she was on her way here because she wanted to hear it from my own lips."

Sunderland blinked, surprised by this verification of Amanda's own story. He expelled a breath; then he walked to a wooden chair and sat down.

"You'd better tell me the whole story," he said. "I had supposed the part about the friend to be a lie."

"Oh, no, no," said Maurice. "Emile is quite ill, I'm afraid."

Just then Sunderland's gaze fell on a portrait of a Greek goddess. The gauzily clad female form was sensuous, basking in a cloud. But the face was startlingly familiar. Blood coursed through Sunderland's veins once more.

"You," he said accusingly. "You are her lover."

Maurice went from Sunderland's angry face to the painting he had been staring at. He smiled, realizing the conclusions one might be led to.

"That is Mademoiselle Amanda, *oui*. But I am not her lover."

Sunderland was on his feet, towering over the painter. "Don't lie to me, man. If you do, I'll call you out. Only a lover would see her that way."

He gestured toward the curves of the woman in the canvas, the delighted smile on the radiant face. Everything about the face in the painting expressed love of a sensuous nature.

But Maurice was not at all perturbed. "Or an artist who sees the potential for such sensuousness in the face."

He faced Sunderland squarely. "I assure you, monsieur, I have only set eyes on Mademoiselle Whitney three times, and never in any intimate way. She is an acquaintance only."

The blood throbbed more slowly in Sunderland's temples. His furious glare still met Maurice's sincere expression.

"Then if you are telling the truth," he said slowly, "I demand the full explanation. And quickly. There is no time to lose."

Maurice sighed, unhappy again at the thought of Amanda's plight. "I met Mademoiselle Whitney at a soirée. I had been sent there with a message for her."

"A message."

Now came the sticky part, but Maurice tended to agree with the duke that they'd best have all the cards on the table.

"My friend, Emile Reveillere, became acquainted with Mademoiselle Whitney at an earlier party. When Emile became ill, he was not able to attend the soirée. He knew mademoiselle would be concerned. So"— Maurice shrugged—"I went in his place."

Sunderland glowered. "Who is this Emile?"

"A poor scholar, known for his joie de vivre and very popular with the rich hostesses for his quick wit and ability to be an entertaining dinner partner."

Insulting words came to the duke's lips, but his natural breeding made him quell his rage. He could hardly duel with an invalid, if he were truly in the so-called sanatorium. The least little doubt still lingered. He would not like to have the wool pulled over his eyes.

"What's wrong with Monsieur Emile?"

Maurice looked very sad. "Dr. Machard assures us it is consumption. The doctors at the sanatorium confirmed it. His very life is in danger."

The melodrama of the situation frustrated Sunderland, and he was seized with irritation that he could not do anything about it. But they were wasting time. They must find Amanda.

Skipping over the issue of Amanda's paramour for the moment, he went on. "Then you have no idea where these ruffians have taken Amanda?"

Maurice raised his arms in a gesture of helplessness. "*Non*, monsieur. I do not understand it. Paris is full of ill-reputes. But one does not expect them to attack ladies in fine neighborhoods."

"Well, they did," said Sunderland. "I will deliver the ransom, of course. We shall have to hope that whoever fetches the ransom is telling the truth, and she will be delivered safe and sound. If the culprit is lying. . . ."

He could barely stand the thought of the alternative, and cut off his words, turning to glare out the paned window to the gas-lit street below.

Maurice uttered a curse through his teeth. Then, to the duke, he said, "I would like to be of help. What can I do?"

Sunderland stilled his roiling emotions long enough to formulate an answer.

"You must make whatever inquiries you can. Perhaps some of your friends can ask questions where the police would be turned away."

Maurice frowned in thought. "It is possible."

"Loan sharks, prostitutes," said the duke bluntly, for there was no time to stand on ceremony. "See if anyone can find out anything. I am at the Ritz Hotel. Send word there if you discover anything. If I do not see you before, be at the park in the rue de la Capitale at eight o'clock tomorrow night.

"I am to bring the money at ten o'clock, but I have been instructed to come alone. You get there two hours before me and be inconspicuous. And do not appear to notice me when I appear. But you may see something. Be ready to spring to action. We must catch the culprits. And—" the duke looked pointedly at Maurice—"if you can, conceal a weapon. You might need it."

Maurice nodded. He was not a man of action, but for the lovely Mademoiselle Whitney and for his dying friend, Emile, he would do this even if he himself took a bullet tomorrow night.

"Do not fear, monsieur. I will be ready."

"Good."

Sunderland prepared to go. Then his gaze fell on the likeness of Amanda again. He was extremely annoyed that this little minx was causing such a stir in his life. Perhaps he should leave her to the culprits that snatched her. Her behavior had disqualified her for the position of duchess of the Sunderland estates, and there were other heiresses to choose from. Why, then, did he resent the fact that her attentions were elsewhere? Was it a matter of pride that he had wooed her but not won her?

Impulsively, the duke strode back across the room, glaring at the portrait of the Greek goddess.

"How much do you want for that?"

Maurice lifted his brows in surprise and quickly thought of a price. "It is not quite finished. There are a few highlights to be done yet."

"When it is finished, deliver it to me at my hotel. I will write out a bank draft for the amount."

Then he turned and left. As he descended the dingy staircase he cursed under his breath. He couldn't hang the thing at Elsenheim. Not that they didn't have semi-nudes on both canvas and in statuary, but the likeness would be recognized by anyone who'd met Amanda. And the painter had given her an unmistakable come

hither look. Perhaps he should go back upstairs and order the painter to change the expression. If the Greek
goddess wore a pure, classical expression, the painting
would be more fitting.

But his footsteps continued on down the street to the
boulevard where he could get a cab. He knew very well
that one of the appeals of the painting was the pose and
the expression. It aroused him just to think about it.

"Damned little hussy," he whispered to himself. She
had gotten her claws into him, and he knew it. Then a
pain twisted his heart. Where was she now? The
thought that some wretched kidnappers might put a
knife to her delicate throat filled him with rage.

After checking again at the police station to make
sure Captain Vallet was doing his job, Sunderland returned to his hotel to catch a few hours of sleep before
the banks opened in the morning. When the manager of
the Banque Metropol, Monsieur Lesard, stepped into
his office the next morning, he found Sunderland and
Captain Vallet waiting for him. They showed the
banker the ransom note, and Sunderland gave a bank
draft for the amount, which the banker furnished in
small notes.

"Are you sure you want to fill the entire package with
bank notes, Your Grace?" asked Lesard.

"Yes, of course. Her life may be at stake."

Lesard nodded sadly. Captain Vallet explained their
plan.

"My men will be in the vicinity, but not where they
can be seen. We hope to apprehend the culprit when he
leaves the scene."

"I just hope that your men don't make a mess of it,"

said Sunderland, who wished he were entirely in charge of the operation. He hated leaving anything to the police. Since he was not in his own country, he was being accorded the respect due his rank, but none of the decision making was his.

The banker did as Sunderland wished, and the notes were tied in bundles and packaged in a nondescript brown wrapper, easy to open.

The search continued for men fitting the description of the kidnappers, but they had covered their tracks well. However, as they were leaving the bank, a member of Vallet's force came up with an urgent message. A street Arab had seen two men abandon the cab they had stolen for Amanda's abduction. He had followed the men for a while and finally caught up with them to beg for coins. The cab, of course, had been found by the Seine early this morning, and the neighborhood searched. But the urchin was the first person who admitted to having seen the men.

"Take me to this boy at once," demanded Sunderland.

"He is being held at the station," said the gendarme who had come to deliver the news.

"Then we must go there right away."

"Very well," said Vallet. "And I believe that package of money will be safer in the police safe until you need it this evening. I would hate to think of you walking around Paris with it in your possession for some pickpocket to finger."

At the station, the dirty urchin was being fed, which greatly encouraged him to talk. He had an intelligent face with eyes that darted everywhere, and his hands were quick. He met Sunderland with a cocked head and a swift glance at his pockets.

"This is a gentleman from England," said Vallet, not bothering with the duke's title, which Sunderland agreed would probably only intimidate the boy and make him clamp his mouth shut.

"Tell him what you told us, young man, and you'll have another cup of that porridge."

"Why should I have to tell it again?" asked the boy, his eyes full of distrust.

"The gentleman is a friend of the lady who's been abducted. He has a great deal of interest in finding her," said Vallet.

The duke took a seat opposite the young man and attempted to take his measure. In that moment, the growing frustration he had experienced in trying to deal with the errant Miss Whitney turned to complete ineptitude.

He realized he was not in his own world and did not know how to deal with a boy who'd lived his life on the streets. For the first time in the duke's life he realized how limited his sphere was. Not that he hadn't been aware of less fortunates. He took care of the tenants on his own lands, but he knew what their lives were like. And his family had donated time and money to charity. But how to talk to a ragamuffin like this was beyond his ken. He searched frantically for some common ground, for a fast friendship must be made.

"Well, my boy," he began. "These footpads you followed the other day have abducted a beautiful lady."

Round blue eyes assessed him, while the mouth still chewed. "Is she your lady?" the boy finally asked.

A corner of Sunderland's lip went up in wry amusement. "Well now, she might be. She hasn't agreed to that yet." Now, Sunderland realized, was the time to use his rank. "If she marries me, she'll be a duchess. What do you think of that?"

Interest flickered in the round eyes. "A real duchess? In England, then?"

"Yes, and she'll live in a palace."

"A palace?" Another spoonful of porridge found its way to the urchin's mouth and dribbled down his chin. "You're either rich, then, or you're lying."

"Hmmmm. What's your name, lad?"

The boy shrugged. "Dunno. Don't have a mother. Sometimes my name's Jean, sometimes it's Sigibert. He was a king. And sometimes I'm Henri."

"Ah, aliases for different jobs, eh?" Sunderland leaned closer and lowered his voice, as if the policemen who were standing in the back of the room could not hear. "Have you ever done a job for these two men who stole the carriage?"

The boy shook his head, and Sunderland tried hard to estimate whether or not the boy was telling the truth.

Jean Sigibert Henri lifted one shoulder and dropped it. "I've seen 'em o' course. And I know their names."

Sunderland lifted his brows. The police had not gotten any names out of the boy. "What are these names, my boy?"

The urchin leaned forward in the same conspiratorial pose the duke was using. "What'll you pay for the information?"

"Aha, a bargain? But of course you'll be paid. Name your price."

The boy thought this over, but while he was trying to decide how much to pinch the duke for, Sunderland was drawing his own conclusions.

"I've got an idea, Jean Sigibert Henri. A really splendid idea."

"I'm listening," said the boy.

"How would you like to help us rescue the beautiful

lady, yourself? You would be a hero like the great King Sigibert, who you're named after."

The stubborn young face was trying not to give anything away. "What would I get for being a hero?"

The duke sat back, assessing the lad. "How would you like a job, and a comfortable place to live?"

"What sort of job would that be?"

"A job in England, in the country. I have a need for a bright boy like you in my palace."

The mouth fell open a trace, and the spoon clunked on the table. Clearly no one had ever offered the urchin a home in a palace. But in another instant the veil came down over his eyes, and his mouth clamped shut.

"You're making it all up. I don't believe the lady is going to be any duchess."

Sunderland thought quickly. "We'll make a contract and have it witnessed. Then you can take me to court if I'm lying."

The boy still didn't trust the offer. "I'd have to have some proof. Besides," he said, sitting a little more stiffly, "I can't go to England. I'm a Frenchman."

Sunderland smiled, beginning to lose his cool reserve. Why was he making such mad promises? "I understand. You don't speak English. But the lady will teach you. She speaks both languages very well."

For a moment more Jean Sigibert Henri weighed the offer. Sunderland could see the boy attempting to assess him without giving himself away. Then the lad must have decided the offer was worth a risk. If it were just more dreams that would dissolve after a while, he was used to that. But the temptation must have proved too great. It was a chance to see a palace and a great lady.

The boy was off his chair. "Let's go. I might know where they've kept her."

Hope leapt to Sunderland's breast, and the police sprang into action. But before the boy darted out of the station, someone laid a hand on him.

"Wait up there, Jean Henri," said Vallet. "We must get ready. We can't go into the neighborhood looking like policemen, can we? We've got to go incognito. Go with the matron there and we'll fetch you when we've dressed for the game."

But Jean Henri would not be parted from the duke. "I'll go with monsieur," he said, walking back across the room to where the duke was conferring with the commissioner.

Sunderland became aware of the presence beside him and looked down. "Well, young man?"

"If it's a disguise you want," said Jean Henri, "I can help you."

In short order, Sunderland was out of his creased gray trousers, stand-up collar and frock coat and into a torn, stained jacket with an old scarf tied around his neck in French fashion. His hair was ruffled, and a bit of grease smeared across his chin so that he and the plainclothes men who accompanied him would better fit into the neighborhood where they were going.

They piled into a carriage and, with the boy directing them, soon left the fashionable district behind. In the poorer section of Paris shutters were in need of paint. Brothels abounded. Warehouses with faded lettering were boarded up.

"We walk from here," said Jean Henri. And following his orders the older men got out, sending back their carriage, which was beginning to appear conspicuous.

A light drizzle had begun, and the men turned up their collars as they walked along narrow, wet brick streets. The sun had gone behind black clouds, and in this warren of streets and alleys the three- and four-story buildings made it seem much darker. Sunderland was uncomfortably aware that time was passing, and he must appear with the ransom at the appointed place if this little invasion failed to produce their quarry.

Jean Henri stopped under an underpass. Above them, carriages rolled past, for the streets in this section were stacked one level upon the other and crossing at odd angles. He stuck his head out into the next street, looking both ways; then he gestured for the duke to come forward. Evidently, he didn't trust the gendarmes.

Sunderland bent over to hear what the boy said. "That's where they went. Don't know if they got your duchess in there or not. But I see 'em coming out of there most times."

The duke squatted down to observe the building the boy pointed out. It was a very old house, built of stone and patched with lime and plaster with the lower-story windows boarded up. It was squeezed into slightly newer brick and stone structures in a corner surrounded by a high wall.

He let his eyes roam upward. The steep roof of the house was gabled, and he couldn't tell from here if a back door gave onto the upper street; but it was possible, for an outside staircase zigzagged up from the street on the side of the house where a narrow alley separated it from the one next to it.

"Good work, Jean Henri," said Sunderland. "We'll separate and watch the house for a while, see if we see anything suspicious." He straightened and addressed Vallet, taking charge, as was his habit.

"I'll take the boy with me," he said, "and investigate the back where it must give onto that street up there." He remembered now that Vallet was supposed to be the man in charge. "I'm sure you've already decided to place your men on this level where the house can be watched."

Vallet cleared his throat, wearied, and yet aware that there would be no satisfying this English duke unless he had things his way.

"*Oui*, Your Grace. We will do as you suggest. Give a shout if you should run into any danger. And keep the boy out of harm if you can."

"Don't worry, Captain," said Sunderland, making sure Jean Henri heard him. "Jean Henri is now my employee, and if we succeed in the rescue, he has a grand reward awaiting him at Elsenheim, my home in England."

The party split up as planned and surrounded the building to watch for anything suspicious. If nothing happened, then the captain would take his men in.

Inside the decrepit structure, Amanda sat in terror where she had been tied to a chair since last night. Certain that her life was over, she thought that perhaps it was better so, for even if she survived this ordeal, where could she turn? Her greasy captors had told her nothing, and she pretended she didn't understand much French. But she had heard them talking about the ransom.

The thought horrified her. If they sent to Aunt Zoe's house for ransom, then everything would come out. The household would be forced to look into where she had been going alone at night, and poor Delcia would be forced to tell everything. Her tears had long since dried, and she laughed bitterly to herself about the mess she was in. It even occurred to her that her mother would refuse to send the ransom, thinking she would be better off dead than scandalized.

And so she waited in dread, being allowed out of her chair only for necessities, which included the most primitive plumbing. For food, they gave her only cold soup, which made her choke. Now she sat dizzy from hunger and lack of sleep, her mind turning fears and fancies into hallucinations, her limbs stiff from remaining in the same position, her wrists red from the bonds that held her.

One of the ruffians named Jacques paced the dark, dingy room, talking to his colleague, who had the name Tiny. The house had no gas or electric lights, and they didn't waste fuel on a lamp. And they kept the shutters closed, except for a crack that emitted a tiny bit of light. Their voices had ceased to penetrate Amanda's haze except when they brought their dirty faces close to hers and shouted instructions. Every once in a while, she would rouse from her half-sleep and listen to their exchanges. From the testiness of their words, she could tell that they, too, were getting impatient and wished for the ordeal to be over.

Jacques sat on a stool sharpening his knife. When it began to gleam in the thin ray of light that penetrated the room, he grunted in satisfaction.

"If your rich friends don't come through with the money, it'll be this across your throat, girlie."

Amanda watched him through half-closed lids but pretended she didn't understand. He seemed to want to make his point, so he rose and crossed the room toward her.

Holding the knife up to her throat, he said in more emphatic tones. "You get this if we don't get the money."

"You should kill her anyway," said Tiny, in his wheedling voice. "Now that she's seen our mugs."

"Can't kill her. They won't give us the money 'til they've seen her, safe and sound most likely. It'll have to be an exchange."

"What if they have the gendarmes there, too? Then what'll we do?"

"We'll be able to see if there are any gendarmes," Jacques growled. "If there are—" he whipped the blade in an arc in front of Amanda's face—"she gets it. That was clear in the note."

"What if they don't come?" Tiny hunched down in a chair, peering out the crack in the shutters. He was obviously getting worried and beginning to fear the consequences of the job.

"They'll come," snapped Jacques. "You said the gentleman picked up the note and read it."

"He read it, all right. But how do we know what he did with it after that?"

"Well, they know she's missing. Surely they'll put two and two together," said Jacques with growing impatience. Then their conversation broke down into an argument in clipped words sprinkled with thieves' argot that Amanda truly did not understand.

Suddenly they broke off. "What was that?" said Tiny, his nose stuck into the crack in the shutters.

"Get back, you fool." Jacques replaced Tiny's face with his own. "There's nobody there. Just the old men waiting for their wives to bring home some bread."

"There was a boy and a man. I saw 'em take the stairs to the high street."

Jacques glared into the gray scene outside, but saw nothing. "Means nothing."

Tiny grunted. "I just never seen the man before. We

know all the other folks who come and go. This one was a stranger, I tell you."

"Hmmmm." Jacques scratched his head, narrowing his eyes.

He thought they had covered their tracks. How anyone could trace them here, he couldn't think. They had been careful to abandon the carriage in the wee hours of dawn and sneak back through the streets with no one following. Course when they got back to their own neighborhood there had been that boy Jean. But he was a familiar figure in these parts. Sometime chimney sweep, sometime pickpocket, he knew where they lived. The thought caused him a moment of concern.

"Who was the boy?" asked Jacques.

"Could be the sweep, Jean. Looked like 'im from here, leastways."

"And the man?"

"Tall, black hair under a cap. That's all I seen."

That was enough for Jacques. He suddenly flew into action. "We got to get out of here. Take her with us. That boy was bad luck. I knew it when we seen him this morning."

Tiny blinked and watched, being the slower of the two to register very deep meanings. "Why do we have to leave?"

"Because if that boy has someone with 'im, we don't know who it is. Might be someone who paid him to lead 'em here."

Tiny still frowned thoughtfully. "That boy wouldn't truck with no gendarme. He's as slippery as they come."

"No, but he's not above a bribe. Come on, get off your arse. Tie the gag around the girl and bind her hands. We can get out the back."

Amanda was alert now, hearing every word. What

boy were they talking about and what man? Most likely it meant nothing, and the kidnappers were simply growing frenzied after the long hours of being cooped up here waiting for the appointment where she gathered the ransom money was to be exchanged for her person.

"Come on, girlie, get up."

Jacques didn't wait for Tiny's help, but produced a rag, which he stuffed into her mouth and tied tightly around her head, making her cry mutedly.

"Shut up," he growled.

Then he untied her from the chair and jerked her to her feet, tying her hands in front of her with ropes that chafed. "You'll do as I say or you'll hang yourself."

And to prove his words, he put another rope around her neck, looping it so that if he tugged on the rope's end, the loop tightened, threatening to strangle her.

She almost crumpled, for she hadn't stood in some hours, but her limbs were forced to follow Jacques' lead as he led her to the door.

"This way."

With Jacques leading and Tiny bringing up the rear, they marched down the dingy hall to the back of the building.

"Wait here."

Jacques handed the rope to Tiny and climbed up on a window ledge to peer over a board that crossed the window opening. Then he muttered a curse. When he came back to them, he snarled.

"We've been found out, all right. There's a snitch watching the back door. They think they can get away with it in their plain clothes, trying to look like one of us. But I can smell a gendarme when I see one. We'll have to use the roof."

He picked up the rope and jerked on it, making her stumble after him with a muted squeal.

"Shut up," he said, jerking on the rope again. This time she tried to swallow, and nearly choked instead. But her numbed feet followed up the narrow stairs that led to the roof. There he opened a small door and then hunkered down.

"On your hands and knees, girlie, we can't let the whole world see us."

She did as she was told and then followed him at a crawl out onto the wet tarpaper. Blinded by the drizzle, she had no idea where they were going until they came to a low ledge. Jacques raised his head to look over.

"Crawl over here. It's not a far drop to the next roof."

She lifted her head and saw that it was indeed only a foot to the next roof, but how she could manage with her hands tied, she didn't know and gave him a bedraggled, pleading look. For answer, he lifted her up like a bag of flour and rolled her over. She landed on her shoulder and cried out in pain. Then the other two were over and pulled her up.

"Come on. Pick up your feet." And they started to run across the building. But a voice behind them shouted.

"You there, stop!"

Jacques spun around, grasped Amanda and held her in front of him, the sharp knife blade at her throat.

"Hold your fire," yelled Jacques as Tiny scampered behind him and crouched. "Or the girl dies."

Through blurred vision Amanda saw a man with a pistol pointed at them. For a moment, he seemed to hesitate; then his arm slowly lowered. Just then she turned her head to the side and saw another man and a boy flattened against a chimney. The dark-headed man held another pistol pointed in their direction. The boy crouched at his feet.

It took her some seconds to register that the tall, dark man against the chimney had a familiar face, and she thought she must be hallucinating. But when he raised a finger to his lips to caution her to silence, she nearly swooned. For never in her life would she have expected to see the Duke of Sunderland on a Paris rooftop pointing a gun at her captors.

Jacques was backing slowly toward the edge of the building, pulling Amanda with him. "Throw the gun down," he yelled.

He stood purposely near the edge of the roof where he could toss Amanda four stories to the brick street below if he had to. And now she looked to her right, her heart spinning over and over as she looked at the street below.

"No," yelled Sunderland, suddenly emerging to Jacques' left. "Let her go."

Jacques turned so that Amanda now faced the duke, trying to make a split-second decision. He cursed in her ear. Even if he cut her, one of the men would be able to hit him. Her life tottered on the brink.

Chapter 14

Amanda stared at Sunderland across the distance of the roof, her heart in her throat. Then her gaze dropped over the side to the street below where, if he decided to, Jacques could send her. And with her hands tied, she would be unable to stop herself. Or, a more grisly notion, he might send her over and hold on to the rope so that she would be hung by the side of the building.

She glanced back at Sunderland, desperation in her eyes, while Jacques tightened his grip on her and pulled her closer to the edge, the knife point at her throat. He maneuvered Amanda so that she would be in the way of either pistol shot. Vallet had lowered his gun, but Sunderland still held his aloft.

"Drop the guns, I tell you," Jacques snarled, "or over the edge she goes."

Slowly Vallet leaned over and lowered his gun to his feet, then raised his hands, not wanting to take any chances. Amanda's attention went to the boy who accompanied Sunderland. She saw the lad glance at the gendarme's gun, as if trying to assess how far it was from where he crouched.

Sunderland's pistol came down to his side. "All right," he shouted. "I'm throwing my gun down. Just let her go. You'll have a fair start."

Taking no chances, Jacques dragged Amanda away from the edge and toward the other side of the roof. His cohort Tiny snuck away in the confusion.

"Keep your distance now," Jacques shouted to the two men and the boy who watched.

Behind them Vallet's other men had clambered up but stood back, watching the scene. Jacques made it to the edge of the roof where he stepped over onto an iron fire escape. Then, pulling Amanda along with him, he started to back down. She saw to her horror that the fire escape jutted off the side of the brick and stone structure right over a wide canal with fast-moving muddy waters, hurrying out of the city.

As soon as the culprit's head disappeared over the edge, the policemen ran, their pistols now in their hands again. But there was no way to get a clear shot, for the man still clung to Amanda for a shield. Jacques hauled her so that she was more scrambling than walking. She screamed into her gag, certain that every backward step her feet sought out on the open fire escape meant certain death. For if she were thrown into the water, her hands would still be tied, and she wouldn't be able to swim.

On the roof above them, Sunderland watched helplessly until Jean tugged at his coat.

"Quick, this way," said the boy and sprinted off. Sunderland lost no time following.

They pulled open a wooden door and plunged into a dark stairwell. But man followed boy down half-broken stairs.

"Watch that railing," said Jean. "It won't hold you."

So Sunderland half slid down the opposite wall, his feet following where Jean led. Two stories down, they raced along a dingy hallway, and now Sunderland could see their objective. It was the same iron stairway. When they came to the window that let out to it, Sunderland stuck his head through. They had been faster, and the kidnapper and Amanda were just coming down above them.

Sunderland stepped through and aimed his pistol again. "Stop right there and put down the knife," he ordered.

Jacques cursed, but halted, and Amanda pitched to the left to lean over the railing, staring at the swirling waters in the canal below. Above him Captain Vallet poised on the landing, his gun pointed at the culprit's head. Jacques looked from one side to the other, maneuvering Amanda around so that he leaned against the railing.

Then in a single movement, he shoved Amanda forward toward the brick wall opposite, while with his right hand he flung the knife upward toward the captain, who ducked. Then he rolled himself over the railing, and with a cry that seemed to bounce off the buildings, he fell, feetfirst, toward the canal.

Stunned, everyone watched him descend, until with a splash, he went in. Still no one moved for what seemed like a very long minute. Finally, Captain Vallet gave the order.

"He'll swim downstream. Quick, after him." And the police captain ran back to the roof, his men going ahead to take the staircase down, evidently not trusting that much weight on the fire escape.

Then Amanda was in Sunderland's arms, gently crushed against his chest, her hard breathing against his racing heart. For a moment neither spoke as he cradled her, touching her hair, struggling to get his fingers around the knot in the gag.

"You might use this." Jean Henri had scrambled upward to pick up Jacques' knife where it had landed on the roof ledge and now brought it back to Sunderland, who expelled a breath.

"Indeed, thank you, my boy." After removing the noose from around her neck, he took the knife and sawed through the rope that tied Amanda's wrists. "Don't move, my dear, while I use the knife to slit the gag. I don't want to cut you accidentally."

She shut her eyes and stood still, her blood still throbbing in her temples, while he maneuvered the blade so that the cloth finally ripped. He pulled the hateful thing away, and she emitted a half-cry, half-groan and started to fall against him. His heart still pounding in fright that she had been in so much danger, he held her, kissing her temple, pressing her against his chest.

"Shhh, shh," he whispered. "You're all right now. All safe and sound."

He fought the tears of emotion that threatened to moisten his own eyes. How close they had come to losing her. A moment more, and the kidnapper might have decided to send her over the brink instead of himself, evidently thinking at the last moment that he could swim better without her encumbrance.

"I was so frightened," she said, her mouth hurting from the gag.

Now that it was over, she gave way to the trembling that she had fought to withstand for the duration she was with the criminals. Her bravery had carried her through the ordeal with thoughts mostly of how she had humiliated herself. That she had actually been in physical danger only now came to the forefront of her mind as she let Sunderland's strong arms and gentle kisses comfort her.

"Don't try to talk," he said. "Can you manage these steps back to the roof? It will be safer that way."

She nodded and let him guide her with his arm about her waist, back up the open steps. When they came to the ledge, he scooped her up into his arms, then stepped across. She clung to his neck fiercely, almost hoping he wouldn't put her down. But once on the roof he set her on her feet, keeping his arm about her waist.

Now she became aware of the small boy trailing along beside them, and she glanced down at him. He raised his smudged face to hers and looked at her out of bright blue eyes. Blond hair tangled across his brow. Sunderland realized it was time for introductions.

"May I present Jean Sigibert Henri," said Sunderland, very formally. "Your rescuer. Jean saw the kidnappers leave the carriage and brought us here. Jean, this is Miss Amanda Whitney."

"Oh," said Amanda, still feeling dizzy and struggling to gather her wits. "I see."

Jean peered intently at her. "Is this the duchess?"

Amanda blinked, and Sunderland grinned. "Not yet, she isn't." He turned to explain to Amanda, and found himself filled with an embarrassment he was not used to.

"You see, I promised Jean Henri a job if he would help us. I am making him a page boy at Elsenheim, where he will live and learn to be a useful member of my household. If he does well, he will be promoted in position as he grows older."

For the first time in days, a hint of a smile broke into the shadows of Amanda's face as she gazed at the boy. In the young face she saw excitement that he was doing his best to hide, and she saw at once the kind of boy he was. Homeless, an orphan, picked up by the police and probably guilty of many crimes himself. But somehow the Duke of Sunderland had managed to persuade him to change sides in the game he was used to playing and lead the police to her. She knelt to eye level with him, which made him back off in shyness. But she extended her hand.

"I am very grateful for your help, Jean Sigibert Henri. I should like to add my own reward to that of the duke's. You helped save my life, you know."

Jean Henri's face turned red, and he brushed his hair off his face, still trying to maintain an air of cocky indifference. He lifted one shoulder in a shrug.

"It was nothing," he finally said.

But he took her hand, and she shook his solemnly. She felt inclined to grasp his shoulders and give him a kiss and a hug, but sensed that this would be too overwhelming for the lad. So she kept her thanks formal.

"Now, as to a reward, what would you like?"

This thought brought his head up again. His eyes widened, and then he looked up at the duke and back at her again. Then to Sunderland, he said, "When I live in the castle, will I have a horse?"

Sunderland raised a brow, and Amanda smiled. "If the duke approves, after you go to Elsenheim, I will get you a pony, provided, of course, that you learn to take care of it yourself."

Light came into Jean's face; then it fell again as he looked down and scuffed his foot on the tarpaper roof where they still stood. "I don't know how to ride a horse. Never been on one."

"Well now," said Sunderland squatting down. "That can be rectified. I have very good grooms to teach you."

"Really?" said Jean Henri, still disbelieving. He had the cautious look of one who had been made many promises only to have them broken.

Amanda saw the moistness in the corners of the boy's eyes and knew instantly that he was afraid that this had all been a dream, and that he would once more be disappointed. Her own eyes clouded with emotion.

"I promise," said the duke somberly. Then he extended his hand, which the boy shook.

Sunderland rose. "Come on now, we shall have to escort Miss Whitney back to the police station so that the officers can ask her questions. These kidnappers must be apprehended, and they will want to know all the details. And, of course, we must take her to a doctor to have her examined."

He glanced at Amanda. "To make sure she is all right."

Amanda stood, meeting his eyes. At that moment a bond formed between them. Just what it meant was not clear, but something had happened, perhaps because of Jean Henri. Her heart filled with emotion, and for a moment she could not speak, only smile with bittersweetness.

Then she reached a hand down for Jean Henri's. Sunderland did not extend a hand, knowing that the boy would consider himself too old to hold hands with a man, but he felt pleased when Jean consented to hold on to Amanda as they walked to the door that would lead them down to the street.

When they came out, the drizzle seemed to have stopped. Tiny had been apprehended and taken away in handcuffs. An officer remained to make sure Amanda and the duke were all right and to escort them back to the police station. They got into the carriage, and Jean sat next to Amanda, his thin body against her side, his leg against her skirt. Every so often his eyes would dart up to her face, but when she looked down to smile at him, he looked away quickly, afraid to be caught.

A physician examined her and pronounced her fit except for the scrapes and bruises she had sustained. Then she faced the police and was able to describe what had happened from the moment she had gone out of the house. Sunderland insisted on remaining in the room, claiming he was responsible for Miss Whitney.

Captain Vallet grudgingly assented. He had, of course, sent word to Zoe that Amanda had been found and was all right. She would be released as soon as she told the police her story. And Sunderland sent word to Letiens, so that he did not go to the park and wait.

"You say you were going to the address of Maurice Letiens when the unfortunate incident occurred?" said Captain Vallet.

She nodded. "That is correct."

The police captain cleared his throat. "May I ask why you did not take your aunt's carriage?"

Amanda's face burned, and she dared not look at Sunderland, whose eyes she felt on her face as he took in every word she said.

"My aunt did not know where I was going."

"I see," said Vallet. He cleared his throat again. "Well, where you were going or why has no bearing on this case. I believe we have gotten all the details. With one of the men apprehended already I believe we will catch up with the slippery Jacques in no time. He cannot get far in that canal. I'm sorry, but it may be nec-

essary for you to appear as witness when he is brought
to trial, to identify him. Would you be willing to do so?"

Unconsciously, her eyes flicked to Sunderland, then
back to the policeman. Appearing in court would be
tantamount to scandal. It would drag her name through
the papers.

"Of course I will do it, if I can avoid mentioning my
aunt's name. I do not want to bring her any scandal if
possible."

Vallet grunted, giving her a look that said she should
have thought of that when she set out alone in a cab,
something no self-respecting lady did. But her morals
were no concern of his. Why the duke was still here,
taking responsibility for her, when she was obviously behaving as ill-befitted a woman of her class, he did not
know, nor would he ask. It was his job to put the culprits in jail.

"Then I will let you know of any eventualities," he
said. "You have been most helpful, and I thank you for
your cooperation. I will contact you if we have the need.
You may go, as long as you keep this office informed of
where you can be reached."

Amanda dared not look at Sunderland. But when she
got up Vallet thanked the duke for his part in the affair.

"Of course, I, too will be glad to appear as a witness,"
said Sunderland as Vallet showed them out.

"Thank you, sir," said Vallet. "I know that appearing
in the courtroom is not a pleasing prospect to one of
your social position. But I appreciate your offer."

The captain shook hands with Sunderland, sent
Amanda a curious look and then turned on his heel.
Sunderland gathered up Jean Henri, then escorted
Amanda out of the station and down the steps.

"Well," he said, when they had reached a street. "I'd best get you home. Your family will be expecting you."

Amanda's face fell. "How can I face them?" She desperately tried to think of a way to forestall the inevitable appearance at her aunt's house, but could think of no way.

Sunderland had a few words with Jean Henri. He offered to send the boy directly to his hotel, where he would meet him for a nice meal, but the boy refused to be separated from him. Again the look of distrust came into his eyes, and Sunderland understood that the boy wouldn't let him out of his sight for fear of being betrayed.

"Very well," he said. "You'll come with me to take Miss Whitney back to her house. Then we'll go to the hotel, where you can have a bath, and we'll see about some new clothes. Will that be all right?"

At the word "bath," Jean's mouth came open and his face registered protest. But then he closed it again. He would stick by the duke, no matter what. "Yes, sir," he said.

"Good. Then come along."

A cab rolled to the curb, and Sunderland gave the address, then helped Amanda in. Jean Henri clambered in and sat looking out the window.

"My poor mother," said Amanda. "I suppose she will disown me now, that is, if she is strong enough to receive the news." Tears formed at the corners of her eyes, but she swallowed and tried to keep from crying. "Perhaps Jacques should have thrown me over that railing. My life is surely over now in any case."

"Don't say that," Sunderland said sharply.

His words helped her snap back to reality. She hadn't gone into the canal. She would have to face her aunt and her mother. She would tell them the truth, of course, except the part about Emile being her lover, a fact about which she was beginning to feel terribly embarrassed.

It was just possible that Zoe could be persuaded to understand. After all, it was at a society soirée that she first met Emile. She would just say that when she learned he was ill, she took pity on him, wired her father for the money and that the duke had loaned the sum in the meantime.

"Could you," she said suddenly, turning to Sunderland. Then, "No . . . no. It would be too much to ask." She faced front again, staring at her hands in her lap.

"What would be too much?" he said, in a low voice that rumbled with a range of emotions from exasperation to anger with himself. "I just risked my life, which wasn't too much to ask. Surely if you have any other favors you wish of me, you might as well put them forward."

She cringed with self-consciousness. "I'm sorry. I haven't thanked you. You didn't need to do what you did."

He laughed ironically. "You didn't ask. I did it voluntarily. Couldn't leave the job to bungling policemen. And besides, we needed Jean Henri, here. I was the one who enlisted his help."

Her expression eased a bit; then her face clouded again.

In a gentler voice, remembering the horror she had just been through, Sunderland said, "What did you wish to ask me to do?"

She hesitated. "Come to the house with me. I'll have to tell . . ." Her voice drifted off at the thought of the confrontation.

Sunderland saw her discomfort. He wanted to say she deserved it, for she had brought all this on herself. But whatever it was that had sprung between them wouldn't let him desert her in her hour of need, which he perceived was not over.

Though it sounded cruel, he thought it fortunate that the hard-hearted mother was ill; perhaps they could avoid telling her if she'd been kept in her bed. The aunt would be easier to deal with. And Amanda was right. If he was there, it might be easier for the aunt to listen to the incredible story. Though why he was lending his support was a curious mixture that he could not begin to sort out. He sat back in the carriage. Why did a man have to feel so helpless where women were concerned?

The cab pulled up in front of Zoe's house, and as soon as they got down, the door flew open and Zoe rushed out, meeting them on the steps. She gathered Amanda into her arms and squeezed her tearfully.

"My dear girl. What a fright. Are you all right?"

"She's all right, madame," said the duke. "The doctor found only a few scratches and bruises."

Zoe stood back to wipe away a tear and help Amanda into the house. Sunderland started to follow and then remembered Jean, who stood shyly by the gate. He turned around and stretched out a hand.

"Come on, Jean Henri. We must tell the lady about your part in all this."

Jean's eyes gaped, but his first step toward the fancy town house was tentative. If he ever went into such a house, it would be to see what he could steal. Now the door was open to him, and the duke was holding out a hand.

Sunderland understood what was going through the boy's mind, and also realized the risk they took. Trusting such an urchin would have its dangers. But he saw deeper into the boy than the dirty rags he wore. When Jean looked at Amanda, Sunderland saw a need for love that raked his heart. He also saw the fear in the small eyes, masked by the streetwise cockiness. Though the feeling was new for the duke as well, Sunderland was determined to change all that.

When Jean came even with him, Sunderland nodded and stepped up to the door, which the footman still held open. Inside, they followed Zoe and Amanda into the parlor, where Zoe was fluttering all over Amanda and calling for tea.

"You'll need to regain your strength, my dear." She nearly bumped into Sunderland. "Oh, Your Grace, I'm sorry. I didn't see you."

"It's all right, madame. Your first concern should be for your niece, who is now back, safe and sound."

Zoe nearly tripped over Jean Henri, who slipped behind Sunderland for safety. Then when Zoe had finished with her orders and shut the door, she turned. Going over to Amanda, she sank onto the sofa beside her.

"You are truly all right, my dear?"

Amanda nodded, saying little. "Yes, Aunt. I am. And I am very sorry for all this. I know it has caused you much worry and . . ." She couldn't bring herself to say the word "scandal" just yet. "Inconvenience," she finished.

Zoe began to calm down. "Yes, yes, well, we shall see about all that. I was so worried."

The duke walked farther into the room and cleared his throat. "There is someone we must thank," he said.

Zoe looked up, surprised, as if she had forgotten her

manners. It was only then that she saw the ragged boy beside the tall, strangely dressed nobleman.

"Oh," she said.

Seeing that he had her attention at last, Sunderland continued. "May I present Jean Sigibert Henri, whom I have now hired as a member of my own household staff. He saved Amanda's life. Without him, we should not have found her."

Zoe's hand flew to her breast. "Oh, my. Then I thank you, monsieur. Whatever you have done will be repaid."

She wasn't used to dealing with street urchins. But from the looks of this one, she imagined a reward was what he was here for.

"Actually, madame, he has already been promised his rewards."

Sunderland wanted to temper generosity with some discipline. He didn't want Jean to become greedy.

"He has no family, and so is to work as page boy at Elsenheim. And your niece has promised to buy him a pony."

"Oh, I see," said Zoe, still flustered.

There came a knock on the door, and a footman entered with a tray. As Zoe poured, she watched Jean's eyes light up.

"Well, now, Jean, you must be hungry. Help yourself to sandwiches."

He approached the table and stared at the food. Then he snatched a sandwich and crammed it into his mouth. Sunderland watched him out of the corner of his eye as the rest took their food. The boy must be starving, and so he did not correct his manners; but he smiled inwardly when, after two sandwiches being thus consumed, the boy took a plate as the others had done and, while the adults were engrossed in talking, placed several more sandwiches on his plate and sat on a hassock, balancing the plate on his knees.

With food in their stomachs and tea to warm them, they were drawn into conversation. Zoe wanted to hear every detail, and while Amanda related the story, she left out certain more grisly details. Sunderland played up Jean Henri's part. Zoe simply nodded and punctuated the conversation with, "Oh, my," her hand on her breast.

When all had been said, the tale came round to its beginning, and to the obvious but painful fact that they would have to tell Louisa, who was not yet allowed out of bed.

"Does she know?" asked Amanda apprehensively.

Zoe shook her head. "When she asked for you, I told her you had gone out. And then she slept. I was beginning to grow desperate, however. Thank goodness you've returned, for soon I felt she would see through my fabrications."

"I will see her," said Amanda.

"But she needn't know that anything has happened," said Zoe.

Amanda frowned. "Won't the newspapers report it?"

Zoe pinched the fabric of her dress. "Perhaps I can have a word with the police commissioner. He might agree to keep it out of the newspapers."

"I'm sorry, madame," said Sunderland. "But I do not think that will work. Both Amanda and I have agreed to appear in court as witnesses when they put the culprits on trial."

"Oh, dear," said Zoe. "Then I suppose everyone will know."

"I'm sorry, Aunt Zoe," said Amanda, squeezing her

hand this time. "If I hadn't been so foolish . . ." Her words drifted off.

Zoe seemed to realize then that they had not discussed where Amanda had been going, and she knew that it was up to her to impose some discipline on the girl. Amanda's safety had come first. But now they must face the ugly truth if they were to lay out plans as to what to do. Zoe cleared her throat and poured more tea to brace herself.

"And who is Maurice Letiens?" she asked. "The man you were going to see."

Amanda sighed, prepared to tell the truth up to a point. "He is the friend of a young man I met at Madame Fichet's. Emile Reveillere is a poor young scholar. It happens that he is consumptive but could not afford to go to the sanatorium the doctor recommended."

Amanda gave a little shrug. "I could not bear to see him suffer, for it was clear that unless he received treatment, he would die."

She squared her shoulders. "I decided to help him. I wired father to ask for the money, but when I did not receive it"—she glanced sidelong at Sunderland—"His Grace agreed to help. He advanced the sum."

Zoe blinked, trying to follow the complicated story. "Well, I see."

Knowing that had not explained her trip into the night when she was abducted, Amanda plunged on.

"I was worried about Emile, who had gone to the sanatorium. So when I had the chance, I was going to see Maurice, to inquire about Emile. Maurice had just returned from getting him settled, you see."

Zoe creased a brow. "I'm not quite sure I see, but I will take your word for it." She was relieved that the story had such apparently altruistic motives. Perhaps there would be a way to avert scandal after all. She cleared her throat. "Is that all?"

Amanda nodded, looking at her plate. "Yes. I was on my way to see Maurice when that horrible Jacques pushed me into the carriage."

Zoe sighed. "Oh, dear, yes." She bit down on a sandwich, thinking. When she had swallowed, she continued. "You say you met this Emile at Madame Fichet's?"

"Yes, Aunt."

"Well."

Her mind worked quickly, and she glanced at Sunderland, who was watching her. That he had stayed around for so long was beginning to amaze her. The entire situation was starting to take on qualities of the bizarre. She looked at the street urchin, who was now stuffing rolls into his mouth. Then she focused on the dirty, dilapidated state of all of them.

If there were relationships here she did not quite grasp, even if she suspected them, she did not need to delve further. Her niece had tried to be discreet about the poor young man she had suddenly taken such an interest in, but had been foiled. Fortunately she had a knight in shining armor in the duke, although at the moment he was dressed more like a pickpocket. And somewhere along the way they had picked up a street urchin, who on the way out would probably try to steal her good silver. But the whole situation struck her as suddenly funny, even though it paralyzed her to think of trying to explain it to Louisa.

"I'm afraid things will be most difficult," she said, fiddling with her napkin. "Especially if you must appear in court, oh, my."

"That will not be for some months," said Sunderland. "In the meantime I must return to Elsenheim." He winked at Jean. "I have a new employee to fit out and train."

"Er, hem, yes, that would be best." She turned her gaze on Amanda. "And as soon as Louisa is better, then the two of you must return to New York."

"But I can't go now," said Amanda, trying to think quickly of a way to stay on French soil. "It would take too long to get back for the trial, and I don't think Mother can yet travel."

Just then, they felt a waft of air as the door moved inward. Like an apparition, Louisa stood there, wan, yet straight-backed, dressed in a wrapper.

"You may be right about my inability to travel, as yet," said Louisa in a voice only slightly less forceful than it usually was. "But I am not too weak to be up and about in this house, and I demand to know the meaning of this little gathering. And why are the two of you dressed as if you'd just been rooting through the coal bin?"

Chapter 15

"My dear Louisa, you should be in bed." Zoe was the first one on her feet and approached her sister.

"It seems my place is here," said Louisa huffily. "I heard enough to realize that things have gone on here that I have not been informed of."

"Now, now, Louisa. Everything is taken care of. Amanda had a bit of a run-in, that's all. But she's back now safe and sound."

"Nevertheless, I demand to be told the truth."

"Please sit down, Mrs. Whitney," said Sunderland, seeing the pallor on Louisa's face.

Though he felt little patience with the woman, he wanted to prevent a collapse if possible. There was enough to worry about without that.

She allowed Zoe to lead her to a chair, but when she settled herself, she leveled her piercing eyes at them all. "Now, please explain the meaning of all this."

She would hear it anyway, thought Sunderland. Best that she hear it from them.

"Your daughter was kidnapped. A ransom note was sent while you were confined to your bed. Fortunately, we discovered the hiding place and retrieved her. No harm was done other than a few scratches."

Louisa's jaw worked silently for a moment. She placed her steely eyes on her daughter.

"How did you come to be kidnapped, pray tell?" And without waiting for an answer, she turned to stare at Jean Henri. "And who is this boy?"

"That is Jean Sigibert Henri," said Amanda, answering the second question first. "He led the police and the duke to find me. We are indebted to him."

"I see."

Amanda twisted her hands together.

"I was outside," she explained. "The criminals leapt upon me and threw me into a carriage and forced me to their hiding place, where I was tied to a chair. Nothing worse than that happened."

"Thank goodness," said Louisa. Still, the judgmental look did not leave her face. "And what were you doing outside?"

Amanda lifted her chin. How dare her mother take such a haughty approach to this inquisition!

"I was visiting a friend. That is, he is a friend of a sick friend of both of ours. I was going to inquire as to the health of the invalid."

Louisa's brows lifted, and her cheeks tinged feverishly. "Alone? At night? Why did you not at least have your maid with you? And why wasn't I told? Zoe, what are you thinking of to allow her to run about unescorted?"

"I . . . oh, dear." Zoe fluttered a hand and then reached into her bodice for a handkerchief. "Louisa, you mustn't get upset. You know the doctor said . . ." Her words trailed off.

Amanda snapped, "You weren't told because you

were ill, and I did not take Delcia because I left her here to explain in case anyone asked."

Mother and daughter locked their eyes in combat as if no one else were listening. Louisa's displeasure with her daughter built into a frenzy.

"Do you care nothing at all for your reputation? What kind of friends could you possibly have that would lure you out into the night? Respectable people would call on you properly or at least expect you to be chaperoned when you called on them. What is the matter with you?"

Amanda was on her feet, a retort on her tongue, when suddenly her mother's face screwed up in pain, and Louisa gave a horrible gasp. She lifted her arms and then started to topple sideways. They all rushed forward, and Zoe caught her.

"Oh, dear, this has been too much for her. Quickly, help me get her to bed."

They lifted the gasping Louisa up, and then Sunderland and Zoe helped her toward the stairs.

Zoe looked back at Amanda. "Send someone for the doctor. Marie knows the address."

"Yes, yes," said Amanda, following helplessly. Then she looked around to find the housekeeper, who was not in evidence. A footman passed through the hall and, seeing the commotion, stopped.

"The doctor," said Amanda. "We must send for the doctor."

"I can go," said a small voice behind her, and she turned to look down at Jean Henri, who had come out into the hall with them. She pressed her lips together, then hesitated no longer.

"Yes, you go." She turned to the footman. "Please get me the doctor's address."

The footman bowed and went for the address. Amanda kneeled in front of Jean Henri, who had not even been cleaned up yet.

"Are you sure you can find the doctor's house?" she asked.

He nodded, and she saw the need to be useful come into the shy, slightly belligerent, blue eyes. "I can find it."

The footman reappeared, and Amanda held out her hand for the piece of paper on which was written the address.

She read the address out to Jean Henri and then handed him the paper, though she doubted he could read.

"If you get lost, show this to some gentleman or lady. It's only two streets over. Do you understand?"

Jean nodded. "Rue St-Antoine. I know it."

Once Jean was out the door, Amanda started for the stairs and then hesitated, wringing her hands. Her mother's collapse was her fault, for Louisa wasn't supposed to be confronted with anything unpleasant. Leaning on the railing and staring into space, Amanda sighed. Why did this have to happen? Chained to a way of life she had been brought up in, she was threatened now with her mother's nervous collapse just when she tried to spread her wings.

What was wrong with her? Was her own stubborn selfishness going to be the cause of her mother's demise? And yet something within Amanda refused to tolerate her mother's rigid views and ambitions. The strictures she placed around her daughter only made Amanda resent her further.

With clenched fist on the polished carved railing, she uttered a groan of frustration.

Only when she noticed her dirty arm did she remember that she had not yet cleaned up. Zoe's first thought had been to feed them, which was wise. But then they had gotten embroiled in discussion, and she had forgotten to bathe. Inhaling enough breath to get her body moving again, she pushed her way up the stairs. She was about to place her foot on the landing when a pair of long legs and torso appeared before her. She raised her eyes to Sunderland's.

"How . . ." Amanda moistened her lips. "How is she?"

Sunderland looked as perturbed as Amanda felt. "She'll be all right. No doubt the doctor will sedate her again."

"I sent Jean Henri for the doctor. They should be here soon. Oh, my." Amanda sank in a heap on the top step. "What shall I do?"

The doorbell rang, and the footman answered it. Just as they expected, Jean Henri stood there with the doctor, who, after a few words with the housekeeper, climbed the stairs.

"This way, Doctor," said Sunderland and led the man past Amanda, who looked up from her place against the wall, but did not rise.

The doctor looked curiously at Amanda, but hurried on to his patient. Sunderland returned, paused, and then sat down tiredly. Both of them looked like rag pickers, but their minds were on other things.

"I must take the boy back to my hotel and get us both a bath," Sunderland said. Still, he did not get up.

Jean Henri had taken a seat on a chair in the hallway looking for all the world like he had been raised with good manners. He could see Amanda and Sunderland, but could not hear them.

"Yes," she said.

Sunderland could not bear her piteous look, and was not sure how much of it was a result of what had happened to her and how much a result of the malice between mother and daughter.

"First Emile, and now my mother," said Amanda as if to no one in particular. "What shall I do?"

"You shall have to get your life in order," he answered, sounding more harsh than he meant to.

But as a man of discipline, he'd had quite enough of these histrionics. He longed to return to his well-ordered household, yet he was now entangled in the threads of this less than well-ordered one.

"Easy for you to say," Amanda answered with more spark than she had evidenced before. Her life was falling apart—rather, had fallen apart—and here this man was simply ordering her to put it back together.

"Indeed." And he got up.

Instantly she felt bad. "I'm sorry. It's my fault I dragged you into this. After today, I'm sure you will want nothing more to do with this family. Please be assured that I am more than grateful for being rescued. But of course, I have . . ." Her voice started to shake, and she was afraid she would break down again.

Sunderland's heart turned over even as he took two steps downward. "Please, say nothing more. Any gentleman would have done the same."

"Would they?"

Smudged brown eyes met his dark ones, and again both of them drew back from that rising accord that was pulling them together. She looked away first. He cleared his throat and glanced at Jean Henri, swinging his legs from the chair where he sat.

"I'll take the boy and call back later to find out how your mother is doing."

"That is very kind."

She started to get up, and he gave her his hand to help her. She looked at the hand and then accepted it, flushing with warmth at his touch. How could he even be polite to her? This man who knew everything about her, who knew she'd disgraced herself.

Their eyes met briefly, and then Sunderland dropped her hand and continued down the stairs.

"I'll see myself out," he said.

She watched him go, watched him extend a hand for the boy, who jumped off the chair and walked with him toward the door. As the footman opened the door, the boy glanced back at Amanda. She pressed her lips together, her emotions filling her breast as she gulped a sob and lifted a hand to answer the boy's salute.

With Delcia's help, Amanda bathed and then got into bed, for she had not slept very well tied to a chair. Though the maid was fascinated by her mistress's adventures, she tried not to ask too many questions, seeing that Amanda needed rest.

"I will make sure no one wakes you, miss," said Delcia, drawing the covers up.

"Thank you, Delcia," said Amanda, tired, both emotionally and physically. "I'm not sure I can sleep." She yawned as she said it.

By the time the maid pulled the door shut, Amanda slept. But her dreams were filled with confused images. She was ministering to Emile, and he would not wake up. She called and called to him. Then she herself tried to wake up and could not, and someone was calling her.

It was the duke. "Amanda," he said, leaning over her bed, his face close to hers. "Wake up, Amanda."

She gasped, her eyes flew open and she sat up. But the room was dim and still. No one was there. She trembled and lay back on the pillows.

Then she turned on her side and let her mind drift, trying to sort things out. When she decided she wouldn't sleep anymore, she threw the covers aside and got up. The house seemed incredibly still. She went to sit before the dressing table mirror, where she pulled her hair out of the braid Delcia had put it in and began to brush it, stroking and stroking, and contemplating.

How had things come to this pass? What an entanglement she was in. And what did the future hold? She realized that she had hoped to be able to go and see Emile, but now she knew that would not be possible. Her mother might have a more serious attack next time Amanda stepped out of line, and while she rebelled against the way her mother was trying to make her live, she knew in her heart she could not live with the guilt if she caused her own mother's demise.

And what about Emile? In the days since she'd seen him, his image had become vague. Not that she didn't care, she cared very much about his well-being, but she wondered just what he was to her. A sweetness remained with her that he had been her first lover, and she would think of him every day. But the feelings she thought she bore for him already seemed unreal, distant. When she'd gone with him that first morning it had been as much for the excitement of doing something daring and rebelling against the prim role she was expected to maintain as it had been infatuation with Emile himself.

"But what if I never see him again?" she whispered to

the mirror. Her melancholy face stared back at her. Yes, what if?

How she missed the comfort of her cat, Morgan, whom she'd had to leave behind in New York.

The door moved slowly in behind her, and Zoe entered. "You're up," said Zoe. "How do you feel, my dear?"

Amanda swiveled on her vanity bench. "I'm all right, Aunt Zoe," she said in a low voice. "How is my mother?"

Zoe shook her head and clucked her tongue, coming across the room to take a seat in a wing chair near Amanda.

"She's resting."

"I suppose she hates me," said Amanda, shrugging. Why try to keep up any pretense?

"Your mother has a temper, just like you. But I know that the reason for her actions is that she wants what's best for you."

"How can she think she knows that?" Amanda laid down the hairbrush with a clatter.

"How can you be sure you know what is best in the long run?"

Amanda fiddled with the combs on the dressing table. "I know what you are thinking, Aunt Zoe. I was just thinking about it myself."

She took a very deep breath and sighed, staring at her reflection in the mirror again. "What am I to do?"

"Nothing, for a bit, until your mother is better. And then perhaps the two of you can talk things out."

Amanda shook her head. "We've never been able to talk things out. We're both too stubborn."

"Is that why you . . ." Zoe chose her words carefully.

"Is that why you chose to help a young man in need whom you had just met?"

Amanda could not help the blush that came into her cheeks and tried to keep her eyes averted from Zoe's. Still, she knew her aunt would be able to read her feelings.

"Perhaps it was," answered Amanda. "I met him at Madame Fichet's soirée, and he promised to show me a side of Paris I would not otherwise have had a chance to experience."

Zoe chuckled softly. "You may not think it, but believe me, I do understand. He represented the daring cafe society from which a young woman of your class is protected."

Amanda nodded. "Yes."

"And no doubt he fell in love with you on the spot. Frenchmen, especially young and handsome ones, are known for their romantic tendencies, you know."

Amanda moved her shoulder in a shrug. "I suppose he did."

"And did you fall in love with him?"

She pressed her lips together and now sought Zoe's eyes, for she felt the older woman really did understand. And besides that, she had some sort of wisdom to draw on that Amanda had never been able to get from her mother.

"I don't know," said Amanda honestly. "He seemed so sweet, and so devoted."

Zoe studied her niece wisely. "Who could not afford to be devoted in the first few days of adoration? I won't ask how he expressed this newfound love. Obviously, he moved you very much for you to become so concerned about his welfare."

Amanda's eyes widened innocently. "Who would not

be concerned to see someone like that taken so ill? And the illness is very serious. Anyone with the resources who knew him would have done the same in paying for the treatment."

"Perhaps. I do hope he appreciates it."

"Oh, Aunt, I'm sure he does."

"Well, we must think of what to do. We cannot prevent scandal, especially since you must appear at the trial of the no-good who abducted you."

"Yes, I'm sorry to have to drag your name into this."

Zoe sighed. "We might think of a way to minimize the scandal." She looked directly at Amanda.

"The duke had asked your mother for permission to pay court to you. Since he rescued you, your names will be linked. If an engagement were announced, then your appearance at the trial would draw attention to an act of heroism on his part. Any gentleman would go to the ends of the earth to save his beloved."

The combs in Amanda's hands scattered to the floor. "Engagement? Impossible."

Zoe lifted a brow. "Perhaps not. I might be able to have a word with him and explain the situation. If we don't do something quickly, your reputation will be ruined."

"But ... but ... Sunderland would never want to marry me after this. Nor I ... him. I ... I couldn't."

Whether or not Sunderland still wanted her for a wife, which she very much doubted, she couldn't marry him now. He would be expecting an innocent wife, something she was not.

"Now, now. Perhaps not. But an engagement, you see, would forestall scandal. Most engagements are long ones, as yours would be. At the end of a suitable period, the engagement could be broken off, if necessary, and no one hurt, as long as the arrangement was understood up front."

Amanda's jaw dropped. She hardly knew what to say. Of course she owed this sort of solution to her aunt. And to herself if she really wanted to save face. And it would give her mother time to recover. She could hardly deny the cleverness of her aunt's idea. She shut her mouth, then opened it again.

"Just an engagement in name only, you mean," she said.

Zoe nodded. "Exactly. If the duke will agree."

Amanda shut her eyes. "Oh, he'll never agree."

And what about poor Emile? What would he think? She ignored the fact that Emile had never broached the subject of marriage. Of course, she might be able to explain what had happened, that the measures they were taking were temporary only, until she could live down her disgrace. She opened her eyes and sighed.

"Very well. I appreciate your concern, Zoe, and if you think it's for the best, then I don't object if you talk to the duke."

Zoe leaned over and patted her knee. "Don't worry, my dear. You shan't have to see him until we find out his answer."

"That's good."

That evening Amanda composed several drafts of a letter to Emile. Tossing most of them out, she finally finished one she was as pleased with as she could be in these circumstances. While minimizing the danger she had been in, she explained that her name was going to be dragged through the gossip columns due to her family's social standing. They had decided that if the duke would agree, a fake engagement to him would save face.

She assured Emile that the duke did not really want

to marry her, nor she him. She ended the letter by promising that she would come to see him as soon as was possible. In the meantime, he was to concentrate on getting well.

She posted the letter the next morning and spent the rest of the day quietly. When Louisa woke up, Amanda was allowed in to see her, but both made sure they spoke of nothing inflammatory. Zoe had presented her plan to Louisa, who agreed that this was the best solution. And so after inquiring as to her mother's health, Amanda said nothing. Rather, she sat beside Louisa's bed and read to her until she fell asleep.

Late that afternoon, Zoe came to inform Amanda that she had spoken to the duke, and he was coming to dinner that evening. He would have his answer then.

Amanda's heart began to patter nervously. "Dinner? And he didn't say yes or no?"

"No, he did not. He listened attentively, quickly grasping the situation. But, of course, he had to consider his own position. His name too, is at risk here. I don't blame him for wanting to take some time."

"He understood that it is only to be for appearances?" said Amanda. "That at the end of a proscribed period of time, we would break it off?"

"Yes, he understood that."

"I see. Then I suppose I should dress for dinner."

"Yes," said Zoe. "And, my dear, it would not hurt to dress attractively. Even though he may not actually plan to marry you, he will want to be thought to be engaged to an attractive young woman."

Amanda appeared for dinner dressed in one of the gowns designed by Worth. The pale blue tulle and satin flattered her face and figure without the daring neckline of some gowns. She went down to the sitting room where the duke was examining a small painting by Renoir. He turned when she came in, and she was aware at once of the dark, sensual eyes that took in her appearance. A smile came to his lips.

"Good evening. How lovely you look. Much better than when I last saw you."

She couldn't help a nervous smile. "Thank you. You look considerably more presentable yourself."

He chuckled.

"And how is the boy?"

Sunderland's smile widened. "Just fine. I left him playing pinochle with one of my footmen. I think the footman is going to learn a few things."

Zoe joined them looking elegant in black satin with jet beads and rubies. Sunderland bowed. "Good evening, madam. What a brilliant costume you wear. The settings for your rubies are very fine indeed."

"Thank you, Your Grace." She rang for drinks to be brought on a silver tray, after which the footman withdrew.

"Since this is a private dinner, and Louisa is not up to joining us, I did not invite anyone else. Thus we will be an odd number."

Sunderland cleared his throat. "Altogether appropriate, under the circumstances, I believe."

Seeing no need to make chit chat, Zoe waited until they had all taken a few sips of their drink and then set their glasses down. "Shall we go in, then?" she said.

Sunderland offered his arm, as she was the oldest present, and there were no ladies of rank. Thus, Amanda was left to trail behind. In the dining room, Zoe sat at the head of the long dinner table with Sunderland to her right. Though there were only three of them, the table was set with her gold dinner plates and the full service. The serving man poured wine into their glasses after Sunderland passed his approval on the vintage, and the soup course was served.

They sipped the delicate mushroom soup silently, and it was not until it was taken away and the next course served—with instructions for the servants not to interrupt them—that Zoe broached the subject they had come together to discuss.

"I have put the case before my niece," Zoe began. "I have made it clear that we are under no illusions here. An arrangement is sought for everyone involved in this most unfortunate incident in order to be able to save face."

Amanda stared at the forks, too embarrassed to look at either of them. Zoe continued.

"It will appear odd when the story goes out that Amanda was alone in a cab at night. The unscrupulous reporters who sniff out news of the doings of people of our class may even be able to wrench from the driver in the case the address to which she was going. We must be prepared for the worst. In which circumstance, Amanda's reputation will be ruined."

"We must prevent that," said Sunderland. His voice made Amanda start, and a rush of surprise went through her. For she was certain that he cared nothing about her reputation.

"Therefore I have suggested an unusual solution," said Zoe in a regal voice. "But one which may be workable if we all understand the conditions."

She paused for a space before continuing. "If a formal engagement is announced, then respectability will be maintained. The more glamorous news of the

engagement of an American heiress to an English nobleman will take precedence over the circumstances which
led to the abduction. The duke's heroism will be emphasized, Amanda's reputation will not suffer, and in time it
will all die down. At which time the engagement can be
quietly broken off and no one the worse."

Amanda felt flushed from head to toe. Though she
understood that this was a business arrangement, it was
still humiliating to have put everyone in this position.
She could not bear to look up.

"A clever solution," said the duke. "I could not have
thought of anything better myself, madam."

"Then you agree?" said Zoe, a note of surprise in her
voice even though she herself had solicited the duke.

There was the briefest of pauses, during which
Amanda's heart skipped a beat.

Sunderland took a drink from his wineglass and
looked across the table at the unwilling young woman,
feeling a mixture of emotions he could not explain.
However, there could be only one answer if he was any
sort of gentleman at all.

"I agree to a period of engagement for, say, six
months? By which time society and the newspapers will
have forgotten all about this sensational occurrence that
brings the three of us together tonight."

Zoe sighed in relief. Amanda jerked her head up, eyes
wide, to meet the ironic gaze of the man opposite her.
Her expression was a combination of disbelief and
fright. Still, logic told her this was the best solution. The
engagement was temporary and not binding. But as she
met Sunderland's dark, questioning eyes, she felt a tremble.

Since Amanda was not speaking, Zoe answered. "Six
months sounds very reasonable to me. We can inform

the society editors immediately. And I speak for Amanda's mother, who agrees to the proposal as well."

Amanda tried to open her mouth to speak, but shut it again. What good were words anyway? She was a pawn in this drama of her own creation. And now she was the duke's fiancée.

Chapter 16

Zoe rang for the servants to bring in the next course, and more wine was poured. When they were left alone again with platters full of artichoke stewed in white wine and porkstock with onions and carrots, the duke raised his glass.

"A toast, shall we?"

Amanda glanced at him, still flushed, but she managed to raise her glass.

"A toast," responded Zoe.

After sipping the wine and taking a few bites of the delicious dish, Zoe turned to her niece.

"I understand the ordeal you've been through, Amanda, but surely you can say a few words."

"I'm sorry," said Amanda.

She looked hesitantly toward the duke. "Your offer is very generous, Your Grace."

She quickly reached for the wineglass, to help cover her embarrassment.

"Say nothing of it," he said. "Sensible, if I say so myself."

Amanda drank more wine than she might otherwise, and her mind became slightly fuzzy. Still it helped her relax, and she was able to join in the conversation more easily. They spoke of the trial they must appear in if Jacques were caught, and other arrangements that must be made.

"The engagement must appear real," said Sunderland. "It would be best if Amanda could make an extended visit to Elsenheim, to see how the prospective duchess might settle in. Chaperoned, of course. You, madam, might take her mother's place if Mrs. Whitney is unable to travel and to perform the duties of chaperone."

"Oh, that is very kind, Your Grace," said Zoe, her expression animated at the invitation. "I will discuss it with Amanda's mother."

"Good."

That settled, the duke wandered into conversation about art, opera, English politics, Parliament and a smattering of talk about Elsenheim.

Amanda half listened as he itemized the difficulties of running such a sizeable place and the cost involved. He was not hiding the fact that he still needed an heiress's money to keep up the palace. Zoe seemed fascinated, and while Amanda said little, it seemed the other two were working up to a state of high interest in the proposed visit, during which Amanda would play the part of fiancée.

Coffee and dessert came and went, and then they returned to the sitting room, attractively muted by the orbs of light shining from milky-globed gas lamps. Zoe entertained the duke with anecdotes of the artists who had contributed to her art collection, and shortly excused herself.

"I believe I shall retire," she said. "But seeing as how everything has been so amicably settled, I will leave you

two young people to any further conversation you may
desire."

The duke rose with Zoe and bowed. "Then I thank
you for your hospitality and for a most delightful evening of brilliant conversation."

Even a woman of Zoe's age could be flattered by the
impeccable manners of a handsome nobleman. She
waved a hand. "My pleasure. And a great relief to have
our little burden lifted."

He bowed again as she exited; then the door shut behind her.

Amanda pressed her back further against the brocade
chair where she sat near the fireplace, her eyes returning
demurely to the carpet as Sunderland noiselessly crossed
the room.

"Well," he said, as he came to a stop before her. "It
will not be so painful to be engaged to me, will it?"

Already her heart hammered in her chest. She shook
her head quickly. "No, no, of course not. You are most
generous."

"Hmmm," he said, resting a hand on the mantel and
studying the Renoir. "I hardly understand it myself," he
murmured more to himself than to her. "In any case we
must make the best of it."

He reached for her right hand as if to shake it on the
agreement they had made, but when she put her hand
in his, she was suddenly pulled to her feet.

Sunderland looked into her face and felt a surge of
desire. His lips curved upward as all thoughts were banished except for the pretty, flushed face tipped up toward his.

"Shall we seal it with a kiss? We are, after all,
engaged."

Her eyes rounded slightly, and her lips parted, perhaps to protest. Her own senses had deserted her at the dinner table due to the wine, and now she felt herself coming under his power in a way that was not unpleasant, but was frightening, to say the least.

"I couldn't," she said, the blood throbbing in her temples.

She could hardly say that she belonged to someone else, for legally, she was now betrothed to the duke.

"Hmmm," was all he said.

His hand slipped to her waist, and he parted his lips to taste hers. He responded to her warmth as he pressed his mouth against hers, and then he pulled her closer, enjoying the feminine curves against him.

Made like any other man, his own desires flashed powerfully, and his kiss deepened. He had been aware of the complications when he had agreed to Zoe's proposal, and he had told himself a dozen times on the way here that the idea was mad. If they actually broke off the engagement in six months as planned, he would have wasted precious time in gaining the money an heiress could bring to him. And he knew instinctively that Amanda, while perhaps not unattracted to him, was not in love with him, nor perhaps would she ever be. The truth was, he now had six months to win her. And he had never backed off from a challenge.

Of course love had not played a part in his plans for marriage. Or perhaps love born of respect might grow later after his bride sired sons to carry on the title. And he was more than aware of the havoc being engaged to this hoyden might create. Why, then, had he said yes?

Was it because of the feel of her hair and her soft skin against his lips when he kissed her? Or the look in her eyes whenever he confronted her? A look he felt could engage his attention for many years. Was it the womanly quality inside the girlish behavior, and the tantalizing feel of her tempting curves when his hand brushed her skin. It was all of this and something else he didn't quite understand, except that he'd be damned if he'd let her slip through his fingers now.

Though he had meant this to be a brief kiss to seal an agreement, her breathless response was having its effect on him. He somehow moved her to the sofa, and mid-kiss they both sat down, his arms now wrapped around her, hers entwined about his neck.

"No, no," she whispered in a confused voice when he took his mouth away from hers for breath and then placed his lips against her throat, unable to stop his explorations.

But her mind roared with sensations she could not stop. She knew this was wrong, but at the same time she reached out for the comfort he gave her. Somehow his warmth strengthened her, lit a fire within her that she now understood was linked with her newfound sensuality.

But how could she indulge in this passion? Wouldn't she always belong to Emile, no matter what happened? Desire and fear raged within her. Her face twisted in anguish as she tried to stop herself from hungering for more kisses.

Sunderland understood some of Amanda's inner struggle, but he was unable to stop his advances. He held her close. "You are so lovely, I cannot help myself."

His hands set her body on fire, and everywhere he touched her, the flame of passion was kindled.

"I can't," she breathed even as her thigh pressed closer to his. "I can't."

"I understand," he said, his voice hoarse with emotion now.

He meant to stop, but his hand strayed down hip and thigh, pushing against the thick material of dress and petticoats. Then in a quick movement, he flipped skirts aside and discovered her leg, coming in contact with an array of stockings and garters that might as well be a chastity belt.

"Hmmm, lovely and formidable," he said, a smile in his voice. It occurred to him that he might never have her money, but at least she could repay him with pleasure. She owed him that, did she not?

Grief, regret, intoxication and a desire for solace all combined in Amanda to the point that she didn't know what she was doing. This was how it was between a man and a woman, she realized. Those first experiments with Emile had taught her that much, and of their own accord her hands and limbs did what Emile had taught her to do. Only fuzzily did she realize that this was not the man she should be doing this with. Or was it?

Slowly her responses changed from resistant to eager, until Sunderland pressed her back on the sofa, his own body half covering hers. So lustful did he feel after an evening of wine, stimulating beauty and conversation, that he was hard-pressed to check his responses. He indulged in the petting for as long as he could before he knew he must break off. It would be unseemly to take her here on the sofa, even if they were engaged. In the dim recesses of his mind, he knew she would hate him for it.

He enjoyed one more deep kiss, his tongue probing hers, his body moving against her thigh. Then he summoned restraint and took his mouth from hers.

"I must stop, my dearest," he whispered into her ear.

"Yes," she breathed. "You must."

He knew then that she did not have the power to stop

him, and for a moment he was tempted to go further. But no, when he took her in passion, it must be with due ceremony in a place where they could take their time and savor their lovemaking. But he was deeply pleased about one thing. He had got himself engaged, even if only temporarily, to a passionate woman. And he was determined to enjoy that passion.

He sat up and pulled her with him, holding her against him until their pulses slowed. She leaned her head against him, the heat he had aroused in her slowly cooling. Then she found words, for now shame at her own behavior penetrated her haze.

"We shouldn't have," she said with slurred words.

"Hmmm," he murmured against her ear. "Why not, my dear?"

"Wrong," she managed to get out.

"No, no, my pet. It's not wrong at all. We are engaged, you remember."

His words helped to sober her, and she struggled to sit up by herself.

"Appearance only. You don't expect me to behave as a wanton," she said and then swallowed, her throat dry.

He smiled in pleasure. "I would never consider you wanton, my dear. Just a normal woman with healthy desires, enough to match my own. And as to whether this engagement is temporary, we shall see." He let the suggestion dangle.

It was on the tip of her tongue to tell him about Emile. But she remembered in some confusion that he already knew about Emile. In her own defense, she suddenly knew she must tell him the truth.

"There's something you must know," she said, pulling herself to the edge of the sofa.

"And what is that?" he asked, still not surrendering her hand.

"I . . . the . . . money you sent . . . to the sanatorium. I . . . well . . . that young man is in love with me." There, she'd said it, or almost.

Sunderland smiled indulgently. "Of course. Why would he not be?"

She gazed at him in stupid surprise. "You don't mind?"

"Of course I mind." He drew her fingers to his lips. "But I intend to make you forget him."

"How can I—" She couldn't find the words, his kisses warming her fingers. "I . . . we . . ." She reddened all over; she simply could not say it.

But he guessed her thoughts. "You were his lover, before he became ill, were you not?"

She gasped, stunned that he could so casually mention it. "How did you know?"

He laughed softly. "I knew it the first time you mentioned him. I saw it in your face, in your eyes. You practically admitted it to me, do you not remember?"

She shut her eyes and pressed her lips together. "I'm so ashamed." She opened her eyes again, looking at him doubtfully. "How could you . . . ?"

"How could I consent to become engaged to a woman of, shall we say, experience?" His light tone changed, and his look became intent. "Because I knew that whatever had happened between you and this young man was understandable. And I also knew that he was not meant for you. Not in a permanent sort of way."

She simply stared at him, stunned. But he laughed again and went on.

"A night of passion? But you would never be allowed to marry this penniless scholar, even if he wanted to do so. And you would not be happy."

The same words she had heard from her aunt and her mother. She could hardly believe she was hearing them from the duke himself. But she choked on her response, giving him time to press his argument.

"I knew that if I wanted you, I could have you. Did I not just prove that? And once you were mine, you would not see your erstwhile lover again. You would forget him."

"I'll never forget him," she said defiantly, hating the power Sunderland seemed to think he had over her.

"No?" He stood up, pulling her to her feet and pushing a loose tendril of hair away from her face. "I see no reason to argue further tonight."

He looked at the snapping eyes with relish. Why did he enjoy her temper so? Perhaps because it made it more of a challenge to subdue her, to see her begging for his love the way she had a moment before.

"Enough for this evening, don't you think? I must leave. But soon, my dear, you will be at Elsenheim for all the world to see that you are engaged to me."

Her spirit returned to her. "Engaged, but never married," she said haughtily.

He smiled. "If you wish." He bowed formally. "I will call tomorrow to inquire after your aunt's plans to bring you to England. I must spend some time at Parliament, where I am badly overdue. But there will be time for my duties at the estate as well."

She didn't answer, but saw him to the door. As she opened it to let him out, the scent of lilac filled her nostrils, the perfume stinging her with its overpowering sweetness.

"Good night," he said from the top step. Then he turned to walk toward the gate to the street.

She sighed, but did not answer as she watched him go. How dare he treat her as if he held her in the palm of his hand? She was his fiancée, but that did not mean she was supposed to respond to him like some hungry beast. Her actions were shameful, and she reddened all over again, even in her still slightly intoxicated state.

Now was not the time to think about it, she told herself, as she climbed the stairs and stumbled to her room. Tomorrow, when she had a clearer head, she would sort this all out. Upstairs, Delcia came to help her out of her gown. If the maid noticed her hair in disarray, or the extra tinge to her cheeks, she said nothing, and soon Amanda lay in bed, the lamps extinguished. Seeking refuge in the comforting dark, she soon fell asleep.

In the morning her head throbbed, but the cook sent her a drink concocted of strong black tea with sugar. And after a few strong sips, she felt better. Still, she blinked in the sunlight when she pulled back the curtains to look out at the sunny street below, the rest of the world walking by as if nothing had happened.

"Ooh," she groaned, wanting to go back to bed and pull the covers over her head. What would she do now?

She donned a modest day dress and after breakfast went into her mother's room, where Louisa was doing considerably better. The mother met the daughter with a pleasant look as she sipped tea from a breakfast tray across the bed.

"Well, good morning, my dear."

"Good morning, Mother. How are you feeling?"

"Much better, thank you. I was pleased to hear from Zoe that last evening's dinner party went so well."

"Yes."

"And so we have an engagement to announce." Her mother looked secretly pleased, and Amanda tried not to show her annoyance.

"It is only temporary," said Amanda. "I am quite sure he does not really wish to marry me."

Louisa fluttered her linen napkin. "Well, one can never tell. At least the man is gentlemanly enough to agree to our plan. You must realize, my dear, that your name has been salvaged from being dragged through the mud in a horrible scandal." She took a breath, and Amanda was afraid she was going to get upset.

"Yes, Mother," she said hurriedly, taking a seat near the bed. "Please don't think about it. Everything is all settled. The doctor said you weren't to upset yourself."

After several deep breaths, Louisa seemed more herself again and took some more tea. "Ah, that's better."

"Perhaps I can read to you later," suggested Amanda. "What would you like to hear?"

They discussed several possibilities, and after settling on a few books that Zoe might have in her library, they moved on to discuss trivial matters such as wardrobe and plans for the day. When Louisa began to feel fatigued, Amanda took herself away, promising to come again after lunch with the books.

Back in her room, Amanda sat down at her writing desk. It seemed impossible that she might be able to get away to see Emile. She would be carefully watched. No one would approve of such a journey, and if she went, her mother would have another attack. She stared at a blank piece of paper, the inkwell filled, and could not think of how to begin.

Oddly, the more she tried to think of Emile, the more her thoughts were filled with the duke. Wasn't she betraying poor Emile? And yet what else could she do?

Finally, she put the pen down in exasperation. Emile was beginning to seem so far away, as if he were drifting from her. Suddenly she felt as if a cold hand wrapped around her heart. He was dying. She could feel it as certainly as if he were in the room with her. She stood up, staring at nothing, as rigid as a stone. Something was happening, and she must find out what.

Still fearful of going to see Maurice herself, although this was the middle of the day, she decided to send for him instead. And she would do it without secrecy.

She sat down again and penned a brief note to Maurice, asking him to call on her with any news of Emile that he had. Then she found Marie and asked that the message be sent round to him. Next she found Zoe and informed her that she expected a caller.

"A friend that I met at Madame Fichet's will be coming to call today. I have asked him for news of our sick friend. I expect he will come after lunch if he can get away from his sittings."

"Are you sure that's wise?" said Zoe doubtfully, vaguely understanding the connection.

"I don't know if it's wise, but I must know what is happening to Emile, the young man I sponsored at the sanatorium."

Zoe frowned. "The young man that has caused us all so much consternation?"

"He didn't mean to cause consternation. That was my doing entirely."

"I suppose so." She fidgeted.

"Don't worry, Aunt. Maurice is merely coming to see me. He is a respectable artist, or else he wouldn't have been invited to Madame Fichet's. If anyone sees him here, you can tell them you are considering having a portrait done."

Thus mollified, Zoe said no more. And when Maurice appeared in the afternoon, the house was quiet. Zoe had gone out, and Louisa had been read to sleep. Thus Amanda and Maurice could speak quietly in the drawing room.

Maurice looked pale, and Amanda sensed his anxiety.

"You must tell me what you know," said Amanda. "How is Emile?"

Maurice shook his head. "Not well. I'm afraid his condition has worsened."

A dagger struck Amanda's heart. "Worsened? How can that be?"

Maurice shrugged. "Who knows? He has the best doctors, and they say they are doing everything for him. There is—" Maurice looked at Amanda meaningfully— "his state of mind to consider. He must want to live."

"But surely he wants to live," said Amanda, stunned by Maurice's words.

"Who knows? Emile was not exactly satisfied with his life. From the beginning he had pressure from his family and was always thought to be a failure."

"Why, that's ridiculous. He was . . . is a very good teacher. He had the best of recommendations."

"Yes, but in the eyes of his family that was not enough. His parents are no longer living, but he is left with the guilt of not having pleased them."

Amanda was on her feet, fists clenched. "Why must families dominate everything? It isn't fair. Oh, dear, I thought Emile was so gay."

"Few things in life are fair, mademoiselle."

She realized that getting angry would not help matters and sat back down. "You must tell him to live."

Maurice smiled faintly. "So I have."

She pressed her lips together. "Does he speak of me?"

"Oh, yes. You are on his mind constantly. And that worries him."

"What do you mean?"

"He knows he has placed you in a compromising position, and he can do nothing to rectify it."

"It has been rectified already," said Amanda with a great deal of cynicism. "I have become engaged to the Duke of Sunderland in order to save my reputation."

"Oh?"

"In name only. It is a temporary arrangement. When the gossip dies down, we will break off the engagement."

"Ah, I see. This will relieve Emile."

She wrinkled a brow. "What do you mean?"

"To see your good name salvaged. He would not want to have ruined your reputation."

She blushed. "That would not be his fault."

Maurice smiled. "But in his eyes it would be." The smile faded to melancholy. "He is also aware that you must marry in your social class."

She blinked at this, surprised at the pragmatism. But, then, maybe that was what made Emile want to die. Her heart twisted inside her.

"It isn't fair, is it?" she said once more.

Maurice shook his head. "You must not worry about Emile. He would not want you to. He would want you to be happy."

"How can I be happy, when I harbor so much guilt?"

"Oh, no, no, you must not feel that way. It is the way of things."

Amanda felt deeply confused. She had expected to hear that Emile was anxious to see her, was calling her to his bedside. Instead, why these noble words? Why this bitter view of life?

"Does he not want to see me?" she asked.

Maurice frowned. "He would like to see you, of course. But I think he believes it would be too painful."

"But what if he dies?" she blurted out suddenly.

"Then he would carry thoughts of you to heaven."

"Oh!"

She was suddenly frustrated at this poetic view of things. Was this how these Frenchmen took everything? Philosophically? And yet what had she expected? That an ill scholar would rise up out of his bed to fight for her? She swallowed, trying to be as realistic as Emile was trying to be. Or at least as Maurice said he was. That gave her an idea.

"Perhaps I shall go see him anyway, if I can," she said.

Maurice nodded. "Yes, if it would make you feel better."

They said a few more words, but there was nothing more that Maurice could say to enlighten her. After a short interval, he took his leave. But as she shut the door behind him, she made up her mind about one thing. She would find a way to see Emile. She had to.

As it turned it out, it was easy. When Sunderland came round to call at tea time, she managed to see him alone. He leaned back casually, one leg crossed over the other, finishing his tea as she paced to the window.

"I must take a journey," she said to the window. "There is someone I wish to see."

"A journey?" he inquired.

She turned to face him. "I must see Emile at the sanatorium. His condition has worsened. I am afraid he may die."

Unperturbed, Sunderland put down his cup. "I see."

She waited for him to respond. It took him only a few moments to realize how this must be handled.

"Then I will accompany you there."

"You?"

"Of course," he said. "It is the only proper way. We are acting out a charade, are we not? We can travel together if you are chaperoned. Where is the sanatorium?"

"The Maritime Alps, I believe," she said.

"Ah, perfect. Then I shall take you and your dear aunt to Monaco to visit the casinos and bathe in the Mediterranean. You can see your friend."

She was surprised it was so easy, too easy. What did the duke have up his sleeve?

For his part, Sunderland knew quite well that it would do no good to try to keep her from seeing this young man. He was prepared for the challenge of having her choose between himself and this rival, whoever he was. Though the duke had never met the young man, his own determination and confidence born of his nobility assured him he had little to worry about.

No one bested Sunderland. It just wasn't done. And now that he had seen with his own eyes how he could affect Amanda, he was willing to play her little game. She might fancy herself in love with this unfortunate suitor, but Sunderland would change her mind. He knew he could, for hadn't she melted under his attentions before?

He met her querying look with a sweep of generosity and suavity. "We can leave immediately," he said.

Chapter 17

Sunderland's agreeable attitude left Amanda nothing to fight. Her struggle to see Emile dissipated in the face of it. Yet she remained suspicious. Surely the duke's self-confidence was born of arrogance, and she looked for other reasons to remain on guard against him.

Persuading Zoe and Louisa would be another matter, and Amanda was again surprised when Sunderland suggested they not tell them the real reason for the journey.

"I've invited you and your chaperone for a holiday in Monaco. It is perfectly natural. Once there, we can arrange for your little outing to the sanatorium."

She watched him carefully, still unsure why he was being so generous.

"Very well," she said.

"Good," said the duke. "Then let us speak to your aunt at once. Better yet, if your mother is up to visitors, I will see her for a few moments. Once I penetrate that battlement, our success is assured."

Amanda could not help but be amused by his description of her mother. But she quickly smoothed her smile away.

"That is a good plan. Wait here, and I'll go see if my mother will see you."

Amanda crept upstairs and tapped lightly on Louisa's door. She found her mother resting, but not asleep. The eyes flew open when Amanda came in.

"Hello, Mother."

"Hello, dear. I understand the duke is here."

"Yes, as a matter of fact, he wants to see you."

Suddenly Louisa's color improved, and she pushed herself higher upon the pillows.

"In that case, bring Delcia to help me arrange my appearance. I would be most happy to see His Grace."

Amanda fetched the maid and then returned downstairs. "She is preparing herself to receive you," she said.

The look they exchanged was tinged with conspiratorial humor, and Amanda couldn't help but feel his empathy. He seemed to understand Louisa's tyrannical moods almost as well as Amanda did. She had to admit he was perceptive, and it made her feel as if, together, she and Sunderland shored up defenses against her mother. It was a comforting feeling, and it drew her to him.

But she quickly pulled her eyes away from his. "I think you might go up now. The maid will admit you."

While Sunderland was closeted away with Louisa, Amanda whiled away the time. After three-quarters of an hour, he returned, raining a smile on her with no doubt the same charm he had just been using on Louisa.

"Your mother is flattered at the idea that I wish to entertain you and your aunt. She was most annoyed that her health prevented her going herself. But since I must be back in England in a matter of weeks, we must leave for Monaco almost immediately. Since the doctor himself has stressed that she must not do anything unusual for some time, she could hardly jump up out of bed and pack her own bags to accompany us. Most unfortunate."

Again the twinkle of humor in his eye. Amanda could not help but respond with a laugh. "Then I'll tell Aunt Zoe."

He nodded. "I will make all the arrangements. I will send word as to when you should be ready, after I have ascertained the train schedules. Would three days' time at the resort be enough?"

She had momentarily forgotten that the trip was her doing. "Yes, I think so. Thank you."

"Then start making preparations, and I will let you know what hour of the day we should leave day after tomorrow. That will give you a day to pack your things. I suggest that rather than returning here, we should proceed to Elsenheim from Monaco. I shall have to be in London to go up to Parliament, and would like to give you a decent interval at Elsenheim first."

She could only agree to the way he took matters in hand. There was a tap on the door, and Zoe joined them.

"Hello, Aunt. We were just making some arrangements that involve you," said Amanda.

"So I've already heard. An expedition to the Mediterranean."

"Then you've been in to see Mrs. Whitney," said Sunderland.

She nodded. "I am so sorry that Louisa cannot chaperone. Therefore, I must accompany you myself."

Though she tried to appear sincere, her obvious pleasure at the idea showed through. The three of them smiled at each other mischievously, as if they had just gotten away with a grand scheme. Then, after chatting briefly about the plans, the duke took his leave.

"Well, my dear," said Zoe, after he had left, "this is an added bonus."

"Indeed it is," said Amanda, disciplining herself to remember that the reason they were going in the first place was so she could sneak off and visit the sanatorium.

The next day passed quickly in a flurry of preparations. By noon the following day, the trunks were ready, all arrangements and farewells made. Delcia was all agog that they were now going to the Riviera. The duke called for them, and the trunks were loaded. Louisa sat on her lounge by the window to wave at them as they stepped into the carriage that would convey them to the train station.

"Poor Louisa," said Zoe, a lilt to her voice in spite of her formal words. "I'm sure she would have wanted to come."

And to make matters worse for us, thought Amanda as they rode through the streets. At the station, Sunderland's footmen took care of everything. Jean Henri was no longer in evidence, as he had been sent on to Elsenheim to begin his outfitting and training as page boy. Sunderland entertained the ladies with anecdotes of how the boy was taking to his new, more affluent life, which made both Amanda and Zoe smile.

"He'll have to work for a living, that is certain," said Sunderland.

"Aren't you afraid he'll try to steal the family silver?" said Zoe.

"Ah, a good point. I had him watched carefully while we were here so that he wouldn't make off with anything. But once in England, I feel we are fairly safe. He will no longer be on his own turf, and he'll soon see that his stomach is full, he has a place to sleep and is properly dressed. He wouldn't know where to go to sell purloined items. The villagers would immediately report him to me."

They arrived at Monte Carlo late in the evening and were quickly settled at the fashionable Hôtel de Paris, where the duke had engaged an elegant suite for Amanda and her aunt. His suite was across the hall. Tired from the journey, they went to bed early.

But the next morning the sun greeted them, and Amanda stepped out to her balcony to see the blue Mediterranean spread at her feet. Glorious was the only way to describe it, and with her face tipped to the blue sky, she breathed in the luscious sea breezes.

"My, my," said Zoe. "This is indeed promising. I haven't taken a vacation by the sea in a decade. Oh, my. We must dress for breakfast, my dear. Try to look smart."

Amanda obeyed. Delcia helped her into her morning costume, striped tan in thin linen, trimmed with a yoke of embroidered silk. Delcia was beside herself at being by the sea.

"Oh, miss. Just to be here is something," she said excitedly. "To see all the elegant ladies and splendid gentlemen promenading!"

She chattered on and on as she wound Amanda's hair into a chignon that would accommodate a graceful feathered and beribboned hat to protect her face from the sun. "It will be so exciting to see some of the professional beauties at the casinos, will it not?"

"I suppose," answered Amanda. She had been too preoccupied with her own problems to consider much of what she would see or not see in this fashionable spot.

Sunderland met them for breakfast in the elegant dining room amidst a lively crowd of men and women. In spite of the real reason she was here, Amanda found herself ogling the incomparably bejeweled women and the handsome men who escorted them. Truly Monte Carlo seemed a lively place.

"I trust you both slept well," said the duke after their breakfasts had been ordered.

"Oh, yes," said Amanda.

"Quite," said Zoe.

"Good. And what would you like to do today? There is the beach, later on the races and of course the casinos."

"You young people decide," said Zoe. "I can't take too much sun, myself."

She seemed to want to say more, but hesitated. Then her eyes widened over Sunderland's shoulder, and she gave a little gasp. "Why, if it isn't my old friend Madame LeBlas. I swear it is she."

They turned to look at a group of women, all wearing enormous flowered and feathered hats, and now taking seats at a nearby table.

"Excuse me," said Zoe, "I must go and say hello."

She got up and rustled across the room to where the table in question broke into feminine chatter. The women at their seats turned to peer at Amanda and Sunderland, who nodded his head toward them.

"Well," he said, turning back to Amanda. "It seems as if your aunt may find herself amused by friends while she is here. All the easier for us to slip away, no?"

"Yes," said Amanda, already nervous about their plan. "But now that I am here, I don't even know how to get to the sanatorium."

"Don't worry," he said in a low voice. "I will drive

you there myself. I inquired of the concierge last night and have ordered a gig for us."

"Thank you." It still made her feel odd that her fiancé was taking her to see her lover, but there was no way to express her discomfort.

Zoe returned to their table, chuckling brightly to herself. "Well, what good fortune. Madame LeBlas has invited me to go to the casino with her group." Then she caught herself up. "That is, I don't mean to neglect my duties as chaperone, but surely during the day . . ." She let it drift off.

Sunderland grinned. "Not to fear, madam. I will take Amanda to the races. You enjoy yourself at the casino."

Zoe tried not to give herself away, but finally leaned forward and whispered, "I did bring a little extra money to spend at the casino. It's a tiny weakness I have." She leaned back. "But I always know when to quit."

Sunderland laughed, and Amanda smiled in relief. At least one obstacle had been overcome.

After breakfast they strolled along the terrace, greeting acquaintances of both Zoe's and Sunderland's. For Monte Carlo was a very popular spot. Amanda leaned on Sunderland's strong arm and was introduced as his fiancée, which brought smiles of congratulations from the men and looks of envy from the women.

She tried to remember that this was a ruse, and was confused at the pleasure she felt and the way Sunderland seemed so attuned to her every whim. The sun, the pleasant breeze and the gay atmosphere were intoxicating. But underlying it all was a growing nervousness about their little adventure.

Just before lunch, Zoe's group of friends came to meet Amanda and the duke. Zoe made the introductions.

"A pleasure," said Madame LeBlas, as the duke bowed over her hand.

"The pleasure is mine," said Sunderland smoothly.

"And I am ever so glad to meet Zoe's niece. I have heard so much about you, my dear," she cooed over Amanda.

"Thank you," said Amanda.

"You are a favorite niece, in case you didn't know. And now to become Duchess of Sunderland, you must be very excited."

Amanda felt that her smile was wooden, and hoped it didn't show. "Yes, quite."

"Have you set a date yet?" asked the matron.

Amanda glanced quickly at Sunderland. "We . . . haven't yet decided."

"Oh, well, there's time enough for that."

"Yes," breathed Amanda.

Clearly she had not thought of all the questions she might be asked in this circumstance. She really must prepare some answers.

"I am sure Zoe and your mother will enjoy putting together your trousseau. I hope your mother will soon be well. A pity she could not join you here."

"Yes," said Amanda again, beginning to feel like a marionette.

"But then that might have deprived Zoe of her little games," teased Madame LeBlas. They all chuckled at that, and Zoe bid her niece good day.

"Have a good time, dear." She turned to look up at the duke, who was considerably taller than she was. "I'll expect to join you for dinner," she said, remembering her role. "You will have her back by then?"

"Assuredly, madam. You can trust me."

Zoe glanced at her niece, a look of uncertainty fluttering over her face, but her friends were urging her to come along to lunch, and so with a weak wave of the hand, she was off, leaving Amanda alone with her fiancé.

"Well," he said with humor. "At least that part is over. Shall we go? A carriage is waiting. I ordered a picnic lunch for us to have on the way, so that we can save time."

She looked at him with that same mixture of awe and confusion that plagued her. "How thoughtful."

He placed his hand on her waist in a familiar manner and steered her through the crowds and out of the hotel. They went down the front steps to a hooded phaeton where a footman held the door for them and a groom held the reins. Since it was a warm, sunny day, the hood had been rolled back so that they could enjoy the scenery and the breezes. Sunderland sat beside her, and a basket with their lunch rested on the compartment behind the seats. He took the reins from the groom, touched them to the matched grays, and they were off.

Sunderland consulted directions he had scribbled on a piece of hotel stationery, then gave the paper to her to hold. Now that they were actually on their way, Amanda had little attention left for the palm-lined avenue and the delicately hued, stuccoed villas of the wealthy. They drove along the Avenue de la Costa, wound past Saint Dévote and then turned into the Boulevard du Jardin Exotique, where they climbed toward the exotic gardens laid out on the rock above the Condamine quarter.

Here the view was exquisite, and even Amanda felt her breath taken away. Neither of them spoke as the carriage continued to climb, and soon they had left the tiny, bustling principality behind and were up into the magnificent hills that shielded the playground for the wealthy below. As the road twisted, Amanda continued to look back at the breathtaking view until they finally took the turnoff that would lead them to the sanatorium.

The thought struck her suddenly, and a sense of dizziness overcame her. It was hard for her to believe that she was finally here. After a few moments, Sunderland pulled off the road, taking a trail that curved behind a shelf of rock onto a flat space, sheltered by rising, rocky slopes and leafy trees.

"You will want to take some nourishment before we reach the sanatorium," he said. "This spot looks as good as any for a picnic."

"Yes, I suppose," sighed Amanda in a martyrlike tone. Though her stomach didn't feel like digesting anything, she knew he was right. She would need her strength.

Sunderland spread a blanket on the spot, secluded from the road, but which opened out to the southwest. From here they gazed at a cleft between the mountains where an inviting path led upward.

"How beautiful," she said softly.

Sunderland spread out the wine, bread, cheese and cuts of meat, which Amanda arranged on plates. She accepted the wine and took a tiny sip. Then she attempted to chew her food. Unfortunate that her situation was so complex. Otherwise she might have enjoyed the setting more.

"You are very quiet," said Sunderland, stretching out against a rock, and turning his face to the sun.

How she envied his casual attitude. "Wouldn't you be?" she blurted. Away from the crowds before which they must act a charade, she felt the desire to speak more frankly.

He turned and gazed at her, his hair falling over his brow. "You mean being driven to a rendezvous with a former lover by your present fiancé?"

She turned scarlet, at first unable to speak. His look of ironic amusement infuriated her. How dare he take it so casually.

"Must you be so indelicate?" she said, lifting her chin haughtily.

He laughed out loud at that. "It is not I, but the situation that is indelicate, my dear. I cannot help it if you entangled yourself in your little indiscretion. I am simply the innocent bystander who was kind enough to help you extricate yourself. You should be grateful."

"I did not say I was ungrateful."

"Oh," he said in a tone that sent warning signals. "Then perhaps you will one day show it."

Her heart trebled its beat, and she knew that there was simply no way she could feel comfortable under the circumstances. Remembering her own betrayal of her better instincts in Sunderland's arms, she flushed at his suggestion.

"If you mean there is to be a repeat of our actions on the night of our so-called engagement, you are wrong. That will not happen again. I was the victim of too much wine and over-wrought nerves."

"Oh?" he said. "I was hoping you were victim of my own charms."

She could hardly look him in the eye. "You are despicable, taking advantage of my situation."

Sunderland put aside his plate and glass and sat up, shifting closer to her. She could not back away, for she was against the rocky hill.

"If you mean being engaged to you, I see no reason why a man would not want to show his feelings to his fiancée."

"But I am not your fiancée," she said, her blood racing as he moved nearer.

"Oh, but you are. We are formally engaged."

She turned her head away. "Not in reality. You don't really want to marry me."

"How do you know that?"

"How could you want to marry me? You already know about my past."

"I, too, have a past, my dear. It's not so unusual. It's just not talked about."

She briefly remembered his mention of the shopkeeper's daughter. But his words were distracting her.

"It isn't fair," she continued, still edging away from his encroachment. "You think I am perhaps a woman of easy virtue. You are playing on our compromising situation."

He chuckled low. "I think no such thing. I understand your upbringing, and I believe your heart is sincere."

He broke off from his forward movements and laughed as if at himself.

"It is true, I don't know myself why I persist. There are hundreds of other wealthy young ladies. Why is it that since I've met you, I have not been able to concentrate on any of them as prospective wives?"

Suddenly he lay back, sprawled on the blanket beside her, face toward the blue sky above them. He closed his eyes, but he did not doze. She looked at the length of him there and felt things she knew she shouldn't. How simple it would be to stretch out beside him, to nestle into his side, to listen to his breathing.

She turned her face away. Truly she was losing her

mind. Sunderland wanted to use her, as he would use any mistress. It was Emile who loved her, she must remember that.

In a moment Sunderland spoke again. "I suppose I keep wondering just what kind of a duchess you might make. If I am to marry, I want a sensual woman, someone with whom I can enjoy siring offspring. You can't deny you had as much pleasure as I did the other night, Amanda. You can't deny you desire what that little encounter promised."

He opened his eyes, turned on his side and gazed up at her, a small smile on his face. He lifted his hand to touch her chin, letting his fingers brush the hair under her bonnet.

"You could actually marry me. I have the feeling it would be agreeable."

While part of her gave way to the tempting caress of his fingers, the other part of her rebelled. Finally she frowned at him.

"Agreeable, you say. But what about love? I believe a man and woman should be together out of love for one another."

"Hmmm," he said in an encouraging tone. "Not a bad idea. But how can you know if you love someone at first? Do you think you love the poor fool who is ailing up there in the sanatorium? You only knew him for a matter of days. Surely you don't think that's the kind of love on which to base a long-term match, do you? Come now, tell me the truth."

She winced, felt moisture in her eyes. "I don't know," she admitted, a great sob suddenly clogging her chest. "I don't know."

Sunderland saw her grief and felt moved. He sat up.

His arm went around her, and he pulled her against him. "Shhhh, shhhh," he said.

He removed the bonnet, which threatened to become a barricade, and kissed her hair. "There, there, don't cry."

She leaned into him, the warmth of the sun and the strength of his arms seeping into her. Why did he always have to affect her this way? Why did he always seem to be there when she needed him? Tears streamed down as she attempted to sort out her feelings and explain herself.

"But I don't love you," she said. "I ought to love Emile."

"Ought to?" Sunderland repeated, a smile coming to his face. Victory beat like a drum in his chest. Hope and pleasure filled him. "And why ought you to love him?" he asked.

"Because," she said, her clenched fist on his chest. "He loved me."

"You mean he made love to you," said Sunderland in a throaty voice. He held her a little away so that he could look at her face. "It is not the same thing."

She swallowed, not looking him in the eye, her chin thrust forward. "It ought to be."

Sunderland gazed at her gently, wiped a tear with his finger. "Of course you would think so, darling Amanda. Because the experience was new. But it is not so that you must love him."

She closed her eyes, shame filling her. How could Sunderland talk about this so rationally?

He let go of her and leaned against the hillside again.

"Your lover introduced you to a new world. A world that makes you truly a woman. I know that. Perhaps I even regret that it was he and not I that did so. But we won't dwell on that. But because you have sampled such love from one man does not mean you must love him forever. It does not mean you cannot give your heart to someone else, someone who will take care of you and cherish you for the rest of your life."

She shook her head. His words were confusing her. "I don't understand," she said. "How can you say that?"

He shook his head. "I don't know. Why is the sky blue? Why is it that when I see you I want to kiss you? I want to make love to you a thousand times, show you things you could not possibly have experienced on that first, clumsy occasion. Why do I want to possess you? Win you from whatever consideration keeps you from me?"

She tried to laugh, but it came out a choked hiccough. "Perhaps you like a challenge," she said. "Then, when I became yours, you would tire of me, put me aside for some new mistress."

He considered the possibility. "I used to feel that way," he said honestly. "But now I'm not so sure. I swore to give up my mistress when I married. And there might be a woman who would make me revel in that promise, who would keep me by her side in ever new, ever deeper discoveries of each other."

Suddenly he was beside her again, his arms around her. "It might be possible, Amanda, with you."

She didn't know how it happened, but suddenly their mouths were together, hungrily kissing each other. The warmth she had wanted a moment ago was now hers as he embraced her, holding himself back no longer with deep, probing kisses and urgent caresses.

Not having the excuse of too much wine this time, for she had taken only one sip, Amanda could not help the response the infuriating duke aroused in her. Could it be possible that he was right? That she only felt obliged to Emile because of their impetuous escapades? If she were truly devoted to Emile, why was she kissing Sunderland? Why was she entwining her arms around him, allowing him to lay her out on the blanket next to the earth that cradled them?

"Edward, Edward," she whispered, using his given name, as she writhed beneath him. "Why do you do this?"

"Because I must love you, my dearest," he answered in a hoarse whisper, kissing her ear, his hand on her breast as his legs covered hers. There, he had said it, but he did not regret it as they wound themselves around each other in the secluded spot.

She returned his kisses, did not resist as his hand found its way under her clothing. Indeed, she seemed as needful as he when he guided her hands to his skin.

She feared she was lost to this man who was making her look at life through new eyes. Was she so weak that she was this easily molded in his hands? Hands that felt stronger, more determined than Emile's. Kisses that were more full of ownership, that promised more. Slowly, slowly, she felt herself slipping away, the promises she'd thought she'd made to Emile broken down.

"You will forget him," said Sunderland when he had her under his spell.

He had pulled apart his clothing, kissing her bared breasts and caressing her thighs, working his magic while throbbing with his own desire, evident now in the instrument she held in her hands, her eyes glazed with passion, her mouth parted.

She did not resist as he climbed atop her, still moving slowly, gently, his tongue dancing from her delicious mouth to her upturned, waiting breasts. Her head was thrown back at both new and remembered sensations as she felt him against her thighs. And a full pulsing deep within her craved more until she moved herself toward him, inviting him in a way that was unmistakable.

"You will forget him," he said once more, finally entering her as he would enter a glorious palace where all manner of teeming luxury and satisfaction awaited.

"Ahh," he said as he at last achieved his goal, his hand sliding down to brace her against him.

So long had he waited that now he was unable to control the thrusts that his body cried out for. But her movements matched his own, and he quickly lifted them both to a pinnacle of ecstasy.

Amanda was beside herself, no longer questioning why this was happening, but giving of herself fully. He had won, and she knew it. She could fight no longer. And now the emotions he aroused in her and the sensations exceeded words. Her mind numbed as her body took over. She heard her own cries and moans from a distance, while she herself floated away on a white, fluffy cloud that moved in the pristine sky above.

There was nothing but the man atop her, his body commanding her with more assurance and experience than she had known before, though she couldn't have described it coherently. Edward was everything, his kisses, his skin against hers, his body, his caring that conveyed itself through the passion he shared with her and through his many acts of consideration and chivalry. Emile could no longer save her from herself.

Chapter 18

Sated, but afraid to open her eyes, Amanda lay in Edward's arms. Now she was truly his. Carried away on the feelings he'd succeeded in arousing in her, she allowed thoughts that she had refused to consider before. As the sun tugged at her eyelids, Edward moved beside her. One arm still cradling her, he smoothed their clothes. And when she finally opened her eyes in embarrassment, he smiled down at her.

"Didn't I tell you we would find passion together?" he said gently, outlining her cheek and chin with the tip of his finger.

She blushed and glanced downward and then struggled to sit. She could hardly protest. She had let this happen. Her cheeks still felt flamed, her limbs warmed by him. What could she say that would explain away the situation?

Instead of speaking she busied herself arranging her skirts and then hunted for the pins that had fallen out of her hair. While Edward put away the picnic, Amanda made herself as presentable as she could. What was happening inside her she could not explain. Did she love or hate this man who had such a hold on her? And how could she explain the rapport that had seemed to grow between them from the first? The way he anticipated her every thought, understood her feelings as if he could read her mind like a book?

He poured some wine into a glass.

"Shall we have a toast?" he asked, a jubilant tone in his voice as he held the glass out to her.

"Why?"

He lifted a brow, a devilish look in his eye. "Is it not enough to toast our rendezvous?" he said. "To the beginning of a long and fruitful engagement."

She reddened. "We're getting ahead of things, don't you think?" she said tartly. "Most engagements are a chaste period during which a couple gets to know each other."

"Hmmm," he said, taking a sip. "But how much more delightful to get to know each other this way."

She had no answer, but sipped the wine to steady her. However, she refused to finish the glass and poured the rest on the grass. About their engagement she was not inclined to think. Right now she had the horrific task of getting up from her fiancé's love nest and going to see her former lover.

It was all she could do to rearrange herself as best she could and then climb into the carriage while Edward put the picnic things in back. She wished it were so easy to rearrange her feelings as well.

Edward, whom she could not help but think of by his Christian name, now that they had crossed the line of intimacy, moved with his usual easy grace, and looked as unruffled as if he had just come from his valet. No one would guess he had just had a tryst by the side of the road.

When they were ready, he slapped the reins to the

team, and they pulled back on the road, on their way once more to the sanatorium. Amanda had the urge to tell Edward to turn around and go back to their hotel. For now, more than before, she did not know how to face Emile. Even in his condition, she felt so guilty she was sure he would be able to tell. She had betrayed him. How could she live with herself? Tears sprang in the corners of her eyes as she confronted her dilemma. What would she say to Emile?

They climbed higher in the mountains, but Amanda was too wrapped up in her emotions and fear of what was going to happen next to appreciate the beauty surrounding them or to glance back to peek at the sea when clefts in the rocks allowed a view. They saw the sprawling buildings of the sanatorium above them on the side of a hill, sun shining on its fresh white paint, and then they turned into the long drive that led onto the grounds.

Visitors strolled about the gently sloping lawn, and convalescents relaxed in rocking chairs on a wide verandah that stretched around the front and sides of the two-story structure. They pulled into a stableyard, and a groom came to take care of the horses.

"We're visiting for a few hours," the duke said to the groom, who nodded and took charge of the carriage. Then he took Amanda's arm to escort her to the front steps.

Rigid with fear that one of the patients in dressing gowns on the front porch might be Emile, she searched the faces, but none of them was familiar. Inside the lobby, nurses in uniforms with short capes and kerchief head coverings flew about. Beyond, a large sitting room, amply provided with more rockers, settees and comfortable sofas, was half-filled with both patients and visitors in street dress.

Edward approached the large mahogany desk and spoke to an attendant behind it. "We're here to see a patient." He glanced at Amanda to provide the name.

"Emile Reveillere," she said with a small voice.

The attendant nodded, consulted a box of cards and then said, "Just a moment. I'll bring you the nurse. Please make yourselves comfortable."

He took himself off, and Amanda and the duke looked around at the nearby seats, choosing an upholstered wicker settee.

In a few moments a middle-aged-looking nurse came back with the attendant, exchanged a few words with him and then floated toward them. They stood up.

"Miss Whitney?" said the nurse.

Amanda was momentarily surprised that the nurse knew her name, but of course they would know who she was since she had indirectly supplied the money. She nodded.

"Yes. And this is the Duke of Sunderland." She almost added, my fiancé, but bit her tongue.

"Your Grace," said the nurse with a nod. "I am Elizabeth Migenes. I've been seeing to your friend Emile."

Amanda winced. "How is he?"

The nurse's eyes were very grave. "Not well, I'm afraid, though he has had the best of care. He seemed to improve at first. But now he has had a setback, I'm sorry to say. Perhaps you will be able to cheer him."

All thought fled from Amanda's mind except Emile's welfare. The complexity of her relationships suddenly did not matter. What mattered was his health.

"May we see him?"

"Yes," said the nurse. "But please don't tire him."

"I'll wait outside," said the duke. "You've a fine lawn here, and I've the need for fresh air."

Amanda glanced at him. Of course he would allow her privacy. Her distracted mind had not even considered it.

"Very well."

"Take your time," he said generously.

His air was one of indifference. Only when she looked into his eyes did she see a glimpse of concern, a small flash of jealousy. But there was no time to address that concern, and even if she did, what would she say?

"Follow me," said the nurse, starting off toward a set of double doors.

Amanda had no more time for words but hastened after the nurse, catching up to her as they passed into a long, light corridor. She pressed her lips together, glancing into the small rooms where doors were open. Many of the inmates did not seem to be in a serious condition. And indeed the airy cleanliness and pleasant ambiance of the place impressed her.

They turned a corner and went through another set of doors. This wing seemed quieter. The doors to the patients' rooms were closed. Indeed a more somber air pervaded this part of the sanatorium. Amanda shivered, and she knew why. The spell of death hung over these rooms, and she felt the life and death struggles that went on behind each closed door.

They stopped in front of one door, and Nurse Elizabeth turned to her.

"He knows you are coming, but please be prepared for what you will see. He has lost much weight."

Amanda nodded somberly and braced herself. Then the nurse moved the door slowly inward and stepped back for Amanda to enter. She blinked, almost not seeing the dark head that leaned against the back of his lounge chair, eyes closed. Her heart lurched. Even wrapped in the long dressing gown, she saw that he had indeed lost weight, for the thin hands that clutched the blanket over his knees were bony.

"Emile," she said, not much more than a whisper as she moved into the room.

The door shut softly behind her.

"Oh, Emile," she sobbed, coming to her knees beside him and taking one of his chilled hands.

His eyes opened, and he coughed. His voice, when he spoke, was weak.

"My angel," he said.

She looked up at him with tears in her eyes. He smiled, but she saw that it took much effort to do so. Gone was the rosy look in the face so full of joie de vivre she had known. What had caused this pall to come over him? She could not help but shake her head helplessly.

"Emile, why are you sick?" she sobbed. "I thought when they brought you here, you might regain your health."

He tried to squeeze her hand, and his voice was a little stronger this time. "It is not to be so."

"Don't say that, Emile."

He shook his head, lifting her chin so he could look at her face. "You must not grieve so, my pretty one."

"Oh, Emile," she said, a fresh round of sobs claiming her.

But she used the handkerchief she had thought to bring and dabbed at her eyes. She didn't want to spend the entirety of her visit crying.

"So much has happened. I feel I must tell you."

"I know," he said with a wan smile. "Maurice has written me."

She lowered her eyes, still dabbing at them. "How much do you know?"

"That you did what was best."

She got up from her knees and took a seat beside him.

"Then you know I was forced to become engaged to the Duke of Sunderland." There, she had said it.

He nodded, his look full of understanding. "Of course. It was the sensible thing to do."

Her face was crimson now. "But I felt I had betrayed you after . . . we . . ."

He smiled gently. "Do not worry, my little dove. What happened between us will always remain in our memory. It is ours to keep."

She pressed her lips together to keep from crying. "But I don't know what to do now. Oh, dear, I've made such a mess of things."

For the first time since she'd seen him, his face lit with a touch of bittersweet humor.

"You must go on living. Life offers you much; you must take it. Is that not what all life is about?"

She swallowed. "But I don't want to marry the duke. Our engagement is for appearance's sake only to save my reputation. He came after me, you see, when that horrid criminal had me tied up."

"Yes, very brave. I am glad he saved you, since I could not do so myself. If I had known . . ." He let it drift, but his tone conveyed some of the futility of it all.

For a moment neither said anything; then Amanda tried to think of a fresh outlook.

"You'll get well," she said. "And in six months' time I will be free of Sunderland. Then we—"

But Emile lifted his hand and touched her lips, shaking his head as well.

"Hush, my sweet," he said, looking into her eyes. Then he lay his head back. "I fear it will not be so."

Fresh horror touched her breast. "Emile, you must not give up."

He didn't look at her, but a peaceful look came over his face.

"This illness of mine," he said, his eyes unfocused, as if he looked beyond the room where they sat. "It has been my nemesis all my life. I believe it is fated to take me."

"No, I won't listen to you."

He gave a laugh that turned into a strangled cough. When the spasm passed, he continued.

"I have always known that my journey on this earth was to be a brief one. Ah, but how beautiful it has been."

"Nonsense," said Amanda. "You will get better. Things will be as they were."

He turned his head to look at her, and this time, she felt he saw into her soul. "No, things will never be as they were."

"Why not?" she asked, her lips trembling.

He moved his head slowly from side to side. "One cannot go back."

The meaning was clear, and she felt as if a hand wrapped about her heart, squeezing it.

"But we must." Her words were a hoarse whisper. "We could start over."

"No," he said again. "No regrets, mademoiselle. You must not punish yourself. You must live for me. You must taste all the sweetness life offers."

She shook her head, feeling her own determination slip away.

"You must marry this duke who is your hero," said Emile. "It is for the best."

"No, no, never," she said, taking his hand again and slipping off her chair to lay her head in his lap. "I couldn't."

"Yes," he said.

He was seized with coughing again, and it was longer before the cough subsided. Then he lay his head back and closed his eyes.

Her anguish great, Amanda hardly knew what to do. She uttered a silent prayer, but the coldness of her heart told her it did no good. A faint anger tinged the sadness she felt. He mustn't give up so easily. He mustn't be so resigned to his fate. New determination seized her.

"No," she said in a stronger voice, rising again to sit on the chair. "I will wait for you, Emile. You will get well and you will take up your old life again."

For a moment peace came over his sallow face. But he did not speak. She squeezed his hand. Finally he opened his eyes.

"It is a pleasant dream, my dove," he said. "I shall take it with me to heaven."

A cry of anguish escaped her. Guilt assailed her. She suddenly wanted very badly to confess that she had been unfaithful to him. As if reading her thoughts, Emile struggled for a few more words.

"Do not worry, my pet. I know how these things are. This duke seems a very determined man. If he wants you, he will make you his, I've no doubt. You must forgive yourself, for I have forgiven you."

"I . . . we . . ." She could not say it.

But Emile understood. "He will take care of you and give you a position I never could. You must not compare our few days together with the life that stretches before you. Promise me you will be happy. And you can do much good in the world as a duchess. You will wear the title well."

She choked on her words. Happiness was so far from what she felt, it seemed inconceivable. Finally her anger at the unfairness of it all surfaced, and she aimed it at the only target she knew.

"I hate the duke."

"Shhh, shhh," whispered Emile. "You must not hate him. There is not room in our hearts for hate, only forgiveness. Do not feel you have betrayed me."

It seemed all he had strength to say. He lay back his head and closed his eyes. His breathing was raspy. Amanda sat beside him, holding his hand, watching the wan face she had once loved. It seemed so long ago.

But even now the wisdom of his words was beginning to sink in. Could it be possible that he was right? Was she hanging on to an incident from the past that symbolized something she could never have? Had she not taken perverse pleasure in it for the very reason that it was opposed to everything about her life that was ordered?

She watched Emile, studied his face, looked at the thin hands that had once caressed her body. Could they bring that back? Something had come between them now, and as her heart lurched again in anguish and anger, she realized that perhaps Emile was right. They could not go back.

Perhaps they never could have lived out the idyllic life she spoke of. Perhaps it would remain a dream, never to be reality. She shook her head to herself, hating the thoughts Emile himself was making her face, loving him for his wisdom as well as for what he had once been to her.

She had no more words, only emotions, and the realization that things had happened too fast. How could Emile at such a young age see things as she could not? Of course, he'd had many days to do nothing but think. Perhaps his contemplation had gained him wisdom that she had not had time to attain. And he insisted that he was dying.

New determination found its way into her grieving heart. At least she could fight that notion. She leaned close and whispered to him.

"I must not tire you. I must let you rest."

She patted his hands, and he opened his eyes to gaze at her. A faint smile flitted over his tired face, and his eyes seemed to drink in the vision of her.

"Rest now," she said, drawing away. "I will come back tomorrow. You will be better then, won't you? And we can talk of other things. I will read to you."

He said nothing, only watched her in his peaceful gaze until a fit of coughing set on. She waited until it passed and he leaned his head against the back of his chair. She stood beside him and brushed back his hair, soothing his brow with her palm.

"An angel," he whispered, his eyes still closed. Gradually his breathing evened, and he seemed to relax. She backed softly out of the room and closed the door.

The corridor was quiet as she made her way back the way she had come. Only a few nurses seemed to float along, taking steaming mugs of herbal concoctions to their patients, for the doctors who practiced here believed in naturopathic healing.

She met Nurse Elizabeth near the lobby. The nurse stopped and waited for her.

"How was your visit?"

"It was a good visit," said Amanda, melancholy in her voice in spite of her attempt to sound hopeful.

The subject of the visit was none of the nurse's concern, but Emile's condition was. "He coughed some, but I'm afraid he believes he shan't recover."

She entreated the nurse with her look, and Elizabeth nodded gravely. "Come with me," she said.

She led Amanda to the roomy, comfortable sitting room and guided her toward a pair of cushioned rattan chairs in a grouping around a small table with a fringed lamp. They sat down, and Elizabeth assessed Amanda.

"His condition is not good," the nurse said. "It is at times like this when the patient's own will has much to do with how the illness goes."

Again the lurch in Amanda's chest, for she knew what was coming. "He thinks he will die."

The nurse nodded. "I see." She sighed as if she had seen this many times before. Sometimes all the sympathy in the world did not change things. "He must want to live."

Amanda felt herself on the brink of tears again. "I don't know why he feels so fatalistic. He seemed well-liked by his friends. I've known him so briefly I only know what he told me. But he was devoted to his students. I thought he could have been happy. Oh, dear," and she broke off into a round of sobs. When she had gotten most of them out, she snuffled into her handkerchief.

"I thought he was in love with me. That's why I felt so guilty . . ." She wandered off into personal problems the nurse knew nothing of.

But the nurse was more perceptive than Amanda realized.

"Ahh," said Elizabeth. "A star-crossed love affair."

She said it matter-of-factly, without judgment. Then, "I'm sorry, it's none of my business."

Amanda took a deep breath and sighed. "I don't know what to think anymore." She shook her head. "But I can't let him die."

"My dear," said the nurse with compassion. "It is out of your hands now. I certainly hope he pulls through this crisis period. But I'm sure you have given him all the encouragement you can. If he dies, it will not be your fault."

Amanda bit her lips and looked at the nurse with anguish. If only that were true.

They got up. "I do not advise you try to see him again until tomorrow. We will know then whether . . ."

Amanda nodded and walked with the nurse to where the carpet gave onto the polished wood floor, and then after saying she would come again in the morning, she crossed the lobby.

Outside the sun blinded her. She stood for a few moments on the wide verandah, blinking against its brightness. She approached the steps and grasped the railing, walking down slowly. Then she crossed the drive and stepped onto the green lawn that stretched down toward the stream beyond. Around her the mountains rose to lofty peaks.

She walked forward without feeling, sensing only the sharp contrasts of blue sky, soft, green turf and jagged rocks in the distance. She had almost forgotten the duke until she was quite a way from the buildings of the sanatorium and approaching a stone bench situated near some trees. She was not the only walker on the grounds. Many of the inmates and their visitors took the air, but there was so much space between them that Amanda felt she was alone with nature, a nature that did not have the power to soothe on this day.

She had been sitting on the bench for some time when the sound of a footstep came from behind. She looked up with a start to see Edward standing there. His hand was against the bark of an elm, and he leaned his weight on one leg as he watched her, his expression neutral. She blinked at him, her lips slightly parted, saying nothing.

Finally, he moved. He lowered the hand and took a step nearer, but did not sit down beside her. Then he turned to face the view she had been looking at.

"Well?" he said. "How is the patient?"

"He's not well," Amanda said in what sounded like a squeaky voice.

"I'm sorry to hear that. His stay at the sanatorium has done no good?"

She shrugged. "His condition was worse to begin with than anyone realized, I suppose, except for the doctor. But no one had the money to send him until I borrowed the funds from you."

Sunderland frowned. "Has he no family?"

She shook her head. "Only a sister, and she hasn't a great deal of money in any case. I don't even know if she's been informed he's here."

"That's too bad."

His words sounded sincere, but Amanda was aware of a certain distance he was keeping. Absorbed in her own emotions, she only now stole a look at Edward, observed his face, saw the tightness of the skin over his cheeks, the set to his mouth.

His look drew her out of herself, and she swallowed. How awkward this was for him. She felt a flush creep under her skin and had to look away. He was trying not

to show his jealousy. And yet he had to suffer the humiliation of bringing his fiancée here to see her former
lover. Suddenly Amanda felt a little of his own anguish,
and her heart could not help but go out to him.

It wasn't possible to love two men at once, and she
knew she did not. She had resented the duke, but he
had a power over her that was swinging her around to
see his good qualities. She felt ashamed of making him
suffer. This was all her problem; she hadn't meant to
bring him into it.

"Oh, Edward, I'm sorry," she said, unable to keep silent any longer. She buried her face in her hands as she
said it.

Instantly he was on the bench beside her. He put an
arm around her shoulders and pulled her toward his
chest. Words stopped in his throat, and he simply held
her. She did not so much cry, as gulp breaths and grasp
his shoulder with one hand, burying her head against
his neck.

"It's not your fault," he said at last, grasping the tur-
moil inside her. "Things have a way of happening."

She was more in control now and sat straighter. "You
mean the way they did between us."

"Perhaps," he said. "Though I meant that to happen."

She shook her head, the fight gone out of her. "But
why?"

He gazed at her tear-stained face, his fingers drifting
through disheveled hair.

"I ask myself that," he said, unable to cover the emotion in his own voice.

She faced him, beseeching him to understand when
she knew she had no right to expect it.

"Emile may not live," she said.

Edward's jaw tightened. Then he said, "I hope it doesn't come to that."

She shook her head, pressing her lips together. "He seems to think it is meant to be this way. He's so philosophical. I mean, he has so much to live for, but he seems to have given up." She had to stop to take a breath. "He knows about us, about you, I mean. He forgave me."

She reddened, but she knew that the words were better spoken aloud.

An ironic smile touched Edward's lips. "That was generous of him."

She flinched at his callous teasing. "How would you know?"

"I'm sorry," he said sincerely. "I honestly don't want the poor man to die."

His hand came down on hers. "I want to win you, Amanda. If this Emile of yours lives, I'll never let you go back to him, do you understand that? Not by force, but by the bonds forged of your own choosing."

He reached for her, turning her whole body toward his, vibrating now with his passion.

"I want you for my own," he said in that resonant, commanding tone he could assume. "If he dies, I won't have you grieving your life away. Rather, I hope he lives, so that you can see for yourself that you were meant for me. I want you to choose between us, Amanda."

She stifled her confused grief. How dare he talk so harshly at a moment like this? In defense, she lashed out at him.

"He won't die." It seemed the only argument she could summon.

"I hope not," said Edward, releasing her. Then he stood up and held out a hand to help her up.

"Come, let us go back. Will you visit the patient anymore today?"

"No, he needs to rest. I will come tomorrow. That is," she said with a reluctant glance, "if I may have a carriage."

"I might as well bring you myself," he said. "I wouldn't want you out in the country unescorted. Unless you'd prefer to bring your aunt, in which case I can rent a couple of footmen to accompany you."

"I really don't care," she said and then was sorry she was so snappish.

In spite of her own upset, she saw what Edward was trying to hide. His jealousy was natural, but his certainty was tinged with just the shadow of doubt that he might not be the winner, that his rival might still have her heart.

Amanda walked through the grass in a tumble of emotions, empathy for Edward, a growing desire to turn to him for support, worry for Emile, self-doubt, and shame. And then it all went back again to antagonism for this man she had trapped herself into becoming engaged to. This man who wanted to make her a duchess.

Edward left her to her own thoughts as they returned to the drive in front of the sanatorium. He went off to have their carriage brought round. When it came, he helped Amanda into the seat, then took the reins from the groom. As shadows lengthened in the mountain valley, they traveled back down the road they had come.

When they passed the spot by the rocky hideaway where they had picnicked, Amanda kept her face averted. She didn't want to be reminded of the passion she shared with the man beside her. And yet, as they silently drove down the switchbacks that lowered them to the oceanfront of Monte Carlo, she again perceived the rapport she was beginning to know with Edward Pemberton, Duke of Sunderland. Perhaps Emile was right, she thought as they watched the sunset cast glitter and shadows over the water. It was fated to be this way.

She rued her inability to handle men. Everything had gone wrong with every man she'd known since she came out. Wrong about Francis, doomed with Emile and trapped by Sunderland. She was nothing more than food in the lion's den.

They returned to the hotel in time to retire to their rooms and dress for dinner. By the time Aunt Zoe found her, Amanda had bathed and changed into a gown of brocade and lace for dinner. Her hair was done up in ringlets, wound with pearls, a velvet ribbon and cameo at her throat.

"Well, my dear," said Zoe, coming in from her long afternoon of adventures with her friend, "did you have a pleasant afternoon?"

"Hmmm," said Amanda, putting down the book of poetry she had been thumbing through. "I would not call it pleasant, Aunt. But it was revealing."

She had decided to tell Aunt Zoe the truth about why they had come here. This far away from the rules and regulations her mother had always forced her to live by, she felt freer to be honest. Also, events were at a crisis. She might be called to Emile's bedside at any moment and didn't want to have to fabricate a reason to go.

"We went to a sanatorium in the mountains where the young scholar I met at Madame Fichet's lies in great peril. Edward, I mean, the duke, drove me. He knew all about this, and indeed it is the reason he brought us here. You may remember Sunderland lent the money for his treatment. We'd heard that Emile had grown worse."

She stopped. Zoe stood with her bonnet half-lowered from her head, staring at her niece. She looked startled, as if not quite grasping all of what Amanda had said.

Amanda smiled gently. She had spoken rather fast; she didn't mean to be confusing. "Sit down, Aunt Zoe, and I'll explain."

Her aunt sat, and for the next half hour Amanda repeated most of the truth about what had happened after she'd met Emile at the soirée, leaving out intimate romantic details of course, explaining how she'd confided it all to Sunderland. Her aunt's eyes grew rounder and rounder, her cheeks displaying pink and then a white pallor followed by pink again.

When Amanda was finished, she simply blinked, moistened her lips and tried to think of something to say.

"Good heavens," she finally managed. "You mean to say that your fiancé not only loaned you money, but brought you here to see this young man who lured you out of my house and across to that risqué Latin Quarter?"

"Yes, he did. He knows all about it."

"Well," said Zoe, her hand fluttering to her chest. "Then our duke is either more of a gentleman than I ever dreamed, or else he is a great fool."

Chapter 19

Though her aunt had some time adjusting herself to the news her niece gave her, Amanda felt a burden lift from her shoulders. Dinner would be strained in any case, but there was not the added problem of subterfuge. Even Sunderland looked relieved when she whispered to him that she had told Zoe everything.

When they reached the dining room, the maître d' had a table ready for them. They were seated at the end of the room near an open arcade that gave onto a balustraded terrace. The room glittered with women in low-cut gowns, jewels about their persons and handsome men in evening dress.

"I hope this view is satisfactory," said the duke after they were seated. "I thought a view of the water would be restful."

"Quite," said Zoe.

Amanda gazed out at the moonlit sea and the lights flickering from farther along the curved beachfront. A round moon, cleft by wispy clouds, shone down on the dark water, its rays a blanket of spun silver. Such a romantic night, and such a night as to tear at her heartstrings.

The wine steward brought the wine list, which Sunderland studied. After selecting a crisp Chablis, the duke indicated that the waiter might describe the specialties of the house. A quick discussion followed, and they settled on cold leek and potato soup, grilled red mullet with wine sauce and chopped shallots, watercress, and salade verte, all of which would be followed by cheeses, fruit and nuts.

The food matters out of the way, the three dinner companions were confronted with awkward silence until the wine was opened. Sunderland tasted it and passed his approval.

Amanda's gaze wandered from the romantic view on her right to the rest of the glittering assembly of diners at tables situated on her left. She began to realize that the women seated at the various tables with their escorts were among the most beautiful she had ever seen. She observed heads that came together in intimate conversations, and then here and there a gay, coy laugh would ripple from the jeweled throat of one of the lovely women.

When the wine was poured, Sunderland let his gaze follow that of Amanda, and he frowned.

"Well," she said, trying to break the silence. "This is quite a gay crowd."

"Yes," he said, clearing his throat. He lowered his voice but projected it so that Amanda could hear him. "I suggest you do not stare too closely at the women."

She lifted her brows and set her wineglass down. "I did not mean to stare."

"I'm sure you didn't," he continued. "A word of warning only, my dear. It would not be fitting for you to appear to acknowledge one of the ladies of the demimonde. Especially if any of them are with gentlemen with whom you have any acquaintance."

"Oh." Understanding came to her. "I see."

But rather than act nonchalant as she was supposed to, the knowledge that she was in the presence of some of the great courtesans of the demimonde who vied with each other in beauty, wit and charm only intrigued her. And she continued to inspect them out of the corner of her eye.

Their beauty did seem enhanced by artifice, which of course was forbidden to any woman of gentility. And yet she could not bring herself to feel self-righteous. For was she herself not guilty of the same sins they were? The difference was that they gave their love in exchange for riches, whereas Amanda had fallen from grace with one man who claimed to love her, and another who claimed to have a right to her favors.

She pulled in her wayward curiosity and tried to concentrate on the dishes placed before her.

"Shall we pay a visit to the casino after dinner?" said the duke, including Zoe in his invitation.

She looked up guiltily from her soup. Then she gave a little shrug. "I've already been," she reminded him.

Sunderland smiled. "And how did you do?"

She threw him a look of consternation. "Not well. I shall have to attempt to win back what I lost."

"Ah," said the duke. "Perhaps your luck will change."

"Perhaps," said Zoe, lifting her fan to flutter it before her face, which had grown warm.

The waiters removed bowls, spoons, and glasses, then refilled wineglasses, all with a smooth coordination of practiced elegance. They were halfway through the meat course when Amanda allowed herself another glance at the gay flirtations going on at nearby tables. A lovely dark-headed woman with a feather boa draped down her back gave a tinkling laugh and leaned to her right to greet a friend at the next table. Amanda nearly dropped her fork.

Sitting opposite the woman was none other than her erstwhile suitor, Francis Newton. Amanda tried to swallow, choked and coughed. Concerned, Zoe handed her niece a glass of water.

"Are you all right, my child?" said Zoe.

She tried to shake her head, her napkin in front of her mouth, her eyes wide. Sunderland watched, his look a mixture of concern and curiosity. The waiter appeared to inquire if there was anything he could do, but Sunderland waved him away.

When she managed to get her food down, Amanda took a gulp of water, wiped her lips and whispered, sitting very stiffly, "I saw someone I recognize."

"Hmmmm," said Sunderland. "That was what I was afraid of. Where is he sitting?"

She jerked her head without turning it. "There, with the blue-feather boa."

"Yes, I see the one you mean," said Sunderland. "It is as I said before. If he is with a demimonde, as I expect he is, you must not recognize him."

"That will be difficult," said Amanda in a more normal tone. "Since he was once my suitor."

Sunderland lifted his chin and frowned. Another suitor? Then he remembered the American Amanda had thought she once loved.

"You will say nothing unless he approaches us," he commanded in that possessive tone of his.

Amanda was half-amused that he was so concerned with protecting her. However, she hadn't the slightest desire to speak to Francis at the moment. She was in fact stunned that he was here.

They managed to complete the meal in great formality, but the time came when they would have to rise. Surely Francis would recognize her. She would just have to make the best of it. Fortunately, Sunderland was with them, so at least she would not have to suffer the humiliation of meeting Francis with no prospects for her own future. Indeed, it would seem to him that her future was most grandly assured.

The waiters held their chairs while the party rose. Sunderland offered Amanda his arm, and they proceeded to cross the room, eyes straight ahead. But just as she expected, she heard a great gasp of surprise as they started past Francis's table.

Lifting her chin higher and tightening her grip on Edward's elbow, she was prepared to continue until she heard the clink of crystal on china as Francis set his glass down suddenly and scrambled to his feet.

"My word, Amanda Whitney," came the once familiar voice.

She stopped, and Edward came to a halt beside her, covering the hand that was crooked in his elbow with his other hand and half turning so that she could respond.

She blinked, appeared to only just then recognize him, then smiled condescendingly.

"Why, Francis Newton, what a surprise to see you here." She fluttered her eyelashes. "I didn't know you were on the Continent."

He still seemed not to have gathered his wits about him as he came around the table, trampling on his companion's feather boa. The lady, evidently used to such meetings, kept her back to them, pulling the feather boa up over her naked shoulder once Francis's foot lifted from it.

"Why, I, that is . . ." His embarrassment at the situation he had so injudiciously placed himself in now became evident. He fumbled to a stop.

Every inch the lady when the situation called for it, Amanda ignored his loss of face.

"Francis, you will remember the Duke of Sunderland, whom I believe you met in New York," she said, adding, "my fiancé."

She then gave a very sweet smile as Sunderland inclined his head.

"Oh, why yes, of course," said Francis, recollecting. He finally regained control of himself. "Yes, yes, well, I had no idea. An engagement? May I congratulate you."

He extended his hand to the duke, who shook it.

Amanda went on airily. "It was just announced. Word would not have reached the States."

"Yes, I'm sorry," said Francis. "I'm rather behind in the news."

He blinked, seemed to become aware that he had not introduced his companion, knew he could not and knew that Amanda and the duke knew he could not. Fortunately it was Zoe who saved them.

She had been waylaid by a table of her friends, but after promising to meet them later at the casino, she now caught up to the group. Amanda introduced her to Francis, explaining that they had been staying at her house in Paris and that her mother was ill. The conversation distracted them all from the demimonde, who waited patiently at the table behind them.

"Well," said Sunderland. "We must not keep you from your dinner. I am taking these ladies to the casino. Since Amanda is chaperoned, there's no harm in it."

"No, of course," said Francis. "Well, please send my best to your mother. I hope she recovers soon."

"Thank you," said Amanda.

The party started to move on, and she expelled a sigh of relief. Again she felt a certain satisfaction that she had been able to rub her engagement into Francis's cocksure conceit. Not one word of apology or explanation. Not that she cared anymore. Enough had happened since. More than enough, she thought ruefully.

But she was determined not to punish herself unduly. While in his room at the mountain sanatorium Emile's life hung in the brink, she must pass the night away on the arm of the handsome Duke of Sunderland, bring him luck at the casino and hope he did not gamble too much.

They strolled the short distance to the casino, and when they entered the richly decorated gambling room, Amanda's eyes sparked with interest. If she thought the diners at the hotel looked elegant, this room fairly glittered with diamonds, rubies, sapphires and other priceless gems in stunning gold settings. The clatter of dice, the slap of cards and the click of the roulette wheel accompanied the din of dealers' calls and the murmurs of those who watched the intent games.

Zoe fanned herself as she looked around for the party of ladies she had said she would meet. At the same time her eyes inspected the various tables where she might decide to try her luck. Sunderland bent to whisper a few words in her ear, to which she nodded distractedly. Then he turned to Amanda and ushered her toward the caged window where he handed over a sheaf of money in exchange for several piles of small round counters. He placed them on a tray and then nodded in the direction of a table he had decided to join. He took a seat, and Amanda stood behind him, watching.

None of the players spoke, but chips moved; the dealer drew his stick along, called out numbers and spun the wheel. Then all waited with baited breath to see on which color and number the pointer would land. After a while, Amanda noted that Edward was not doing badly. He lost a few times, but had also managed to accumulate a larger pile of counters than when he started. She amused herself by watching the others at the table, their expressions stony when they lost, satisfied when they won.

At last, Edward had had enough and rose to cash in his counters.

"Perhaps you would like some refreshment?" he asked, signaling to a uniformed waiter who moved in the crowd.

"Champagne please," he said without waiting for Amanda's reply.

He moved her toward a small oval table next to a potted fern, and they sat. The waiter brought the champagne glasses, and then they each took a sip.

Amanda noticed that the room seemed to be buzzing with conversation. Soon heads began to turn in the direction of the grand staircase. Amanda caught the name on everyone's lips: "La Belle Otero."

The casino had no footman to stand at the top of the staircase to announce names, but there was no need; for when the leading demimonde in Monte Carlo appeared at the head of the stairs, she was the focus of all eyes.

Amanda saw that she was a dark young woman with the look of a gypsy, flamboyantly dressed in clinging green silk, which set off her voluptuous figure. And she was covered from head to foot in priceless jewels. Amanda leaned closer to Edward.

"Who is she?" she asked.

He muttered some words under his breath and then stood up, pulling Amanda with him.

"Come, we must get out of here."

"But we've only just gotten our champagne," she said.

"It doesn't matter," he said tartly. "We can have some more at the hotel. Come on."

He started in the direction of a side entrance, but Amanda was aware that the crowd beside them was parting. She almost felt as if the beautiful dark woman floated toward them on the warm sea wind. They didn't walk fast enough, because as Sunderland and Amanda reached the center aisle between the gambling tables, Otero arrived at the same spot. Her calm, dark eyes were fixed on him. Amanda's glance flitted up to his face, and she saw the flinch of his jaw. He stopped, having no choice but to stare at the ostentatiously arrayed courtesan.

She gave him a slow, seductive smile, her eyelashes half covering her mysterious dark eyes. Slowly a willowy arm came upward lifting a graceful hand.

"Edward," she said in a sensuous voice.

Sunderland straightened his shoulders, bent from the waist in a low bow. However he did not take the hand that was extended toward him.

"Mademoiselle Otero," he said with great formality.

Then he straightened, tucked an arm about Amanda's waist, averted his gaze from Otero and directed Amanda toward the exit. The room that had fallen to a hush now buzzed behind them as he hurried her out.

"Do you know her?" asked Amanda as soon as they

were through the velvet drapes and in the plush, carpeted corridor.

"I knew her," said Sunderland gruffly. "That was a long time ago."

"Oh," said Amanda, blushing.

Obviously, the woman had at one time been his mistress and had attempted to reacquaint herself with him. She knew that he had hurried her away in embarrassment.

They came out in the lobby and went down the stairs to the sidewalk in front. At last Sunderland slowed his pace.

"We forgot Aunt Zoe," she said, just now remembering.

"Don't worry about her. She'll come back with her friends," he said. "I gave her to understand that I might want a little time alone with you."

"And she agreed?"

"Of course. We are engaged, you know."

Amanda swallowed. Thinking of the brilliantly arrayed courtesan inside made her feel suddenly plain. She took Edward's sudden annoyance to mean that he was now sorry that they were engaged. As they walked toward the hotel, she began to reflect on all the beautiful women here, and how their use of artifice combined with expensive clothing and jewelry made them outshine their more modest sisters.

"Oh, why should I care," she murmured to herself.

Sunderland was not conversant as they took a path that led to a terrace above the water. His mood was brooding, and she opened her mouth to speak, then thought better of it.

They strolled silently, and Amanda could think of nothing to say. She felt she had become an enormous burden on him, but it was too late to extricate herself now. Perhaps the least she could do would be to make herself scarce and allow him to spend the rest of his evening as he pleased. Perhaps he would seek out La Belle Otero.

The instant she thought it, a pang of jealousy shot through her. Yet she fought it. If he preferred to seek the more glamorous company of the beautiful courtesan, she was powerless to stop him. She ought to let him go. After all, he was being generous in letting her visit Emile. Of course, the situation was different, and even Amanda was smart enough to see that. Emile was in no condition to try to claim her as a lover. Were he so, she suddenly realized Edward would not be so generous.

As if sensing her thoughts, Sunderland stopped at the corner of the balcony and raised his head to look out at the glittering sea.

"As soon as matters are resolved here, we must proceed to Elsenheim."

She gave a jerk of the chin. "If you're certain you want to carry out this mock engagement," she said.

Suddenly his manner changed. He turned to her and slid his hands around her waist, pulling her against his chest so that her head was thrown back and his face bent over hers.

"Of course I want it. Can you not see what I want? I thought I showed you adequately this afternoon, and before that when we sealed our engagement. Are you still so resistant to my advances, Amanda? Do you still mourn for the poor chap who lies in the sanatorium bed? What must I do to make you forget him?"

And with that his mouth came down on hers, causing her a pang of surprise, while at the same time awakening familiar feelings within her. His mouth claimed hers more harshly than usual, his grip on her so tight she found it hard to breathe. But as their breathing began to quicken, he relaxed his grip and held her so that his hands could roam the length of her as he traded harsh demands for more sensuous persuasion. His mouth searched for her throat and ear, his arms cradling her.

Unable to think, she could only respond to a need that seemed to become more powerful each time he did this to her. But still, she felt the traitor to herself.

"I can't," she murmured, her cheek against his temples. "I can't."

Surprisingly enough, he listened. And instead of pressing his desires on her, he cradled her head against his shoulder, holding her gently, comfortingly.

"You are mine, Amanda." His voice was persistent and confident, but gentle. "I want you to see that."

She knew she was his, but she also knew that he wanted her just because he couldn't have her completely. He was the kind of man who must possess everyone and everything around him. Find pleasure in her he might; but he did not really love her, and she did not expect him to.

As she leaned into the strong arms, she almost wished he did love her. Then she winced. That would just make matters worse, wouldn't it? With two men loving her, who would she choose? As it was, it was easier. She could not give her heart to the duke, for he would tire of her as soon as she did so. And then she would have lost everything.

Forcing her mind to stop its cogitations, she tried to lift her head.

"Perhaps you should see me to my room now," she said.

"If you wish."

They broke off their embrace, and he tucked her arm

under his. Then they strolled back to the hotel entrance, crossed the lobby and took the lift to her floor.

At the door to her suite, she nearly changed her mind. "What will you do now?" she asked, her eyes fixed on his ruffled shirtfront.

He shrugged. "Go to the casino, most likely. I am not ready to turn in. If you have changed your mind . . ."

She shook her head. "No, no. That's all right. I am very tired."

He held the door for her and then followed her into the sitting room. As she turned up the lamp, his eyes roamed about the room and then flicked to hers hopefully. She extended her hand.

"Good night, Edward," she said.

He lifted his lips in a smile and took her hand, bringing it to his mouth for a kiss.

"I like the sound of my name upon your lips. You must say it often."

Afraid to allow him to stay, afraid to let him go, she simply nodded. And as if he knew that now was not the time to press her, to say nothing of the possibility of being walked in on by her aunt, he bowed and turned to go.

Once out of her dress and into her dressing gown, she dismissed Delcia and then turned down all the lamps. She stepped out onto her balcony to commune with the night. A ripple of laughter rang up from below, and she glanced down to see the bejeweled figure of Otero moving across the terrace. For a moment Amanda felt a pang of fear. What if Edward followed her? But the next moment an older man with balding head sprang after the courtesan, caught her and laughed. She smiled up at him, and as he bent to kiss her, she slipped out of his grasp, leading him on a chase down the steps to the beach.

Amanda felt a sense of relief that it wasn't her own fiancé going after the courtesan when she herself had refused him. But she shook her head. Even she could see that she made no sense. But then matters of love were, as she was beginning to learn, not always sensible.

In the wee hours of the dawn, Amanda awoke, sensed a presence in her room and got up. An intense grief assailed her heart, and it was as if Emile were calling to her. She donned her dressing gown and stepped out to the terrace.

"Emile," she whispered.

A breeze touched her face, and she imagined that she heard him speak to her.

Be happy, the words came to her. Never in her life was she so certain that she was in touch with another being far away.

"Emile, don't go," she whispered, reaching out to the wind.

But then the spirit was gone. An overwhelming grief descended on her, and she gave a cry, sinking to the balcony floor.

When Zoe found her, Amanda was crumpled in a heap, tears staining her face. Terror penetrated Zoe's heart as she reached for Amanda.

"What is it?" she asked. "Are you all right?"

Amanda blubbered, but Zoe managed to get her back to bed.

"A bad dream," said Zoe, tucking her in again. But the tears on her niece's face were real, and she washed them away with a warm cloth.

Amanda made no attempt to explain, but lay heartbroken, holding her aunt's hand. Zoe fell asleep in the chair, and eventually Amanda rose and tiptoed out to the balcony again to watch the dawn.

When the sun was well up in the sky a knock was heard at the door. A uniformed hotel servant stood with a small tray upon which lay an envelope with Amanda's name upon it. She took the letter and closed the door.

Opening it up she found it was from Nurse Elizabeth, and it confirmed what Amanda already knew. Emile had died in the night, peacefully, in his bed.

When Zoe awoke, she found Amanda seated in a chair, staring at the sea, the crumpled note in her hand.

"Amanda, what is it?"

She handed her aunt the note, which Zoe read.

"It's the young man," she said. "The one you went to see?"

Amanda nodded.

Her lips pressed together, Zoe was afraid to say anything else, but left her niece there, fearing for her sanity. She summoned Delcia, who helped her dress and then sent a note to the duke, across the hall. When he came, Zoe met him at the door.

"Oh, dear," she said. "Someone has died. Amanda's out there. You'd better see what you can do. I fear she is taking it hard."

The duke's color faded, and his jaw tightened. He looked toward the inner bedroom off which Amanda would be sitting. But he turned his gaze on Zoe.

"I don't think I should see her just now. I shall wait until she asks for me."

And with that he was gone, leaving Zoe, mouth open, feeling at a loss as to what to do. She murmured to herself, paced across the sitting room and then sent for Delcia again. Breakfast, that was the thing. Amanda must eat and then come to her senses.

Chapter 20

Sunderland stayed away from Amanda that day, letting her mourn alone. Zoe drove with her to the sanatorium to see to the arrangements. Maurice was notified and asked to inform Emile's sister. A memorial service was planned.

Amanda moved through it all in a daze. They returned to Paris without Sunderland, who, after a talk with Zoe, went on to Elsenheim. Riding in their compartment back to Paris, Amanda felt as if she were in a different world.

Back at Zoe's house, Louisa had recovered and received her sister and daughter with great expectations, but when told of the events that had transpired, she took to her bed again, refusing to speak to Amanda, who, she decided, had determined to ruin both their lives.

Amanda sat in the small chapel in the Latin Quarter where the memorial service was held, listening to the words spoken as if from a great distance. When the service was over, she walked along with Maurice. Flowers rioted in gardens next to the little church, and spring was in full glory. They said little as they walked along the little streets, finally coming to the Seine. There

Maurice stopped and leaned on the stone railing overlooking the water.

Maurice sighed. "We must let him go, you know. He would not like us to mourn."

"Yes," said Amanda tonelessly. "It is all so strange. My life since I left New York seems not to belong to me, but to all the people who have touched it."

Maurice smiled sadly. "Perhaps now you might reclaim it."

"Odd, but that is what Emile told me he wanted me to do. He knew he was going to die. I don't know, Maurice. I don't know."

He paused. "Did you love him very much?"

She shook her head. "I don't know that either. Of course, I did in a special way, but love that lasts? I'll never know, will I?"

She had spent all her tears and now spoke out of a leaden heart, one that looked neither forward nor back. Maurice squeezed her hand comfortingly.

"It doesn't matter. What matters now is that you pick up your life and move on. He would want that, I know. You must love again."

She looked at Maurice. "Is that possible? It seems so wrong. I feel I should mourn for Emile."

"Why mourn? Is that not a waste of life? We don't know what happens to the spirit after death. Emile believed he would exist somewhere else. If that is true, then he will not benefit by your tears. Life is to be lived to the fullest. That is what he always believed."

She tried to take in his words. "Yes, I can try."

"He would expect no less of you."

"I am engaged to the Duke of Sunderland. But he does not love me. He only became engaged to me to save my reputation." She shook her head. "It is all so confusing."

"Then he must at least care for you if he would link his name to yours just to save your good name."

"Perhaps. I don't know why he did it. He might even marry me after all. He once told me he needs to marry a fortune."

Maurice chuckled. "And you have one to offer?"

"Unfortunately, I do. Oh, it is terrible, Maurice, never to know if someone cares for you or your money. At least with Emile I knew he cared for me."

"Hmmm. But you must forget about that now and go on. If Emile cared for you, then it means that you have qualities that a good man can care about. You might give this duke of yours a chance."

"Oh, I don't know, Maurice. How will I know if I can love again? Or if another can love me when there has been so much in the way?"

"All you need is time, *ma chérie*. Time is the great healer. You must have patience, and then you will see."

Amanda did not want to go to Elsenheim, nor did she want to remain in Paris, which would forever remind her of Emile. And the gossips in social circles were atwitter with the story of her abduction. So rather than face them all, she ordered Delcia to pack her trunks.

There was one piece of good news. Her father had returned to New York from a business trip to Chicago. When he belatedly received her letter explaining why she needed the sum of money, he cabled that he could now send the amount if she still needed it. She cabled him to send it to the Duke of Sunderland, from whom she had borrowed the sum to take care of the sick friend. She didn't bother with further explanations; she would think of something to say later in a letter. But at least Edward would be paid back now.

The thought occurred to her, of course, that she might go home to New York; but Louisa had decided to leave Europe behind, her daughter now safely engaged, and return to New York society, and Amanda could not imagine traveling back with her mother. It would be far too unpleasant.

She wrote to Emily and her friends, saying she would be staying at Elsenheim and perhaps some of them would come and visit her, and she hinted that she might be lonely in spite of being the guest of her fiancé. She couldn't tell them the truth in a letter, so she said only that she did not know the duke very well, but would try to keep herself busy learning about his estate.

And so in a matter of a week, Amanda found herself once again on English shores. She traveled with Delcia and Zoe to the little station at Woodhaven, near Elsenheim, and as the train pulled in, she became aware of a great deal of commotion outside. A band was playing, and a banner had been hung across the station.

"Dear me," she said, beginning to worry, "either there is a dignitary aboard, or we are going to get a rather large reception."

"The latter, I would suppose," said Zoe uncomfortably. "The duke said something about a welcoming committee."

Amanda rounded on her aunt. "You said nothing to me."

"Well, my dear. I did not want you traveling all this distance in a despondent mood. Besides, it is only courtesy. Many of the people met you when you were here before. They are simply honoring you now that you are the future duchess."

There was no time for protest. The compartment door opened, and she stepped off the train. Her eyes flew at once to Edward, who stood some distance away with a short, squat man she remembered as the mayor. Edward broke off mid-sentence and came toward her. The crowd parted between them, and she found herself the center of attention.

He bowed and then took her arm, and as he escorted her back to where the mayor stood, the crowd began to cheer. She tried to smile, and then she was planted before the mayor, who handed her a huge bouquet of roses.

"Welcome to Woodhaven, Miss Whitney," said the mayor. "In anticipation of your arrival, I have prepared a few words, if you will follow me across the square to the steps of town hall. The people want to welcome you."

"Of course," she said.

He turned, Edward urged her forward, and they found themselves at the front of a procession. Though it was only across the road, the wind had picked up, and as she took her place on the steps facing the crowd, she felt the wind tug at her bonnet.

"Ladies and gentlemen of Woodhaven," began the mayor. "We have assembled here to congratulate the Duke of Sunderland on his engagement to Miss Amanda Whitney and to give them our best wishes for their future."

The faces turned up toward them, and Amanda read the excitement in the townspeople's eyes. She wished she might close her own eyes. This was not what she'd bargained for. The mayor droned on, the wind pulled harder, and the bouquet began to get heavier.

Through it all, Sunderland stood erect, hardly noticing her, and by the time the ceremony came to a close and the people applauded while an open carriage was brought for them, she wished she could die. She had thought this pseudo-engagement was meant to save her own reputation. Why was Edward getting everyone's hopes up when he knew those hopes would be dashed come six months' time?

To her astonishment, the team was unharnessed from the carriage, and the townsmen took up the harness and began to pull them.

"My word," she said, feeling awkward seated in the heavy carriage which must create a strain on the men's backs.

"They're showing their respect," said Edward to her. "It is a tradition."

She started to complain that it was not democratic, then held her tongue. Instead she asked, "Do they intend to pull us all the way?"

"Of course."

Now more townspeople gathered to cheer. Children ran along beside the carriage, shouting and waving. Laborers stopped their work to gawk.

"Smile at them and wave, dear," said Edward, who did the same.

They left town soon enough, but some of the crowd clung, especially the children, who found it a great game to race ahead and wait for them. Finding the smiling and waving fatiguing, and the great bouquet making her want to sneeze, she sagged back a bit until they rounded a bend and the house came into view.

"Was your journey satisfactory?" asked Sunderland to fill the space.

"Yes, quite," she said.

She threw an embarrassed glance toward him. She had hoped their first moments together might be in private, so that they could at least clear the air; but instead they had been thrown into this public reunion, and she felt awkward.

They pulled into the first court, and then as the men dragged the carriage into the second court, she drew in a breath. Of course, she ought to have expected it, but lined up in their best uniforms and standing in a semi-circle on the steps were the servants. More tenants lined the drive below.

"Just a few more speeches, my dear," said Sunderland. "The servants will want to avow their service for as long as you are here."

Instantly the flares went up in Amanda's mind. A trap. He had done this on purpose and intended to embarrass her. Anger shot through her, but she didn't let it show. It wasn't the servants' or tenants' fault. She must get through the rituals somehow.

The townsmen who had pulled the carriage came to a halt and held the doors for them so they could step down. Sunderland took her elbow and escorted her up the steps. As they moved, the crisply uniformed members of the household curtsied and bowed until they came to the top step where the housekeeper, Mrs. Gunderson, and the butler, Jeds, waited.

Jeds stepped forward. "Greetings," he said, in his formal monotone. "I speak for the entire staff in saying that we wish to make your stay at Elsenheim as enjoyable as possible. We place ourselves at your service in the hopes that the arrangement becomes a long and fruitful one."

He stepped back, and Mrs. Gunderson moved forward a step, her little speech likewise prepared.

"May I add my personal congratulations, miss," she said in a prim manner. "And hope that you find the staff at Elsenheim, which has served the family, together with visiting royalty, for two hundred years, acceptable."

A reminder, thought Amanda, of their longevity. She was suddenly made more aware than before of the English caste system. Everyone had their degrees, even the servants, and she nodded formally, assuming what she hoped was the proper amount of superiority.

The welcomes were not over, as she discovered when they entered the great hall. A red carpet had been rolled across it, and two footmen stood at the entrance to the grand salon. Of course, the family members themselves would be wanting to see her. So she took a deep breath, and gladly relinquished the bouquet to the housekeeper.

"I can have these put in a vase for you," said Mrs. Gunderson. "When you are ready, I will show you the vases you would want to choose from and the worktable in the greenhouse where you will want to make your own flower arrangements. But for now, you will have too many other duties, one would assume."

Now was the time to assert her command. Amanda, having lived with servants in her own family, only too well realized that not to assert authority would show them she was weak and incapable of running such a household. That she did not actually intend to run it did not matter at the moment.

"Thank you, Mrs. Gunderson. I plan to make many flower arrangements and would kindly appreciate your showing me the greenhouse. I would appreciate it if you would take care of these for me this time. Please shorten the stems and send me a single bud in a vase to my room."

The housekeeper nodded. If Amanda hadn't been watching for it, she might have missed the look of judgment that flitted across the woman's face. She dipped in a small curtsy without losing any of her upright bearing and took the bouquet away to do with it as she was told.

Amanda allowed Sunderland to escort her into the salon. She remembered her first visit to this awesome room. As before, the family was grouped at the far end around the massive marble fireplace, the furniture opening out to the room where the couple approached. All stood, except the dowager duchess.

Lady Norah came forward and extended her hands. "My dear Amanda. How lovely to have you back. And may I be the first to offer my congratulations."

Amanda warmed at her welcome. Evidently these people had heard nothing of Edward's chase through the slums of Paris, and of course he would not enlighten them.

"Thank you, Lady Norah, I am glad to be here."

"Please call me Norah. I think now that we are almost related, we can drop the formalities."

"Well, come here, child," said the dowager duchess, evidently not liking to be kept waiting. She held up the ear trumpet.

Amanda moved forward. "How nice to see you, madam. I am very pleased to be here," she spoke loudly into the trumpet.

Edward handed her into a wing chair next to his grandmother, who inspected her.

"Now that you have agreed to marry my grandson, I

assume you have decided to shoulder the burden of seeing that Elsenheim upholds its reputation and prestige."

Surprised that the older woman was being so blunt, Amanda could only nod and say, "I will do my best, madam."

"Hmph. I certainly hope so. It has been my dream to see the place restored to former glories, but of course that will not be your first duty."

"I understand." She thought she knew what the dowager duchess was about to say and prepared herself for the shock of it.

"Your first duty," the woman continued, for all to hear, "but not until after you are married, of course, will be to have a child, and it must be a son."

If it weren't for the strain of the conversation, Amanda would have found it amusing that the grand lady thought she could command even the sex of the unborn child they were discussing.

"If we should . . . that is, I would, of course, hope for a son," she managed to shout.

Just then she caught Edward's eye out of the corner of her own and thought, to her consternation, that he was enjoying her discomfort, thus fueling her suppressed anger at him.

The other family members moved toward her one by one to give their congratulations and welcome until at last the men formed a grouping around Sunderland while the ladies remained with Amanda. Servants appeared with tea. While Amanda was indeed hungry and thirsty, she resented being trapped with the family when what she really wanted to do was take off her shoes and relax. But a future duchess did not have such choices, as she was beginning to be made aware.

"How was your stay in Paris?" asked Norah.

"Very pleasant," Amanda said. *I snuck out of my aunt's town house, was abducted by a thief, and made love to a Bohemian. How would that sound in this august company?*

"And Monte Carlo?" said Lady Isabel. "Such a gay place."

"Yes," said Amanda, sipping her tea.

She had to fight the sudden grief that welled up at the mention of that place, and again resentment flared. Instead of going off by herself and mourning for a young man she had known briefly, but intimately, as might be his due, she was forced to enact this charade.

A few more moments of conversation passed until she thought she could bear it no longer.

"I am very tired," she said suddenly to anyone who would listen.

Norah was the quickest to respond. She took Amanda's cup and saucer and handed it to the maid who was serving.

"Of course. I'll show you to your room. You'll want to rest before dinner. Tonight after dinner is soon enough to share your wedding plans with us. And tomorrow we can answer any questions you might have about redecorating Elsenheim."

A dull throbbing asserted itself in Amanda's head. She was barely engaged to a man she didn't even plan to marry when suddenly she was thrust into the role of interior decorator. The ludicrousness of the situation would have made her laugh if she weren't so angry with Edward, whose fault she was certain it was.

"Thank you."

She did manage to remember to turn and dip in a little curtsy to the dowager duchess before moving away with Norah, who proved to be more sensitive to her feelings than she had expected.

"I know how you feel," intimated Norah. "All the pomp and circumstance. Americans are never used to it. All expected of nobility over here. I do hope you become used to it. The people actually have good hearts, you know. They love us in their own way. And Grandmother has her eccentricities, but then she is allowed them, due to her age and position."

"Of course," said Amanda. "I'm sure I'll be up to it after a little rest."

They climbed the grand staircase and proceeded along the main corridor until they came to the turn that led to the family wing. The halls seemed longer and draftier than she remembered, and she gave a little shiver.

At the carved and gilded door to the suite that would be hers, Norah reached for the handle and pushed it inward. It was a large room with good Louis XIV furniture, damask hangings and faded carpet. An inner door led to the boudoir where Delcia was already unpacking.

Amanda marched forward and sighed. Life seemed to be never-ending unpacking. She turned to thank the duke's sister.

"Thank you for your kindness. I will see you at dinner?"

Norah smiled and squeezed her hand, holding it for a moment. Her eyes were searching. She lowered her voice so that the maid would not overhear them.

"My brother intimated to me that this engagement is somewhat, er, you might say, fragile. He did not explain. Whatever the circumstances are, I hope I might add my influence for a happy engagement and a welcome marriage."

She paused, cocked her head, seeming to try to put forth the right words.

"Edward can be, well, difficult, demanding, you might say. He was raised to the title, you know. But he really has a very good heart. I hope you can see that." Her lips quivered with the hint of a smile. "He has had his rather wild side, but I always suspected marriage would settle him."

Amanda felt moved by Norah's sincerity and felt all the more guilty. Still, she fought the softening that threatened to dismantle her anger, for she was quite prepared for a confrontation with Edward. The sooner the better.

Another thought occurred to her. "The boy, Jean Henri. Is he here?"

Norah smiled. "Yes. Edward told me something of what happened. Quite amazing. The lad was put to work in the stables. He has quite a knack with horseflesh. And he's picking up English fairly quickly. He's a bright child."

"Oh, I'm so glad. I didn't know . . ."

Norah laughed. "How a city urchin might fit in here. Well, he is a bit shy. And he wouldn't dare let you catch him staring. He's quite taken with the surroundings. I'm pleased Edward thought to bring him here."

"Well," said Amanda with a trace of a grin. "He helped save my life."

"Yes. We haven't mentioned that to Grandmother, of course."

"Then I take it Edward told you the whole story."

"Well, enough of it for us to gather it was rather exciting. But Isabel and I know what not to talk about among acquaintances. Whatever misfortunes you ran across in Paris, your secret will be safe with us."

Again she appreciated Norah's genuine feeling. She knew how to keep up appearances without seeming snobbish. Yet she wouldn't press for personal details that Amanda didn't want to discuss.

A bath had been run for Amanda in one of the two bathrooms the palace possessed, and as she went along the corridor with Delcia in her wake, she commented to the side.

"I must rate. On our last visit I wasn't allowed in here."

Delcia could not resist a conspiratorial giggle. "Perhaps you timed it right. The others had a chance for their baths before you arrived. Only the duke and yourself must bathe for dinner."

"No doubt you are correct."

She pushed open the oaken door and stepped into the marble-tiled bathroom. Only two there might be, but at least this one had been done with grandiose taste as well as convenience. A long tub sat encased in mahogany in the middle of the room, which curved in a bay on the other side. A ledge beneath a small, high window displayed large porcelain vases and Greek statuary. Brass fixtures regulated the water temperature.

A marble sink was likewise encased in a mahogany stand with a marble countertop for soap and creams. Thick, snowy towels were folded over ebony racks, and a private partition separated the bath from the commode. The walls were wood-paneled halfway up and papered with a green and gold floral pattern up to the moulding. The plasterwork ceiling echoed the floral print with wreaths of foliage and flowers.

Steam rose from the hot bath, and Amanda handed Delcia her dressing gown and stepped in.

"Ahh," she said, sliding down into the porcelain tub. "This is more comfortable than that awful copper thing they brought to my room last time."

"No doubt, miss." Delcia handed her the soap and picked up sponge and long-handled back brush.

"Thank you, Delcia. You may leave me here. I think I'll just lie here and soak for a bit."

"As you wish, miss. Are you sure you have everything you need?"

"Yes, thank you. Go ahead, you'll be wanting to join the rest of the staff for your own dinner before we have ours."

"Thank you, miss, I'll do that. I'm just beginning to find my way around this big place again. I swear it's a mile to the servants' hall."

Amanda was left mercifully alone. So she thought. She leaned her head back on the edge of the tub, tendrils from her chignon trailing in the water at her shoulders. She had just achieved a relaxed state, with warmth seeping into her limbs, when she heard the sound of a latch, followed by a draft of air. Thinking that Delcia had returned, she turned her head. But it wasn't the door to the corridor that opened.

Turning to glance behind her, she gasped. Sunderland stood on the tiles in bare feet, his dressing gown knotted at his waist.

"Well," he said, looking surprised, but not embarrassed. "I see the bathroom is occupied. That door wasn't locked. Sorry if I intruded."

She sat up, sloshing water over the side of the tub, and reached frantically for her towel. But in two steps, he was there, picked it up and handed it to her.

"Oh," was all she could say as she tried to stand up and wrap the towel all around her. But she slipped and had to sit down on the edge of the casing, which was wide enough to provide a seat. The towel dragged half into the water behind her.

Edward laughed, stepped casually to the outer door and locked it, then sat down beside her, picking up another towel to help her dry herself. But she swiveled around, putting her feet onto the thick mat beside the tub.

"What are you doing?" she asked indignantly.

"I thought I'd assist you," he said with a devilish sound to his voice. "Your towel is soaking wet."

She tried to edge away. "This is hardly decent," she said, aghast at his behavior. "I'm not dressed."

"So I see." His meaning was all too apparent, and it made her cheeks flame.

"Don't you think it improper to be caught in the bathroom with a woman who is not your wife when both of us are in a state of undress?"

He lifted a brow, the invitation in his eyes not in the least masked.

"My dear, if I am not wrong, we have been in such a state before, or near to. Though I find the simplicity of the towel even more appealing than layers of clothing and petticoats between us."

"Edward," she snapped.

He smiled, pulled her nearer. "My, how I like the sound of my name on your lips."

"Edward." This time it was more pleading. "What do you think you are doing?"

His hands slid across her still-damp shoulders. "I think, my dear, I am going to make love to you."

But her question of protest was cut off by his mouth

coming down onto hers as he grasped her and pulled her harder against him. She gave a gasp when his mouth lifted, for he was making no attempt at subtlety. He, too, had been dressed for the bath, which meant there was nothing under the dressing gown he wore. And the physical expression of his desire was evident to say the least.

When he moved the silk of his robe aside and she felt him between her thighs, her heart leapt in spite of herself. His hands took control of the towel, and he began to rub her dry, the motions as much caresses as strokes to rid her body of the remaining soapy water.

"Hmmm," he said, his mouth busy kissing her temples and hair. "I like you this way."

Words of protest tangled within her. All she could do was stare at the bare chest before her as his own robe parted. Her hands were somehow on his chest, splayed across male nipples and muscular pectorals, her mouth open, gasping for breath.

"How can we do this . . . ?" she asked, more of herself than of him.

She was angry with him, wasn't she? She hated him, didn't she? But when he was with her like this, she seemed unable to remember the commanding side of him that she resented. Why did he have the power to dominate her life in this as well as in every other way? Rationale fleeing, her body began to respond to the fire he was lighting.

The towel having done its work, he cast it aside. Down came his robe, and he stood next to her, naked masculine prowess making her breath quicken. How he made her want him, regardless of her reluctance. Her hands reached out to touch his steam-moistened skin, his lips parted, her tongue moved to taste of his. Bliss seemed imminent, and as he lowered his mouth to taste of her nipples, all resistance was cast aside.

Arms and legs entangled, tongues tasted. The need for him seemed deeper this time, a release from the pent-up emotions she'd been living with. In the dim recesses of her mind she realized that there was a great rightness about what he was doing, for if nothing else, he was showing her what a woman she had become, how she was meant to love. Hadn't that been what her earlier experimentation had been about? Was that not why he did not hold her earlier affair with Emile against her?

His urgency knew no bounds, and with the bathroom door fastened, he did not fear someone walking in on them. The setting titillated him, and he rejected the idea of moving to the bedroom. How much more exciting to take her here, now, in the heat of passion, for his body read from her half-closed eyes, her quick breathing, her trembling, that she was caught up in the release of her passions.

"Amanda, you drive me mad," he murmured, lowering her to the soft mat beside the tub and kneeling over her. Then he quickly entered her as she wrapped her legs around him. He couldn't get enough of her, breasts, thighs, mouth as his own body began moving, moving against her.

"This is how it should be," he said, breathless with effort. "With me," he emphasized with a thrust, "with no one else."

Her mind numb with feeling, her body used to the tight friction between them, she could only claw, moan, thrill at the undeniable effect he created. Madness, yes, that was it. Though whether it was the act or the man that caused it, she was not yet sure. But as he took her, she gave and gave of herself, hardly aware of the words, "yes, yes, yes," that she uttered in his ear, driving him to further heights until he could stand it no longer.

The one precaution that neither of them took was to muffle their cries enough not to carry through the thick oaken door.

As Jeds happened to pass by, his ear picked up the sounds within, but being the superlative butler he was, he continued on his way. Then seeing Lady Isabel approaching in dressing gown and slippers, he stopped, forming a barrier between her ladyship and the bathroom door.

"Hello, Jeds," said Lady Isabel. "Is the bathroom free?"

"I'm afraid not, madam. His Grace is busy within."

She cocked her head, peering past his shoulder as if to assess how long the room would be occupied. He waited implacably until she turned around and went back to her room. Then he proceeded with dignity down the hall.

Chapter 21

Their passion sated, Edward held her and kissed her as her breathing returned to normal.

"The mat is narrow and the tiles are cold, my dear," he finally said, raising himself so he could reach their dressing gowns.

He placed an arm around her shoulders and lifted her up, handing her dressing gown to her. Then he threw his around his shoulders and stood up, offering her a hand.

"Back into the bathtub with you," he said. "I believe you were in the process of rinsing. Ah, the miracles of modern plumbing, of which this place needs more."

And he pulled the chain that was attached to the drain plug so that the soapy water could drain out. Then he turned the handle to allow fresh warm water to fill the tub.

Amanda had difficulty looking him in the face, but stepped into the warm water. He took the dressing gown from her, so that she slid down. But he did not leave her to bathe alone. Instead, he seated himself on the edge of the tub behind her and picked up the sponge to wash her himself. His naked arm slid into the water, and he kissed her temple, murmuring his pleasure.

"There can be many such baths, my dear."

"Oh?" her voice was shaky, uncertain.

She daren't admit to him that she'd enjoyed it as well. She daren't even admit to herself that if she could prolong the intimacy they shared and could block out all other thought and responsibility, she could dwell in this warm cocoon forever.

"Of course, when you are my duchess," he continued.

She winced. "Why do you persist in this game?" she asked.

"Isn't it obvious?" he replied, stroking her with long, sure strokes, gently avoiding the parts of her body that he knew must be tender at the moment. "We were made for each other."

"How do you know that?" she said.

"You must trust me."

She bit her lips together. Then she said, "I'm not sure I can."

"Why do you say that?"

She swallowed. "You told me yourself that you did not plan to marry for love, that you had a mistress."

"Ahh, just as you have had a lover. What is so wrong about that? It is the present and the future that count. I have told you, I intend to make you forget your lover. He is dust now, I am sorry for that. Even had he lived I would have taken you away from him, my dear Amanda, such are my feelings for you."

She ducked her chin to the water. "And you," she felt brave enough to say. "Will you forget your mistress?"

He chuckled. "When I am with you, I forget everything."

And when you are not with me?" she said, the defiance returning to her voice.

His laugh was louder now. "Can it possibly be that you actually care enough now to want me to forget her?"

He was baiting her, and he knew it. His sense of honor and sportsmanship demanded that he put her through the same hoops she had put him through if that was possible. Who was the fox and who was the hound now?

She lifted her head, her sense returning. "I can't marry you, Edward, and you know it."

"Why ever not?"

Their voices were louder now, but neither seemed to consider the fact that they might be heard on the other side of the door by those who still wanted to use the room for themselves.

"You think you own everyone around you. I am nothing more to you than an heiress who will add bathrooms to your palace."

He gripped her shoulders with his strong hands, giving her a light shake. "You silly fool, you know that's not true. I just proved it to you."

"You proved only that you can woo me. I've no doubt you've made love to many women, possibly some of them right here."

That made him angry. "What I have done before this moment is of no account and certainly no business of yours."

"It is my business," she said, suddenly sloshing about and coming to a stand. She jerked a towel upward and around her. "If I'm to marry you, everything about you is my business."

He opened his mouth to argue and then paused. Instead, his lips formed into a sly grin.

"Yes," he said with cunning. "When you marry me, everything about me will become your business. Then you will deserve all the answers you want."

Seeing the trap into which she had gotten herself, she simply expelled a breath, stepped out of the tub, rubbed herself quickly dry, turned her back to him and donned her dressing gown. Then without looking back she stepped to the door, fumbled with the lock and opened it, hardly caring if she moved too fast for the duke to be exposed to anyone who might be in the corridor.

Fortunately there was no one, but as she passed Lady Isabel's half-open bedroom door, the duke's eldest sister came to the door and followed her with a look of curiosity.

Seeing that her mistress was fuming, Delcia said little as she helped her dress. Then when Amanda realized she had gotten ready an entire hour early, she paced about, trying to decide what to do with herself. Remembering Zoe, whom she had entirely forgotten the moment they had stepped off the train, she went into the corridor and then stopped at the length of hall with the confusing doors, all of which looked alike. Fortunately, a footman was just coming along, carrying a tray with a crystal carafe.

"Excuse me," she said to the servant, who stopped. "Do you happen to know where my aunt is housed?"

The footman inclined his head and marched ahead, pausing two doors down from hers. "Here, miss."

"Thank you."

As he continued on his errand, she knocked on the door. A familiar muffled voice called, "Come in."

She entered the room, which was a large bedchamber

with the bed on a platform at one end of the room. The other end had a seating area round a large fireplace similar to the one in her bedroom. Zoe was rummaging through her jewelry case, her things spread out on a dressing table.

"Oh, come in dear," she said, then turned back to the table and heaved an exasperated sigh. "I am such a bad traveler. I just cannot seem to find anything in a foreign situation."

Amanda threw herself into a chair beside the dressing table. "I'm a bad traveler, too," she said, her foul mood displaying itself. "Oh, why did we ever come here?"

"What?" said Zoe, only half listening. "I'm sure I don't know."

A knock sounded at the door, and Amanda rose to answer it. Jeds stood there. "Excuse me, miss. I was informed that you were in this room."

"Yes, what is it?"

He extended a silver tray that had two cards on it. "You have some visitors. I've asked them to wait in the long parlor downstairs."

Curious, she reached for the cards. "Who could be visiting me here?"

As soon as she saw the engraved names she nearly dropped the cards. "Oh, no."

Jeds bowed and turned, and she shut the door after him. "Oh, no," she said again, leaning against the door she closed.

"What is it, dear?" asked Zoe.

She clasped the two cards to her breast. "I can't believe it."

Zoe came forward and held out her hand, seeing that her niece was too distracted to answer her question. She peered at the names on the cards.

"Why, it's your cousin Henry. But who is Francis Newton?"

She gulped. "The young man we saw at Monte Carlo. You remember, he was dining with that courtesan."

"Amanda," Zoe reprimanded her.

"Oh, come now, Aunt. The lady's beauty was accentuated with makeup, and he didn't introduce us. Isn't that the normal behavior of a gentleman when he is out with a lady not fit to be introduced to polite society?"

Her aggravation was not masked. "He must have inquired as to where I'd gone and followed us here. The nerve. How dare he?"

Zoe frowned. "Was he some sort of special friend of yours?"

She flung herself across the room. "I thought we were engaged once. At least that was our secret."

"Oh, my."

She shut her eyes and sighed. "I was warned away from him, but I was too stubborn. I had to find out for myself that his words of flattery meant nothing. And to think I nearly threw my life away on the likes of him."

Zoe said nothing to this tirade, thinking only that her niece's life had gotten rather complicated in matters of men. But Amanda was headed toward the door.

"I suppose I'll have to see them."

Then she was in the corridor and making her way along. She nearly turned the wrong way when she came to the intersection, but managed to set herself right and came at last to the grand staircase with murals up to the heavens. She walked slowly down, her hand running along the smoothstone railing. For a moment, she imagined herself as mistress of the palace, and felt surprisingly at ease and in command.

She passed into the long salon and saw the two familiar figures at the far end of the room talking to Lady Norah. That was good, for with several people present, she didn't feel called upon to say anything personal. But what was Henry doing here? Amanda always looked forward to seeing her cousin, but back in New York, he had been no particular friend of Francis's, except that they were in the same social circle. Then she suspected that Francis had run into Henry and had simply used him to get to her. But why, she could not fathom.

The old resentments began to surface, and she lifted her chin higher, feeling even more confident in the gown she wore, one of the Worths they had purchased in Paris. She lifted the lace-trimmed skirt and marched slowly and with dignity toward the visitors. When she arrived, she dropped the skirt so that it swished about her feet.

"Hello, Henry, Francis. What a surprise to see you both here."

Henry turned in the direction of her voice, squinted and then stepped forward, narrowly missing the corner of a low coffee table.

"Hello, Amanda."

"Henry." She reached to give him a hug, as much to prevent his tripping as out of affection for her cousin. "How good to see you."

When he had reclaimed his balance, she held him away from her and confronted Francis, to whom she held out her hand formally.

"Welcome to Elsenheim, Francis," she said, although there was no welcome in her voice. "I'm surprised to see you here."

"I daresay you are. And I apologize for the hour of

our arrival. The blasted train from London broke down, or we would have been here much sooner."

"I see. And you have met Lady Norah, I see."

"Oh, yes. She's been quite entertaining."

Amanda nodded. "Well, seeing as dinner will be served within the hour, I'd better inform Jeds that we need two extra places."

She glanced at Lady Norah in a quick exchange as if to see if that would be all right. When she saw Lady Norah's subtle nod and amused smile, she gathered courage and went on.

"It's short notice to Cook, but I'll see what can be done."

She proceeded to the bell rope as if she were already in possession of the palace and quite used to ordering things. When Jeds appeared, she addressed him.

"Jeds, I have unexpected visitors from my country. As they arrived at an awkward time due to a travel mishap, do you think Cook can do something about the menu so that they might dine with us?"

He bowed, giving her a grave look. "I will handle matters, miss. Two more at dinner."

"Thank you, Jeds."

Then she returned to the group around the fireplace. Lady Norah spoke up.

"I'm sure you'll have much to chat about with your compatriots," she said. "I'll leave you alone."

"Oh, no," said Amanda, beginning to show her panic. "That really won't be necessary."

While Lady Norah could be extremely perceptive, at the moment Amanda was finding her dense. She wasn't reading Amanda's pleas of desperation.

"Nonsense," said Lady Norah cheerily. "You'll have so much to catch up on. I must change for dinner in any case, but I look forward to the added company at dinner."

She shook hands with both gentlemen and then took herself off.

"Have you both been shown rooms?" said Amanda, finding a way out of personal matters. "It's rather primitive here, owing to the age of the building. Not enough plumbing, I'm afraid. And you'll want to change for dinner."

"Sorry to inconvenience you," said Francis. "As I said, when I ran into Henry in London, we wondered if you might be missing your countrymen and decided to run down for a day's visit. But the best laid plans often go awry."

"Yes, don't they?" said Amanda with a touch of sarcasm. "Well, I suppose we'll have to save our visiting until after dinner."

She pulled the bell rope again. In a moment Jeds appeared.

"These gentlemen will need rooms in which to change for dinner. They'll be spending the night."

Knowing better than to sympathize with the efficient butler, who would inform the housekeeper, who would then place the burden on the already overworked maids, Amanda kept a formal demeanor. "Do you think rooms can be found for them?"

Jeds took matters in hand. "The rooms have already been anticipated, miss, and your guests can be housed quite comfortably. If they will follow me." And he turned without looking at them and started for the door.

"I'll look forward to dinner, then," said Amanda.

She reached out for Henry and took his arm, giving it an affectionate squeeze.

"Dear Henry," she said, with feeling. She lowered her

voice so that Francis, who was ahead of them, gazing at the paintings in the room, might not hear them. "It is good to have you here, cousin. I've been needing someone to talk to. You will stay for a few days, won't you?"

He looked at her in some surprise. "If you want. I was rather afraid we would be imposing. Thought you'd be wanting to spend time with your fiancé."

"On the contrary," said Amanda. "I cannot talk to him."

Henry said nothing, but concentrated on where they were going as he followed Francis up the stairs. He did strain his neck to look at the murals in the great hall, and Amanda had one bad moment when she feared he would miss the turn on the landing and walk into the wall; but he rounded just in time, his hand on the balustrade, and managed to continue up the stairs.

She sighed, less in relief that near-sighted Henry was in good hands with the capable Jeds than that she had gotten through the brief interview. But what Francis wanted here, she could not fathom. She went along to her room to check her appearance and then went to report to her aunt about the arrival of the guests.

"Good," said Zoe. "I haven't seen Henry in years. He must have changed."

Amanda grinned. "He has a heart of gold, my favorite cousin does. But his near-sightedness has grown worse. You have to watch out for him lest he meet with an accident, especially in places where there are low tables and delicate statuary. But one grows used to it."

"I'll be careful with him, then," she said with a smile of amusement. "Steer him away from sharp edges and steps."

They chuckled, and Amanda enjoyed having something to take her attention. In one way, having so many people present relieved some of the pressures of Sunderland's family cross-examining her. When it was time, they all gathered in the long salon again before dinner.

Sunderland was the last to enter, and by that time Amanda was deeply involved in a talk with Henry, who was telling her about the grand tour he was making. His telling of it was so amusing that she was beside herself with laughter when Edward approached. She tried to break off in order to introduce him; but the amused flush still showed in her face, and tears of laughter stained her cheeks.

Edward approached the little group, his attention arrested by her gales of laughter. When he saw the delight on her face, something twisted in his heart. She had never looked at him that way.

She gathered breath to remind him of where he had met both gentlemen before, and he greeted them with all of his inborn graciousness. But he looked suspiciously at the American who was unrelated to her. Had this fellow been the one to draw her out so? If so, he must find out why he was here. Instant possessiveness pushed all other thought aside, and he began to exert that manner of assertive authority that never failed to remind everyone present of his rank and position and, more importantly, of the breeding that could, when needed, put others in their place.

"I'm glad to see Amanda cheered by some of her friends," he said kindly. "The thought of taking on the responsibilities of being a duchess can be somewhat daunting," he said. "She'll need bolstering and amusing."

The little group sobered at the word duchess, and it had the effect Sunderland wanted until he could fully evaluate just what was going on here. Dinner was announced, and he offered his arm to his grandmother. Even at family dinners, they went in to dinner according to rank. Lord Isington took his wife, who was second in age and rank. That left Francis Newton to escort Norah, who went before Amanda. Henry wound up with both his aunt and Amanda, and while Sunderland didn't feel jealous that she might have romantic feelings for a first cousin, he felt a pang of consternation at the way she seemed to flutter about him, anticipating his every move.

Out of the corner of his eye while he waited for the grand duchess to arrange herself on his arm, he saw the look of mutual warmth and affection that passed between Henry and Amanda, and he read instantly that theirs was a long friendship. They'd probably grown up together. He felt jealous that she saved her tender looks for such as her cousin.

Tightening his jaw, he remembered that she probably had had many such looks for the unfortunate young man who had not lived to delight in any more of them. It was blasphemy to be glad that her lover was dead, yet he could not quell a sense of displeasure that for all his being noble and eligible, he had not truly won her heart. That he possessed her body was not enough. It gnawed at his pride.

At the same time he chastised himself for such foolishness. When he'd entered the marriage market, he'd never given a whit for the feelings of a prospective bride. And now Amanda Whitney had gotten under his skin. It was a matter of personal honor that he win her. For she would become his duchess, of that he was certain.

The procession went in to dinner. They took their places, and Amanda was seated between the duke and

Francis. And even though the dowager duchess was at the far end of the table, conversation stopped when the old lady took it into her head to ask Amanda a question. She would simply shout down the table.

Abruptly interrupted from her conversations, Amanda jerked her head around to answer.

"When you marry my grandson," said the dowager duchess during one of these intervals, "you'll be expected to redecorate. I do hope you can do something to the dismal north rooms. You'll be wanting to have house parties, and the north rooms will have to be used."

Amanda blinked. "Of course," she said. "What do the north rooms look like?"

"Dismal light, dark furniture."

"I see," said Amanda. "I'll be happy to take a look at them."

"Have you much experience in redecorating?"

None, thought Amanda with sudden panic. Having lived under the domineering eye of her mother for so many years, she felt unprepared for this task. She felt Edward's gaze, and tried to remind herself that she might not be doing any decorating at all. But she had to say something.

"Yes," she said. "We always procured the latest in interior design in our house on Fifth Avenue in New York."

"You must illuminate us about your country," said the dowager duchess. "Do you have slaves?"

Amanda blinked. "Why, no," she answered, startled. "No one has had slaves, even in the south, for nearly thirty years."

"The south? I never did understand your war with South America."

"We didn't fight South America, madam. Perhaps you are referring to the War Between the States."

"Yes, yes. And North America won."

Amanda gave up, feeling she'd rather defend her ability to decorate than explain American history to this provincial aristocrat.

The conversation seemed to satisfy the dowager duchess, and she turned to Lord Isington to press him about local matters, leaving everyone else free to resume their conversations.

The dinner dragged on, mostly due to the fact that after a long interval the dowager duchess would suddenly decide to eat every morsel on her plate, thus frustrating the footman who had just reached to remove it. The next course was inevitably delayed, and Amanda marveled at how the kitchen managed to keep it hot.

At last they were finished. The ladies followed the dowager duchess along the long stretch of chilly corridor to a withdrawing room that had a bright fire waiting for them. There they took seats to enjoy their coffee while the gentlemen remained in the dining room over their port. Amanda could hardly keep her mind on the talk at hand for wondering what kind of quizzing Edward was putting Francis through. Wishing she could overhear, she knew she must wait until later to discover the meaning of his visit.

When the men joined them, music was suggested. As there was a piano in this room, it was often used for after dinner entertainments.

"Perhaps Amanda will play or sing for us," said Lady Norah.

But Amanda shook her head. "Sadly, I have no musical talent, though I enjoy music very much. I can only just carry a tune. You play, Lady Norah."

"Norah has all the talent in the family," said Lady Isabel. "Go ahead, sister. We shall listen to you."

Norah took her seat and did indeed play very well, classical pieces first and then some popular English tunes. Amanda noticed that Francis did not remain seated but rather strolled the length of the room looking at the collection of paintings that adorned the walls. Feeling restless herself, Amanda rose after a while and joined him at the end of the room where a door led to a long gallery.

At her approach Francis spoke. "Ah, Amanda, I was hoping you might show me some of the palace. Truly an amazing art collection. The duke's family must be great collectors."

"I believe so, for many generations."

She refrained from mentioning the paintings Edward had told her he'd been forced to sell to raise funds to manage Elsenheim.

They slipped into the next room. The door being open, she did not think it looked inappropriate. Anyone might join them at any moment, but the music was less distracting here.

"Why have you come?" Amanda hissed in a low voice, determined to get to the point. "I never expected to see you again."

"Yes," he said, taking on a hangdog look. "I can understand your feelings. But that is why I came. I wanted to mend any misunderstanding between us."

She walked a little way in exasperation. "Oh, for heaven's sake, Francis. Don't you think it's a little too late for that? I found out, thank goodness, that you were less than sincere back in New York. Fortunately our secret engagement went no further than it did."

"That's why I came here, Amanda. I had to see for myself that it was true about you and the duke."

She opened her eyes wide. "Surely you're not trying to tell me that you still care."

"Of course I care, my dear. Why else would I follow you here?"

"Oh, Francis. Don't be ridiculous. I heard from my good friend Emily that you were escorting Abigail Van Ryck about Newport. Evidently my fortune wasn't as big as hers. Admit it. You wanted to marry me for money."

He smiled contritely. "Surely it's no mistake for romance and wealth to mix. I've been placed in that unfortunate position of being born into a good family, but one whose financial opportunities are limited. I must do something to assure my future. But that does not mean I wouldn't marry a woman I loved."

"Provided she had enough to keep you in style as well."

"Well, true. I must be realistic."

She shook her head. "Then if I hadn't a fortune, you wouldn't have looked twice at me back in New York."

He followed her as she paced along the gallery. "Of course I would have looked at you."

"But not married me."

"Now, Amanda. That temper of yours gets the better of you. Surely the duke is no different. Only he's giving you a title in exchange for your money. I'd say it is you who are the ambitious one."

She turned and stamped her foot, nearly tearing her train. "I am not marrying him for ambition's sake."

"Surely you cannot love him."

"Why ever not?"

He shook his head. "You cannot love a title, and I daresay you hardly know the man."

"Whether or not I love him is none of your business." Her face began to warm.

He frowned. "That is too bad. I had hoped to beg forgiveness, thinking perhaps it might not be too late for us."

"What happened? Did your wealthy widow refuse you?"

"Amanda, you're being too harsh."

She turned from him. "Oh! You must think me very stupid indeed."

He cleared his throat. "I can see that you are upset. Well, I shall remain through tomorrow, and though I know my position is hopeless, the least you can do is grant me the day to recuperate from my travels; then I shall take myself away, wishing you happiness if my rival is to win your hand after all."

"The sooner the better."

They stood awkwardly for a moment, and then Francis turned in the direction of the sitting room from which the music drifted faintly.

Not wanting to return to the company, Amanda took a set of stairs that twisted upward to a loggia above. The loggia ran along the outer wall of the palace, where tall windows admitted moonlight. During the day the light would be just enough to show the paintings below to advantage. She moved along in semidarkness, for the lamps here had not been lit. But she found a window seat at the end and sat down, leaning her back against the cold stone wall.

It might as well have been a cell in a dungeon, she thought, feeling trapped. She shook her head, despairing of the flaw in her character that she saw clearly as her undoing. She had no ability to judge or to manage men. Only nineteen and she had made three mistakes already.

She'd trusted Francis and been deceived. She'd thought herself in love with Emile and realized only at the last that she had only been in love with the freedom and liberty he represented. And now she'd trapped herself into an engagement with a man who could easily overpower her.

A tremble passed through her when she thought of the way she responded to Edward when she was in his arms. It frightened her that her traitorous body and emotions were so easily manipulated by him. Where was the easy partnership she thought she'd find in a marriage between consenting parties who might, if they were fortunate, come to love each other one day?

What frightened her even more as she sat in the dark contemplating what was happening to her was the fact that she was falling in love with Edward. But not true love. She knew now that she could not count on her heart to tell her what true love was. Besides, Edward was out to prove something, to own her. For did he not admit he needed her fortune?

She gave a start at the sound of footsteps below and instinctively shrank back against the embrasure, for she didn't wish to be disturbed. But whoever was below crossed the room slowly, but purposefully, and began to climb the stairs. The tall figure appeared at the top, and then the moonlight lit Edward's face as he moved toward her. Not seeing her at first, he seemed to gaze into the darkness. When he spotted her in her window seat, his face changed.

"So there you are." He joined her and lowered himself to sit beside her, glancing out at the night.

"Hiding from your guests?" he asked, a trace of mockery in his voice.

"Yes, if you want to know the truth."

"I always want to know the truth with you," he said, taking her chilly hand and pressing it with his own.

A jumble of emotions shot through her. "I'm glad to see my cousin," she said truthfully. "But I never expected to see Francis Newton here."

"Another of your suitors?"

The suggestiveness of his voice implied something she did not like and she grew embarrassed.

"Not that way." She almost said not like Emile, but couldn't bring herself to say it.

"Hmmm." He took her meaning. "That's good to know. I was beginning to wonder."

She could hardly face him. "It's not like that."

She could hardly defend herself, for he knew exactly what kind of passion she possessed. But she had a sudden, desperate desire for him to understand that Francis aroused no such feeling in her.

"That is good," he whispered in her ear. "I like to think that I am the only one to possess you that way. While I'm willing to let bygones be bygones, I don't like to think of you as having been in many other romantic interludes before our own."

She pulled away from him. "Unlike your own interludes as you call them. I won't bother to ask how many you've had."

He chuckled. "I assure you it does not matter. Only the present and future matter."

She was on her feet now, progressing along the dark loggia.

"And if we married, how long would you remain at

my side? When would you tire of me and return to your other interludes?"

He caught up to her and grasped her arm, pulling her around to face him in the darkness.

"I would have no need for others, my dear." He pulled her close. "Can't you see, Amanda, that we could build something together here?"

"You mean we could build onto your palace. That is what you wanted me for, my fortune, is it not?"

"To begin with, but we have grown far past that."

"Have we?"

Already his arms around her threatened to bestir her once more.

"Of course we have, and that is why I've become persuaded that you are right for me."

She turned her head to the side, avoiding his mouth. "But you don't love me. You told me that."

He laughed against her throat. "That was before. Love between a man and a woman grows, my dear. Marriage, hopefully children, all those things bind a man and a woman together."

Unbelieving of his caressing words, she felt herself slipping. Her heart began to twist as his breath fanned her cheek. If only he meant it. If only she could trust him and herself. If only it were all true. But the only demonstrable truth was that he fanned a fire within her that she was powerless to fight. And in the end if she lost to him, it would only mean one more mistake in her seemingly long chain of mistakes when it came to suitors. She must not be ruined again.

Chapter 22

Early the next morning, Amanda wandered outside. After taking a wrong turn and nearly ending up in the laundry room, she found the way to the stables. Always comforted in the presence of horses, she decided to see if she could find Milady Gray, the mount she had used when she'd ridden with Edward's sisters.

The grooms were about, leading some of the horses out to walk them. As she neared the door, a familiar figure peered around it. She stopped, smiled.

"Jean Henri," she said and then spoke in French. "How good to see you."

A smile lit his face and then was replaced with a more dignified expression, but she could tell by the way he approached that he was glad to see her.

"*Bonjour,* mademoiselle," said the boy. "So you've come. Are you going to marry the duke?"

She laughed. "That's a complicated question, Jean Henri. Come, sit down with me so we can talk. I want to hear about your new life here."

They walked toward a bench by the stone stable walls, and Amanda sat down. From here they could watch the grooms walking the horses and polishing tack.

A bit of sun was beginning to penetrate the clouds, and it promised to be a fine day. Jean Henri hopped onto the bench beside her and sat up straight.

"I understand you've been learning English," she said. "And that you're very good at it."

He gave her a sideways glance. "Maybe."

"We could practice it if you like. I could help you."

He considered. "All right," he said. Then he frowned, forming a question. Finally he looked up at her.

"How long did it take you to learn?"

She understood him to mean how long had it taken her to learn a second language. She gave him an honest answer. "I studied French with a tutor when I was a little girl. But I didn't learn it well until we traveled in France. The best way to learn a language is to live with the people speaking it, the way you are here. It will come much quicker."

He sighed, and she sympathized with the exasperation he must be feeling, to have to learn English and at the same time be given jobs to do. It was quite a change for him. Her heart went out to the boy, and she longed to offer him friendship.

"Now that I am here," she said, "I'd like it if you wanted to show me some of the things you do. You see, I am like you. I don't have any friends here. All these people are strangers except for my aunt who came here with me. It can be lonely being in a strange place."

He considered this and faced front. She could see that he didn't want to be too hasty in his answer. The poor boy was so used to being bottled up in himself that his defensiveness showed in everything he did. Impulsively, she put an arm about his shoulders and squeezed them.

How could he understand that spending time with him would also comfort her? Although he was a painful reminder of her escapades in Paris, she had taken a liking to him. And since they were both foreigners to England, she thought they could offer each other a lot.

Jean Henri's rigid shoulders began to crumple against her. In spite of himself, he leaned into her warmth. But she knew better than to expect any commitments. He wasn't used to trusting anyone.

"Tell me, what do they have you doing here?" she said, letting him sit up straight again.

He shrugged. "I feed the horses. The other day I pointed out where a horse had a limp. It had something in its hoof that the groom removed. But if it hadn't been for me, the horse might have gone lame."

"That's very good." She paused, thinking. "And have you seen much of the duke?"

He shrugged. "He went to London, to sit in Parliament," he said in an authoritative voice. Then he frowned, turned to Amanda.

"What do they do in Parliament?"

She grinned. "Parliament is part of the government. They make laws to help rule the country."

"Oh."

"You see," Amanda went on, "the Duke of Sunderland has responsibilities not only to Elsenheim, but to the country. He has to spend part of his time in London, at least until August when Parliament takes a recess."

"Then what does he do?"

"Why, he takes care of the estate."

Now she was the one to sound authoritative when, in fact, she actually didn't know what he did in late summer. Perhaps he took a hunting trip to Scotland. She would have to ask.

"He's here now," said Jean Henri. "He came back to get ready for you. Will he go to London again soon?"

Amanda smiled. She could see that Sunderland had become a hero in Jean Henri's eyes. She wondered if he knew it. How nice it would be if Edward would spend some time with the boy, but with all he had to do, he had probably already forgotten about the imp, having turned him over to the grooms in the stable. It made Amanda even more interested in looking out for him.

"Shall we take a walk?" she asked. "We could look at the gardens."

"Maybe later," said Jean Henri, trying to sound indifferent. "I have to help water the horses."

"Oh, of course. I don't want to interfere with your duties. What about later? Do you have free time during the day?"

"After supper," he said, not looking at her. "I'm in my room then." He said it with importance, and Amanda wondered if perhaps he had never had a room of his own before.

"Well, then, I should like to see your room. If you would like to show it to me, of course."

He hopped off the bench, fairly bursting with pride. "All right. You can ask Mrs. Gunderson the way."

She stood up as well. "Very well. And what time do you have your supper?"

"Six o'clock."

"Then I shall come to your room at seven, and we shall practice your English. You can show me your lessons."

She realized that her appointment with Jean Henri might mean that she miss dinner with the family and her guests. But she didn't care. At the moment she would rather go see Jean Henri where she thought she could do some good. The rest should take care of themselves. And once having made the appointment with

Jean Henri, she would rather die than break it. For the
boy could do with seeing someone keep a promise.

She waved him off, and then went into the cool stables. She wandered down the row of neat stalls, finally
asking a groom where she might find Milady Gray.

"Would you like me to saddle her for you?" asked the
groom.

She hadn't planned to ride, but then why not? She
had arisen earlier than everyone else, and she hardly
cared if she put in an appearance at breakfast. Let them
all see her independence. She needed to be by herself at
the moment.

She went to her room to change into her riding habit,
then back down to the stables, where the mare was waiting. She gave the horse a lump of sugar, spent a few
moments talking to her and stroking her neck. Then she
led her to the mounting block and got into the sidesaddle.

"If you would send word to the duke that I've gone
out," she said to the groom, "I would appreciate it."

"Yes, miss."

Then she turned the horse in the direction she had
gone with Norah and Isabel. The sun succeeded in
breaking through, and the scent of lush foliage was intoxicating. She crossed over the little bridge and rode
into the park. She had no intention of going into the
woods where she might get lost. It was better to keep
the house in view so there was no question of which way
to go when she was ready to return.

Alone in the park, she was able to meditate on all the
recent events. She'd had no time to mourn Emile because of the predicament she was in. And because scandal was not to be tolerated she could not even wear
mourning for him. She dismounted near the stream that

wound toward the fields and the village beyond. Hobbling Milady Gray, Amanda found a flat rock to sit on. The babbling brook was a comfort, and as the sun rose, she simply sat there, thinking of nothing, letting her mind wander, letting her soul heal.

Rest was what she needed. To be thrown from the frightening experience in Paris into Emile's death and then into the engagement with Edward was too much. No wonder she was having difficulty being civil. She was simply trapped in a circumstance that allowed no vent to her emotions other than the erotic outpouring she experienced in Edward's arms. A sob escaped her throat, and she dabbed at her eyes.

What she needed was a good cry, an outpouring of emotions. Tears formed and another sob escaped. Soon she bent over, holding her head in her hands, letting the tears fall. Grief rushed out, released from within. She had thought she'd cried out her loss of Emile, but this was more an emotional release from the changes she faced.

Milady Gray stretched her neck and nuzzled Amanda, and she reached up to caress the horse, finding comfort in the soft muzzle. The animal did much to communicate sympathy, and Amanda continued to cry, to murmur to the horse, and finally got up to wipe away her tears. She walked to the stream, then bent over to scoop up cold water and wash her face. Feeling somewhat purged, she went back to the mare and mounted up.

She had sat there nearly an hour, though she wasn't aware of time, and clouds that she hadn't noticed before had snuck across the horizon. A breeze touched her face, and she felt the air temperature cool. Milady Gray rotated her ears forward and responded to the change in the weather.

Now Amanda looked at the sky and felt a drop of rain touch her face. She patted the mare's neck.

"We'd better get back to the house, girl. Looks like a shower."

But just as she turned back, she noticed the hunting lodge, situated up the hill on this side of the lake. It was closer than the palace, and she thought they might make it there before the rain broke.

"Go on, girl. We'll see if we can get into the lodge." And she urged the horse forward.

They skirted the woods and went up the slope to the lodge. Passing the well, Amanda guided Milady Gray toward an arch that led to a covered brick courtyard. Though the courtyard was open on two sides, the horse would be sheltered. Amanda dismounted and tied the reins to the ring of a hitching post. Then she went to the solid oak door with its brass knocker.

She didn't bother to knock, but tried the door, which was locked. Muttering her bad luck, she went along the lodge and turned a corner. Here were some steps leading downward, and she followed them. To her good fortune, the door at the bottom was unlocked, and she pushed it inward.

She found herself in a pantry and paused to let her eyes adjust to the gray light from windows at ground level. Then her eye spied a lantern.

"Hmmm," she murmured to herself. "I wonder if it's got fuel." Lifting it down, she saw that it did, so she searched about for matches, which were not hard to find.

She struck a light, adjusted the wick and then felt better, for the rain was coming down harder now, and she would have been soaked if she'd tried to make it back to the house. With Milady Gray sheltered, there was little to worry about except that the family at the great house might be looking for her. But surely the groom had told Edward she had gone riding, and they would trust her to find shelter from the rain.

Unconcerned, she held the lantern before her and passed from the pantry into the kitchen and followed another set of stairs to the main floor. The hunting lodge was well furnished, and there was no trace of dust, so she judged that it was kept up. Still there was the sense of disuse about the place. The cushions of the chairs were plumped up as if no one had sat on them in some time. While the carpets were worn, it was the same wear she had seen at the palace, looking as if it had been done by feet of decades ago rather than recently.

She wandered from room to room, saw several clocks that had not been wound, confirming that the place must not be much in use. And yet, she found it comfortable. It was cold now, but that could be remedied with a fire in one of the brick fireplaces. She even debated building one, but walked to the windows of the front parlor to look out at the rain.

When she did so, she gasped in surprise. Riding hard for the lodge was a dark horse and a rider who could be no other than Edward. As he came nearer, she confirmed that it was he, and she wondered what he was doing out in the storm. She set the lantern down and found her way down the passageway to the side door that had been locked.

She opened it and stood on the sill as he rode into the courtyard. "Edward," she called out.

He drew rein and dismounted, hitching his horse as she had, and then he strode toward the door, his collar still turned up against the rain, his deerstalker cap pulled low over his brow. He moved past her into the entryway and then stopped to remove his hat.

"We were worried about you," he said. "Thought you'd met with trouble when the storm came."

She suppressed a smile. "You needn't have worried. I'm a good rider, and Milady Gray is a good mount. But when the rain came I realized it would be quicker to come here than to try to make the house. Fortunately a pantry door was unlocked."

He shrugged out of his riding cape and hung it on a coat tree. Then he led the way down the passage.

"Well, so now you've seen our hunting lodge. I would have brought you here myself eventually."

"Hmmm. It is very cozy. Is it used often?"

She noticed a flicker in his eyes before he shook his head. "Not often, except in hunting season. The woods are near, as you have noticed, so it is a favorite spot for hunting parties. The prince likes it."

"Oh, the Prince of Wales. Does he come here often?"

Edward gave a grunt. "The official royal visit. One does not invite the prince; one is commanded to entertain. Usually through an attendant, he expresses a wish to visit a country estate. Of course one agrees. Then one draws up a tentative list to send to him and to Princess Alexandra, if she is accompanying him."

"You mean he, himself, approves the guest list?"

"That's right. He might eliminate names of those he doesn't wish to meet, or add new favorites."

"I suppose it is quite an undertaking to have the royal personages here."

"Quite." Edward threw himself into an easy chair and put his booted feet on a leather hassock. "It is a chore."

"Do you not get along with the prince?" she asked out of curiosity.

"In public one has no choice. In private, let us say, it is a relief to choose my own guests."

She sat on the sofa in front of the empty fireplace. "Has he been here to hunt, then?"

Edward nodded, his eyes searching the room. "There, on that table, there is a photograph."

Amanda retrieved the framed photograph and looked at the figures in black and white. A group of people were seated in front of what she recognized to be Elsenheim. She picked out Edward among the row of men standing behind the seated ladies. In the center was the prince with his bushy beard. But she didn't see Princess Alexandra and commented on it.

"No, she wasn't present. The prince brought his mistress instead."

Talk of mistresses distressed Amanda, and she placed the photograph back on the table and came to sit uneasily on the sofa again. Edward spoke in soft tones.

"If you become my duchess, you will be expected to play hostess to the prince, who will one day be our king."

She sighed, pressed her lips together. "I know I wouldn't be a very good hostess. There are so many rules to learn."

His hand drifted from his chair to the arm of the sofa where she rested hers. "I realize that. It is why I also want you to see the more pleasant sides of life in the country. It might help balance out what would be expected of you as a duchess."

Again the honesty accompanied the persuasion. She swallowed. "I just don't think I could adjust to living here." She felt grief threaten to claim her, and she felt suddenly very lost.

Edward saw the emotions pass over her face, and he moved from his chair to the sofa beside her, leaning back and stretching his arm across in back of her.

"You are homesick, no doubt."

"Well, not homesick exactly." She remembered that Louisa was at home in New York, so she could hardly want to go back there.

"I miss, I miss ..." But she couldn't name exactly what she missed, and she felt foolish, thinking that Edward would think she referred to Emile and all he symbolized in her young life.

But instead of talking of the things that weighed on her, Edward began to enumerate other details having to do with a royal visit, in an effort to distract her.

"To make for really good shooting, birds must be raised, fed, and keepers and beaters trained. Elsenheim's beaters are so skilled they can fly the birds over the guns high, medium or low on a shooting weekend. A very good day's shooting might number one to two thousand dead birds."

"I can imagine the prince's pleasure in that," she said. Thinking of sport reminded her of Jean Henri.

"I met Jean Henri at the stables this morning."

"Ah, and how did you find the lad?"

"He seems to be trying. I hope his work has been satisfactory."

"I've heard no complaints."

"It was nice of you to arrange English lessons."

"Well, I didn't want to leave him to the grooms for that. His teacher says he is bright."

"I've agreed to help him after his supper. I'm to be at his room at seven o'clock tonight."

Edward gave a wry smile. "You mean to say you are going to another man's bedroom this evening so that I am to be deprived of your company?"

"Only for two hours. I imagine he must go to bed at nine o'clock."

"The family will be displeased that you are going to miss dining with us. And what about your cousin and your friend?"

"I'd nearly forgotten about them. I'll try to see Henry today. As to Francis, I don't care if he leaves without saying goodbye."

"Good. That's one rival disposed of."

"He's no rival."

She hadn't meant it to sound that way, but Edward did not miss his chance.

"Well, then am I to believe I am gaining in the race to attain your heart?"

The heart he spoke of began to hammer, and she stumbled over her words. "I didn't mean it that way."

"Well, I hope I am not to be deprived of your company for the entire evening. After you tuck Jean Henri in, perhaps you will join us afterward for coffee."

"If you wish."

"I wish."

His other wishes were demanding expression, and he reached for her shoulders, pulling her toward him so that his mouth could rest on her cheek. The flutter expanded to encompass her trembling limbs, and he turned her face for a kiss on the lips.

"Amanda," he said gently, desire and love filling his heart.

He let his fingers drift up through her hair, and she closed her eyes, soaking up the warmth. Her confused feelings drifted, but she did not resist as he crushed her to him, and let her hair fall over his face. Soon his hands explored the curves bound up in the riding habit, and his tongue probed between her moist lips.

He got to his feet, pulling her up with him. She experienced a moment of dizziness, steadied by his strong arms.

"Amanda," he said again, this time more firmly. "Come with me."

If she had doubts as to what was going to happen, she did not try to fool herself, giving in to the building desire within her. Something had changed, and she did not understand it herself; but as he led her by the hand up the twisting stairs to the upper floor, she felt that part of herself had drifted down the brook with her tears earlier that morning.

Perhaps it was the past that she had finally let go, for as they entered the bedroom, shrouded in heavy drapes, and he pulled her into his arms again, she felt none of the guilt or hesitation she had before. Instead his kisses and caresses built an urgency in her that was becoming familiarly comforting and exciting. He led her to the bed and then undid her jacket, his hands straying under her breasts, his touch lighting a fire within her.

He pulled back the jacket, unwound her neck stock. Now her hands ruffled his damp hair. He got her out of her complicated costume, and when he removed his shirt, she thrilled at the sight of the dark curls on his muscular chest. He stretched out on the bed and pulled her onto it with him. Then his hands sought the soft material of her camisole while her hand strayed down his chest, reveling in the feel of it.

He pushed her hand lower to the tight bulge in his trousers, and this time she felt more confident as to what to do. Then his hands slid up under the camisole, seeking her taut nipples, and she threw back her head, emitting a cry of passion as he tweaked them. Gently he laid her on her back and pulled the camisole upward so that he could gaze at her lovely breasts. He took one and then the other in his mouth, tantalizing her until the erotic thrill was too much to bear.

"Edward, Edward," she cried again and again, her hands pressing his head closer and closer to her.

She was aware of the power within him, like a coiled spring that would soon release a torrent of passion, and this time she was not the shy, hesitant neophyte she had been before. This time she participated, urging him on, guiding him to do what she wanted, what she knew would give her pleasure.

His hands sought her erotic center, and his touch seemed to lift her off the bed. Responding to her movements, he slid his hand under her, pressing himself against her.

His hair drifted across her face, and she thrilled at the touch and the scent of rain. When he gazed at her face his heart leapt at the passion he saw there. His lips grazed her face while his hands and his body did the rest. It seemed they left not an inch of each other unexplored.

"I want you, Amanda," he said. And she tingled at her name on his lips. "Do you want me?"

She gave a little nod, but he looked into her eyes. "Say you want me, my dearest. It would make me so happy."

"I want you," she whispered, feeling her heart would rise up into her throat.

"Ohhh," he moaned, shifting so that he slid into her open center. "My darling, my love."

Amanda felt as if a bolt of lightning moved through

her, and she cried out in passion. The sensation was still new, and the feeling of being completely one with a man was so delightful that she closed her eyes to savor every movement.

He moved his thighs against hers, relishing the feel of her. This was what he wanted. This was what he needed. Warmth engulfed him at her grip on his shoulders, at her moans and writhing body beneath him. He felt he could spend eternity this way.

He stretched out time as long as he could, until his desire mounted, and he found himself moving faster and faster, quick, beating thrusts jolting her as he took them both to a pinnacle of sensation. Then madness beat in his ears; he left his body and poured his liquid into her, shuddering, half rising, both of them crying out.

Amanda shook, shattered, drinking in the warmth and moistness, hanging on to him so that her spirit would remember where to return when it came down from the heavens. Finally he stretched out on her, the throbbing still descending as she held him as long as she could between her legs. She kissed the dampness on his forehead, relishing at holding him in her arms.

At long last he rolled from her, flinging his arms out on the bed beside her. She turned on her side, her arm resting on his shoulder. He lifted her hand to kiss it.

"I love you, Amanda," he said.

Her heart cracked, and she felt she could not speak. I love you, too, Edward, she thought. But she could not bring herself to say it. Passion, passion made two people say such things to each other on the heels of ecstasy. But as she had learned it did not mean real love, lasting love. It might be only a fleeting love. Something she was not prepared to undertake again.

She closed her eyes and nestled against his shoulder

as he drew her hand across his chest. She wondered if he would ever say those words again. In the cold, brittle sunlight that seemed to be what only occasionally warmed Britain, he might forget. His body loved her, but what about his soul and mind?

For Amanda knew now what was lacking in her life, and she felt bereft, as if knowing she might never attain it all. Sensuality and sex with a man was heaven. That was not to be denied. But she still wanted everything. Love, commitment, loyalty, trust, happiness, hope, family. The thoughts mingled as she drifted into a doze. It was human nature to want it all.

After some time she awoke to find that Edward had arisen. His clothing was gone, so she presumed he was dressed. For a moment she feared that he had abandoned her, and she sat up, reaching for her garments. But in the next moment the door opened, and he appeared with a tray. On it was a teapot in a cozy and two cups.

"I thought you might want some tea to warm you," he said.

"Oh. That was thoughtful."

He set down the tray and came to the bedside as she got up to dress. "Let me help you dress. It is as much pleasure to dress you as to undress you."

Feeling embarrassed in spite of what had just occurred between them, she let him help her on with all the complicated clothing. When she was attired, she sat in a chair and poured the tea. It tasted wonderful, the cup warming her hands.

"I suppose we should get back to the house," she said.

"That is too bad. I was enjoying looking at you."

She gave an embarrassed smile, burying her face in the teacup to take a sip.

"I want to see Henry. He will be lost by now."

Edward lifted his sensual lips in a grin. "You seem to cater to him."

"Henry and I are very close."

Now that he had satisfied himself with Amanda, he wasn't quite so jealous of the attentions she might wish to lavish on her cousin. If only she would lavish them likewise on him.

"In a cousinly friendship, I assume."

"Of course." She blushed.

"Well then, let us not keep our guests waiting." He stood, extended a hand and helped her rise. "And you must prepare for your English lessons later this evening."

"Yes, it seems as if I have a rather busy day ahead," she said.

"Then I am glad I got my time in first." He smiled, dropped a kiss on her forehead and led her downstairs.

Chapter 23

By the time they returned, they had missed lunch, so Jeds served them in Edward's sitting room. Back in the big house Amanda felt more constrained, and thought she noticed more formality in the duke's manner as well. It was as if neither of them wanted the family to read their thoughts or guess what they had been about.

The shower ceased after lunch, so in the afternoon, Amanda decided to escape with Henry to the village. Zoe caught up with her on the way to her room and said Francis was looking for her.

"Well, I don't think he shall find me. Where is Henry?"

"I believe he said he was going to the library."

"Good, then I'll fetch him. Are you amusing yourself, Aunt Zoe?"

"Well, yes. The day is so dreary that Lady Norah and Lady Isabel have invited me to help with flower arrangements to brighten things up."

She looked down the hall as if to see that no one else was listening and then said in a stage whisper, "It seems that the two ladies are adept at cards. We might have a game later on."

Amanda grinned. "Just don't play for money."

Zoe put a hand to her breast. "Oh, heavens no. That would be gauche." She lifted her head in the air and sailed off to her room.

Amanda went down the corridor, but before she took the staircase she hugged the wall stealthily to make sure Francis was nowhere in sight. The way was clear and she went downstairs. Remembering which way to turn for once, she located the corridor that led to the library. She found Henry in a wing chair reading and closed the door behind her.

"There you are, Henry," she said. "Zoe told me you were in here."

He shut his book. "Hello, Amanda. I didn't know where you were, so I thought it best to find something with which to occupy myself."

"I apologize for not coming down to breakfast. I went for a ride." She sat in the chair drawn up next to his. "I needed some time alone, you see."

He nodded, readjusted his spectacles. "Understandable. I suppose you have to get used to living in a palace."

She winced. "I'm not sure I'm going to."

He decided to take off the spectacles and clean them with his handkerchief. "Oh?"

She stood up. "Come on, Henry, let's go to the village. We can talk on the way."

"Fine with me."

"It really is a charming village, and the people are so hardworking. You will be impressed with their crafts."

When they reached the door, she opened it a crack to peek out.

"It's all right," Henry said. "They shouldn't mind if we go to the village."

"It's not that. I just don't want to run into Francis."

"Oh, well then you don't need to worry. I believe he is inspecting the duke's gun collection."

"Just so he doesn't aim at us. Come on, then."

They went out into the corridor, proceeded down a long oak hallway covered in worn runner and, after some moments and another turn, came out the door that led to the stableyard. Jean Henri saw them and came out to greet them.

"Hello, Jean Henri."

"Hello, miss."

She spoke in French to make it easier for Jean Henri. "Henry, this is Jean Sigibert Henri. He saved my life in Paris."

"Really?"

"I'll tell you the story later. Jean, this is my cousin Henry from America."

Henry bent, stuck out his hand, and the boy shook it, looking at him solemnly.

"What are you doing here?" he asked.

Henry's French was good enough to carry on a simple conversation, and he responded. "I've come to visit your future duchess. I was touring Europe, you see, visiting the cathedrals and seeing the great works of art. I spent some time in your country as well."

Jean Henri replaced his hands on his hips and examined Henry as if he wasn't sure what he thought of a man who visited cathedrals. But he held his head up proudly and said, "I don't live in Paris anymore. The duke brought me here."

"Well, that's good," said Henry.

"Jean," said Amanda. "Do you think you could get us a carriage? I want to show Henry the village."

Jean Henri scratched his head. Of course, he was too

small to harness a wagon, but he raced off to ask one of the grooms to help.

Henry smiled. "A likeable boy. You say he saved your life."

"Yes, it's rather a long story. But Edward brought him here as a reward for his part in it. I'll tell you as we drive."

"My, my. What were you doing risking your life?"

"Visiting a sick friend."

"Is it that dangerous a thing to do in Paris?"

"Well, not normally, but a footpad attacked my carriage."

"Dear me, I didn't know."

"We're trying to keep anyone from knowing. You must promise not to breathe a word, especially to Francis."

"Whatever you say."

Unfortunately, Amanda would not get her chance to bring Henry up-to-date, for Francis appeared in the stableyard.

"Ah, there you are," he said. "Fine day after that rain stopped, isn't it?"

"Hello, Francis," she said. "I understood you were occupied with the gun collection. I was going to show Henry the village."

"Oh, capital. Mind if I go along?"

"It won't be very exciting, I'm afraid. Life in the country is probably rather dull to your way of thinking."

"Oh, well. Variety is the spice of life."

The grooms had harnessed the carriage and led the horses out. Jean Henri appeared as if supervising. He checked the harnesses and bustled about the carriage, very proud to be the one to have ordered it up for

Amanda. He came to announce that the carriage was ready and then saw Francis. Amanda introduced them.

"Francis is an old friend from America."

"What's he doing here?"

A smiled of amusement crossed her lips. "He came to visit Elsenheim, to see what it was like."

Jean Henri eyed Francis and finally stepped back to allow the party to climb into the carriage. Francis drove, and soon they were on the road past the fields. The tenants looked up out of curiosity, and some tipped their hats. Amanda smiled and waved back, and then felt a twinge of guilt. If she didn't marry Edward and left at the end of her six months, she wondered what the country folk would think. She'd no doubt that the palace provided them no end of gossip, and found she was concerned about them talking about Edward behind his back.

But she pushed such thoughts aside and tried to enjoy the outing. When they came to the edge of the village, Francis slowed the horses from a trot to a walk. Here again, the villagers looked up from their conversations or their work, and those on foot or horseback made way for them. Amanda felt like she was on display, and knew that the entire town would be wondering who her guests were.

They drew up near the church, and Amanda decided to take Francis and Henry to meet the vicar's wife, since she was the only person in the village she was on social terms with at present. So they hitched the horses to the post, and Amanda opened the gate to the vicarage and walked up the path to the porch.

Agnes Dumbarton was delighted to see Amanda and invited them all in for tea. She had on a gardening dress and apologized for her appearance. But her house was neat as a pin, and she scurried off to the kitchen to boil water for some tea.

Amanda, Francis and Henry settled themselves in the parlor. When Agnes came back, Amanda explained that she had run into Francis in Monte Carlo, refraining from mentioning his companion, of course.

"Oh, my, Monte Carlo. I've never been there, but they say it is a beautiful place. And a little sinful." She gave Amanda a quick wink.

The comment seemed to embarrass Francis, who cleared his throat. Amanda enjoyed his discomfort.

"Actually the duke took me there so that I could visit a friend who was in a nearby sanatorium." She managed to say it without giving way to a lump in her throat.

"Oh, how thoughtful of him. I hope your friend is better?"

"Sadly, no. He . . ." She thought she could say it, but choked. Still she made herself go on, only the cold dullness in her heart a reminder. "I'm afraid he worsened. There was nothing they could do. He passed away a few weeks ago."

"Oh, dear. I am so sorry. What was his name? I'll say some prayers for him."

Her kindness overflowed, and Amanda appreciated it. "His name was Emile Reveillere. He was a gentle soul, a scholar in Paris."

Her conversation with Agnes excluded Henry and Francis, and when she became aware of their curious stares, she sat back, trying to explain.

"The duke helped sponsor Emile at the sanatorium, at my request," she said by way of explanation.

"Generous of him," said Henry.

"Yes, rather." Francis eyed her curiously, and for a moment she felt as if he saw through her.

She managed to turn the conversation to other things. "The candles, how did they do at the church?"

"Oh, wonderfully. And they smelled so nice."

"I'm glad. I did enjoy helping with them." A mischievous thought occurred to her. "Tell us, are you busy making something for the church today?"

Agnes tittered. "Well, since you asked, I am. I've been making soap in the back room. We'll sell it to raise funds for a new organ for the church. We've been raising money for quite some time." She gave a little chuckle. "If you heard our organ, you'd agree we need a new one."

"Oh, how interesting," said Amanda. "I'm sure we'd love to see how you make it."

"Soap," said Henry. "Well, now, indeed."

"Well, our tea will be steeped by now. Why don't we pour our cups, and after we refresh ourselves I'd be happy to show you the soap making."

They spoke of matters concerning the village while they munched on cakes and drank delicious strong tea. Agnes answered Amanda's questions about the soap. Henry was familiar with the scientific principles involved and explained them to Amanda.

"Soap is basically fat, you see, which is classified as an acid. You combine it with an alkali, which is needed to neutralize the acid."

Amanda glanced at Francis, who was beginning to look bored and restless, crossing first one leg and then another.

"Please continue, Henry. If I am to live in the country for a good part of the year, I feel it is important to understand these principles."

"Yes, well." Henry cleared his throat and adjusted his spectacles. "Tallow, which is beef fat, is best. Second to that, and Mrs. Dumbarton may correct me if I am wrong, you can use sheep fat or pig fat."

"That's right. We use sheep fat as we've so many sheep here. Sometimes pig fat. Of course, olive oil can be used, but we don't grow many olives in England."

"Yes, yes," said Henry, warming to his subject with such a willing audience, except for Francis, of whom he took no notice. "Now, in Africa—"

Amanda interrupted, not wanting the conversation to stray too far. She knew Henry's tendencies. "Once you get the fat, Mrs. Dumbarton, then what?"

"Well, you must make your alkali from ashes. Very simple. Drill holes in the bottom of a barrel and put a layer of gravel in the bottom, then a layer of straw. Then fill the barrel with hardwood ashes. You have to pour rainwater on top of the ashes. You need a good deal of patience because you have to wait for the liquid to drip out of the holes in the bottom. You collect this liquid and boil it down until it is concentrated enough for a fresh egg to float in."

"Good heavens," Francis finally said. "You don't mean to say you actually do all this."

"Of course she does," said Amanda. "How else would you get soap."

"I don't know," said Francis. "In New York we get it from a manufacturer."

"Well, I daresay they follow the same process," said Agnes, unperturbed by the city gentleman. "Only they will have it on a bigger scale. But then our soap is probably better for the scent of the country that gets mixed in."

"Naturally," said Amanda. "Please go on. You float the egg in it."

"The whole egg or just the yolk?" inquired Henry.

Francis gave a sound that was somewhere between cough and choke.

"The whole egg. Well, then you have lye, you see."

"Of course," said Henry. "That is the traditional liquid employed in the making of soap."

"Have you ever made it yourself?" Agnes asked him.

"No, madam. I've only read about it."

"I've some lye that needs testing in my workroom. Perhaps you'd like to see it."

"I really think—" began Francis, but Amanda cut him off.

"We'd love to see. Perhaps we can be of some help. We've no other engagements until dinner." She laughed. "After that I'm helping the new French page boy with his English."

Agnes got up, and they were on their way through the kitchen to the workroom, Francis trailing reluctantly behind, cursing under his breath. But Henry's natural interest in anything the least bit complex held his attention, and so Francis was outnumbered.

In the workroom, Agnes showed them the barrel of ashes and the collecting basin that had already done its job. Now the basin was on a worktable with the lye in it.

"Don't touch it," she warned, handing aprons all around. "It can eat its way through most anything."

Francis kept his distance, refusing to put on the apron.

In a separate bowl, Agnes dissolved salt in water until no more would dissolve.

"Ah, a saturated solution of salt," said Henry, bending over it, his apron tied around his neck and waist.

Agnes handed him a stick with a small weight attached to one end of it. "Now drop the stick into the solution."

Henry did so. The stick bobbed upright with the weight at the bottom. She took out the stick and made a mark exactly at the waterline.

"The stick is our instrument for measuring the strength of the lye. You need the lye at exactly the same specific gravity as the saturated salt solution."

"Fascinating," said Henry.

"Now," she said, handing Henry the stick again, "drop the stick into the concentrated lye."

He did so. It floated with its mark above the surface of the liquid.

"See there. We must add rainwater very carefully, stirring as we do so until the stick floats to its mark. Then the lye will be correct for soap making."

Francis uttered a sigh, and Amanda, though amused with his discomfort, felt she had achieved her point. She turned around.

"Francis, you sound as if the fumes are affecting you. Perhaps you need some fresh air."

"Yes, well, that would be nice."

She turned to Agnes. "If you like, I can leave Henry here to help you with the rainwater. I believe I'll show Francis the grounds of the church."

"Of course, of course," said Agnes, fluttering her hand. Evidently she was enjoying showing Henry the workings of her little laboratory and didn't care a whit if the others left them.

"Do you mind staying a while longer, Henry?" she asked.

But Henry already had a cup and was dipping into the rainwater. He looked up distractedly.

"What? Oh, go ahead. I'll just stay here and see the process to its completion."

She grinned. "We'll fetch you before it's time to return to dress for dinner." She doubted he even heard her, but led the way back to the kitchen, where they replaced their aprons.

"Good heavens, Amanda," Francis said when they were once again through the house and standing on the porch. "You can't really care about all this cottage industry, can you?"

"Of course I care about it, Francis."

They walked back down the path and through the gate. He gestured to the quaint village. "But this is so far removed from New York."

"Exactly." She faced him squarely.

"But, Amanda, you'll turn into a frump here."

She lifted her chin. "Not entirely. There is the season in London."

"My point exactly. It's at its height, and here you are buried at this place."

"Edward will be going up in a few days. I shall accompany him, of course."

Indeed, she had only vague notions about his plans to go up to London. But she didn't mind expounding on the idea for Francis's sake.

"Well, but that's only until August. Then what will he do, abduct you to some Scottish castle for hunting season?"

She shrugged. "I don't know." They walked a little way toward the center of the village. "Really, Francis. I'm sorry if you're jealous. But it is too late."

"I'm not jealous."

"Then why all this fuming about how I spend my life?"

"Because it's such a waste . . . of money," he finally said.

She turned, her cheeks warm. "So that's it."

"You know as well as I do that he wants to marry a fortune, Amanda. It's so typical. English lord bargains his title for American heiress. You're one of many who flock to these waters to marry an English lord."

"Really, Francis. I could do worse." She was angry now, impatient and tired of him. And she hadn't really forgiven him for his earlier betrayal. "You don't care about me at all. It's my fortune you want for yourself. Well, you're not going to get it. It's just a good thing I woke up to your conniving motives before it was too late."

She started down the street, and he caught up to her, hissing in her ear. "At least keep your voice down. All right, we'll drop it. I can see this argument is getting nowhere. I won't mention it again."

"Francis, why don't you go back to New York where you belong?"

"I think I'll do just that. I just wanted to make sure you hadn't forgotten that you belong there, too."

She stopped and faced him again, an array of emotions passing over her face. "I don't know, Francis. I don't think I do belong there anymore."

"Where do you belong, then? Here in that drafty relic of a palace in a bit of isolated countryside?"

She considered him seriously. "Perhaps I do, perhaps I do. In any case I shall be here and in London with Edward for the next six months. Surely that's time enough to see."

Too late, she realized she'd let the truth slip.

Francis eyed her curiously. "Six months? And then what?"

She blinked. "Um, I mean that we have arranged our social calendar for the next six months. Surely by that time I'll see what my routine as duchess would be. It will give me a feeling for my responsibilities."

Francis seemed to accept that. They broke off their conversation to smile and nod at villagers who passed. They gazed with interest in some of the shop windows, then made their way back.

"We'd better rescue Henry before she finds something else for him to do," Amanda suggested.

"Strange chap, your cousin. Doesn't seem interested in all the normal things."

"You mean he doesn't like to drink and chase women?" she snapped. "Maybe you ought to try reading a book sometime yourself."

"Amanda, don't be churlish."

They gathered up Henry, and thanked Agnes for showing them her work projects.

"Why, any time, my dear. And the parish appreciates your help."

Back in the carriage, Henry explained the rest of the process of making soap to Francis and Amanda. When they pulled into the stableyard, Francis excused himself. Amanda broke into peals of laughter.

"I never saw someone so anxious to be relieved of our company, Henry. Now maybe he'll go home."

"Hmmmm," said Henry. "I don't think he and I get on. Can't seem to come up with any subjects in common."

"That's because you're so uncommon, my dear Henry." And she reached up to kiss him on the cheek affectionately. Then she took his arm and led him into the house.

On the way upstairs they ran into Norah, who stopped to hear about their outing. She seemed pleased that Amanda was taking such an interest in Agnes Dumbarton's work.

"Oh, and Norah, I won't be at dinner. I promised Jean Henri, the French boy, to help him with his English after supper. Since his supper is at six o'clock, I told him I'd be in his room at seven o'clock. I'll come down in time for coffee."

"We'll miss your presence, but that is good of you. I'll tell Jeds to send your dinner to your room at six, then, so you won't starve."

"Thank you. Oh, and how was your game with my aunt?"

Norah twisted her face into an ironic smile. "She beat us shamefully. Took everything we wagered."

Amanda gasped. "I told her not to play for money."

"Oh, we only played for a few pence. But I gather she's had experience recently at Monte Carlo."

Amanda gave a wry laugh. "Well, I didn't think she broke the bank there." She shook her head. "I hope her little entertainment doesn't become a problem."

Norah laid a hand on her arm. "I don't think it will be. She is just a delightful companion, interested in the game. It's better than having some boring, self-righteous chaperone who isn't any fun."

Amanda spared a thought for her mother. "Yes, things could be worse. Well, I was just going to return Henry to the library until it's time to change for dinner."

Norah's face brightened. "Why, I would be glad to show him the way. I know this house sprawls. It takes some time to get used to. You probably want to visit with your aunt."

Amanda could take a hint and experienced a sense of wonder. Norah and Henry? Was there some interest blooming here? She hadn't thought about going to see Zoe, but she willingly turned Henry over to Norah.

As they went separate ways, she reflected on how comforting it was to have Henry here. With Zoe and Henry about, she at least felt she had some family to turn to. It helped fill the desolate feeling inside her that had seemed to take root. Emile's death combined with the strangeness of this place still left a hollow feeling in her chest. And despite her confused feelings for Edward, she dreaded being left alone here.

If Henry and Norah became attached, that would give him a reason to stay on. She contemplated the possibility as she reached Zoe's door and knocked.

From an upstairs window Edward had seen the party return and watched Amanda kiss her cousin. He expelled a breath and muttered an expletive. Not that he suspected that she had any romantic notions for Henry. What he saw in her concern for Henry was a nurturing warmth that one might have for a sibling. But what he was jealous of was her commitment to that relationship.

He turned from the window and ran a hand through his hair, feeling exasperated. He had thought he had almost won her, and certainly the ecstasy they experienced in lovemaking showed her what married life might offer. But he knew he had not won her to be his duchess. Perhaps she was still frightened of the responsibilities she would encounter in being married to a duke and in running such a large estate.

Perhaps she had not healed from the death of her lover, and he knew he ought to give her time. But he was running out of patience. It was the reason he had delayed his attendance at Parliament. He had attended the opening and then left London to meet Amanda in Paris. Then after Monte Carlo, he'd managed to squeeze in a few days in London before having to come here to meet her again. But he could not do that much longer. The prince would notice he was missing and send inquiries.

He longed to take Amanda with him, and once the weekend house party was over, he would pack her up and go up to London, Zoe trailing as chaperone. At least the witch Louisa was out of the way, safely back in New York nursing her wounds over Amanda's adventures.

The thought brought a trace of amusement to Edward's face. Amanda succeeded in raising hackles on everyone around her, including her mother. He strode down the corridor to his study, trying to settle his nerves. Once alone in the study, he pulled the bell rope for Jeds. When the butler appeared he ordered a glass of sherry. He needed to steady his nerves before dinner. Then he remembered he wouldn't be seeing Amanda at dinner because she would be tutoring Jean Henri.

He threw himself into his leather chair. Her altruism seemed boundless. He supposed he ought to admire the attention she was paying to the boy. But he felt left out. He wanted her to pay some attention to him.

When the sherry came, he drank it down and refilled the glass from the carafe.

* * *

Amanda dressed in a high-necked, long-sleeved gown. At least she didn't have to put on an evening dress, since she wasn't going to appear at dinner. And the more practical cashmere gown trimmed with black velvet ribbon was more suitable for her task. She left her hair unadorned, pulled up into a top knot and left full and soft around her face.

She rang for Mrs. Gunderson and asked the way to Jean Henri's room, explaining her mission.

"How nice of you to help him. He seems a bright lad. I wasn't sure about him at first. His Grace didn't explain much about the boy's background, only that he was a Parisian orphan."

Amanda knew better than to tell her anything Edward hadn't. "Yes. It was generous of His Grace to offer Jean Henri a position and a home."

The housekeeper didn't pry, but led her to the servants' wing and up the stairs to the top floor. Here the halls were narrow and dark, and exposed beams gave the halls a rather medieval look. Mrs. Gunderson indicated the plain brown painted door, and Amanda knocked.

"Come in," a young voice said.

Amanda opened the door and entered a small, narrow room. Jean Henri was sitting on a narrow bed. The only other furniture in the room was a small wooden table, a wooden chair and a plain chest of drawers.

"Hello, Jean Henri," she said. "Are you ready for your English session?"

He shrugged. "Uh huh."

"This is a nice room," she said. "And you've got a window."

"Looks down at the stables, it does," he said with perhaps more enthusiasm than he meant to show. But he pushed back the plain curtain to show her.

Lanterns were lit in the stableyard, so she could see his view. A better view than the gutters of Parisian slums, no doubt.

She sat on the edge of the bed beside him. "Do you like it here, Jean Henri?"

He shrugged, then nodded.

She was curious about one thing, but she was careful how to put it. "Do you like, well . . . working? It must be different from what you're used to."

He veiled his expression and cocked his head to the side. "It ain't too bad."

From his look, she gathered he knew what she meant. She looked around the room, wondering where he might stash anything his previously sticky fingers might have decided to attach themselves to.

"When you lived in Paris, you must have done various jobs for people. But, of course, then you didn't have a real home and you had to scrape for a living. It isn't the same here, is it, Jean Henri?"

He gave her a sideways glance. "If you mean have I filched anything, no, I haven't. The duke talked to me, you see. We made a bargain."

"Oh?"

"He told me that living here was my reward for helping him save your life. But I had to be square with him. He'd see I had everything I needed long as I didn't try to steal from him. And no matter who I might steal from in this place, it all belonged to him because everyone here works for him."

"Ah, I see."

"So if I went back on my promise, and he caught me

with something that didn't belong to me, he'd send me back to Paris. I wouldn't get no second chance."

"And so he let you decide whether you liked it here well enough to behave honestly." The duke's cleverness in handling the situation impressed her.

He nodded. "And then I wouldn't get my pony."

She was reminded of her promise. "Of course. The pony, we must arrange that right away. I'm sorry, Jean Henri. I've been so distracted with my guests that I forgot the pony. Would you like to look for one tomorrow? I'll discuss with the duke about which of his tenants might have horses with foals."

He turned round eyes on her. "I knew you'd forgot."

"I'm glad you reminded me. I would never go back on a promise."

He shrugged, but she could see he was satisfied. "Could it be a black pony?"

"Well, I don't know what kind of horses they raise here. But if we can find a black one that you like, I don't see why not. I'll speak to the duke. Now, how about that English?"

Jean Henri seemed anxious to show what he knew, and the next two hours sped by with quick conversations, broken up with explanations in French.

When his eyes began to droop she left him, again reassuring him about the pony. Then she found her way out of the servants' quarters and into the main part of the house.

The family had gathered in the withdrawing room they most often used, the one connected to the painting gallery with the little loggia above it. She discovered that Norah was showing Henry the portraits. Isabel and Zoe were playing cards, and the dowager duchess was grilling Francis about America. Edward rose from his seat and greeted her.

"I trust the English lesson went off well."

She gave him a contented smile. "He is doing very well. But I was reminded of my promise to buy him a pony."

"Oh, yes, of course."

"I told him I would speak to you about it."

"I'm glad you did. We shan't disappoint him."

He led her through a door to a small anteroom, and from there they wandered into another sitting room with tall windows facing the darkened garden. He shut the door behind them, the room in darkness with only the moonlight spilling in.

"Now," he said, pulling her down into the sofa beside him. "I think I deserve some of that tender attention you've been lavishing on your cousin and our ward."

"Oh?"

He gently took her face in his hands, his eyes on her lips. "You know what I mean."

Amanda didn't resist as he lowered his mouth to hers and pulled her closer to him. She was growing used to his ministrations and found she could not help but look forward to them. Truly, they were growing closer, in spite of all her doubts. And she cast her doubts aside as he began his gentle caresses that seemed to set her heart on fire.

Chapter 24

The next morning found Amanda closeted with Lady Norah as they went over the dinner list for a weekend house party, for the dowager duchess had deigned it fitting to entertain, so that local society might meet the duchess-to-be. After going over the lists and arranging a chart of the seating, Amanda's head began to ache. Lady Norah was going on about rules of precedence.

"There will be four earls present," she said thoughtfully, "but see here, I believe I have given each the status due him."

Amanda considered the seating chart, which began to blur before her eyes.

"Now," said Norah, "we should attend to the matter of room assignments."

Feeling stricken that she was expected to learn how to arrange all this in the future, Amanda became more and more depressed. It actually began to appear that she must go through with a marriage to Edward, for as she became more and more involved with him and with Elsenheim, she realized that it would be harder to undo what was being done. Norah's voice began to sound far away as Amanda chafed at the role she was playing in her own life.

Suddenly she held a hand to her head. "Norah, you must excuse me. I have an excruciating pain in my head. I'm afraid I can't go on."

Norah dropped the chart and looked up very solicitously. "Oh, I am sorry. Shall I fetch you an herbal concoction? Cook knows some splendid remedies."

She stood up. "No, thank you. I think I shall be all right with a bit of fresh air." Then, feeling a little guilty, "Perhaps we can continue with the plans after luncheon if I am rid of my headache."

"Of course. One forgets that all this is a bit foreign to you. And there are the menus yet to prepare for the coming weekend. After luncheon would be quite satisfactory."

Amanda smiled thankfully, feeling that Norah was truly a friend. If she did have to spend time in this place, she would certainly rely on the duke's sister a great deal. She almost expressed the thought in words and then pressed her lips together.

In the corridor, she happened to meet Henry, dressed in tweeds, who was moving along, looking from side to side as if lost.

"Henry, what are you doing here?"

He looked relieved to see her. "I've just been with the duke in the stables, but I'm afraid that once we came in through the green room I quite lost my way. He was called out on some matter of the estate, and I ended up in the laundry wing."

She suppressed her mirth and squeezed his arm. "Come with me, Henry." She sighed. "My goodness, it is good to have you here. I'm almost glad you ran into Francis. Where is he today, by the way?"

"Out for a ride, I believe. I declined."

"That was smart."

Francis loved to jump, and with Henry's sight impairment he had to stay away from jumpers.

"I was just going out for a walk. Will you join me?" she asked.

"Certainly."

She led him along the corridors, a little more sure now of the turns to take that would finally bring them to the French doors that led to the terrace above the gardens. But at last they came out right. The gardeners were busy trimming the box hedges, and Amanda and Henry went down the steps to walk along the gravel walks.

The gardens were in full bloom, and they admired the sunken topiary laid out in curving patterns, punctuated with the occasional vertical shrub. On the other side of the low brick wall that separated it from the formal flower beds, they followed a rose walk. Finally they came to brick pillars with ball finials leading to the lawn.

"Oh, this is better," she said once they were under the bright blue sky. "I was getting such a headache inside."

"Oh, dear."

"Nothing to worry about, Henry. I fear it was the circumstances rather than anything to do with my physical being."

"Hmmmm. Well, then. You must tell me about it."

"Dear Henry. That is exactly why I want you here." She shook her head as they paused to admire a sculptured nymph playing in a pond. "I don't know where to begin. I feel I've been such a pawn in the game of my own life up until now."

"Oh?"

She sat down on the stone bench nearby, and it all came tumbling out.

"You see, Sunderland wants to marry me for my money. He needs an heiress to give him an heir." She rushed on. "But he's really only engaged to me now because I was abducted in Paris, like I told you before. My name was in the newspapers, and we were afraid it would be linked to Emile, the young man I had met there. All so complicated."

"I daresay." Henry took off his spectacles and polished them with a white handkerchief.

"It's such an awful mess, Henry. I don't believe I understand men at all. It's such a burden to be wealthy."

"Yes, well I hadn't thought of it that way, but I see your point."

"It wouldn't be so bad if only . . ." She sounded wistful.

"If only what?"

She took a deep breath. "If only he loved me."

"Hmmmm. Surely in time . . ."

"I wish I could believe that. But I'm afraid time will breed boredom in a man like the duke. He's so used to having everything at the snap of his fingers. It simply wouldn't work."

"This sounds quite serious, then. I am sorry for you."

Of everyone she knew, she believed that Henry was the most sincere. There seemed little more to be said. Her mind turned to Francis.

"What does Francis really want with me?" she asked. "Yesterday he tried to persuade me not to marry Sunderland. But I know now that Francis was also only after my money."

"Well now, I don't know," said Henry. "Seemed

rather anxious to come down here. Perhaps he had to satisfy himself that you had really gone and gotten yourself engaged to a duke. Only just realized what he let slip through his fingers, I suppose."

"Good thing, too. Oh, Henry, I've been so wrong about so many men."

"Well." He seemed unable to think of anything else to say to that. "Pity."

She grinned at him. "And you've been getting on with Norah, I see."

He blushed unmistakably. "She's a very nice lady."

She didn't press the matter. "Henry, would you like to ride with me? I can get you a gentle mount, and as I'm in no hurry to gallop, we can go easily about the countryside. You might enjoy it. And the woods are very nice."

"Well, if you'd like."

"I think there's time before luncheon. Let's change for a ride. It would help lift my spirits."

Trusting himself to Amanda, who knew his limitations as a horseman, he agreed. They walked to the stables where she asked for two horses to be saddled, explaining Henry's near-sightedness and the need for a gentle mount that knew the trails. Then she walked Henry back to his room where he could wait while she changed, and a half hour later met him outside his door, for she didn't want to risk him bumbling about the palace and getting lost again.

Back at the stables, Amanda mounted Milady Gray while Henry climbed up on a docile mare named Posy. They set out at a walk through the arches and took a path that wound down by the lake, with the woods their destination. Feeling little need to speak, Amanda kept her spritely mount at a pace that would not outdistance Henry's.

She had not seen her fiancé this morning and wondered what he was about. Business, Henry had said.

There, she was thinking of herself as his fiancée. A momentary image came of their lovemaking, and she was glad her face was averted from Henry's, for the thought brought a blush. How would she feel if Edward did go up to London and leave her here? She realized suddenly, she would miss him. Surely he wouldn't leave her behind.

They passed the lake and came to the edge of the trees. She turned to Henry.

"It looks like a path goes here. I'll look ahead for bogs."

"You lead," Henry agreed, and pulled in behind Amanda.

The ancient oaks and elms raised their lofty branches in gentle shade, and as they penetrated deeper into the forest, she became aware of a sense of timelessness. There was something almost mythological about a forest this old, and she imagined for a moment gallant knights, old women living in huts, the fires of bandits from less civilized times.

Spots of sunlight forced themselves through the trees, but the trees were close together, only the path having a clear way. The forest offered the solace that Amanda needed. She gave Milady Gray her head, and the horse kept to the path, which made an occasional turn. But there was little danger of getting lost, for the horses could find their way home. Her thoughts turned again to Edward.

She thought about the feel of his arms about her, of his kisses, which she so hungrily answered. Thinking of

him now, she felt a craving about her, a looking forward
to their next encounter. For now she had to admit there
would be a next encounter. They seemed to have a need
for each other that had grown since he had first kissed
her. And with a sudden awareness, she realized she had
come to accept that.

She had fought him because of her reckless indiscretion with Emile, feeling guilty and ashamed. But
Edward had said a hundred times that he did not hold
that against her. Indeed, he seemed to relish the fact
that he could show her more, could lead her into more
mature and ever exciting ways of love.

She stopped her musings, remembering Henry and
feeling that he in some way might be able to read her
thoughts. Though Henry was her confidant, she certainly wasn't going to confess what she had been doing
with the duke in private.

After all this time of resentment, now his face seemed
to appear before her; words he'd professed rang in her
ears. She began to recall the many expressions of his
face. She drew in a breath and nearly missed ducking to
prevent being slapped by an overhanging bough. Could
it be that he really might love her after all?

The woods began to thin out, and the path widened.
Eventually they found themselves through the woods
and out into a grassy meadow again. A great outcropping of rock on her left looked unfamiliar, and she drew
the conclusion that she had never seen this part of the
estate before. Indeed, she didn't even know if they were
still on Elsenheim lands.

Turning left, they rode across the meadow and then
came to a field marked off by a low stone wall. In the
distance among some trees was a cottage with smoke
curling upward from the chimney. Trees still dotted the

landscape, and above the cottage sheep grazed on a hill. More hills rose behind, green and lush. Above them the sun was climbing to its zenith.

"We should turn back," Amanda said. "It will be nearing lunch by the time we arrive at the house."

"Very well," said Henry easily, evidently agreeable to whatever she decided. "The countryside is most pleasant."

They turned the horses and returned the way they had come. Entering the woods, Amanda again gave Milady Gray her head, and sensing that they were going home, the little mare picked up her pace, her ears forward and alert. After the slow pace, Amanda didn't mind a brisker ride. But she turned in the saddle once or twice to make sure Henry was all right.

"Don't worry," she called to him. "The horses know the way. But watch out for the low branches."

This time she watched where they were going, all musings about Sunderland aside. The way seemed longer than she remembered, and she chided herself mildly for not paying more attention. But surely there was nothing to worry about.

But when they came out of the trees, they were confronted with a hill she didn't remember. Where was the long sward and the lake below the house?

"Home," she said to Milady Gray. "Find your way home." Still, Amanda wasn't worried. The worst that could happen was that they would be late for lunch.

Milady Gray tossed her head, shaking the bridle. But she seemed certain in her direction. Amanda peered around her, looking for some landmark. Then she studied the sun and tried to ascertain in which direction the house might lie.

Suddenly both horses became nervous. They snorted,

and danced sideways, and fear shot through Amanda. Something was wrong, though she couldn't tell just what.

"Easy girl, easy."

She was enough of a horsewoman to know that something was making the horses skittish, perhaps an animal in the woods. She guided the horse along the path, down a slope to a little vale through which a stream ran.

"Hold on to your horse, Henry," she called. "Something is bothering them. Head for that stream. Once we cross it, perhaps the scent of whatever they don't like will be less."

She urged her horse along, and began to feel more in control when a sudden yapping bark followed by a shrill howl made Amanda's hair stand on end. Then red fur flew out of the woods and streaked across the path, paws flying, bushy tail swishing behind. The red fox.

The vixen's howl and its darting almost under Milady Gray's feet caused the horse to rear on its hind legs, and Amanda leaned forward, desperately attempting to hold her seat, clutching at the horse's mane, the sidesaddle providing no balance. One of the reins slipped from Amanda's hand and slapped on Milady Gray's withers, and the horse jolted down on all fours and leapt forward.

Nearly thrown from the saddle, Amanda clung, leaning over the horse's neck, the loose rein slapping her face. She gave up on the reins and hung on for dear life to the flying mane. As they neared the stream, she saw that it was wider than she had thought, but still her horse did not slow. As the gray horse bore down on the rocky stream, Amanda felt the animal gather its legs under it to prepare to jump. With horror she gazed at the sharp rocks pointing upward from the little waterfalls, and she tried to hold on to her seat to jump the horse.

But she had never jumped a horse over a long

streambed before, and never jumped with the reins flying about the horse's head, contributing to the runaway. She could not scream, and in vain she tried to command the horse. Instead, all she could do was hug the sidesaddle as best she could, cling to the mane and lean over the horse's neck as the animal stretched itself out for the leap across the river.

And then they were up, flying across the stream, the sharp rocks beneath the horse's belly. With a jolt, the forefeet and then the hind feet came down, and the sidesaddle did no good in helping Amanda keep her seat. Feeling herself slide, she managed to extricate her foot from the stirrup, knowing that a free-fall was better than being dragged by the heel.

Then the ground came up to meet her, and she felt her bones jar against each other as she rolled on the grass coming to a halt near a rock outcropping. Even as the pain began to overtake her, she felt the thunder of the horse's hooves on the ground next to her ear, heard Henry's shout and tried to focus on the hill and the sky above her; but everything went hazy, and then it was gone.

Amanda awoke some time later with a dull throb in the back of her head. It took a moment to remember anything, and when she did, she did not seem to recognize the surroundings. Sunlight came in from a curtained window, and she tried to move in the narrow bed with clean linen sheets.

Giving up the effort, she closed her eyes again. Then she became aware of muffled voices. A door creaked open. She opened dry lips to speak.

"Edward," she croaked. For she knew it was him without even looking.

He sat on the wooden chair beside the bed. "Amanda, you're awake."

She fluttered her eyelids open. "I fell . . ." Her speech felt slurred.

He grasped her hands. "Don't try to talk, my dearest. Just rest. The doctor has been here."

Ignoring his command not to talk, she struggled onward. "Where am I?"

"In a tenant's cottage. Now don't say anything more. Shut your eyes. That's it."

When she had complied he lowered his head next to hers and gently kissed her cheek.

"Edward," she whispered, or so she thought she did. Perhaps the word was only in her mind. She slept.

The next time she awoke, the room was dark but warm. There was no more sun pouring in. But as she focused her eyes, she perceived the twinkling of stars through the glass-paned windows. She sensed she wasn't alone in the room.

"Edward?"

He stirred, a shadowy figure beside her in the chair exactly where she remembered him. He came awake instantly and bent down toward her.

"Amanda?" he whispered. "Are you awake?"

She tried to nod, but it hurt. "Yes," she managed.

A match was struck, and then light glowed in a kerosene lamp on a small wooden table next to the bed. He adjusted the lamp so that it was dim, only enough so that she could make out his shape. He sat back in the chair again, reaching for her hands.

She gazed at him and now saw the deep circles under his eyes, his open shirt collar without a tie. His tweed jacket hung unbuttoned, and his hair had been mussed.

She realized in her foggy mind that he hadn't really slept, but had been dozing in the chair by her bed.

"How long . . . ?" she conveyed her question to him.

His face took on a more hopeful look, and he leaned close so that she could hear him. "You've been here since yesterday midmorning. It must be about four A.M. now. How do you feel?"

She tried to smile at him. "Headache," she said.

But he could see that her eyes were clear, her face was taking on some color, and he sighed in relief. His own expression was full of emotion. His hand came up to tenderly caress her brow.

"You had a nasty fall. We brought you here. Henry was afraid to move you."

"Henry?" she asked, remembering that he had been with her on the ride.

"Your cousin is a hero. Evidently when your horse bolted, he dismounted, saw that you had hit your head and yelled for help. My tenant and his wife were working in the next field and came running. Henry gave Mullins his horse and sent him to the house for help while he waited by your side, bathing your face with water from the stream. He was frightened to death, poor bloke."

She grinned. "Dear Henry."

A whiteness seemed to pass over Edward's face as he recalled the scare. He himself had mounted the fastest horse after sending Mullins to Woodhaven for the doctor. He had reached Amanda, stretched out by the stream, and his heart nearly stopped beating. When the doctor came and examined her, Sunderland had carried her in his arms to Mullins' cottage, which fortunately was not far, much closer than the palace.

After the doctor had done what he could, it had been

a matter of waiting. But as he gazed at her dear face, he gave a prayer of thanks that she had regained consciousness. He felt her fingers squeeze his hand, and felt a tear slip over the rim of his eyes. If she died. . . . He could not bear the thought.

Amanda saw his eyes brim, and her heart turned over. She felt a wave of emotion and could not find words to speak. She owed him some words and tried to form them on her lips, but his finger pressed against them.

"Don't try to speak, my dear. The important thing is that you rest and recuperate." Noticing that her lips felt dry, he turned and poured water from a ewer into a glass.

"Here, take a drink of water."

She gave a little nod, and he slid an arm around her shoulders to help her sit up. Then he held the glass so she could drink. Her own hand came up to cover his strong one, and she sipped gratefully, her eyes closed, drinking more than the water. For she drank in the warmth and love he conveyed.

He laid her back on her pillows, and her eyes flew up to his. *Edward*, she cried out in her own mind. "Don't leave me," she said aloud.

He smiled then, a heartwarming, loving smile, one full of concern. "I'll never leave you," he said.

She slept again, but this time full of comfort and warmth, and in the deep recesses of her mind was the knowledge that she was loved. Near morning, images floated in her mind, images that used to be confused. Somehow just before she awoke, they all settled into their proper places, and became clear.

When she came fully awake, sunlight streamed into the little window, and someone had opened it so that a fresh breeze also aired the room. Edward was gone, but

Norah bustled around the small room. Amanda shifted; Norah turned from where she had just folded a blanket.

"Amanda," she said, coming to the bed and taking a seat in the chair. "How do you feel?"

Amanda moistened her lips. "Much better." Her eyes scanned the room, and Norah smiled.

"Edward is in the other room. I made him go have something for breakfast. He spent all yesterday and all of last night in this chair, but I promised I'd fetch him if there was any change."

Foolish relief spread through her that he was near. Norah continued. "Shall I get him?"

"No, please," said Amanda hastily. "Let him eat. He must need his strength."

Norah smoothed the covers over her. "He was quite worried about you, my dear. We're all glad you're mending."

She blinked, feeling ready to shift upward. Norah perceived what she was about and brought an extra pillow to stuff behind her against the plain little headboard. Then she helped Amanda sit up.

"Be careful, now, and don't move about too much. Are you hungry?"

Amanda grinned. "Ravenous."

"That is good. A healthy appetite is a sure sign of recovery. I'll tell Mrs. Mullins. They've been so kind and so concerned."

Looking down, Amanda realized that she was no longer in her own clothing. Rather a simple cotton nightdress clothed her. Who had undressed her, she wondered. Norah went out, and an instant later Edward appeared. He was still in the same clothes, but his hair was combed and his face washed. Some of the lines of concern had lessened, and the dark circles now looked like those of fatigue instead of deep worry. In two strides he was beside her.

"My darling, how do you feel?"

She clasped his hands warmly when he gave them to her and smiled. "Much better."

He hesitated a second, drinking in her face, and then he came forward to kiss her lightly on the lips, afraid to do anything to hurt her wounded head. But her arms went to his shoulders, and she accepted the kiss joyfully, hungrily. His arms went about her body, and he carefully lifted his mouth from hers and cradled her head against him.

"Amanda, I was so worried."

Her heart felt full then, and she thought she would cry. "Edward, I—" she began. But he stopped her.

He sat back, kissing her temple and forehead. "Shhhh. Time enough to talk later. You must eat and regain your strength."

Then he simply smiled at her. She couldn't take her eyes off him, and she knew finally that she loved him and always would. It seemed so simple. And it had taken so long to arrive. Laughter began to bubble up in her, and she knew with certainty that she would become a duchess.

He met her grin with one of his own. "What's so funny?" he asked.

Her laughter was music to his ears. "Morgan."

A brief look of consternation flitted over his face, but he said, "Who's Morgan? Another rival?"

"My cat. If I am to become a duchess, I shall have to send for him to be brought over to live here. I cannot leave him in New York indefinitely. He wouldn't be happy there without me. Especially now that Mother's gone home."

Chapter 25

Then Sunderland was on his knees, his face near hers. He picked up her fingers kissing them. "If you will marry me and be my duchess, you can have whatever you want." Then he raised an eyebrow. "That is, within limits."

She took his meaning and lifted a hand to caress his face, but she shook her head, meeting his gaze with her own solemn one.

"I don't need anything but you. I've learned that now."

There followed many private words and looks. Gentle kisses, owing to the fact that she was injured. He never asked what changed her mind, what made her suddenly so sure. After an hour or so, Edward sat up straighter.

"When you were lying there unconscious, it was my darkest night," he said. "I want that never to happen again."

"I'll try not to fall off a horse again, my lord," said Amanda, already her old sense of humor returning.

He grinned and squeezed her hand. "Evidently your mare was following the scent of a stallion we'd recently purchased for breeding. You rode too close to the fox's young and frightened her. An unfortunate accident."

And yet ironically, because of the accident she had witnessed Edward's devotion, had had time lying there between waking and dozing to sort things out.

"I want to get better," she said suddenly. For the first time her future looked bright.

When she could be moved, they took her to the palace where the staff and family were all solicitous concern. Once Zoe saw that her niece was out of danger, she relished talking about the proposed wedding.

After a long enough period recovering in her room, Amanda sought the out of doors. Edward was at her side as they strolled through the gardens. They passed under a little archway and sat on a stone bench supported by two lions. From here they could gaze at the lake and the countryside, so green it almost hurt her eyes after being indoors for so long.

Edward held her hand in his. Dear Edward, always so strong. Always there. It amazed her that she had taken so long to see it.

"You're sure you still want to marry me," she said for the hundredth time.

He was used to the question and only turned a quizzical brow to her. "How can you doubt it?"

She gazed at the face she loved. "We've not had an easy time," she said.

He laughed. "Perhaps courtship is never easy."

She gave a small frown. "But ours was particularly difficult."

"No matter. It was an adventure." His tone turned more serious. "I'm glad that's over. I'm glad I convinced you at last."

She shook her head. "I just couldn't see that you loved me for myself."

"What made you finally see it, my love?"

"You were persistent. I suppose I finally believed you."

"Believed me about what?"

"The past," she said with only a slight change in tone. "We've finally been able to lay it to rest."

He pulled her close to him. "I've laid it to rest; have you?"

She thought seriously for a moment. No more regrets. What had happened had happened. No reason to be ashamed of it or to withhold herself from Edward any longer. "Yes," she said. "I've laid my past to rest. But what about yours? You've always been so evasive about it."

He hugged her. "You mean my erstwhile mistress, Charlotte. I don't think of her anymore, my dear. She's moved to another county and is happily married, according to her father. There, does that satisfy you?"

"I suppose," said Amanda. "And you don't miss her?"

His kisses drifted across her brow and ear. "I haven't missed her, or for that matter, had room in my heart for any woman, since the day I heard you arguing with your mother at Mrs. Astor's."

"Oh, Edward, that's not quite true. Admit it."

"All right." He sighed. "I honestly don't remember when it was that I fell in love with you, my dear. Was it when we danced? When you were held over the edge of the building in the Paris slum by that rascal Jacques? Or was it when you shouted at my grandmother at my own dinner table? How can I say? There've been a thousand things. And we've only just begun."

"Yes," she said, snuggling in his arms. "We've only just begun."